SEA DRAGON

RIDERS OF FIRE
BOOK SIX

EILEEN MUELLER

CONNECT WITH THE AUTHOR

EileenMuellerAuthor.com

Website, newsletter and free books, including *Bronze Dragon* and *Silver Dragon*, *Riders of Fire* prequel novelettes

Facebook:
www.facebook.com/groups/RidersOfFire

Follow Eileen on BookBub:
www.bookbub.com/authors/eileen-mueller

SEA DRAGON

RIDERS OF FIRE
BOOK SIX

EILEEN MUELLER

Sea Dragon and the *Riders of Fire* series are works of fiction. All characters, events and locations in this book are fictional. Any resemblance to persons or dragons, living or dead, is purely coincidental. No dragons were harmed in the making of this book, although there may have been a few injuries to tharuks.

This book is copyright. No part may be reproduced or transmitted in any form or by any electronic means, including photocopying, recording or by any information retrieval system without written permission from the author, except for short excerpts for reviews, in fair use, as permitted under the Copyright Act. Dragons' Realm, the Riders of Fire world, and its characters are copyright.

Sea Dragon, Riders of Fire © 2020 Eileen Mueller
Typesetting © Phantom Feather Press, 2020, American English
Cover Art by Christian Bentulan © Eileen Mueller, 2020
Dragons' Realm Map by Ava Fairhall © Eileen Mueller, 2018
Phantom Feather Press Logo by Geoff Popham, © Phantom Feather Press, 2014
Paperback ISBNs: KDP: 9798653412585
NZ Edition: 9780995115293

Phantom Feather Press
29 Laura Ave, Brooklyn, Wellington 6021, New Zealand
phantomfeatherpress@gmail.com
www.phantomfeatherpress.wordpress.com

Magic, every time you turn the page.

Dedication

For everyone fighting darkness.
Keep your light shining and don't let it go out.
You may feel alone,
but there are friends out there,
waiting for you to discover them.

DRAGONS' REALM

Red Guards

GREAT SPANGLEWOOD FOREST

Tooka Falls

DEATH VALLEY

THE TERRAMITES

Devil's Gate

Monte Vista

Waldhaven

Fore Edge

THE FLATLANDS

N W E S

NAOBIAN SEA

DRAGONS' HOLD

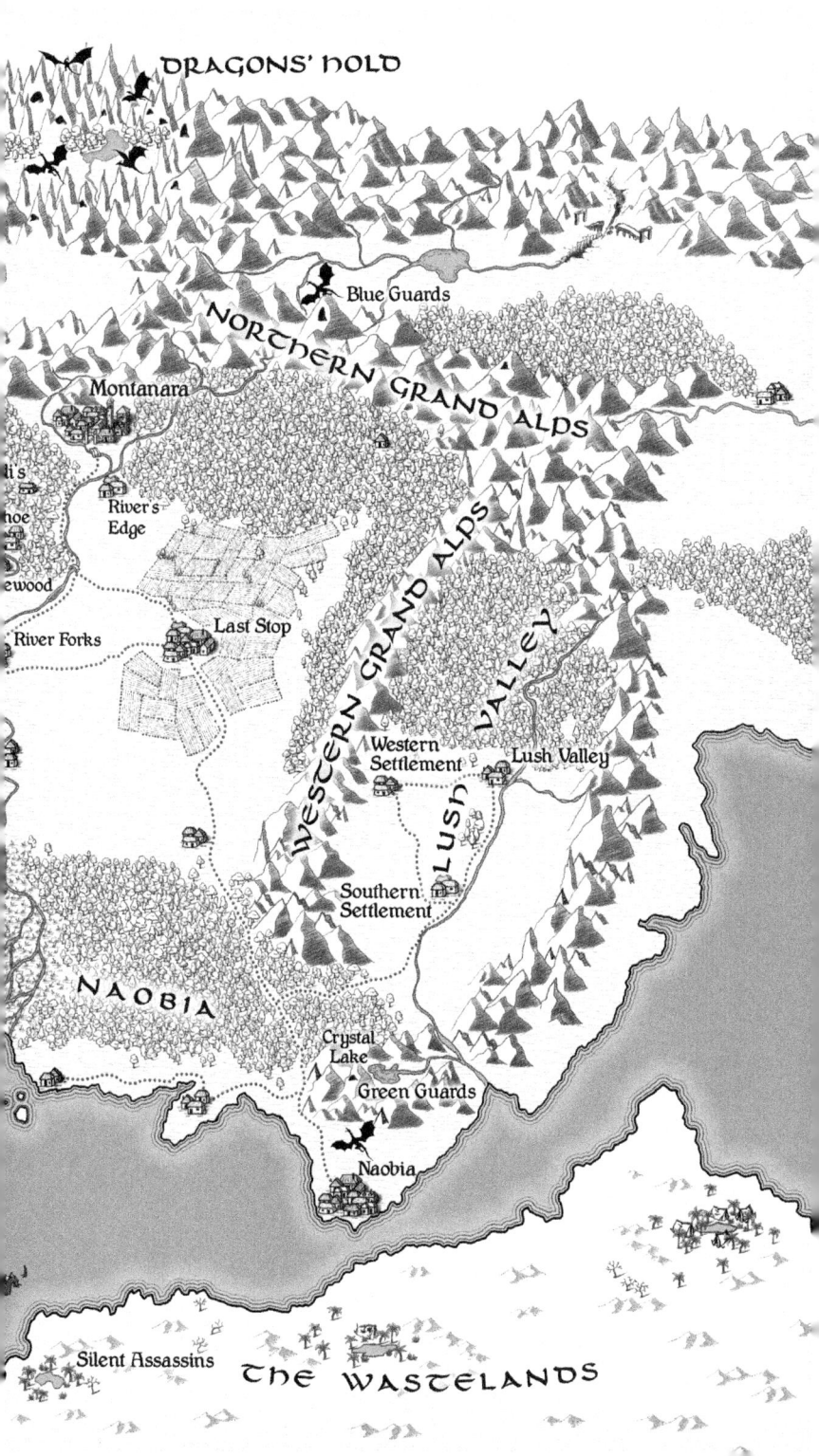

Blue Guards

NORTHERN GRAND ALPS

Montanara

River's Edge

River Forks

Last Stop

WESTERN GRAND ALPS

Western Settlement

Lush Valley

LUSH VALLEY

Southern Settlement

NAOBIA

Crystal Lake

Green Guards

Naobia

Silent Assassins

THE WASTELANDS

Prologue

*These short scenes are repeated from
Ezaara, Riders of Fire book 1*

Ithsar was used to hiding in the tunnels. Used to avoiding the unwanted gaze of her fellow assassins. Used to crawling into tiny spaces to escape their taunting. But she wasn't used to the new strength in her fingers, the strange energy that had surged along her half-dead nerves as Ezaara, she of the golden hair and green eyes, had healed her. Ithsar had never experienced such kindness from anyone. And although the *dracha ryter* from a far-off land had given her a vial of healing juice, Ithsar honored Ezaara, so she hadn't dared use any on herself.

So, Ithsar ran for her life and for Ezaara's. Having hands that didn't work well had helped her hone the rest of her body. Whenever she was off-duty, she practiced the *sathir* dance for hours on end, her limbs nearly brushing the walls of her tiny cavern. Her legs were strong, feet agile, and her endurance was akin to the legendary *Sathiri*, who had established the ancient dance. Not that any of her fellow assassins realized. She'd hidden her prowess, deliberately acting clumsier than she was. Deliberately fooling everyone—especially her mother, Ashewar.

On through the dark, Ithsar ran, through winding tunnels to a hidey-hole they'd never suspect. When pursuers passed her, she doubled back until she reached an alcove near where the Naobian lay healing. Healed. She'd healed him with that little vial of juice. He of the dark eyes shining like ripe olives under the sun. No wonder Ezaara loved this man—Roberto, she'd called him—it was evident in her *sathir* when she'd asked after him. And he had cried, calling Ezaara's name in his fever with such love, babbling about her color. The color, Ithsar had understood. Ezaara's presence radiated all the colors in her mother's prism-seer. Another talent Ashewar was unaware of—Ithsar could see without a prism. And she'd seen a vision of these two *dracha ryter*.

The Naobian had also ranted about banishment, murder and poison. It appeared he'd saved Ezaara, the healer. For that, Ithsar owed him.

Chief Prophetess Ashewar planned to breed him with her women and then kill him.

But no, Ashewar would not kill this man, loved by her healer. Ithsar would see to that. He would go free to love Ezaara. Perhaps one day, she, Ithsar, would have a man like this, who called her name with a voice that ached with tenderness.

Her breathing now quiet, Ithsar stepped out of the alcove. The Naobian had only one person guarding him at night—but tonight it was Izoldia. Ithsar's birth defects meant she was smaller than other girls her age. Izoldia, the largest, had led the bullying, and was always the last to finish beating her—the most savage, the cruelest. Bruises, black eyes, and, later, cuts and burns had been Izoldia's mark—until one day, Ithsar had wrestled the brand off her and burned Izoldia, keeping her brutality at bay.

Ashewar, noticing Ithsar's hurts, had said nothing. Disciplined no one. If Ithsar had been the daughter of another assassin, Ashewar would've been ruthless in punishing Izoldia. But she wasn't.

She was Ithsar, Ashewar's only daughter—the chief prophetess' malformed disappointment.

Perhaps Ithsar owed Izoldia, for driving her to artistry in *sathir*, for making her stronger than she otherwise would have been, but Izoldia had also twisted what the Naobian had said, conjuring up stories so Ezaara—she of golden beauty, the girls called her in hushed whispers over their evening meal—would die.

Not while Ithsar breathed.

Opening the healing room door, Ithsar kept the anger from her face, instead, offering congeniality and supplication.

"What do you want?" Izoldia snapped.

"Did you hear the disturbance?" Ithsar asked, eyes downcast.

"You think I'd miss that lot, thundering around like a herd of Robandi camels?"

"I came to fetch you because you're stronger. You'd be better at fighting an intruder than me."

Izoldia sneered at Ithsar, her chest swelling with pride, but then her eyes narrowed in suspicion.

Although she hated groveling, Ithsar had to be quick. She held out her twisted fingers, hiding the healed ones in her palms. "My hands… I'm useless, afraid…" She let her lip wobble.

"You miserable wretch, Ithsar. I should make you go and face the danger." Izoldia's bark was harsh, loud. She'd never been good at silence—gloating didn't sound right in a whisper. Izoldia got up, hand on her saber. "Watch that man."

The moment Izoldia shut the door, the Naobian's eyes flicked open.

"I am Ithsar," she murmured. "Ezaara's friend. I'll take you to her so you can escape."

"My hands and legs are fastened." His whisper was papyrus-thin. He was obviously used to stealth—good, that would serve them well tonight.

The ropes on his hands and feet were quick work for her saber. Ithsar thrust the cut ropes into her pocket and pulled some clothing and a headdress from a drawer. He threw them on. On close inspection, he wouldn't pass for a woman, but it was better than the *dracha ryter* clothes he wore underneath. She passed him his sword and dagger. They slipped out the door, sliding through the shadows along the walls and nipping into side tunnels or alcoves whenever someone neared.

Finally, they made it back to Ezaara, hiding under the bridge.

When she'd crawled out and they'd retreated to a nearby side tunnel, Ezaara whispered, "Ithsar, quick, give me your unhealed fingers."

In the darkness, something dripped onto Ithsar's fingers, then Ezaara rubbed the oil into her skin. The slow healing burn built until her bones were on fire and moved and straightened. An ache pierced her chest and her eyes stung.

She was whole.

Ithsar clutched Ezaara's hand for a moment longer, placing it on her wet cheek. "My life is yours."

The Naobian's hand rested atop theirs, enclosing them both. "Thank you, Ithsar," he whispered. "Thank you for risking your life to save ours."

They stood in the darkness, her and these two strangers, their breath flowing and ebbing together in the inky black. And then the vision descended upon Ithsar again—these strangers on mighty *dracha*, with her beside them on another. *Sathir* built around them, tangible, like a warm caress full of color and life, a force connecting the three of them. She belonged to these people. This was her destiny.

From Ezaara's soft gasp and the grunt the Naobian gave, they'd sensed it too.

Footsteps slid over rock nearby. They froze, waiting until they retreated, then Ithsar led them into a tunnel far away from the main thoroughfares. Winding under the heart of the lake, deeper and deeper into the earth, she took them toward a hidden exit on the far side of the oasis.

§

Ithsar and the strangers stooped to avoid sharp rocks protruding from the ceiling and slithered over piles of rubble nearly as high as the tunnel itself. Ithsar led them on, the tiny lantern at her waist a star in the inky blackness.

When they were near the tunnel's end, there was a ripple in the fabric of the sathir, a rip in the cloak that surrounded them. Ithsar turned to the *dracha* ryter, holding up her lantern.

They were no longer holding hands. The Naobian's face was stoic.

Ezaara's… Ezaara's look haunted Ithsar. Hollow-eyed, bereft of hope.

Something terrible had passed between them. "What is it? What ails you?" Ithsar asked. "With such disunity, Ashewar will feel the disharmony and find us immediately. If you are to be reunited with your *dracha*, you must put this pain aside."

They nodded and stared at each other for long moments—counted by the pounding of Ithsar's heart. Expressions flickered across their faces—no doubt they were mind-melding—and the ripple of *sathir* died.

She nodded. "That's better."

Ithsar turned and shone her lamp on a series of handholds and footholds in the rock, leading up a chimney into darkness. She went first, Roberto next, and Ezaara took the rear. Her hands bit into the dusty rock handholds. The footholds were gritty with stone particles, her feet sending pebbles and sand cascading onto the couple below.

They climbed in silence, making their way up to the surface of the oasis.

When Ithsar's new strong fingers brushed the tangled roots of a date palm over a handhold, she whispered, "We're here." She put out the lantern hanging on her belt and reached above her to part the rustling foliage of the desert brush.

The cool kiss of night air rushed in to meet her. Ithsar climbed out to a sky scattered with stars, and date palms whispering in the breeze like hundreds of silent assassins. Moonlight cast a shaft of brightness across the lake. Beyond, a strange new hillock was silhouetted among a fringe of trees—the enormous blue *dracha* that had brought these strangers here. The sky was dark, but it wasn't long until dawn. She had to get them out of here.

The Naobian scrambled up and reached down to grasp Ezaara's hand. As he pulled her up into the open, she stumbled on the edge of the chimney. He grabbed her and she landed with her cheek against his chest.

The Naobian leaned in to kiss Ezaara.

"No," Ithsar whispered, but it was too late. The Naobian's lips touched Ezaara's hair, lighting up the *sathir* connection between them like a million stars. Any assassin tuned into *sathir* would know where they were. So much for stealth.

On the other side of the lake, a sand-shifting roar split the air. A belch of *dracha* flame lit up the palm grove, and the mighty blue-scaled beast took to the sky.

He was coming. Both *dracha ryter* would be saved.

"Traitor." Izoldia stepped from behind a date palm, saber out.

By the *dracha* gods, Izoldia had seen through her ruse. She had to think fast.

Ithsar snatched her own saber and pointed it at the Naobian. "Now, you're coming with us!" she cried.

The Naobian spun, flinging Ezaara aside. He was fast. When had he unsheathed his sword?

"You," he spat at Ithsar, lunging at her. "You've outlived your usefulness."

He was absolving her of blame. Ithsar parried with her saber, letting it fly out of her hand as he struck, as if her fingers couldn't hold it. Izoldia wouldn't know any different.

The Naobian held his sword to Ithsar's throat. "Drop your weapon," he said to Izoldia. "Or the girl dies."

Izoldia threw her head back and laughed. "She's worthless. Kill her. It'll save me the trouble."

The slow burning anger that Ithsar had harbored all these years blossomed like a bruise, staining the *sathir* purple-black. The stain spread across Ithsar's vision, blotting out the stars, blotting out the date trees, blotting out Izoldia.

Ithsar had never deserved such scorn. Despite her deformed fingers, she had tried her best. Izoldia had seen to it that everyone despised her, including her own mother.

A breeze stirred at her feet, whirling the sand into a flurry. It rose, faster and higher around her, whipping her clothes in the wind. It shook the date palms, rustling their fronds and swaying their trunks. Thrusting out her anger, Ithsar's whirlwind made the date palm over Izoldia tremble.

A huge bunch of dates fell, hitting Izoldia's head, knocking her to the ground.

Instantly, the purple stain was gone.

The Naobian released Ithsar and spun, checking for more assassins. Ithsar could sense them across the lake, running toward them.

Ezaara rushed over to Izoldia. "She's unconscious." She hesitated for a moment.

"I'm sorry," whispered Ithsar. "I've never done that before."

"A good job you did," the Naobian said, putting a comforting hand on her shoulder.

Ezaara opened her pouch and took out a tiny sack of powder. "Ithsar, quick," she hissed, "fetch a little water."

Ithsar snatched the empty waterskin at her belt and collected water from the lake.

Ezaara threw a pinch of powder into the skin, and they held up Izoldia's head, letting the water trickle down her throat. Izoldia swallowed reflexively.

"This is woozy weed," Ezaara said. "It will make her sleep and leave her confused about what happened over the last few hours. She probably won't remember any of this."

Ithsar had been prepared to die to free these strangers. She let relief wash through her, not trying to control it. If anyone had seen the dark bruise in *sathir*, they'd believe the *dracha ryter* had caused it. She fished the ropes she'd cut off the Naobian's limbs from her pockets and thrust them deep into Izoldia's tunic. "Hopefully, they'll think she's the traitor who led you here."

Cries carried on the crisp pre-dawn air as the assassins raced between the palms, getting closer every moment.

The *dracha* bellowed and landed with a flurry of wings.

"Fast," said the Naobian, "go back to your quarters through the tunnel." He snatched the dates that had hit Izoldia and flung them into a saddlebag, then helped Ezaara on Erob's back.

Ithsar flung herself down the chimney, and he pulled foliage back over the entrance. Only when she reached the bottom and turned on her lamp did she realize she'd forgotten to farewell the *dracha ryter* and tell them about her vision.

Treacherous Secrets

The roar of the mighty blue-scaled *dracha* shook the ground above Ithsar's head, sending sand into her hair. She clambered down the rough-hewn hand and footholds and scurried along the tunnel, more sand dusting her head and shoulders. Blinking grit out of her eyes, she hurried on. Yells from outside drifted through the foliage and down the dark passage. Another roar came, more distant now. Ithsar was glad—hopefully it meant the *dracha* was escaping, whisking Ezaara and her Naobian lover, Roberto, away from the oasis.

She scrambled over a pile of scree and shale from a fall in, her stomach coiled as tight as a rust viper in the hot desert sand—hoping like the blazing sun that the Naobian had pulled the foliage over the tunnel entrance well enough to fool her fellow assassins. Most people had long forgotten the secret tunnel. She prayed the *dracha* gods would be kind and help it stay that way.

If she got caught aiding the *dracha ryter*—the northern dragon riders her mother had captured—to escape, her life would be in danger.

Although fear prickled along her scalp, Ithsar tried her best to remain calm so no one would detect a ripple in her *sathir*—the life energy binding every living thing—as she made her way along the secret passage under the lake. The lantern at her waist flickered, casting looming shadows on the walls, shadows with long fingers that leaped out grasping as she ran.

When she reached the entrance to the tunnel, Ithsar was panting. She paused to catch her breath and cocked her head. The tunnels riddling the silent assassins' underground lair were quiet. Her only chance was to sneak back to bed and pretend she'd missed everything—but Izoldia was a major thorn in that plan. Izoldia had been on duty watching the Naobian who'd still been tied to his bed in the healing quarters when Ithsar had relieved her. Ezaara had said that after having woozy weed Izoldia may not remember everything, but which of her memories would be hazy? Those in the healing room, or only the recent fight by the lake?

For long moments, Ithsar waited in the shadows. If she went to the healing quarters and pretended she'd been asleep, she'd probably encounter people who'd wonder why she hadn't rushed to help capture the strangers when the alarm had been raised. But if she went to her sleeping alcove and pretended she'd missed everything and then Izoldia later remembered her sitting with the Naobian, she could be accused of treason and executed. Had anyone checked her alcove to see whether she'd still been sleeping? By the *dracha* gods, she should have thought everything through before she released the prisoners, but she'd been so desperate to set them free she hadn't spared a thought for her own life.

It didn't matter. Ezaara, she of golden beauty, the new Queen's Rider who'd healed Ithsar's damaged fingers, was now her friend. Roberto, Ezaara's beloved Naobian man with olive-black eyes that gleamed with love as he beheld the Queen's Rider, was her friend too. Since Ithsar's father had died when she was a littling, she'd yearned for human friendship. With only her lizard Thika to keep her company, she'd been lonely. But now, she had two new friends. A smile traced her lips and she flexed her newly-healed fingers in wonder. Now, she could hold her head high and fight with the other assassins. She need no longer be afraid of not being worthy. No longer be afraid of being the deformed one, the only assassin unable to fight.

Light footsteps and the faint rustle of clothing sounded along the northern tunnel. That ruled out going back to the healing cavern, then.

Ithsar's newly-healed fingers doused the light on her lantern. She plunged into the darkness, fleeing along the southern tunnel, trailing her fingertips along the wall to sense her way to her sleeping alcove. Fingertips that could feel, sense, and move again with newfound freedom.

§

Ithsar woke to something burrowing into her armpit. Thika popped his orange scaly head onto her chest and looked up at her with his yellow eyes. His tongue flicked out and tickled Ithsar's chin. She smiled and rubbed his eye ridges. The lizard's eyes hooded and his body thrummed with pleasure as he leaned into Ithsar's touch. Without the old pain shooting up her fingers, things like stroking Thika were more pleasurable—Ezaara had not only healed her, she'd given her the power to enjoy such simple things.

Ithsar sat up and cradled him in her lap. Running her fingers over the dark bands on Thika's orange back, she whispered, "I'm so glad Ezaara healed you too." Someone had recently poisoned Thika. Ezaara had managed to detect which poison it was by sensing the *sathir* of various poisons and remedies to see how they affected the lizard.

Ithsar swallowed. Everyone knew her father had given her Thika before her mother, Ashewar, the chief prophetess, had executed him when Ithsar was only four. Ithsar blinked, seeing her father's pleading dark eyes as he'd begged her to take care of herself and be strong, before they'd killed him.

The best way to hurt her was to strike at Thika. After enduring Izoldia's taunting and physical torment for years, she knew Izoldia was most likely the poisoner.

Distant footsteps scraped the dry dirt in the tunnel outside her tiny alcove. Ithsar's keen ears caught the whisper of fabric. She popped Thika on the bed and pulled on her orange robe. She tapped her belly. Thika clambered over her legs, along the voluminous fabric, and crawled inside the front of her robe. He flattened his body, settling himself above her waistband as she pulled the stays shut.

The curtains across the narrow opening of her alcove slid open, their iron rings rasping against the brass bar. Thut, one of Ashewar's most trusted guards, thrust her head inside. Thut's eyes slid over Ithsar and, curling her lip, she crooked her finger, motioning Ithsar to follow.

Ithsar nodded demurely and kept her eyes downcast as she rose and left her tiny alcove.

More guards were waiting, one on either side of her nook, flat against the wall. Without a word, they each grasped one of her arms and dragged Ithsar along the corridor toward the chief prophetess' grand hall.

§

"Where were you last night?" Ashewar hissed, her dark fiery eyes burning through Ithsar like the desert sun. The chief prophetess was seated on her grotesque, ornately-carved throne depicting hundreds of female assassins murdering men.

Ashewar's personal guards—a semicircle of stony-faced female assassins standing behind her throne—didn't even look at Ithsar.

Ashewar thrust her chin forward, the diamond studs in her beaked nose glinting and the beads in her hundreds of tiny braids clacking. "I said, *where were you?*" Her whisper echoed off the walls. Torches guttered, as if Ashewar's voice controlled the brightness of their flame.

No one's gaze shriveled Ithsar's heart the way her mother's did.

Ithsar flexed her fingers, keeping them hidden in her long sleeves. Her mother didn't yet know that they were healed, and now was not the right time to reveal that surprise. "Asleep," she murmured, meeting her mother's gaze for a fleeting heartbeat before she lowered her eyes and stared at her dusty feet. Grains of sand clung to her toenails. She marked the passing time with her thundering heartbeats, surprised the rhythm wasn't reverberating off the walls of the grand cavern.

"Asleep? The alarm sounded, yet you slept?"

The alarm—hundreds of feet slapping against the floors as the silent assassins had sought Ezaara and then Roberto in the maze of tunnels between the caverns. The assassin's vows of silence meant they were attuned to hear the faintest noises in the tunnels. Attuned to feel the subtle shifts in *sathir*. Their muted footfalls should have been enough to wake the deepest sleeper.

The guards would be sensing her *sathir* now. Ithsar had to maintain a sense of calm and keep herself as cool as the lake waters above them—or someone would sense a ripple in the colored fabric that joined them together. "Yes, most revered Chief Prophetess." She breathed slowly through her nose and kept her head lowered so her mother wouldn't see the pulse racing at her throat. Her waistband was damp with sweat where Thika pressed his body against her skin.

Ashewar despised Ithsar and Thika. She always had, but Izoldia's snipes and jeers had fueled her mother's hatred into something wild and pulsing that bashed at Ithsar's skull.

The door thunked open. A heavy tread on the stone marked Izoldia's arrival. Two female assassins, both much shorter than Izoldia, guided the burly guard into the cavern. She was sporting a black eye and an egg on her forehead the size of a small sand dune. Izoldia sank to her knees and bowed low enough to scrape her ugly nose on the floor.

One push, and Izoldia would fall flat on her face.

"My honored Chief Prophetess," Izoldia's harsh whisper cut through the cavern. She'd never been good at keeping their vows of silence, but it didn't matter because she could fight. Ashewar overlooked Izoldia's shortcomings because of her size, sycophantic attitude and sadistic streak.

Hands still hidden in her sleeves, Ithsar subtly dug her fingernails into her palms—the only movement she dared make to calm herself. A new movement—her fingers had refused to bend properly until Ezaara had healed them. Thika's tail shifted slightly, his scales slithering across her hip.

Ashewar's voice hissed again. "What were you doing last night, Izoldia?" She snapped her fingers.

A guard stepped forward and dropped to one knee in front of Ashewar, holding out two pieces of hacked-off rope.

Rope that Ithsar had cut to free the Naobian with the olive-black eyes, then stuffed into Izoldia's pockets. Would Izoldia remember what she'd done? Or had the woozy weed numbed her memory, as Ezaara had promised? Ithsar let her gaze slide around the room, examining each guard's face for a reaction, for a sign that they'd seen her shake the very palm trees with the power of *sathir*.

Roshni, a slight guard with piercing blue eyes and ebony skin, from the deep South, was watching her every move. Despite her knees wanting to melt like camel butter in the midday sun, Ithsar met Roshni's gaze squarely, pretending she had nothing to fear.

"What are these?" Ashewar addressed Izoldia, flicking a finger at the ropes as if they were bugs on her robes.

Izoldia's eyebrows rose, and she shrugged. "I don't know. Um, ropes?"

"What were the prisoner's bonds doing in your pocket?" the chief prophetess' dark eyes flashed with venom.

Izoldia stayed on her knees, arms prostrated on the floor before their leader. Her voice shook like palm fronds in a sandstorm—something Ithsar never thought she'd hear. "I—I do not remember." Her face rippled with fear.

Ashewar's dark eyes narrowed, glittering like burning coals. "If you do not remember, why are you afraid?"

Cunning stole over Izoldia's features. "An assassin likes to keep her wits about her, my revered and highly intelligent Chief Prophetess. I don't know what happened and woke with a bump on my head and found out that the scrawny *dracha* and its two *ryter* had escaped while under my watch. It was enough to cause fear in anyone." Izoldia remained prostrated on the floor, her arms practically touching Ashewar's feet. Ashewar flicked a beaded slipper toward Izoldia's hand.

Those slippers, traditional *yokka*, didn't fool Ithsar. Underneath the hundreds of tiny orange beads glinting in the torchlight, there were blades hidden in the soles that would spring out if Ashewar pressed her big toe down. Izoldia's wrist was within a finger's breadth of those blades.

"The prisoner was under your care, my loyal guard," Ashewar crooned, caressing the inside of Izoldia's wrist—along a pulsing vein—with the toe of her *yokka*. No doubt, considering setting the blade free. "How did the Naobian escape if you were watching him?"

Izoldia leaped to her feet. Her head hanging, she whispered, "I do not know. I don't remember anything."

Ashewar's head spun to glare at Ithsar. "And you? Why weren't you fighting last night?"

"I slept deeply."

Ashewar's eyes narrowed, flitting between them both. The chief prophetess' smile turned into a feral grin. "Izoldia, the prisoner escaped on your watch. Although you are my most fearless and courageous personal guard, I have no choice. You will be whipped twelve times and tied to a palm tree in the hot desert sun until mid-afternoon." Leaning against the hideous carvings on her throne, Ashewar waved a languid hand. "If she cries out, rub salt into her wounds."

Ashewar's whisper died, the slap of bare feet the only sound as the guards grasped the stunned Izoldia and marched her from the room.

After the years of torture, burns, and bullying at Izoldia's hands, Ithsar knew she should feel jubilation at Izoldia's punishment. But, twelve lashes in the hot sun? It was her fault that Izoldia's flesh would turn into a bloody pulp. Ithsar tried not to cringe. She wouldn't wish that upon anyone.

Ashewar gestured at Bala, one of the more vicious guards and a close crony to Izoldia. "Once Izoldia has been whipped, arrange for a tonic to heal her head and restore her memory. We must get to the bottom of this."

Her gaze snapped to Ithsar, her black eyes glittering more brightly than the diamond studs in her beaked nose. "Someone who sleeps through the alarm needs to gain strength. You are on drill, doing the *Sathiri* dance in the training cavern until nightfall. No food nor water." She waved to her guards.

"Bala, once you've ordered the healing tonic, you will oversee her dance." Ithsar's mother flashed a terrifying smile that reeked of bloodlust. "If the deformed wretch collapses, leave her. Anyone who helps her is under the threat of death."

Dance of the Sathiri

Ithsar kept her fingers tucked inside her palms and hands inside her too-long sleeves as she executed the movements of the ancient dance of the *Sathiri*. She pointed her toes, kicked and spun, then lifted her knee and swung her arm, pretending to wield a saber. Even though her chest felt as if it would crack in two for causing Izoldia's whipping, the smooth rhythm of the dance soon soothed her. The women around her moved as one, flowing like the tide on a shore, the hissing and slap of their feet against the sandstone floor and the soft huffs of their breaths echoing around the chamber. The other women's sabers glinted in the flickering lamplight, but, due to her mangled fingers, Ithsar had never been allowed to wield a saber. Maybe tomorrow, after she'd danced all day to prove herself, when she showed her mother her healed fingers, she would at last earn a real blade instead of the dagger she'd once stolen from the weapons cache when no one had been around.

Thika stayed pressed against her belly, adjusting his weight to compensate for her movements, the harmony between her and the lizard filling her with quiet peace. Her father had found the tiny hatchling abandoned in the tangerine desert sands and gifted Thika to her. Ithsar had fed Thika, catching flies and bugs for him and oiling his dry scales during the molting season. Sometimes the lizard disappeared for hours to hunt around the oasis, but his favorite place to sleep was nestled around her belly. She carried him under her clothing to help him avoid detection. Izoldia had made more than one attempt on Thika's life. It wasn't enough that Ithsar was scorned and hated by all the women—no, Izoldia wouldn't even allow her the small privilege of loving the lizard her father had given her.

Ithsar's breath caught in her throat as her father's face flashed to mind: his handsome face; the kind smile lines around his mouth; and the way he used to hold Ithsar on his lap and tell stories of his life beyond the oasis out in the wild desert. Stories of taming camels, fighting rust vipers with a knife, or the story of him nearly dying. Dehydrated, he'd been taken in by the female assassins to breed an heir to the chief prophetess. Often, he'd stroked Ithsar's hair, saying, "You are Ashewar's heir. Never forget it. You are the most precious thing in my life." His love had warmed Ithsar's heart, sinking down deep into her bones.

One day, when she'd been a littling of four summers, he'd found her crying.

"What's wrong, my beautiful princess?" He stroked the tears from her cheeks and scooped her into his strong arms, the scent of camel enveloping her.

"The older girls say I'm weak because my fingers don't work. That mother will kill me when I come of age," she whispered, terrified someone would hear her speaking aloud and punish her. Although no one punished Izoldia when she spoke.

"Was it Izoldia, Bala and Thut?"

Her lip wobbled as she nodded. More tears came. "They did this." Ithsar held out her arm, swollen and mottled with rapidly-forming bruises. "They hurt me. They'll snap my arm if I tell anyone, but I can tell you, can't I?"

Her father had nodded, eyes burning with rage, and gone off to find the girls who'd hurt her.

That night, she'd heard voices in Ashewar's sleeping chamber. Raised voices—unheard of in the lair of the silent assassins—her parents arguing.

Her heart had rejoiced that her father was championing her. She'd rolled over and gone back to sleep.

The same heart had broken in the morning when she learned her mother had ordered his execution.

Tears had glimmered in her father's eyes, then, as he stole a few last moments with her. "Remember," he whispered, his voice a flutter against her ear, "I will always love you. Be strong, practice the *Sathiri* dance every day. Even if no one sees you, I will be watching over you. One day, you will rise above your mother's petty hatred, for you are my precious daughter, strong beyond words." He kissed her hair and caressed her fingers with his bound hands.

The guards yanked his rope, pulling him away from her. They dragged him down the tunnels.

And then her mother had collected her and made her watch.

Ithsar faltered, her foot slipping on the cavern's sandstone floor.

Bala's eyes flicked to her as the women around her continued moving in rhythm. Lip curling, Bala snapped her fingers, the sharp sound whipping through the natural echo chamber of the training cavern.

All movement stopped, women freezing mid-pose, arms extended and knees bent. Waiting.

Bala stalked, feet barely making a whisper on the dusty cavern floor. Ithsar angled her head, holding her cheek up, ready.

Humiliation washed over her. She could never be a true Robandi assassin, despite her healed fingers. She was too weak. Too full of what her mother called fool's sentiment. If just the thought of her father made her falter, how could she kill? She didn't have it in her. She was a failure.

The ominous faint scrape of Bala's feet on sandstone reverberated off the cavern walls, reminding Ithsar of the night she'd unlocked the cell in the corner and let Ezaara loose. Ezaara had dropped her saber, the clattering echo raising the alarm for the assassins, but at least Ithsar had helped the Queen's Rider and her lover get free.

Bala stopped in front of her, leering.

Ithsar drew in a breath and braced herself. *You are my precious daughter…*

Bala drew a knife from her belt and slapped the flat of the blade against Ithsar's cheek.

Despite her stinging cheek, Ithsar kept her gaze steady, her spine straight and her chin up… s*trong beyond words.*

A figure moved from the shadows, beads on tiny braids clicking softly as Ashewar made her way through the ranks of silent assassins, still frozen in place. She clapped her fingers and the assassins stood down.

"Not you," Ashewar hissed, glaring at Ithsar. She motioned with a flat hand.

Ithsar quickly raised her arms again and lifted her knee, and froze in *Sathiri* stance.

The other assassins retreated to line the walls, leaving Ithsar standing alone in the middle of the voluminous cavern. One by one, they filed into the barred cell where Ezaara had been captive and helped themselves to a dipper of cool water from the natural spring.

Ithsar licked her lips, throat dry. She hadn't even eaten or had the barest sip of water before the guards had manhandled her to Ashewar, but now was not the time to ask.

Ashewar nodded, eyes glittering with malice, not with the love Ithsar longed for. She motioned Ithsar to continue.

With a heavy heart, hands still hidden in her sleeves, Ithsar spun on her left toe, her right leg flung out, and then landed and raised her arm in a defensive block, flawlessly executing the next *Sathiri* movement.

Ashewar's eyes blazed.

Ashewar had never seen her complete the full dance. Because of Ithsar's bent, scarred fingers, she'd been assigned menial tasks, rarely joining the assassins' training. But since her father's death, Ithsar had practiced every night in her tiny sleeping alcove, her fingertips and toes nearly brushing the walls. So Ithsar continued, sweeping her arm wide in a blow that would dismember any attacker—if she had a saber. But now was not the time to ask Ashewar for a saber. Not until she'd proved she could perform the killing dance. Ithsar spun and leaped again, kicking an imaginary attacker's chest. She landed, following through with a left arm flick as if she were throwing a knife. Keeping her hands still buried in her long sleeves, she twirled and executed a series of slashes. On and on she danced, until she'd executed all thirty movements of the *Sathiri* killing dance.

Ithsar stood before Ashewar, head high and chest heaving, controlling her breathing so she didn't huff. Surely her mother was proud of the way she'd executed the dance. Surely now she could have a drink.

Ashewar's eyes fell to the ends of Ithsar's sleeves. Her lip curled and she motioned for Ithsar to start the sequence over.

She would try harder, and earn her mother's love if it killed her. Ithsar slipped into the starting stance again, and spun, kicked, and slashed. She sprang higher, moved faster, leaped farther until, at last, she stood before her mother, the dance complete. Surely now…

Ashewar's nose wrinkled. She gazed down at Ithsar and motioned her to begin again.

When her mother found out that her hands were healed, Ithsar would join the ranks of the assassins, but now, she had to prove she was worthy. Her hollow belly rumbled, but Ithsar unleashed her full power, spinning, turning, and flying through the air. *Sathir* swirled around her in reddish waves, tendrils flying from her as she attacked imaginary assailants. Waves of pale blue *sathir* flowed from Roshni, her ebony braid glinting in the torchlight as she watched Ithsar's every movement with those piercing blue eyes, stony-faced. More *sathir* flowed from three others, until the blue, red, orange, and greens of their intertwined *sathir* danced in time to the rhythm of Ithsar's movements. Too tired to figure out what the merging *sathir* meant, Ithsar kept dancing.

Her legs shook as Ashewar motioned her to start yet again.

Ithsar made a cupping gesture, the sign she and her silent sisters used when they needed to drink.

The chief prophetess' face hardened and she waved her to continue dancing. The four assassins whose *sathir* was now intertwined with hers shifted against the wall, but said nothing.

Shoulders aching and legs trembling, Ithsar began the dance again, arching her back with more agility, putting in extra effort to impress her mother. *Sathir* swirled as she danced and finished, landing with her head high and a smile on her face. That was it. Any moment now, her mother would smile back, then she'd show Ashewar her healed fingers.

The corners of Ashewar's mouth drew down and she thrust her hand out, motioning her to start over, then held up her hands, her fingers splayed. Once. Twice. Thrice.

Thirty more times?

Ithsar's smile froze, but she didn't dare show her displeasure, so she kept her forced smile in place as she started the next thirty rounds of the *Sathiri* dance. Her head spun from lack of food. Her throat was dry and scratchy, like she'd swallowed sand. Perhaps she'd breathed in the grains that had flown around her as she'd danced. No matter, she could do this—she could prove herself to her mother.

Ashewar gestured to the other assassins to go to the mess cavern for food, as if she knew Ithsar's belly ached from hunger. She gave Bala a grim nod, motioning her to keep watch on Ithsar, and, robes rustling, stalked from the cavern—not toward the mess cavern or her throne room, but out toward the entrance—to witness Izoldia's whipping.

Under Bala's glower, Ithsar finished a cycle and began the dance again, limbs leaden and her movements hollow. Her gnawing belly matched the emptiness of her heart. Her whole life she'd endured scorn, abuse and dismissal because of her deformed fingers. Couldn't her mother see that all she wanted was her love?

No, not love—the chief prophetess wasn't sentimental. Approval—the barest nod or hand motion to show her mother was satisfied.

As Ithsar finished the next cycle, the *sathir* around her washed scarlet. Blinding red pain flashed through her mind. She faltered and gasped. Izoldia—it had to be. The *sathir* was the color of blood. Blood that would be running down Izoldia's back—and all because she'd planted the prisoner's bindings in the burly guard's pocket. Ithsar stumbled as the *sathir* ran off her in rivulets, pooling like water at her feet.

Bala sneered. "Tired?" she hissed, not daring to use a louder voice and have it echo around the cavern and bring assassins running.

Ithsar kept dancing, completing that cycle and the next, and the next, her mind searing with Izoldia's pain and red *sathir* spraying from her hands. Bala's teeth flashed in greeting as a new shift of assassins filed into the cavern. They joined Ithsar in allotted positions, twirling and slashing in time with her. Not one of them gave her a second glance. None of them could see the blood-red *sathir*. None of them could sense Izoldia's pain.

But, from a young age, Ithsar had possessed the gift of seeing without the aid of her mother's prism-seer. Especially when events directly affected her. She'd seen a vision of her future: flying into battle on a mighty green *dracha* with Ezaara flying on the multi-hued queen of Dragons' Realm and Roberto on his blue *dracha* Erob. Ezaara had given her a new chance to be whole, so Ithsar had set them free.

And let Izoldia take the blame.

Limbs nearly giving out and movements growing clumsy, Ithsar drove herself harder. But dance as she might, she couldn't shake the visions of blood-red *sathir* coating her hands and pooling at her feet.

Yes, she was responsible for her tormentor's pain.

Lashed

Four assassins manhandled Izoldia along the tunnels underneath the oasis. Her head spun. The huge bump she'd somehow gotten last night ached, making her head throb in time with the guards' footfalls. She couldn't remember anything past her midday meal yesterday. Her face was covered in bruises and her body as battle-weary as if she'd been on a killing spree. Vague dreams of a storm—palm fronds slashing among purple clouds—flitted at the edges of her mind. But that couldn't be right. She'd even asked Thut, and indeed, there'd been no storm yesterday.

Besides, Ithsar's face featured in those dreams, full of rage and strength. Izoldia snorted. That runt Ithsar was anything but strong. No, it must be just another nightmare about that pathetic heir of the chief prophetess, the useless sniveling thing. Izoldia should have poisoned her too, not just that slimy lizard that Ithsar insisted on carrying around like a crutch. When Izoldia was finished with her lashes, she'd kill the lizard and Ithsar too.

Then no one could stand between her and the chief prophetess.

And, when the chief prophetess was dead, there'd be nothing between Izoldia and the beautiful throne Ashewar sat upon—made from the bones of murdered men and carved with the Robandi Assassins' killing rituals. Deep at night, when no one was around, Izoldia sneaked into the throne room and ran her fingers over the carved patterns, reveling in the exotic depictions of women murdering men. By studying the carvings, she'd learned new methods of torture, and had been hoping to test those methods on the Naobian prisoner as she forced him to breed with her sisters. But now, he was gone.

A sun-blasted shame—she'd hoped they'd spawn fine daughters from him. Daughters they could raise to be strong assassins in true Robandi tradition. Ashewar had assigned Izoldia to kill the Naobian when his time was up. Izoldia had planned a slow and torturous death, peeling his skin under the desert sun while she carved holes in his pretty face.

And then there were the other deaths she would've enjoyed—the newborn babes, his rejected spawn—all males or deformed females. Slicing littlings open while they screamed and watching the vultures pluck their bones clean had been her delightful pleasure when they'd last kidnapped men for their seed. There was no place for men or cripples among the assassins. No place for soft emotions. No place for that runty heir, Ithsar.

Yes, it was a sun-blasted shame, but the guards had found the ropes in Izoldia's own pockets. She couldn't remember releasing him, couldn't remember anything. Had he unbound his own ropes, fought with her and hit her head, escaping? Her cheeks burned with shame. Whatever had happened, it was obviously her fault. She'd failed the prophetess, failed her people.

Their chances of replenishing their ranks were gone. Unless she hunted down more men.

Yes, she'd find more men for her sisters to spawn from, so she could earn her way back into Ashewar's good graces.

As they clambered up the tunnel toward the daylight, Izoldia stumbled, her head throbbing. A guard hefted her arm to help her up—Thut, who wouldn't dare disobey Ashewar, but was a loyal crony. Izoldia kept her head high. She would not falter. She'd take her lashes without a scream. The prisoner had escaped on her watch, so she deserved them.

They stepped through the entrance into the shade of the date palms. Sentinels parted, letting them pass. Izoldia's feet shuffled through the cool sand as Thut and the other three guards led her under the palms out to the edge of the oasis. Vast orange sands shimmered with the sun's haze. Heat beat down upon Izoldia's face. The sand was already burning the soles of her feet. She squinted against the brightness, then bowed her head against a palm trunk. Thut and the others tied ropes around her wrists, and bound her to the tree. Izoldia let them. She deserved this. The chief prophetess' prime breeding stock had been lost on her watch.

Thut uncoiled a whip from her waist, and moved in, murmuring so quietly it couldn't be deemed as treason, "I have no wish to lash you. I am only obeying Ashewar."

Izoldia gave the faintest nod. It made no difference. She'd accept her scars as trophies, a symbol of her submission to the prophetess. But one day, she would no longer submit. Then she would pay back every assassin who had ever caused a wisp of harm to her.

The whip cracked, slicing through Izoldia's robes into her flesh. She clenched her jaw against its stinging bite as rivulets of warm blood trickled down her back.

Another crack. Pain lanced across her shoulders. Gritting her teeth, she kept her head bowed so the whip wouldn't mark her face. When the third lash came, she clamped her teeth down, biting the edge of her tongue. Her mouth flew open in a grimace. She arched her back against the pain, but refused to cry out.

The next strike of the whip cut deep into her flesh, driving Izoldia's body into the date palm. Her forehead smacked against the knobbly trunk. She gasped and shuddered as her back burned.

Sand hissed as Ashewar's orange-slippered feet came into view. She stepped from the shade into the blazing sun, her rings glinting. The prophetess' cool voice rang out, "Not only the tip, Thut. Let her have the full brunt of the lash."

The next stinging lash made Izoldia's knees falter and her body sag. The impact nearly wrenched her shoulders from their sockets, the ropes on her bound arms the only thing holding her in place. The lash bit into her back again and again, agonizing blows that shredded her back, blood splattering the tree trunk and streaming down her legs.

On the twelfth lash, her jaw unlocked and a cry ripped from her throat, shattering the silence between the whip cracks.

"You," Ashewar's voice hissed. "Rub salt into her wounds. It's not becoming for my strongest warrior to cry out in pain." Ashewar turned and strode back under the date palms to their underground lair, her rustling robes nearly kissing Izoldia's face as she passed.

Drida—their oldest assassin, a silver-haired woman who could strike a man dead with one well-aimed kick—paced to Izoldia and untied a pouch of salt from her belt. Not a lick of sympathy showed in the harsh lines of her ancient wrinkled face as her eyes flicked over Izoldia. She rubbed salt into Izoldia's wounds. Roughly. The scrape and grind of the grit made Izoldia scream. Tears of pain ran down her face in rivulets, wetting her orange robes.

And then the assassins left her out under the heat of the beating sun.

A Test of Endurance

Bala was relentless, insisting that Ithsar keep dancing long after thirty cycles were done. After forty. And fifty. Until Ithsar lost count. Until time was measured by the slap of her feet, the whirl of her body and the blood pumping in her ears. Every time she slowed, Ithsar received another smack with the flat of Bala's saber—on her arms, cheeks, or legs. But Ithsar accepted it. It was less pain than what she'd caused Izoldia.

The others filed off for their evening meal. Bala left, and Thut replaced her to watch Ithsar. Still, Ithsar danced, her limbs slow and sluggish. Thut picked at her nails with her blade, leaning against the wall, occasionally gesturing that Ithsar should speed up. At last, the assassins joined her for the late evening dance.

Ithsar swiped a hand at her dry, pounding temples—she'd stopped sweating long ago. There was little fluid left in her. Giant dark spots swam before her eyes, obscuring the assassins to her left. Not *sathir*. Exhaustion.

Her breath rasped, dry and hot in her throat. She leaped and stumbled, then flung her arm weakly. She jumped and thrust out her foot to land. Ithsar's knee buckled and she slammed into the sandstone. Her body flew across the floor, gashing her cheek. A warm gush of blood pooled under her face. Although she tried to push up with her hands, her elbows collapsed and she lay amid the dancers, slumped on the cool stone. At least, here, she could rest.

Thut barked at her, threatened her, but she couldn't respond. So Thut motioned at the other women to keep dancing and ignore her.

Ithsar's head spun as the slap and scrape of feet thrummed through the sandstone against her aching, bloody cheek. Then darkness claimed her.

§

Ithsar woke, cold and shivering, to something scraping her cheek.

No, not scraping, but licking. "Thika?"

The lizard squirmed under her face, trying to rouse her. Ithsar's breath shuddered out of her. Everything ached, her head spun, and the blood on her cheek had congealed. She tried to swallow but her mouth and throat were as dry as the desert sand. Thika wriggled again. How had he squeezed under her face?

The scuff of feet carried along a passage. More than one pair of feet. Were Bala and Thut coming to gloat over her? Gods, what had happened to Izoldia?

Heart pounding, Ithsar froze on the stone, the last nearly-dead torch sputtering. It must be the deep of night. Thika wormed his way under her neck, hiding.

A shadow fell over her body as someone bent over her. Ithsar braced herself for a kick or jab.

"Thank the *dracha* gods you're still with us," Roshni breathed so softly, Ithsar wondered if she'd imagined it. Roshni knelt beside her and lifted her aching head, gazing at her with those piercing blue eyes. "Look," she rasped faintly, her voice croaky from disuse, "your lizard tried to protect you. He slunk under your cheek to stop you from swallowing your blood."

A low moan threatened to escape Ithsar, but she held it in. No need to set the chamber echoing—that would only bring people running.

Roshni held a waterskin to her lips. The cavern dipped and swayed as Ithsar sipped. The cool, refreshing nectar of life slid down her throat.

In the shadows at the edge of the cavern, someone moved. An assassin materialized from the gloom, her silver hair glinting in the torchlight—Drida, holding a blanket.

Drida motioned that they must leave, and Roshni nodded and scooped Ithsar into her arms. Drida tucked the blanket around Ithsar and picked up Thika, depositing him on Ithsar's belly. Then she pulled a bandage from her robes and pressed it to Ithsar's cheek. Her eyes flitted around the cavern and she made the hand gesture for leaving swiftly.

When they were deep in the passage, halfway to Ithsar's sleeping alcove, Drida murmured, her voice as soft as a moth's wing, "I was on duty in the healing cavern tending Izoldia, but all I could think of was you, lying there, broken and wounded."

Ithsar's only reply was a violent shiver.

"You're cold." Drida took her hand. Her brows shot up. Eyes wide, she stared at Ithsar's hand.

Roshni stopped walking, staring too. "Your fingers…"

Although it made her head pound, Ithsar managed a weak nod and wriggled her healthy fingers.

Roshni said nothing more, slipping through the tunnels, Drida nipping ahead to make sure the way was clear. When they reached her sleeping alcove, Drida lifted the curtain without drawing it, so the rings wouldn't scrape along the brass rail. Roshni ducked inside, carrying her, and Drida followed, letting the heavy curtain fall.

Roshni deposited Ithsar gently on her bed, but instead of the two women leaving, Drida took a tiny lantern from her belt and lit it, and the two assassins sat beside Ithsar on her mattress, Drida at her head and Roshni by her belly. Thika crawled straight back into her robes to rest against Ithsar's stomach. Warm, familiar, comforting—despite the raging aches rippling through her muscles.

Roshni held Ithsar's fingers, examining them, wonder in her eyes.

Ithsar didn't dare tell Roshni how she'd been healed. Two of Ashewar's most trusted guards, these women could've been sent by the chief prophetess to wheedle out her secrets.

Drida drew a needle and twine from her robe and stitched Ithsar's cheek, her smile warm and her fingers nimble.

Roshni pulled some flatbread and dates from one of the many pockets in her robe and passed them to Ithsar. "Eat and gain strength, for I'm sure the dawn shall bring new trials." Her blue eyes were concerned—such a strange color for a southerner, vividly bright against her dark skin.

Ithsar took a piece of flatbread and chewed it, nearly gagging.

"Here, more water," whispered Drida, eyes darting to Ithsar's curtain. The water helped ease the passage of the flatbread down her dry throat. As Ithsar chewed the sweet, succulent dates, Drida continued, "You know, you should leave. Ashewar hates you and will find another way to hurt you."

"And if she doesn't, Izoldia will," Roshni whispered.

Drida leaned in so close, Ithsar could barely hear, her breath tickling Ithsar's ear. "We can prepare a camel for you on the far side of the oasis and wake you in two hours so you can leave."

Their *sathir* didn't show the dark shadows of betrayal, just a calm yellow tinge around Roshni and an orange glow around Drida, but where would Ithsar go? What would she do? She'd only ever lived in the lair beneath the oasis. For a heartbeat, Ithsar hesitated. Leaving didn't feel right, despite her maltreatment at her mother and Izoldia's hands. "I can't," murmured Ithsar. "This is my home."

"But what good is a home where you must hide who you truly are?" Drida whispered urgently. "You danced an entire day without food or water. You have great strength and talent, yet you've masked it. And now, Ashewar knows. She will not make life easy for you." Drida tilted her head, her voice a faint breath. "Are you sure you don't want to run away?"

Ithsar nodded.

The women stood and slipped out her curtain.

They'd seemed to be genuine. Their *sathir* had even appeared so, but Ithsar couldn't help a dark foreboding that Drida and Roshni were working against her. That they were scheming for Ashewar, trying to catch her out so they could hurt her.

So far, everyone but her father and Thika had.

Ithsar sipped the water they'd left and chewed the remaining flatbread and dates, cradling Thika against her belly as a lone tear slipped down her cheek.

Agony

With a start, Izoldia awoke, lying on her stomach in the same bed that stinking Naobian had lain in when he'd been healing from his slit gut. The bed he'd been in the night he'd escaped. The night she'd been watching him. Had that only been yesterday?

By those slimy reptilian *dracha* gods, what had happened?

Irritation flashed through Izoldia at the constant dribble of water—the underground stream flowing through the edge of the healing cavern. Despite it being the deep of night, that cursed water made it hard to drift off again. She shifted, her head still foggy—and now throbbing from the long hours under the desert sun. Her back burned. By the cursed sun gods, she could barely move.

With such terrible gut wounds, how had that Naobian managed to run and evade everyone hunting him through the cavern tunnels? Ashewar had reported that he'd flown off on his giant blue *dracha* with that woman of the golden hair, but managing to climb on a *dracha* with such shocking wounds was about as likely as rain in the Robandi desert.

She tried to push up on her hands, but her back screamed in agony, so she slumped down again.

Robes rustled and a cool hand was laid upon her brow. Those same hands held a reed straw to her lips.

Curse it, so much pain that she couldn't even sit up. Glowering, Izoldia tugged water through the straw, then laid her head down again. The healer's footfalls padded away.

Izoldia's eyelids fluttered. They'd put healing tonic in her water to make her doze so her body could recover. She fought the tonic, battling to stay awake as a memory niggled at the edge of her mind.

In a flash, Izoldia remembered Ithsar requesting to take over her post guarding the Naobian, suggesting that Izoldia should fight. With a lurch in her gut, Izoldia knew that despicable worm had betrayed them. That sniveling good-for-nothing hangdog with the broken fingers, that softhearted piece of camel dung, had fooled them. She must have planted the ropes in Izoldia's pockets after helping that foreign scum escape. Izoldia hadn't betrayed Ashewar at all. Ithsar had.

Ithsar had cheated Izoldia of her fun with that man. Cheated her of forcing him to breed and create daughters. Cheated her of the chance to slay any male offspring he would've sired.

And it was Ithsar's fault Izoldia had been lashed. Ithsar's fault that Izoldia's back was a mess of fleshy, bloody tatters and searing pain. Due to Ithsar's cunning, Izoldia had fallen out of Ashewar's favor.

Izoldia's burning back was nothing compared to the hatred that burned through her gut as she contemplated her revenge. Then the tonic claimed Izoldia and, try as she might, she could no longer battle her drooping eyelids, so she drifted into a restless sleep.

Stealth

Izoldia screamed in pain, begging Ithsar not to whip her. But Ithsar gave a grim smile and flicked the whip again, scoring deep into Izoldia's bloody, tattered back.

"Enough! Please!" Izoldia begged.

Ithsar struck her again and again.

"Please, Ithsar, be true," her father pleaded. "You are my precious daughter, strong beyond words."

"Thank you, Father." Ithsar smiled, whipping her enemy's back until she collapsed dead on the sand. Still, Ithsar lashed her, again and again.

Until Izoldia's body disintegrated into tiny blood-red sand grains, carried away by the wind.

Ithsar's chest heaved as she stared down at herself. Her robes were splattered in Izoldia's blood, her whip slick in her hand, and her arms stained red to the elbows.

She turned to her father, but his eyes were dead, soulless black holes that sucked her toward him, step by step. His body grew, towering over her, wreathed in black shadows. A whip appeared in his hands. "Now it's my turn, princess," he crooned, his words as soft as gossamer as he raised the whip to beat her.

Ithsar jolted up in bed, sweat beading her brow, gasping.

Thika crawled out of her robes and clambered up her torso to perch on her shoulder. He nuzzled her neck.

"It's all right, Thika. It's only a dream." She stroked the lizard's soft scales, trying to steady her breath, but it still shuddered out of her. "Gods, Thika, it's my fault. I have to do something." She plucked Thika from her shoulder and put him back on her bed.

Ithsar reached under her bed. Dislodging a stone that leaned against the far wall, she pulled out a slim vial of pale-green juice. She tucked it in her pocket and slipped out of her sleeping alcove, striding quickly on bare feet, ever watchful. She had to be fast.

Footsteps sounded around a corner. Ithsar nipped into a crevice, pressing her body flat against the wall as two assassins passed, returning from night patrol. Then she slipped out and continued winding her way through the tunnels to the healing cavern. She hid in the curtained alcove of supplies just outside the door and waited.

When the night healer slipped out for a latrine break, Ithsar stole into the room, Ezaara's vial of precious green juice clutched in her hand.

Izoldia was asleep, face down on a bed. Two other patients were fast asleep. The sight of Izoldia's swollen back wrapped in bloodied bandages made Ithsar's stomach churn. By the *dracha* gods, she'd been so callous, letting Izoldia take the lash for her own crimes.

But she'd had to rescue Ezaara and Roberto from the clutches of these evil women. Women who were her only family—even though they maltreated her. As she neared the bandaged carnage that was Izoldia's back, Ithsar's belly heaved. She battled, clenching her stomach muscles. After not eating yesterday, she couldn't afford to lose the meager flatbread and dates she'd had only a few hours ago.

Swollen, angry flesh tugged at the sides of the bandages. The lash marks must be deep, then. Whoever had welded the lash would've been one of Izoldia's friends. Ashewar constantly played the assassins against one another, ruling with iron claws of fear that dug deep into the gut of every assassin, teaching them they could never trust, never give in to any emotion—except the terror of being punished by the chief prophetess or their peers. Izoldia may have been different if Ashewar had let her. All of them could have been different if Ashewar had drilled them with love instead of hate.

Ashewar could punish her, but Ithsar wouldn't have Izoldia's lash marks on her conscience. She quickly loosened the bandages, biting her lip at the deep tracks cut into Izoldia's flesh. Too many to count. So many to heal.

One at a time, then.

She let a drop of the piaua juice fall onto Izoldia's skin and rubbed it along a wound. The muscles and flesh knitted over beneath her fingers, weaving the fibers together until there was nothing but a rough red scar. Ezaara had used a second drop of juice on her fingers to rid Ithsar of scar tissue, but Izoldia had so many wounds and she had so little juice, that was a luxury she couldn't afford. Ithsar selected another gash and dribbled another drop, rubbed it in as Izoldia moaned in her sleep. Yes, the healing juice had burned through her flesh as Ezaara had straightened her finger bones and healed her twisted flesh, but the Robandi healers drugged their patients into a deep sleep, so hopefully Izoldia wouldn't wake. Ithsar worked quickly, aware the night healer could return any moment.

When the worst of Izoldia's cuts were healed and only a few small nicks remained, Ithsar shoved the empty vial into her pocket. Izoldia groaned and tossed.

Heart pounding, Ithsar raced to the door. Perhaps she should find Drida, and be rid of this awful place, after all. It was the only home she'd ever had, but there must be a better life out there.

As she eased the door shut, footsteps approached. She ducked back into the supply alcove, huddled under the shelves, and tugged a linen bedspread down to cover her.

The footsteps stopped right outside her hiding place. Someone drew the curtain, the scrape of the brass rings impossibly loud. Through the bedspread, a light shone. Ithsar tensed, ready to run.

A shadowy figure leaned in. There was a rattle on the shelves above. A scrape as the curtain was pulled half shut. Then the door to the healing cavern opened and shut.

Ithsar inhaled. Thank the—

A loud gasp came from behind the healing cavern door, then a muttered curse.

Ithsar clambered out, thrust the bedspread back on the shelf, then raced down the tunnel, every nerve in her body taut. Gods, her *sathir* was brilliant yellow—screaming fear.

Near her alcove, she slowed, letting her eyelids droop as if she'd just returned from a sleepy walk to the latrine. She mentally rolled her eyes—as if she'd need the latrine after not drinking all day yesterday. A sound came from her sleeping alcove. Ithsar ducked back around a corner, just in time to see Bala exit her alcove and slide the curtain shut.

Gods, Thika!

Bala disappeared down the hall toward the larger, more spacious sleeping caverns reserved for Ashewar's personal guards.

Pulse hammering at her throat, Ithsar slipped into her quarters.

Thika was still asleep on her bed, his tail curled around his body. Ithsar crawled back under her blanket, wondering why Bala had been here.

Blessed by the Gods

Izoldia awoke. Her wounds were burning, way worse than when she'd dozed off into a fitful sleep. The pain draught must've worn off. She flexed her back, muscles searing, but different than before. She grabbed fistfuls of sheet. The fabric tore beneath her hands with a satisfying rip.

Something crashed to the stone floor and glass skittered across the healing cavern.

"Izoldia, by the mighty *dracha* gods!"

"What?" Izoldia growled, sitting up. She turned.

A hand flew to the healer's mouth. "Your back. It's healed."

Izoldia snorted. That idiot. "Of course it's healing." It wasn't as if anyone was standing there, making the wounds worse. She stopped, mid-thought. The burning had faded to a warm glow. She flexed her back. The glow slowly faded.

"No, I said it's *healed*."

Surprise rippled through Izoldia. She swung her legs over the edge of the bed and stood, flexing her arms and bending her torso. "The pain is gone."

The healer nodded and whispered, "The wounds have disappeared. The *dracha* gods have blessed you."

Izoldia felt a slow grin spreading across her face. She pointed at the shattered glass. "Then you'd better clean this up, hadn't you? You fool, the chief prophetess won't be pleased you've smashed her glassware." Izoldia backhanded the woman so hard that the healer's head flew back, the audible crack of her blow ricocheting through the healing cavern.

Treason

The heavy tromp of guards woke Ithsar. It didn't bode well, but she wasn't expecting much after yesterday. Thika slithered out from under the blanket, and scampered up the wall to the low rocky ceiling of her alcove. Thika's throat puffed in a brief, brave show of defiance as he angled his head toward the doorway, then the lizard pressed himself flat into a crevice—one of his favorite hidey-holes—his orange and brown striped hide blending with the sandstone.

Ithsar closed her eyes again, pretending to sleep.

Guards stopped outside her curtain and flung it open. One of them strode in and shook her shoulder roughly.

Still clothed in her robes, Ithsar rolled to face them and sat up. A moment later, Thut's saber was at her throat. The guard hauled Ithsar outside. Others grabbed her upper arms and dragged her, like a criminal, along the corridor to the throne room. Ithsar didn't bother asking what they wanted her for. There was no point.

Thut thrust the heavy doors open and pushed Ithsar inside.

Gods, her muscles still ached. She was still shaky. If Drida and Roshni hadn't fed her, her legs would've collapsed. As it was, Ithsar stumbled into the cavern, but regained her footing and straightened her spine.

With fiery eyes burning like the Robandi sun, Ashewar, sitting on her grotesque throne, raked her gaze over Ithsar. Behind her throne, her guards were arrayed like vultures on a dead branch, Drida and Roshni among them, faces harsh and shadowed in the flickering torchlight.

Ithsar met her mother's fiery stare without flinching, without apology.

Ashewar set her elbows on the arms of her throne and steepled her fingers. "On the night the strangers escaped, I saw a purple bruise of *sathir* staining the sky around them, and the palms swaying violently in the breeze. One of those palms dropped a cluster of dates right onto Izoldia's head. I wonder what caused that? Magic from the strangers? Or something, someone, closer to home?"

Oh gods, oh gods, her mother knew.

Or suspected.

"But no, there is no one here with that sort of skill," Ashewar continued, her eyes never leaving Ithsar's face. "I must consider this an act of war from the North. Soon, we must strike back at these *dracha ryter* and their worm-scaled beasts. But first, I've to deal with you, an heiress who sleeps through a vicious attack upon my guards by our enemies. Once you are dealt with, we'll ride to war and slay those *dracha ryter* in their sleep."

Ithsar had really messed things up. Instead of saving Ezaara and Roberto, she'd consigned them to a war against the bloodthirstiest assassins.

The doors thunked open, making the guards twitch. Izoldia was in the doorway, her huge frame rigid with tension. Bala rapidly gestured to her. Izoldia's posture softened and a grin broke out on her face.

Then Izoldia stalked across the tiles to stand in front of Ashewar's throne. "My revered Chief Prophetess, Seer of all, and the ultimate Wise One, I have reason to believe your heiress is plotting against you. She wishes to murder you."

"No!" The cry broke from Ithsar before she could check herself.

Ashewar waved Ithsar to silence. "Does she, now?"

Bala piped up, "Last night, I heard the weakling mutter something about killing you, right before she collapsed."

"No, I didn't," Ithsar cried. "You weren't even there. It was Thut on duty when I fainted."

"Fainted, did you? Not a good trait in an heir." Ashewar's eyes flashed, as hard as diamond. "Bala, take witnesses and search her quarters."

Bala bowed, thumping her hand on her chest, and then exited the throne room, taking two other guards with her as witnesses.

Ithsar breathed a quiet sigh of relief. There was nothing in her alcove that could incriminate her. Nothing except Thika. She swallowed. She hadn't thought of bringing her friend with her.

"My most revered and wise Chief Prophetess, please let me explain—"

Izoldia's words died as Ashewar waved her to silence.

Good. Izoldia's fawning attitude rubbed Ithsar's scales the wrong way.

Ashewar rose from her throne with the grace of a feline predator. Her feet slipped across the tiled floor. Noiselessly, she glided between Ithsar and Izoldia, her quick eyes measuring every breath, every twitch of a muscle, every heartbeat. She stalked, circling them both.

Ithsar's heart thundered. As her mother's icy gaze slid over her, she lowered her eyes, staring at her dirty toes on the clean tiles.

"Izoldia, you appear to be in remarkably good health after just being lashed."

Izoldia preened, meeting Ashewar's gaze. "My rapid healing is a sign of the gods' approval, my revered Chief Prophetess." Izoldia inclined her head and gave a deep bow. "I took each lash with pleasure, knowing you had bestowed them upon me. However, the gods have seen fit to heal me while I slept."

As quick as a rust viper, Ashewar sprang, slitting Izoldia's robe with her knife.

The collective sharp intake of breath from the gathered guards ricocheted like a scream in Ithsar's ears. Her heart raced like a herd of camels, their hooves thundering inside her chest.

Ashewar's eyes narrowed. "Bring a torch," the chief prophetess hissed.

A guard sprang into action, fetching a flaming brand.

"Bend." Ashewar snapped, kicking Izoldia in the back of the legs.

The guard fell to her knees on the tiles, bowing her back. A crisscrossed mash of thin, red scars gleamed on her healed flesh.

Ithsar let her eyebrows shoot up in surprise, staring like the rest of the assassins.

Ashewar spun, her sword a flash in the torchlight as it sliced toward Ithsar.

Ithsar dropped into a defensive crouch, ready to roll, raising her arms to block the blow, her sleeves sliding down her arms.

Ashewar's sword stopped a hand's breadth short of Ithsar. Her mother's control was impeccable. What had she been trying to prove? Ashewar's cackle bounced off the walls, reverberating around the throne room, making the hairs on Ithsar's neck rise. Then her mother's glittering gaze landed on Ithsar's healed fingers outstretched before her face.

Her mother's glare made something inside Ithsar curl up and die like a stray plant out of the shade.

Ashewar sheathed her sword, her eyes never leaving those fingers.

Surely now, her mother would rejoice that she was healed. Ithsar sprang to her feet, smiling. "Mother, I—"

Her smile froze as her mother sneered, "So, you've been healed, too? I wonder how that happened?"

Although her mother's words sounded harmless, the venom of hundreds of rust vipers laced her words, sending icy trickles of fear through Ithsar's bones.

§

Ashewar stalked back to her beautiful bone throne. That scheming snipe of a girl had been healed. In a flash of insight, Ashewar knew the vile blonde Queen's Rider had been responsible. Her limbs shook with savage rage. Her prisoner had not only escaped, but she'd healed her daughter. The girl that, one day, would be the end of her. Ashewar tried to control her trembling hands. She'd heard rumors of the miraculous piaua juice in the northern lands—in Dragons' Realm—but she'd never believed they were true. Now before her eyes was evidence that, not one, but two people, had been healed. Perhaps the man she'd captured for breeding stock had been too. How else could he have negotiated the caverns without his guts spilling out of his belly wound?

She wanted no trial for her daughter. Slaughtering her on the spot would be more fitting for such a despicable runt.

Izoldia rubbed her hands together. "If I may, my revered Chief Prophetess."

Ashewar narrowed her eyes at the fawning sycophant who'd dogged her daughter for years, but had not been able to quell Ithsar's stubborn streak—or break her spirit. The daughter whose long slim fingers now moved with dexterity as she tucked them into her sleeves.

"But, Mother," the girl cried, eyes bright with tears—another weakness not to be tolerated. "Mother, my hands are healed, so I can now train as an assassin. Please let me be a true weapon in your hands."

Ithsar dropped to the tiles, her forehead kissing the floor and her outstretched, now nimble, fingers within a hand's breadth of

Ashewar's deadly *yokka*. An act of trust. A fool's trust. She should snap the girl's neck and end this now. "Stand, you weakling."

As the girl scrambled to her feet, Izoldia crooned, "Chief Prophetess, Ithsar wants to be trained as an assassin so she can end your life. It was Ithsar who set the prisoners free and planted the ropes in my robes. I fear Ithsar has plans to kill you."

The door to the throne room burst open and Bala marched inside, holding up an earthenware pot. She strode between Ithsar and Izoldia and laid it at Ashewar's feet, then bent and touched her temple to the ground near Ashewar's *yokka*. *Yokka* that could slit her throat if a single word from her guard displeased her. Ashewar gave her coldest smile and waved Bala to speak.

Bala swayed back on her haunches. "We found this pot under the runt's bed." At a nod from Ashewar, Bala uncorked it and held it up, waving the fumes toward Ashewar.

The reeking poison stung Ashewar's nostrils. "Dragon's bane," she spat.

Bala bowed. "We believe that the deformed runt was seeking to end your life, dear Chief Prophetess."

Ashewar coiled in her strength, refraining from smiting the rutting snipe dead on the spot. This useless hunk of flesh that had been born of her body with blood, sweat, and pain had been a bitter disappointment since her first cry. Although she hadn't been male, perhaps it would have been just as good if she'd had her guards feed that runtling to the desert vultures.

She needed strong women to fill the ranks of the Robandi Silent Assassins. Women who would not betray her. Unlike this snipe—the spawn of that attractive man who'd produced nothing but male spawn and this useless deformed waste of flesh. She would end this once and for all.

§

No. This was not the beginning of a new life with strong, healed fingers. A life fighting among her cold-hearted sisters, the Robandi assassins. Pain lanced through Ithsar's muscles. If she hadn't already been lying on the floor, then she would have fallen at the ice-cold rage she'd seen in her mother's eyes. For years she'd been working to please her mother, to gain her love. And now? Now, there was nothing.

Nearby, Izoldia smirked.

Izoldia had poisoned her mother against her. Rage built inside Ithsar. She quelled it. She only had one chance. And that was to submit to her right for a trial before her execution. "But, Mother, that poison's not mine. In fact, someone used it to poison Thika."

Ashewar sneered at her. "You named that despicable lizard from that useless man?"

Her father was not useless. Her father had taught her to love, to believe in herself. *Precious, strong beyond words.* Above all else, he had given her Thika, a special friend to carry with her. Ithsar habitually placed her hand against her belly. Her robes were empty.

"We searched her quarters but never found the spiteful lizard," Bala snapped.

Ithsar hid her smile. No doubt, Thika had evaded them. She sprang to her feet. "I request the right of a fair trial."

"I'm sure you do." Ashewar turned to Izoldia. "My most trusted guard, it's the runt's fault I had you whipped. What do you suggest?"

Izoldia bowed so low her hair scraped the floor. "It would be my humble pleasure to assist you in dispatching this traitor. I have long wanted her bleached bones to lie strewn under the hot desert sun."

"I'm aware," Ashewar said dryly. She turned, her cold eyes slicing through Ithsar. "This has been trial enough," Ashewar announced. "Tomorrow at dawn, this outcast will be thrown off the edge of the Robandi cliffs into the Naobian Sea." Ithsar's mother stroked an elegant finger along the carved arm of her bone throne. "Although I pity the sea monsters who will devour her. She won't make much of a meal."

Faithful Friend

Guards dragged Ithsar, kicking and fighting, down the narrow passages in the deepest dungeons. When they reached a tiny cell at the tunnel's end, they unlocked the door and threw her inside. Ithsar landed on the hard stone floor and immediately leaped to her feet, rushing to the doorway. Thut lashed out, kicking Ithsar beneath her rib cage.

Winded, Ithsar stumbled, hitting the stone, then rolled to her feet. She lunged, but the bars clanged shut in her face.

Thut stalked down the passage, laughing with the other guards—they made no attempt to keep their vows of silence now that they were so far from Ashewar.

Ithsar yelled, "No!" But after years of disuse, her voice only echoed in the tunnel like a rasping ghost.

She refused to give up, pacing the length of her cell, running her hands along the crumbling walls, straining her eyes in the flickering shadows of the distant torches. Here, near the back of the cell, the sandstone wall was damp. She scrabbled with her fingers, gouging tracks in the dirt, but Ithsar knew they were under the heart of the lake. Even if she could dig up high enough, the sandstone would cave in, the cell instantly flooding, burying her in a pile of waterlogged silt.

She ran her hands along the back wall and turned toward the cell door again, barking her shin on something hard. Her newly healed hands ran over a natural stone shelf with the remnants of a tattered blanket lying on it.

Ithsar slumped onto the bed and wadded the scrappy blanket into a ball, hugging it against her chest. Without Thika snuggling against her belly, she felt empty. And even though she'd seen a vision of herself flying into battle with the two *dracha ryter* she'd released, it must've been nothing but a dream. Her belly gnawing with hunger, and her muscles still aching from her *Sathiri* dance yesterday, she choked back her sobs and drifted into a nightmare-plagued sleep.

§

The bars clanged open and Ashewar swept into the cell. The blaze of the torches in her guards' hands made Ithsar squint as she scrambled to her feet, still clutching the tattered blanket. Ashewar waved a languid hand and her personal guards filed out of the cell, leaving them alone.

Ithsar considered dashing past her mother to snatch the torch the guards had left in a sconce outside her cell and burning her way out, but there were too many guards waiting along the tunnel. There was no point in fighting here where the odds were against her. Better to wait until she had a chance. For the first time in years, she did not hide her hands inside her sleeves. She would not back down. If she had the chance again, she'd still free Ezaara and Roberto.

Dark shadows played across Ashewar's face. "So, I finally get to kill you. Believe me, the pleasure will be all mine."

Ithsar's chest tightened, making it hard to breathe. Her fingers were healed, so why did her mother still hate her so much? "I would gladly train with my sisters."

"The likes of you? Train with the Silent Assassins?" Ashewar wrinkled her nose. "You're a useless chattel, only worthy to fetch and carry, or bow and scrape. My clan have undergone extensive training. They have discipline."

As if dancing the *Sathiri* dance yesterday from morn until deep into the night had not taken discipline. As if *bowing and scraping* and hiding her strength from these monsters she'd lived with all these years had not taken discipline.

"Izoldia has told me everything. You freed those dirty *dracha ryter,* going against your own flesh and blood." Ashewar pointed to the dusty sandstone floor. "At my feet."

Ithsar complied, prostrating herself for the chief prophetess. There was no point in fighting. Not here. Not now.

"You loved your father, didn't you?" Ashewar gave the feral, wild smile of a panther about to pounce. "Did you know you were his downfall? One day as I sat with my hands cradled around my prism-seer, seeking glimpses of my future, I saw you killing me." Ashewar stalked around Ithsar, a shark circling its prey. "How could a despicable tiny slip beat me, the best fighting weapon the Robandi has ever had? I scoffed at the idea, assuming the vision must be wrong. But I kept seeing it: you, killing me in a hundred different ways." Ashewar paused by Ithsar's head and then lashed out with her foot, kicking Ithsar's chin.

Ithsar's head snapped back. Her jaw clamped so hard, her tongue was already swelling, the tang of blood in her mouth. *Precious, strong beyond words.* She held onto her father's words.

"It was your fault your father died," Ashewar hissed. "I killed him because of you. For impregnating me with such a vial loathsome specimen of the human race. A daughter who could not even hold a weapon properly. A daughter who would turn against her mother. A daughter more treacherous than a rust viper. I, Ashewar, rule the Robandi with an iron heart. I sit upon a throne made of the bones of my enemies. There is no place for weakness in my clan."

Strong beyond words. Sometimes there was strength in waiting, in biding your time.

"I shall laugh tomorrow morning as your body is ripped to shreds by the vicious fangs of those monsters in the deeps. I'll cackle with glee, breaking my vow of silence as they tear you limb from limb and feast upon your flesh and bones."

Ithsar didn't point out that Ashewar was already breaking her vow of silence, right now.

Ashewar towered over her. "Because I'd foreseen your treachery, I decided to systematically destroy you. I fostered hatred among the other girls. Izoldia was a perfect tool in my hands, torturing you for years. You'd come to me, begging for justice, unaware that I was behind her cruel actions." A deep-throated laugh burst from Ashewar's throat. "To your feet, you weak fool." Her mother's hands twitched as if she wanted to throttle Ithsar.

Ithsar rocked back to her knees and then stood. She'd looked to her mother for support.

Looked to her mother for love.

Looked to her for solace from Izoldia's torment. Her mouth grew dry, her tongue thick and clumsy. She tried to answer, but all that came out was a croak.

"Killing your father gave me double the pleasure, knowing it would destroy you."

Ashewar's words stole Ithsar's breath. Pain lanced through her chest. Her knees faltered. Her father had died because of her. There was no blow Ashewar could've dealt that cut as deeply as that truth.

As quick as an asp, Ashewar's foot struck Ithsar's gut with so much force Ithsar flew across the room, crashing into the wall and striking her head on stone.

The walls of the cavern spun as dark memories swirled through her: *Ashewar taking her on a special trip to the desert; seeing her father sinking to his knees, grasping his gut as blood sprayed over the tangerine sand; palm leaves rustling overhead in a hot, arid breeze;*

her father staring at her until his eyes glazed over and he toppled into the sand, unseeing.

One day, you will rise above your mother's petty hatred, for you are my precious daughter, strong beyond words.

Her screaming, screaming.

Ashewar gloating, her face radiant with joy as assassins tied Ithsar's father's dead body to a camel and dragged it over the dunes, leaving him far out in the desert so his bones would be picked clean by vultures. Ithsar, on camelback, being squeezed against Drida's chest firmly, despite squirming and kicking and fighting, as they followed the trail of blood and the camel hauling her father's bloody body away.

Pain throbbing through her skull, Ithsar tried to clamber to her knees, but Ashewar was already there, pinning her underfoot, her pretty *yokka* on Ithsar's throat.

"You deserve to die." Ashewar pressed her big toe down.

The lethal blade from Ashewar's apricot-beaded *yokka* pricked against the artery in Ithsar's throat. One move, and she'd be dead.

"But not now," Ashewar gloated. "I will have no greater pleasure than watching the fanged monsters of the deep rip your body to shreds. You, Ithsar, will not be my downfall. I will be yours."

The blade slid back into Ashewar's *yokka*. The chief prophetess spun, robes swishing, and stalked from the dungeon.

As the cell door clanked shut and Thut turned the key in the lock, leering at her, Ithsar clambered to her feet and cradled the blanket to her belly, blinking back bitter tears.

The guards' footsteps retreated, leaving her alone.

Her mother had never loved her, always hated her. Worse, she'd done everything in her power to destroy her. Sorrow and rage surged through Ithsar. A dry breeze rustled her robes, and she sensed purple bruised *sathir* forming at her fingertips.

Rise above your mother's petty hatred, my precious daughter.

Ithsar quelled her rage and waited.

§

Ithsar woke to a faint rasp across the stone in her cell. Her eyes flew open to something slithering along the floor. Orange scales flashed in the torchlight. A rust viper! She clambered onto the stone bed, standing with her back hard against the wall.

The viper skittered over to her bed.

Skittered? She gasped. "Thika."

Her little lizard leaped onto the ledge and Ithsar gathered him in her arms. He nuzzled against her cheek, his tongue flicking out to tickle her nose. She gave a quiet chuckle. "At least you're here, Thika. I may not have a knife or a weapon, but I have you."

To Ithsar's dismay, Thika cocked his head and scurried off, leaving her alone in the dark.

§

Ithsar's sleep was plagued with dreams of drowning, snapping sharks hurtling toward her body, and scaled maws and talons ripping at her flesh. She woke in a cold sweat. Tugging the scrap of blanket around her, she sat up and tucked her knees against her chest, trying to get warm. Another day without eating or drinking. No wonder her body was so cold and her limbs sluggish and leaden.

Ashewar's words came crashing down on her again, a heavy smothering blanket weighing on her, making it hard to move. She was responsible for her father's death. If she hadn't loved him, held him so tightly in her heart, then perhaps her father with his warm brown eyes and soft laughter would still be alive. She squeezed her stinging eyes tight. Her world had crumbled when he'd died, leaving no one to protect her from the taunts and jeers of Izoldia, Bala, and Thut.

It was worse now, knowing that her mother, driven by hatred and fear, had caused every burn, punch, kick, or knife wound those bullies had inflicted upon her.

Still clutching her knees to her chest, Ithsar rocked on the hard stone bed. She sat there, unable to shake the guilt threatening to choke her.

Something ominous scraped along the corridor. She cocked her head.

There it was again. The only other sound was the guard's soft snoring further down the passageway. The scraping—metal along the stone—was approaching her cell. A blade, then.

Had Ashewar changed her mind and come to finish her off?

A quick kill might be better than the vicious fangs waiting in the Naobian Sea. Ithsar shuddered.

Balancing on the balls of her feet, she tiptoed across the cell and peered out the bars. Something glimmered. There was a flash of silver in the torchlight, light catching on a blade. But low, at floor level.

The blade drew closer, and in the flickering light from the nearest sconce she saw a pale glimmer of orange. It was Thika—tugging Ithsar's knife along the floor, dragging the ornately-carved handle by a decorative tassel.

"Thika!" Ithsar fell to her knees, took the knife from Thika, tucked it inside her breeches, and tightened her belt securely. There, it would be hidden by her voluminous robes. She embraced her lizard, patting his warm, scaly hide.

The snoring in the passage stopped. Stealthy feet made their way along the corridor.

Ithsar slunk onto her bed, and Thika slithered inside the front of her robe. Nestling the lizard against her belly, she drew her knees up and closed her eyes, breathing evenly.

The bright flame of a torch danced, casting yellow and orange shadows behind Ithsar's eyelids. There was a grunt, and the footsteps receded. She cradled Thika, glad of the solid knife hilt against her hip, grateful for her only true friend among these cutthroat, male-hating assassins.

Desert Trek

The unmistakable clip of Ashewar's boots echoed on the stone walls. Faint and weary with hunger, Ithsar stood with her chin high. She tugged her robes so they hung loosely around her waist to disguise her dagger and Thika's presence. She would release Thika in the desert. At least one of them would live to see another day. Because, if she didn't let him go, Ashewar would kill him.

Ashewar and her guards arrived at her cell. Ithsar winced, blinking against the light of many torches. The diamonds glinted in her mother's hooked nose—a nose that wrinkled at the sight of Ithsar.

Keys clanking, Izoldia unlocked the door. Bala's rough hands gripped Ithsar's biceps, sending sparks of pain through her arms. Izoldia bound her wrists far too tightly, the ropes biting into Ithsar's flesh. She tensed her muscles, hoping that when she relaxed the bonds would loosen.

"None of those tricks," Izoldia hissed.

Ithsar ignored her, staring, unseeing, at the walls. *Precious, strong beyond words.*

Izoldia drove her thumb into a pressure point on Ithsar's elbow, spiking pain down Ithsar's arm and releasing the tension in her palms, while Bala bound her wrists more tightly than before.

Resistance was futile. There were too many of them. Her head held high, Ithsar mustered her dignity as the guards led her down the passage. Bala followed closely, her breath huffing against Ithsar's neck. Through the winding corridors Ithsar traipsed, up past the caverns and out into the hot desert. It was still early morning, so the sands didn't burn her feet, but she had no illusions. By the time they reached the Naobian Sea, those same orange sands would be blistering hot. No one offered her boots or sandals.

No one cared whether she died with blistered feet.

Thut mounted a camel. Izoldia hefted Ithsar as if she weighed no more than a scrap of parchment, and threw her over the bony haunches of Thut's camel. Thika squirmed beneath her belly, moving so he wasn't so squashed, as Bala and Roshni tied her to the saddle and bound her feet, so she couldn't slip off and run. Roshni tried to meet her gaze, but Ithsar looked away.

Ashewar's fine camel knelt. Izoldia stooped to let Ashewar step upon her back to seat herself in her elegant leather saddle, ornately painted with desert flowers and encrusted with jewels. Around them, guards mounted their camels.

Ithsar's head spun with fatigue. Dread pooled in her stomach. With each rise and fall of the camel's haunches, Ithsar bounced against Thut's beast's bony rump as they plodded off into the blazing orange.

§

Joy surged in Ashewar's breast. Never before had she had a righteous reason to execute her daughter. At long last she would be free of the visions that had plagued her, showing her daughter's dominion over the Robandi assassins. Although Ashewar had tight control over her assassins, in the visions she'd seen of Ithsar, her women had been devoted to Ithsar, joy and admiration in their faces as they followed her. Instead of fear.

Rage ripped through Ashewar every time she remembered that vision. That girl must die.

She glanced back at the small figure draped over the back of Thut's camel, tied to its saddle, head lolling and limbs flopping in time to the camel's gait as its large feet plodded through the sand. The sun blazed down, warming Ashewar's heart. Tonight she could rest easy, no longer plagued by the nightmares of her daughter usurping her and stealing what she'd worked so long to create—her tribe of loyal well-honed assassins who hated men, cold-blooded killers not afraid to destroy weakness.

Izoldia sidled over on her camel and inclined her head.

Ashewar waved a hand, giving the fawning guard a chance to speak.

"My revered Chief Prophetess, there is dissension among the ranks. Some believe the girl should not be executed."

Ashewar glanced back at the group of orange-robed women traveling behind them. Her best guards were on the perimeter on camelback, bows nocked toward the young figure slumped over Thut's camel's haunches. She lifted an eyebrow.

"Would you like me to name them, most revered Chief Prophetess?" Izoldia asked.

Ashewar inhaled a thin stream of warm air through her nostrils, and gave a half nod.

"Roshni, she of the blue eyes. Bala believes she helped the runt when she collapsed."

No surprise there. Ashewar raised her other eyebrow.

"Drida, she of the silver hair and many wrinkles, helped her as well."

How dare that runt influence one of her best assassins. Ashewar's rage bucked inside her like a wild beast straining to be set free. She pursed her lips, letting Izoldia squirm under the hot sun for a hundred camel paces before she replied. "Tonight we'll purge our ranks of these weaklings. At midnight, slaughter them both in their beds."

Eyes glinting, Izoldia licked her lips. "Yes, most revered Chief Prophetess, it shall be done."

Only when Izoldia had pulled her scarf over her face and fallen back to ride with the clan, did Ashewar allow herself to smile.

§

Ithsar's throat was parched and gritty by the time Ashewar halted at the foot of the enormous slope jutting up against the sapphire sky. They'd reached the drop off, where the steep sandstone cliffs that edged the Robandi desert fell into the Naobian Sea. Although Ithsar couldn't see it, the hiss of the ocean rose over the sand.

Thut dismounted and yanked Ithsar to the ground. She collapsed in a heap, then used her bound hands to push herself up. Gods, the sand was hot. She wriggled her tied feet, burrowing beneath the surface to find a cooler patch, hoping there were no lurking scorpions—although it made no difference, because today she was due to die.

Her efforts weren't much use—her feet still ached from the heat.

Ashewar snapped her fingers.

Bala sprang forward, thrusting a spear at Ithsar's back.

Izoldia's blade flashed, slashing the rope around Ithsar's ankles. The burly guard picked up the pieces and waved them in Ithsar's face. "Cut ropes, just like the ones you hid in my pockets. Now you'll pay for your treachery." Her spittle landed on Ithsar's cheek.

If she could get to her knife…

"You're too afraid to release my hands, aren't you?" Ithsar said. "Afraid I'll beat you."

Izoldia's eyes flashed. Her blade flew at Ithsar's wrists. A moment later, Ithsar's hands were free, the ropes falling to the sand, her wrists throbbing as the blood rushed back into them.

Through her robes, Bala's spear pricked Ithsar's back.

Her hands and feet still prickling with pins and needles, Ithsar stumbled up the sandy dune, trailing Ashewar and her personal guard to the top of the cliff. The rest of the assassins followed them—Ashewar was taking no chances.

Every time Ithsar placed a foot on the burning sand, rivulets of orange grains ran down past her. For every three steps she took, she slipped back two. Ithsar wished she were as small and insignificant as a grain tumbling down the dune. Too small to bother with. Not worth killing.

Bala's spear prodded her back again. She rushed on, feet searing, assassins arrayed behind her and to either side—lethal weapons in Ashewar's hands.

She could never fight them all. Never hope to beat them.

Sacrifice

"Face your destiny." Ashewar's boot-clad feet were planted in the sand above Ithsar on a large flat space at the pinnacle of the dune. Ithsar's gaze traveled up her mother's legs and powerful lithe body to her stony face. "There is no hope for you," Ashewar said. "What use was your love for your spineless father, for that pathetic lizard, if it all led to this?"

Bala's spear jabbed Ithsar's back, and she scrambled up the last few body-lengths to the flat area at the top of the cliff, Bala and Izoldia on either side of her. Behind them, the assassins formed an impenetrable wall several women deep. The front of the cliff fell away in a sheer drop to the raging sea. The thundering of foam-speckled waves crashing against the orange sandstone was drowned out by the pulse pounding in Ithsar's ears.

Her breath stuttered. Her heart fluttered against her ribs like the Naobian starling she'd once seen trapped in a cage at the oasis, beating its wings against the bars—under the illusion it could get free. Dead within hours, that tiny bird had never soared under blue skies again.

Ashewar's chuckle shuddered through Ithsar's bones. Her mother prowled along the cliff, and kicked a loose clump of sandstone. It skittered off the edge and dropped in a spray of orange sand into the sea. "Give the monsters their due," Ashewar smirked, snapping her fingers.

Misha, a slim assassin who'd been adopted into the clan when Ithsar was a littling, took a Naobian flute made of opaline crystal from her robes. She held it to her lips, the sun glittering off the eagles carved along the instrument. Misha's deep brown eyes latched onto Ithsar's. A few high crisp notes trilled from the flute, then broke into a haunting melody that wrapped itself around Ithsar's heart and carried it out soaring above the open sea, sweeping her off to far distant lands. The sea breeze danced through Ithsar's hair. Pink *sathir* wended from the flute, wrapping itself around her in a soft cocoon, then billowing out over the ocean.

If only the melody were a giant-winged eagle that could whisk her far away to Naobia.

Ithsar's knees trembled. *Precious daughter, strong beyond words.* She forced strength into her muscles, holding them rigid. She'd go to her death proudly, honoring her father.

Roshni, of the piercing blue eyes, took a pale-brown satchel from her shoulder and dropped it in the sand, kneeling next to it. Every detail etched itself into Ithsar's mind: the worn, tan leather; the gleaming brass buckles; the pale half-moons on the tips of Roshni's fingernails as she opened the buckles with deft fingers; and the way Roshni averted her gaze.

A cool breeze danced off the sea, clashing with the arid desert air. Izoldia's fingers tightened on the hilt of her saber. Bala's dark eyes scanned Ithsar, missing nothing.

Roshni flipped the lid of the satchel open, revealing dark red stains and a slab of raw meat. The scent of blood filled Ithsar's nostrils—from sacrificial goat flesh, an offering to rouse the monsters of the deep.

As if their appetites needed rousing.

Still kneeling at Ashewar's feet, Roshni held the chunk of meat in her bloodstained hands, her head bowed and eyes down.

So much for Ithsar's camel ride off the oasis. Roshni and Drida's support had crumbled in the face of Ashewar's wrath. Had the offer been genuine, or just a means of trapping her?

A vision washed through Ithsar.

Hundreds of dragon riders wheeled in the air above a forest pockmarked with snow, their colored wings flashing like jewels in the wan winter sun as they fought shadowy, foul dragons with ragged wings and yellow beams slicing from their eyes. Riding the multi-hued queen, Ezaara, with Roberto on Erob at her side, led her dragons and people into battle. Bolts of fire shot through the sky at Ezaara and her dragon riders, the shadow dragons blotting out the horizon with their dark leathery wings. Below, a strange metal chest sat in a clearing with a brilliant beam of golden light streaming from it into the sky.

Ithsar resisted seeing the rest of the familiar vision—the part where she joined Ezaara in battle. This vision was not to be. Ashewar had triumphed.

With a flash of her hard ebony eyes, Ashewar said, "Awaken the beasts from the depths and stir them into a feeding frenzy."

§

Roshni stood, her blazing sapphire eyes connecting with Ithsar's. With a jolt, Ithsar realized Roshni's eyes were blazing with anger— she'd only averted her gaze to hide her fury from Ashewar. Roshni threw the meat high in the air and whipped her saber from her belt. With two slashes, the meat fell onto the sand in four pieces. Blood dripped from Roshni's ceremonial saber, but she did not clean it and sheathe it, as was custom. Instead, Roshni speared the hunks of meat upon the tip, bowed her knee, her eyes downcast once more, and offered them to Ashewar.

The chief prophetess was so filled with glee that she didn't appear to notice the lapse in custom.

Ashewar plucked a piece of meat from the tip of the saber and threw it off the edge of the cliff. The harsh sunlight caught ruby drops of blood as the flesh arced through the air, then plummeted to the sea. Ithsar couldn't tear her gaze from that tiny piece of goat.

It hit the water. Dark fins sped through the sea, and the water foamed as sharks fought over the morsel.

"More," Ashewar spat. "Work them into bloodlust, ready for this traitor."

Izoldia plucked the next piece from Roshni's saber and tossed it off the edge of the cliff, sliding a sly grin at Ithsar. "You're next," she muttered, malice glinting in her eyes.

The sea became a churning mass of thrashing tails and fins as the sharks ripped the flesh from one another's jaws, devouring it.

Farther out, a dark shape rippled under the ocean's turquoise surface. Longer than three camels, it cut through the water toward the frenzy of the fins and snapping jaws. Another dark shadow followed in its wake; and farther out, many more. Those giant, fanged monsters would rip her body to shreds, as Ashewar had promised.

Bala hurled the third piece of meat. It flew from her bloody hands. An enormous shark rose from the ocean, its gray and white maw snapping down the meat.

Ashewar flashed her teeth at Roshni. "You may throw the last piece."

Her saber still dripping blood, Roshni took the meat from the tip. She tossed the flesh high into the air, off the cliff. As Ashewar's eyes tracked the chunk of goat, Roshni whirled, her saber flashing toward Ashewar's heart.

The chief prophetess deflected it. With a kick to the chest, she knocked Roshni off balance, then slammed into her with her shoulder. Roshni teetered on the edge of the cliff, saber flashing as it was flung from her hand, arcing, blade-over-hilt-blade-over-hilt in a spray of ruby droplets. Roshni's body followed, her scream shredding Ithsar's heart, her sapphire eyes stark with fear. Dark hair swirling around her face, her body hit the sea, and her scream was silenced in a spray of white.

Sharks dived in. Within heartbeats, Roshni's body was a churning froth of red.

A scrap of her orange robe floated upon the ocean's surface as sharks prowled, waiting for their next meal. Waiting for Ithsar.

§

Ithsar tried to swallow, but couldn't. She gasped, but couldn't draw air. Her chest felt as if it had been kicked, the life driven from her lungs. She clasped her hands to her breast.

"See what happens to those who disobey me?" Ashewar crowed.

Roshni's only failing had been to show kindness. Despite the broken feeling in her chest, anger flickered inside Ithsar and spread like wildfire to her belly. How dare her mother end lives on a whim. Ashewar hated Ithsar, had always planned to kill her, disobedient or not. Ithsar refused to stand in the shadow of her mother. If she was going to die, she'd go down fighting.

Ithsar spun, facing her mother. Behind Ashewar, the assassins were an impenetrable wall. Drida's eyes were misty, her mouth gaping. The Naobian flute dangled from Misha's fingers, her jaw slack. Nila, a lively assassin with black curls, stood beside Misha, eyes glinting with hatred. The rest of the assassins were stoic, immovable.

"You killed Roshni." Wildfire burned bright in Ithsar's belly, spreading through her core.

Ashewar held a hand out, examining the nails at the end of her long slender fingers. "Oh? So I did." She snapped her hand shut.

Ithsar spun, executing the tenth move of the *Sathiri* dance, kicking out at Ashewar.

Ashewar ducked, and rolled away.

Izoldia and Bala lunged. Grabbing Ithsar's arms and torso, they kicked her knees out from under her, slamming her into the sand,

and dragged her to the edge of the cliff. They thrust her upper body out over the edge. The wildfire guttered and died, leaving Ithsar's belly hollow. There was nothing between her and the raging sea—nothing except Izoldia and Bala's grip. She gasped, head spinning at the vertical plunge into that wild ocean writhing with sharks and the huge, dark shadows of terrifying sea monsters.

"No, no, my beloved guards," Ashewar drawled. "She's mine."

Bala and Izoldia dragged Ithsar back to her feet and spun her to face Ashewar.

With a feral grin on her haughty face, Ashewar whipped her saber from its sheath.

§

As Bala and Izoldia backed off, Ithsar balanced on the balls of her feet, ready. Like a deadly rust viper, Ashewar struck, saber flashing. Ithsar whirled, but the saber caught her robes. A scrap of orange fabric fluttered free, and was caught by the wind and tossed out over the sea.

Ithsar's limbs trembled, not from fear this time, but from rage. The trembling grew until her whole body shook. Her fury pooled in her gut and burned along her veins. She thrust her hand into her robes and yanked out the hidden dagger from her breeches. Ashewar's eyes widened. She slashed again. Ithsar blocked, the reverberation clanging through her blade and running down her forearms into her elbows. Ashewar spun and kicked Ithsar's ribs, then followed through with a lunging swing of her gleaming saber.

The blade whispered past Ithsar's head as she rolled to the side and leaped to her feet, sand crumbling beneath her and cascading down the cliff. She rushed forward as Ashewar struck again, her saber slicing a rent in Ithsar's flowing breeches. Her mother's face was mottled with fury, her cunning eyes slitted as she swiped her wicked blade at Ithsar's legs. Ithsar leaped over the blade and kicked her mother's jaw. Ashewar grunted as her head snapped back, but recovered her footing and slashed at Ithsar again, going straight for her belly.

No! Not Thika! Ithsar shrieked the ancient *Sathiri* battle cry, "Avanta!"

Her robes ripped and Thika leaped out, landing on Ashewar's face. His claws scrabbled bloody gouges in Ashewar's cheeks. Ithsar leaped, slashing at Ashewar's ribs.

But Ashewar grabbed Thika by the tail and held the squirming lizard up, the tip of her saber at his belly. "Move a hand's breadth and I'll spill this despicable creature's guts."

Ithsar froze.

"See, love is a weakness," Ashewar sneered. "Something to be used against you. A weakness I do not tolerate."

Ithsar's heart pounded like a herd of stampeding camels. Ashewar was determined to destroy everything that meant anything to her. Everything precious. Just as she'd killed her father. Rage blazed through Ithsar. A purple bruise of *sathir* built at her fingertips. A dark bruise blossomed on the ground beneath her feet, and the earth shook, tremors running up her legs and through her body. She knew she was causing the quake, but she didn't care. White-hot fury surged through Ithsar's veins. A flurry of sand swirled around her feet, whipping into a dust storm around Ashewar, Thika, and Ithsar.

Ashewar dropped Thika. He scrambled up Ithsar's leg, clinging to her robes.

She slashed her dagger at her mother. Ashewar deflected her knife and barreled into Ithsar. The *sathir* bruise blackened and the sand shifted. The edge of the ledge crumbled, and, in a thrashing pile of limbs, Ashewar, and then Ithsar, fell from the cliff, plunging toward the sea.

INTO THE DEPTHS

Wind tugged at Ithsar's tattered robe as she plummeted through the air, Thika's tail wrapped tightly around her wrist. By the *dracha* gods, what had she done? Ithsar's rage had cleaved the edge off the cliff. She, Ashewar, and Thika would die—and it was all her fault. Ashewar flailed, her saber flying from her grasp and the beads on her braids clacking. The roar of the waves grew louder, water pounding against the sandstone cliff and drenching them in spray. The sea was swarming with sharks and dark ominous shadows.

Ashewar's body hit the water first.

Ithsar smacked into the ocean, plunging beneath the surface, the impact of the water driving the air from her lungs. She flailed and kicked up, holding her hand over Thika's nose so he wouldn't ingest any water. She burst through the surface, gasping, holding Thika aloft. An enormous, wicked fin arrowed toward her.

Treading water, Ithsar spun, but there were more sharks behind her, closing in fast. Beyond them, the giant, green-scaled tail of a sea monster whipped above the water, sending a spray over the sharks. Thika climbed upon her head. Spluttering, Ithsar swam in the only direction she could—toward the sheer cliff. She couldn't scale it, but Thika was nimble, good at climbing. If she could toss him onto the cliff face, maybe one of them would survive.

She glanced back. That shark was getting close. In a few heartbeats, it would be here.

Ashewar burst out of the water behind her, Thika's scratches on her cheeks still bleeding.

Ithsar screamed, "Look out!"

But it was too late. The shark lunged and opened its cavernous jaws. White fangs gleaming, it crunched down on Ashewar's body. Her blood leaked from the shark's maw. It shook her broken body like a dog worrying a big, bloody bone. Fins sliced the water and sharks dived at Ashewar, tearing off her limbs and severing her head. The sleek creatures ripped her apart in a feeding frenzy, snapping her bones and thrashing their tails.

Ithsar turned away, unable to unsee the carnage and clothing scraps—the only remains of her mother. Giant shadows of sea monsters roamed the depths below Ithsar. Gods, she had to flee. She shoved Thika's tail off her face, his claws digging into her scalp as she frantically kicked toward the cliffs. Her arms were tired. Her sodden robes dragged her down. For every few body lengths she swam, the strong ocean currents sucked her back a length or two toward the enormous sea monsters.

Something nudged her stomach. Ithsar glanced down, wanting to scream.

A shark butted her again, then dived and angled back up toward her. This time, it nudged her thigh. It was playing with her, toying, before it closed in for its meal. Her breath rasped as she kicked and thrashed. There was no way to get Thika to the cliff now, the current was too strong. The shark, too close. Should she lie limp on the water's surface, pretending to be a piece of driftwood, and hope the shark would leave her alone?

No, it was hopeless.

Heart hammering and gasping so hard she could hardly breathe, Ithsar plucked Thika from her head and held him aloft while she trod water. A wave crested, swamping them, but she kept her legs moving and held her precious friend as high as she could. Waiting.

Far above her, assassins in orange robes peered over the lip of the cliff. Their cries drifted on the wind, drowned out by the thundering waves smacking the sandstone. One of them gestured, pointing. Ithsar turned as a wave broke over her. She gulped in mouthfuls of salt water, throat burning, and stretched her arm up again to keep Thika aloft. His tail was curled so tightly around her forearm that her hand was going numb.

The shark's blunt nose rose out of the water, the pale underside of its jaw gleaming. It turned, its curved fin speeding away, but then circled around and raced toward her. Ithsar strained, churning her legs and stretching to keep Thika high, but it was no use. This was it.

Sobs broke from her chest. "I'm sorry, Thika. Sorry, Papa. I just wasn't strong enough." Her visions had been for nothing—she would never see Ezaara again.

The enormous fin neared.

A huge shadow rippled underwater.

The shark surged up from the sea, opened its maw and leaped, its jaws angled to crunch through her forearm and snap up Thika.

A giant green-scaled head speared out of the churning ocean and opened a gaping maw, revealing the dark cavern of its throat. Water streamed from pointed fangs as long as Ithsar's forearm. Its fiery gold eyes locked onto hers as it dived through the air, spraying brine. Those enormous jaws engulfed the shark, crunching its body in half. The monster flicked its head, and the shark's remains went flying and splashed into the sea.

Then the sea monster opened its jaws again. Grasping Ithsar in its fangs, it dragged her under the water.

Izoldia's Decree

Ashewar's saber flashed and her arms flailed. A purple bruise stained the sky and sand grains whipped through the air. Izoldia squinted and pulled her headscarf over her mouth. There was no need to intervene. This would soon be over. Besides, if Ashewar died at the hand of that runt, Izoldia would easily finish the girl off afterward. And if that scrawny thing died?

As head guard, Izoldia would be heiress to the chief prophetess—and then only Ashewar would stand in her way.

The dune shook. Izoldia gaped as a chunk of the cliff broke off. In a flurry of sand and scrabbling limbs, the chief prophetess and her daughter tumbled off the cliff.

Izoldia rushed to the edge and peered over. Her sister assassins surged forward to join her, head scarves whipping in that strange wind. Suddenly, the wind died and the purple stain vanished.

Ashewar hit the water first and disappeared. Ithsar's turn came a moment later. The sea turned into a choppy frenzy of snapping jaws. When Ashewar burst to the surface, the sharks made short work of her, turning the sea frothy red.

That deformed fool was down there, struggling in the sea, but the enormous fanged monsters were heading toward her, their tails lashing the water.

Nila and Misha called out, trying to warn her. Izoldia glared at them, but they were too busy yelling and pointing to notice. She dragged her gaze back to the ocean below. A giant green head and shoulders rose from the surging surf. Its jaws wrapped around Ithsar's pathetic, weedy body and dragged her under the surface.

Izoldia's heart thrummed. She waited, licking her lips, but the monster didn't resurface.

The day couldn't have turned out better.

Snatching her saber from her hip, Izoldia thrust it high into the air. "Ashewar is dead. The chief prophetess is no more. And her traitorous heir has been swallowed by the mighty beasts that patrol the depths of the Naobian Sea." She spun, grinning, still holding her saber high.

The women fell into line, staring at her, stone-faced.

"I, as Ashewar's most loyal guard, will take her place. I now anoint myself Chief Prophetess." Izoldia smirked.

Not a brow rippled.

Drida, that wrinkled old crone with ugly gray hair, stepped forward, eyes blazing. "A chief prophetess is not self-declared," she croaked. "The *dracha* gods anoint the new chief prophetess, one with gifts. Stand down, Izoldia, or we will—"

Izoldia flicked her wrist, throwing the blade hidden up her sleeve. Her dagger hit the woman's throat before she finished speaking. A spray of red drenched the nearby assassins and the woman collapsed in a puff of orange sand.

"Any more objections?" Izoldia surveyed them all.

Among the women arrayed before her on the hot desert sand, not a single muscle twitched. They each met her gaze with hard eyes.

She gestured to Bala and Thut. "As the chief prophetess' elite guard, these two women will help me enforce new rules among the Robandi assassins. For too long, the chief prophetess has only let us glean lousy pickings from the desert, but there's fine hunting to be had among these dunes. We shall now take the lion's share, and spill the blood of the male vermin that dare inhabit the Robandi Desert sands. Their spoils shall be ours."

Izoldia twitched her saber at the dead woman whose blood was seeping into the hot desert sand, her glassy eyes staring skyward.

"You two." She gestured at Misha, a young, skinny assassin, and Nila, who was a wild, wicked fighter. "Toss this carrion to the sharks and join us. We'll ride out now, and make men quake and scream with terror."

§

The sun beat down mercilessly. Sweat prickled Misha's forehead and slithered between her shoulder blades, snaking its way down her back. She traipsed over to Drida and Nila. The other assassins were following Izoldia down to the camels, their nimble feet making short work of the steep dune.

Wiping a black curl from her face, Nila leaned over Drida's body and pulled Izoldia's dagger from her neck.

Misha winced, trying to hide her horror at the wet sucking sound. At Drida's beautiful, silver hair now splattered in gore. And the gaping wound in her neck.

After examining and cleaning the blade, Nila gave a sly grin and pocketed it deep within her robes. She shrugged and wrinkled her nose at Izoldia's hulking back as she led the assassins away.

So, Nila wasn't a fan of Izoldia either. That was handy to know. They might as well get this unpleasant job over and done with. Misha bent her knees and slid her hands under Drida's shoulders. There was nothing for it. Even though Drida had held the admiration and respect of all of her sister assassins, she was better off with the sharks than the vultures circling overhead. Anything but vultures. Misha shuddered at memories of her father and brothers' bodies strewn across the sands. They said vultures picked out the eyes first—that eyes were a delicacy for those foul birds. At least those sharks would finish Drida's remains quickly.

Nila picked up Drida's legs and Misha hefted her shoulders, the wound leaking more blood as Drida's head flopped back. They crab-walked over the flat area to the lip of the cliff. Drida was dead.

Roshni was dead. Sharks had just devoured Ashewar, and a sea monster had gobbled up Ithsar. Misha shook her head. Ashewar had been bad enough as a leader, but Izoldia would be worse—way worse.

When Misha was a littling, her father and brothers had died at the hands of these Robandi assassins, but one of their killers had taken mercy on her and adopted her into the clan. Without a choice or a say in the matter, she'd been raised to fight among these violent women. It had been her only chance of survival. She'd never dared disobey.

And the harsh lines that carved Izoldia's face and the hate that glittered in her dark eyes, had Misha obeying now, too.

They tossed Drida's body to the sharks. Misha spun away before it touched the raging ocean, keeping her face impassive.

Nila bounded to her side, sand streaming from every footfall as they half-slipped down the dunes to their camels. But as they mounted, Nila slid her a sidelong glance, raised an eyebrow, and gave her a jaunty grin.

With a jolt, Misha realized Nila's ebony eyes were bright with unshed tears.

Sea Monster

The sea monster's fangs pressed through Ithsar's tattered sodden robes, against her torso. She and Thika were dragged down, down, her heart hammering and lungs threatening to explode. She hadn't even caught a proper breath. They'd only last heartbeats before they drowned. Not that it would matter. This ravenous beast was about to eat them. She clamped her hand over Thika's nose, squeezing his nostrils and mouth shut, but the lizard lashed his tail against her arm and squirmed.

Gods, Ithsar's lungs *burned*. Dark spots danced before her eyes. Her chest ached as they dived deeper.

Thika fought and thrashed. He bucked out of her grip, hooked his tail back around her shoulder, and opened his mouth. No, despite all she'd done, her best friend would die. Ithsar gasped, drawing in breath—

Air filled her lungs—not water.

Another breath. More air.

Ithsar drew in great gulps, easing the pressure on her chest. She was breathing—still alive. A shimmering silver bubble filled with glorious air surrounded her and Thika. Thika nestled against her face. Thank the *dracha* gods, he was all right. Thank the sea gods, too, that they both were. For now.

The sea monster opened its fangs and released her. Ithsar floated, suspended in the water before the monster's golden gaze. Its eyes glowed like a lantern in an oasis welcoming home a weary traveler. Silver *sathir* danced around the creature. A strange surge of warmth bubbled in Ithsar's chest and belly.

A current tugged Ithsar away from the beast. Its forelegs snaked out and it cradled her in its talons. *"You are precious, noble and strong, fated for great things,"* a warm voice hummed in Ithsar's mind. *"I am Saritha, renamed after you, Ithsar."*

This monster was talking to her? She'd heard of the naming convention in Dragons' Realm, where dragon or riders took upon a syllable of each other's names upon imprinting, but surely these sea monsters—

"Sea monster? I'm not a monster. I'm a dragon, a sea dragon."

"You're not going to eat me? But I've seen Ashewar feed other traitorous assassins to your kind."

"True, we have killed some orange-robed women in the past, but only because their sathir had turned rotten, hatred eating like a dark canker through them. But your sathir is pure. You proved it by trying to save our cousin."

Wonder wove through Ithsar. Like the oasis lake's soothing kiss on the hottest day. Reminding her of how she'd felt as a littling, sitting on her father's lap listening to his stories, wrapped in his warmth. Awe filled her and, for the first time, Ithsar *really looked* at this wondrous creature, at her head and body coated in green scales that gleamed silver in shafts of sunlight cutting through the sapphire ocean. Saritha's *sathir* danced around Ithsar and Thika. Now she recognized the source of the beautiful silver bubble: it was Saritha's shimmering *sathir.* *"You didn't want to eat me. You were saving me from those sharks."*

And from a life with cutthroat assassins.

"Just as you saved little Thika, my distant cousin from the desert sands."

The skin along Thika's sides twitched and a groove appeared. Tiny buds sprouted from his body and unfurled into wings. Thika lunged, swimming around in glee, fluttering his new wings like fins. Her lizard looked like a tiny orange sea dragon.

"Land lizards are the ancient ancestors of our kind," Saritha said. *"Some of them have the gift of transformation."*

Despite being underwater, that strange warmth burst from inside Ithsar's chest and radiated through her body, from the roots of her hair to her toenails. She wanted to sing, dance, shout at the top of her voice. And as Saritha's gossamer *sathir* wrapped around her, and Thika swam in happy circles, Ithsar felt as if she could propel herself into the skies, into a life full of wild possibilities.

Her life with the Robandi assassins had been a cage she'd been trapped in for too long. But she wouldn't die like that Naobian starling. She was never going back. She'd swim to the ends of the sea with Saritha. *"You've given me hope and freed me from my shackles. I can now be anyone I want."*

"Ithsar, you need only be yourself. You will always be enough for me." Saritha lowered her muzzle into the silver bubble and huffed warm breath against Ithsar's cheek. *"Always."*

Ithsar's throat caught. A tear slid down her cheek. *"I'm enough?"* Something was unfolding inside her, something small and sweet that had been lying dormant since Ashewar had killed her father and that camel had dragged his dead body into the desert. *"Thank you."*

Someone understood her—Saritha understood. *Sathir* swirled around her in a silvery dance, wrapping her in a warm cocoon and cradling her.

"Yes, I do understand."

She reached out a tentative hand and scratched the sea dragon's nose. This was no monster, just a beautiful giant creature who was now her friend.

"Yes, Ithsar, you are now my rider."

Rider? "So, I should ride you, like I'd ride a camel?"

Saritha snorted, shooting a stream of water from her nostrils. *"Not quite like a camel. Climb on my back."*

§

Saritha swam through waving fronds of green weed, Ithsar on her back with Thika perched upon her shoulder. The fronds brushed against Ithsar's legs, tickling, and she laughed as a tiny yellow-and-turquoise-striped fish darted away into the towering green forest around them. They broke out of the weed and swam along a coral reef. Growths of purple-and-orange-striped mushrooms clung to rocks. Enormous clusters of flat yellow plates formed towers that rose above them. Pink coral formations waved tiny tentacles with white stars on the ends, and red puffy balls drifted along the pale sand of the ocean floor, like tumbleweeds. Orange and tan starfish darted among small trees of pink, yellow, and vibrant turquoise, and turtles swam past Saritha, their mottled shells blending with their surroundings. And the fish—Ithsar had never seen such a variety—banded, spotted, spiky, and sleek, with more colors than the rainbow.

"At home, everything is so... orange."

Saritha's foot disturbed a red tree with undulating fronds, and yellow-and-silver-striped fish burst from its foliage, shooting away. A diamond-shaped ray floated past, its mantle flowing in the current and tail streaming out behind it.

"Avoid those barbed tails—they're poisonous," Saritha rumbled.

As Saritha approached, a school of purple-banded yellow fish with enormous bellies and bulging eyes fled into a clump of yellow and blue coral.

Ithsar gaped. And gaped. This was a whole world she'd never suspected existed. She glanced up to the pale-gray underbelly of an enormous sea creature, nearly as large as Saritha. Mournful keening filled her ears.

"What's that?"

The dragon chuckled in her mind, a comforting rumble. "A whale. They're peaceful, our friends. Although sometimes their songs do get tedious."

The whale's song floated through Ithsar, filling cavities inside her that she hadn't known were empty. Sadness, happiness, pain, and joy flitted inside her. Tears trailed down her cheeks as she remembered her father's laugh, his warm dark eyes, losing him, loving Thika, Roshni's bright blue eyes wide with fear as she'd tumbled from the cliff.

"Who pushed your friend into the ocean?" Saritha asked.

"My mother, Ashewar, who hated me for the crime of being myself." Ithsar saw Ashewar's screaming face as sharks snapped up her body. Her throat tightened and she thrust her hands to her aching chest, trying to staunch the pain. A splintering sob broke from her. *"She destroyed everything I loved, and wanted to destroy me."*

"I'm sad that your mother is dead, but she deserved to die," Saritha said. *"However, crying will only use your air supply faster. Believe me, we don't want you to run out of air down here."*

Her dragon's sweet voice soothed Ithsar. Ashewar was gone. She and Thika had a new life.

Dolphins swam overhead, chittering. Thika darted off, following them. Saritha trumpeted, and the lizard whirled, his tiny wings fluttering, and zipped back to Ithsar's shoulder.

They dived under a coral archway festooned with conical pink spires. Anemones the size of her torso wafted tentacles in the water. One snaked out its tendrils and plucked up a silver fish, forcing it inside its cavernous mouth. The tentacles shrunk, pulling in on themselves and closing over the fish until the anemone was a small dark ball, no larger than Ithsar's head.

"I wouldn't want to get caught by one of those."

"Indeed."

On the other side of the archway was a forest of waving yellow weeds that towered above them. Saritha dived and the plants parted to let them through.

Another sea dragon appeared out of the undulating plants. Then another, and another. Through the yellow fronds, Ithsar spied hundreds of sea dragons in a variety of greens and blues as vast as the ocean's moods, all radiating silver *sathir*.

As Saritha burst out of the forest, the scaly long-bodied dragons formed a ring around them. Sharp talons sprang from their feet, and their tails lashed the water. Their snarls rippled through the water, making Ithsar's head pound.

Queen Aquaria

The sea dragons' snarls rippled through the water. Then turned into roars that crashed through Ithsar's head. The water quaked. Fish darted into hidey-holes. Thika's claws tightened on her shoulder.

Fear rattled Ithsar's bones, making her tremble. *"Why are they so angry?"*

"They say that women with orange robes are murderers, destroying the life energy of living beings. They see your robes and fear you have come to harm us. I've told them you're my new rider, but they're distrustful because it's been so long since any of us had riders."

Thundering roars crashed into Ithsar, ricocheting through the water around her and lashing her like a storm.

"They're insisting I take you to my queen."

"Your queen?"

"Yes, my queen. You didn't think we were a lawless bunch, did you?" Saritha chuckled, her rumbling belly tickling Ithsar's legs, but the bared fangs and slitted eyes of the dragons around them weren't so convincing.

"Am I in danger?"

"Is anyone ever out of danger? You leaped into the jaws of the ocean and found me. Now, prepare to meet Queen Aquaria."

Saritha's reassurance did little to calm Ithsar's racing heart. They dived between two coral spires, the other sea dragons trailing them. They speared down until the water was darker, the fish drab, and the coral brown, then leveled out and swam toward a mountainous rock bigger than the assassins' oasis. Saritha entered a gaping tunnel in the rock, and the sea dragons followed them into pitch black. Thika's tail twined tightly around Ithsar's neck and he nestled into her face as they angled down into the black. Cool currents streamed past Ithsar's legs. Pressure built in her ears, and her lizard squirmed—no doubt, feeling it too.

Glimmers of distant light appeared, growing larger.

Strange fish with vicious jagged teeth and light-bearing stalks protruding from their heads surrounded the sea dragons, illuminating the darkness, and led them through the base of the rock until the tunnel angled upward toward the light.

Saritha kicked strongly and shot up. *"I'll open my mind so you can hear."*

Ithsar was about to ask exactly what she'd hear when they burst out of the tunnel onto a broad shelf of pale sand.

Shafts of sunlight spilled through the water like the pillars in the assassins' throne room, striking a majestic dragon seated on a coral-festooned rock, lighting her green scales with a silver shimmer. The dragon angled her head. *"Be seated, my daughter. Be seated, my loyal subjects."*

"Daughter? Does that make you a princess?"

The barest murmur of assent rippled through Ithsar's mind followed by a whisper, *"Keep your thoughts still. Everyone can hear you."*

A titter from one of the smallest dragons ran through Ithsar's head, but the queen silenced the dragon with a glare. The water undulated as the sea dragons arrayed themselves on the sand in front of their queen.

The queen's voice thundered through Saritha and Ithsar's minds. *"My daughter, what have you done? Why have you brought this creature with you?"*

Ithsar's hand shot up to cover Thika with her hand. Until the queen's gaze leveled at her. No, the queen did not mean Thika. She meant Ithsar.

SEA DRAGON

"Why did you bring this vile beast to our innermost sanctuary?" Venom laced the queen's thoughts. *"These orange-robed murderers are the vermin of the desert sands. For years they've left a trail of carnage in their wake."*

"Their ruler is dead," Saritha replied. *"And this is her daughter."*

The queen's eyes glinted with feral menace. *"Ah, so you brought her as a sacrifice to appease the gods. Well done."*

"No, we've imprinted. She's my rider." Saritha straightened.

Queen Aquaria's head snaked down from her perch. Eyes narrowed, she glared at them. Ithsar's legs trembled, but she held her head high, meeting the queen's blazing gaze. Queen Aquaria's derisive snort wound through Ithsar's mind. *"Rider?"* The queen leaped from her coral throne, the scratch of her talons amplified by the water, skittering through Ithsar's bones. She landed, her mighty talons raking the sand and stirring up a cloud of dust that obscured Ithsar's vision.

Ithsar's traitorous pulse raced at her throat, and despite the shimmering bubble around her, her chest grew tight.

The eddying sand settled and the waters cleared to reveal the queen's giant maw outside Ithsar's bubble of *sathir*. A long tongue darted from her jaws. *"Let me taste you."*

Saritha had tricked her to gain her trust and bring her as a sacrifice to the queen. Swallowing hard, Ithsar knew her time was up. *"Take care of Thika,"* she begged Saritha. Her only regret was not helping Ezaara in battle against those dark dragons, but she would not quake. She would not fear. She had already faced death twice today. And she had lived to see wonders that even her father and Ashewar had not seen. It was enough.

She was enough.

"Of course you're enough," Saritha harrumphed. *"I told you so already. Now stretch your hand out of the bubble so my queen can taste you."*

Ithsar gulped. Her fingers tingled as they brushed through the silver bubble and plunged into cool water, but the bubble stayed intact. She sucked in a deep breath, relieved she wouldn't drown.

The queen licked her palm and gazed at her quizzically. *"I do not sense death upon your fingers, yet you wear orange robes. Please explain."* Queen Aquaria nuzzled her hand.

Oh gods, the queen had wanted to scent her, not eat her. She felt like such a fool. As the queen touched her hand, her life flashed before her: the years of taunting and jeering; Izoldia burning and cutting her; her mother's hatred; her father's brutal death; Ashewar throwing Roshni to the sharks; and finally, Ithsar fighting Ashewar and them both tumbling into the sea.

Her memories swept on, revealing the vision she'd seen.

Above pristine snow-tipped mountains and carpets of lush forest, dark-winged beasts blasted dragons from the sky, beams from their eyes slicing into the dragons' flesh. The foul creatures' screams ricocheted through Ithsar's mind. Amid plumes of flame, Ezaara dived on a dragon with scales that flickered with all the colors from a prism-seer, firing arrows. But there were too many beasts. Ezaara and her troops were nearly overwhelmed. Then Ithsar arrived, riding a beautiful green dragon whose scales flashed silver—Saritha.

Ithsar inhaled a sharp breath. The prophecy was already coming to pass.

They swooped into battle, trails of sea dragons bearing Robandi riders behind them, followed by Naobian green guards. Their arrows found their marks. The sea dragons killed foul beasts, shredding their wings and breathing fire. Ezaara and her warriors rallied, but the battle was not over.

"So you see visions, too?" The queen inclined her head, not breaking contact with Ithsar's hand. A vision swept through Ithsar, and she knew it was the queen's. Sea dragons, wings dripping with water, rose from the sea with orange-robed women on their backs.

"I fought this vision for years, knowing these women were killers, but after meeting you, I relent." Queen Aquaria's eyes were steady, softer. *"You are heralding in a new age where sea dragons will take to the skies with riders again, to protect the freedom of my far distant cousin, Zaarusha, Queen of Dragons' Realm. If we fail, the entire realm will become a barren wasteland."*

Another vision roiled through Ithsar's mind—the same land she'd seen in her vision.

Instead of gleaming snow gracing the mountain peaks, they were brown and barren. At their feet, desolate sludge and swamp stretched as far as Ithsar could see. The oceans were clogged with dead fish and carcasses of dragons, and the waterways were green and stagnant, choked with waving tendrils of flesh-eating plants.

Ithsar pulled her hand back into the *sathir* bubble with a pop, clutching her stomach.

"The visions are upon me now, young Ithsar. I realize that for us to help prevent this awful fate, you must find us new riders among those orange-robed killers, fierce women with pure hearts."

Impossible. How could she ever convince those bloodthirsty women to fight for good? She'd be slaughtered, cut down by Izoldia, Bala, and Thut within a moment of setting foot in the desert. *"I'm only one person. One small, insignificant person."*

Saritha leveled her gaze at Ithsar, then looked at the queen. *"My Queen, I'll accompany her and ensure the job is done."*

The queen nodded sagely. *"To prove their goodwill, these new riders must make a leap of trust: every new rider must throw herself from the cliff into the sea, just as you did."*

Ithsar opened her mouth to protest.

The queen gave a flick of her tail, scattering a school of brown fish. *"Do not fail me or you'll be failing the whole of Dragons' Realm."*

Ithsar snapped her jaw shut and nodded.

"Good," said the queen, stirring. *"My beloved dragons, our fate and the fate of our lands are in the hands of a chosen few. Ithsar is*

one. Zaarusha's rider, the golden-haired girl, is another. There is yet another."

She gestured Ithsar to lay her hand upon her snout.

Ithsar saw an older man with dark hair, a goatee and extraordinarily-bushy eyebrows standing in a forest. His gaze was piercing, his stature, tall, and he wore a forest-green cloak. Green flame danced at his fingertips. A mage, then. *"Who is he?"*

"The dragon mage, Master Giddi. Years ago, he saved my life. Aid him in any way you can and send him my greetings. His role in this war is essential, but without your support he will fail, and Dragons' Realm will be lost. I cannot sense more than that. Let this suffice for now." Queen Aquaria turned and swam back onto her coral throne. *"Bring forth the blade."*

A small green dragon swam from the assembled crowd toward the queen, something shiny flashing in his talons—Roshni's ceremonial saber.

Ithsar's fingers tingled as they passed through the bubble and grasped the hilt. She would use this saber to honor Roshni.

Queen Aquaria's golden eyes glowed. *"Swear you will never use this for cruelty or revenge, only to protect the downtrodden and the weak."*

"I swear." Ithsar pounded her heart with her hand, her head reeling.

"Good. Revenge will never bring you happiness," the queen said.

Ithsar didn't want to go back. She wanted to flee the assassins, never visit the oasis again, but now she had no choice.

A weight settled upon her, like a thick blanket warding off the bitter cold of the desert night—but heavier, much heavier. The weight sank down through her flesh and settled in her bones. She had to face Izoldia and the other assassins. If Dragons' Realm were to survive, she had no choice.

Bloody Trail

Wings dripping and seaweed dangling from her foreleg, Saritha burst from the Naobian Sea with Ithsar upon her back. The bubble around Ithsar popped and fresh air rushed into her lungs. She hadn't even noticed that the air she'd been breathing had grown stuffy and thin, until she was above the surface. The orange sandstone cliffs rose above them—so impossible to scale when she'd been drowning and holding Thika. The blood in the sea had dissipated. The only thing left of Ashewar and Roshni was a shred of orange fabric floating on the sea. As Ithsar watched, a wave crested and swallowed the cloth, dragging it under. Ithsar shut her eyes, drawing in a deep breath. When she opened them, the orange sandstone was rushing past them as Saritha ascended.

Thika curled his tail around her neck and spread his little wings, drying them in the breeze.

"Who would have known you could sprout wings?" She scratched his nose. His wings fluttered and slid back into the tiny slits in his scales. "Now you look like a normal lizard again, but I always knew you were special." He nuzzled her cheek.

Saritha crested the cliff and landed, puffs of tangerine sand stirring at her feet. She held her snout up, nostrils flaring, scenting the breeze. *"I smell fresh blood."*

A dark satin marred the sand amid scuffed footprints, and splatters of blood led from the stain to the cliff's edge. More blood than just the sacrificial goat had been spilled here today. *"Someone's been killed. It looks like they were thrown into the sea."*

There was no doubt in Ithsar's mind that Izoldia had murdered someone. But who? "Stay here." Ithsar popped Thika on Saritha's back, slipped off the sea dragon and dropped to the scorching sand. She hopped from foot to foot. If only she had *yokka* to protect her feet.

"Come here, my littling." Saritha thrummed.

"I'm hardly a littling. If I'm to rally my people for more riders, perhaps you should find another term of endearment."

"But you're such a small slip of a thing to fill such large yokka*,"* her dragon replied.

"You know the name of our footwear?"

Saritha dipped her head in a nod. *"Littling will do until your feet have grown."*

"I never knew sea monsters could be so cheeky."

Saritha disentangled the seaweed from her foreleg, and held it in her jaws. *"Wrap this around those tiny feet, my littling. And, by the way, I told you: I'm not a monster. Sea dragon is the correct term."*

"If you're going to be so cheeky about my size, perhaps monster will do," Ithsar said as she sat and wrapped the weed around her scorched feet.

A low throaty rumble echoed from Saritha's throat and skittered through the dragon's belly.

"You're laughing!" Ithsar tilted her head. *"I never knew dragons could laugh."*

"Yes, my littling, monsters laugh too."

Littling? Hah. Ithsar slugged Saritha's foreleg and sprang to her feet. Although her dragon had tried to distract her from the bloodstain, it was time to face what had happened while she'd been gone. The seaweed wouldn't last long—the hot desert sand would soon dry out its moisture and it'd become brittle. She stalked along the bloody trail and followed it to the stain.

So much blood. It had gushed freely and stained the sand dark crimson. Someone had definitely died here—especially with that awful trail to the cliff's edge. Ithsar knelt and examined the bloody sand. The blood was dry, but that didn't mean much—the hot desert sand would dry out warm blood in a heartbeat. Silver glinted among the red-caked sand. Ithsar picked up strands of silver hair coated in blood.

Her other hand flew to her mouth and her belly tightened. "No. Not Drida." Had Drida paid with her life for helping her? Ithsar swayed and sank to her haunches, dizzy. No…

Saritha pounced, landing beside her. *"You need nourishment. We must find these murderous vipers, but you'll collapse without food in your belly."*

"You're right. I've barely eaten in two days." Gods, oh gods, was Izoldia going to destroy anyone who got close to her, anyone who tried to help her? If she tried to recruit more riders, would Saritha be in danger too?

The dragon flew off and returned with a flapping silver fish in her maw. She tossed the fish into the air, speared it on a talon, then breathed fire over it. The aroma of roasting fish made Ithsar's mouth water. *"I'll just cool it, so it won't burn your fingers or mouth."* Saritha leaped into the air and flew a circle around Ithsar before landing and proffering the fish.

Ithsar bit into the succulent flesh, juice running down her chin. *"Oh, this is good."*

"One of my favorites. I scoffed a couple too." Saritha extended a foreleg.

Ithsar clambered up, reaching up to grasp her spinal ridge. *"It's much easier to climb onto your back in the water."*

"Everything is easier in water," Saritha replied, cocking her head and gazing at the desert. *"Especially hunting and swimming. I don't see any tasty fish flapping their fins around here. Or any water to swim in."*

"Don't worry, at the oasis we have a lovely big lake."

"Any fish?"

"Small ones." Such a huge beast wouldn't survive on oranges, dates, and couscous. *"But we have goats. They're quite tasty and have none of those nasty scales that get caught in your teeth."*

"Nasty scales?" Saritha bristled, her own scales standing on end. *"I think scales are beautiful."*

"Yes, of course, so do I," Ithsar replied hurriedly as Thika nestled inside her tattered robes against her belly. *"Especially the way the sun makes your emerald scales glisten with silver."* Then she realized what her dragon was doing. *"You distracted me again."*

"I don't like seeing you sad about your friend dying." Saritha sprang into the air. *"I spotted camel tracks when I was cooling your fish. Let's hunt down those murderers."*

The breeze of Saritha's wingbeats fanned Ithsar's face, a change from the stifling heat of the desert air. Now *all* she had to do was hunt down her archenemy, and convince a band of highly-trained bloodthirsty assassins to join her in defending Dragons' Realm. Dread pooled in Ithsar's stomach as they swept over the dunes, following the camel tracks across the shimmering tangerine sands.

Coldblooded Attack

To Izoldia's left, camel tracks led up over a dune. A thin trail of smoke rose up into the blazing sky. Good. Someone was making camp. With her hand upheld, she motioned her band of assassins to stop. She shaded her hand over her eyes against the mid-morning sun as the women silently dismounted and hobbled their camels. Izoldia motioned Thut to watch the others and make sure no one slipped off. Although she had them under control for now, it would only take a few to rebel for that control to slip. Tonight, she would make sure any dissent was extinguished.

Izoldia and Bala sneaked up the dune, slithering the last camel length on their bellies, and peeked over the top. Bala's eyes glinted and her teeth flashed in a fierce grin. Izoldia licked her lips as she gazed down at their prey. In a hollow between the dunes, six men were seated around a bed of smoldering coals, heating a steaming pot. A large, dark-bearded man with a yellow headdress took the pot and tipped a thick brew of tea into the waiting mugs of the others. Behind them was a caravan of twenty camels, still hobbled, their backs heavily laden with goods. The rolled tents tied to their beasts' backs suggested that these men had stopped for the night and were ready to head out again after a lazy morning.

What luck. Six men and such a fine caravan laden with goods. A great way to start her reign.

Izoldia and Bala slithered backward on their stomachs until they were hidden from view, then Izoldia motioned to the assassins with a series of quick hand signals.

A third of the assassins headed around the dune and sneaked up the left flank of the hill, a third took the right, and the rest made their way up to join Izoldia and Bala. When they were all a camel length from the top, Izoldia gave a quick flick of her hand, which each woman repeated, sending the message rippling along the ranks. As one, they slid their sabers from their scabbards and rose. They crested the dune and charged downhill, the only sound the rustle of the robes and their feet on the shifting sands.

The man with the yellow headdress and dark bushy beard cried out, dropping his mug, the dark contents splattering his white robes. His companions leaped to their feet. Four of the men drew sabers and faced them, while two raced to their camels, desperately yanking at the hobbles. The assassins swarmed past the hot coals and were upon the men in moments.

Izoldia gave a feral snarl and slashed her saber across the big man's face, laughing as blood sprayed over the sands, coating her hands.

§

The man's yellow headdress was drenched in red. Misha was aghast at the blood, her stomach roiling. Although she'd been raised to fight with these assassins, she'd usually found excuses to stay back at the oasis by tending someone in the healing cavern, volunteering for kitchen duty, making meals, or feigning illness. It had escaped Ashewar's attention, but she knew Izoldia had noticed.

Izoldia's saber plunged into the man's gut and he fell to his knees. Their new chief assassin's grin made Misha even more nauseous.

At her back, Nila whirled to fend off a man, her blade scraping against his saber. Misha slashed her saber halfheartedly at another, disarming him in a heartbeat.

"No, p-please, I have ch-children," he gibbered.

No, not more children left orphaned at these women's hands. Misha pretended to stumble—and let him run. Thut lunged past her, saber slashing another man's calf, and raced after him. The short man's paces were no match for Thut's long legs. She caught up to him easily, and plunged a dagger into his back.

His body hit the sand, a red stain spreading across his white robe. Misha's knees wobbled.

Nila squeezed her hand, then dropped it, glancing around. "Stay standing," she whispered, lips barely moving. "I think Thut's onto you."

Thut kicked the dead man over. His unseeing eyes stared up at the lapis sky.

Thut growled, "You two, come here."

For the hundredth time, Misha wished she were a bird and could fly away from the oasis, these awful assassins, and this terrible life. She mustered up as much bravado as she could and swaggered across the sand, Nila at her side. As they neared the man, she gave a disdainful sneer at his prone figure and nudged his body with her boot. At least his wound was against the sand now, the blood no longer glaring at her.

"You two were too slow," Thut growled, eyes glinting as she twirled her dagger, scattering droplets of the man's blood. "You have a weak stomach, don't you, you coward?" She glared at Misha. "Don't think I haven't noticed you skiving off and missing the action. Let's see how you enjoy this." She plunged her dagger downward and ripped open the man's belly. His pale, steaming entrails spilled over the hot sand.

Misha fell to her knees, retching. Nila reached down to comfort her. But another dagger flashed in Thut's hand, aimed at Nila. "Leave the weakling. We don't need her. Izoldia asked me to kill her in her sleep tonight anyway. This'll save me the job."

Saber out, Nila lunged at Thut. Thut parried, the sun glinting on her flashing blade.

The earth shook. A spray of sand flew over them, pelting them like gnats. Flame surged overhead.

A giant beast had landed, jolting the sand and making it shift between Misha's knees. The green-scaled monster bared fangs the length of her forearm, flame dripping from its jaws. It snarled, sending shivers down Misha's spine.

Ashewar, Roshni, and Ithsar had not been enough to satisfy the hunger of this mighty sea monster. It had come for them. With trembling hands, Misha stood and drew her saber. Nila and Thut flanked her, their fight forgotten as they faced the wild beast with billows of sand clouding around its taloned feet.

§

Ithsar frowned. Something was wrong, dreadfully wrong. There was an agonizing shudder of *sathir* in the desert below them. Screams rent her ears. Someone had just died a violent death. The mighty sea dragon beat her wings upon the hot desert wind, speeding over the dunes. Ithsar strained her eyes. It was difficult to see the Robandi Silent Assassins' orange robes against the sand below; however, their hobbled camels, a large caravan, and the bloody bodies of men who'd been slaughtered were all too clear. The clash of sabers rose on the air.

A short distance from the main fight and the men's smoldering campfire, Thut was attacking Nila and Misha.

Ithsar gasped. *"Saritha, over there. Save those women."*

Saritha swooped between the dunes and landed, showering sand over the assassins. She roared, shooting a jet of flame over Thut's head. Thut dropped her dagger, gaping. Misha leaped up and snatched her saber, tossing it to Nila.

Nila shoved it under Thut's ribs. "Hands up. Misha, grab some rope and bind her."

Misha dashed to the caravan of poor camels, who were bleating at the chaos, and sliced a length from a lead rope, then raced back to bind Thut's hands.

Ithsar whirled. *"Look, Saritha."*

Izoldia was chasing a man, tufts of sand spraying up behind her. He had no chance. She was faster, fitter. She drew a dagger and raised her arm to throw. Saritha swooped and knocked her to the sand with her foreleg. Cursing, Izoldia rolled to her feet and threw her dagger at Saritha's belly. Saritha twisted aside, and blasted fire at the dagger until the wooden hilt burned and the blackened blade dropped to the sand. The sea dragon roared, swooped, and snatched Izoldia in her jaws.

Croaky screams issued from assassins who hadn't spoken in months. They stared skyward, faces rippling with shock and horror. One of the men bellowed in fear, raising his arms in supplication, then fell to his knees.

"I am rather awe-inspiring, you know," Saritha quipped, landing and sending a spray of sand over the smoking fire pit. Izoldia's kicking legs and thrashing arms hung out of either side of her jaw. The burly assassin was still cursing. Saritha gave her a rough shake.

Four men were dead and another's calf was bleeding and his shoulder stabbed. Only one man was unharmed. Ithsar shook her head. How was she supposed to convince these bloodthirsty women that they should trust sea monsters and defend the dragon riders in the North? It would be impossible.

"Shall I finish this miserable wretch now?" Saritha mind-melded, shaking Izoldia again.

Although Ithsar wanted nothing more than to see Izoldia dead, Queen Aquaria's words rang in her mind: *revenge will never bring you happiness.* She sighed. *"Saritha, we shouldn't act in anger or for revenge."*

"Put me down, you great, galumphing, ugly beast," Izoldia yelled, waving her arms at the assassins. "Attack! Kill this beast and free me from its jaws."

Eyes on Saritha, none of the women moved.

"She's asking me to put her down." Saritha's eye ridge twitched. She opened her jaws and dumped Izoldia unceremoniously on the sand.

Izoldia sprang to her feet and smiled, bowing graciously—the last thing Ithsar expected. "Oh mighty fine beast of the sea, there seems to have been a grave misunderstanding. Please take two of these fine camels as an offering to appease you." Izoldia gestured at the caravan.

Those camels weren't even hers to give. Ithsar should've known Izoldia would try flattery, given her fawning, pernicious attitude toward Ashewar.

Saritha tilted her head and asked Ithsar, *"Why would I want those camels? I've already had my fill of fish, and those beasts are stringy and not nearly as tender."*

Ithsar spoke up. "Izoldia, those camels are not yours."

Izoldia's head shot up so fast, Ithsar thought she'd break her neck. The orange-robed assassins shifted, eyes flying wide.

Saritha snorted. *"I believe your friends were so impressed by me that they didn't even see you upon my back."*

"You!" For a heartbeat, Izoldia's lips contorted, then they smoothed into a smile. "Oh, Ithsar, I'm so glad you survived your terrible fall into the sea," she said sweetly. "How awful of your mother to push you."

Now it was Ithsar's turn to snort. She ignored Izoldia, addressing the assembled women. "I've tamed this ferocious monster from the deep. She's my friend and a foe to my enemies. No doubt Izoldia has tried to lay claim to my lineage." Misha and Nila gave surreptitious nods. "However, I am the true heir of Ashewar, our deceased chief prophetess."

Bala, at the front of the assembled assassins, shifted on her feet, looking everywhere except at Ithsar. Thut, hands still bound, glowered.

"You're a liar, a traitor," Izoldia screeched, hand drifting to her empty scabbard. "You fought your mother. She hated you."

Thika pounced from Saritha's back, his wings unfurling, and flew at Izoldia, scratching her arms with his claws. Izoldia's eyes nearly bugged out of her head. Then she whirled and batted Thika away. Saritha snarled.

All the assassins except Bala and Thut leaped into action, drawing their blades and surrounding Izoldia.

The lizard flew back to Ithsar, panting and heart thrumming. Ithsar stroked Thika, crooning.

Misha and Nila tied Izoldia's hands together. The assassins led her and Thut over the dunes and tied them onto the back of their camels. The camels harrumphed and shifted their hooves in the sand.

The remaining man turned to them, trembling. "Anything you want, anything, I'll give it to you." He gestured at the heavily-laden caravan and brightly-colored burdens stacked high on the camels' backs.

"The sea dragon thanks you for your kindness," Ithsar said. "We apologize for the tragedy that has befallen your companions. You may depart in peace. Please, feel free to take your dead with you."

The man hefted his injured companion onto a camel and unhobbled the beasts. His hands shook as he waved farewell. "No, no. Thank you, thank you for sparing my life." He mounted the lead camel and the caravan plodded over the dunes, leaving his dead companions behind.

Ithsar sighed. *"I didn't want their bodies to be picked apart by vultures."*

"That, I can fix," Saritha replied. She piled up the bodies, and then incinerated them, dark smoke scorching the sky.

A New Stand

Saritha flew above the desert, dancing in the hot breeze. Ithsar's hair ripped loose from her headscarf as they rode the thermals, lazily spiraling up on the warm air, then swooping down, making her belly somersault. Growing up in the subterranean caverns and narrow tunnels of the assassin's lair, she'd never imagined such freedom. Even among the dunes, there'd always been hills closing her in. Flying in this vast azure sky with her hair whipping in the wind and the world spread far below made her heart soar.

The assassins rode their camels, trailing between the dunes toward the oasis, as tiny as dates. In the distance, the oasis beckoned, the turquoise waters shining among the palm groves.

Saritha mind-melded, *"You did well back at that skirmish. We quickly stopped those bloodthirsty women."*

"They only listened to me because you were there." Ithsar sighed. "Once I'm back in the lair beneath the oasis and you're above ground, how will I retain control? Bala, Thut, or Izoldia could kill me at any time with a flick of their wrists and a well-aimed dagger."

"You have a noble spirit. Count upon your friends to rally around you and protect you."

Friends? Up until now, she hadn't had any. What part of persecuted and despised had Saritha not understood?

They spiraled down to the edge of the palms and waited for the assassins to arrive.

Soon the camels traipsed over the dune and descended into the oasis. Ithsar signaled for the women to tether the camels in the shade of the date trees near the water's edge. The women moved with efficient well-trained movements, their muscles packed with power.

"I'm not fit to lead them. Look how they move, how strong they are."

"You move similarly," Saritha said. *"You have the same strength and power in your frame."*

"I do?"

Saritha's only reply was a chuckle.

Ithsar remained on her dragon's back between her spinal ridges, with Thika on her shoulder. She stroked the lizard absentmindedly as he nestled into her neck.

Once the camels were settled, the assassins quickly fell into a disciplined formation in front of Ithsar.

Ithsar's voice rang out, "As Ashewar's heir, I claim my place leading the Robandi Silent Assassins. We will break from tradition, so be prepared for change, and change with us—or be left like a tumbleweed to be blown in the hot desert sands without purpose or meaning to your existence."

Women shifted uneasily.

"The first change I'll introduce is that we need not maintain the vow of silence. Ashewar demanded silence unless it was necessary to speak. I expect to hear your voices, raised in speech, song or laughter. I suggest you now speak to the women on either side of you."

At first there was stunned silence, then murmurs flitted between the women. A nervous laugh broke out. Thut and Izoldia, hands still bound, glowered at her from the back ranks, Bala beside them.

"You must show them they have no chance, or they'll be forever scheming against you," Saritha rumbled in her mind.

"I know." Ithsar gestured to Misha, Nila, and two other guards, who fastened Izoldia and Thut to the trunks of two nearby palms.

Ithsar stood on Saritha's back and raised her arms for quiet. "My mother used her power to maim and harm others. We've been trained, honed as weapons, to spill men's blood. Ashewar pledged to hate men and honor women, yet you're all aware of the suffering I've endured at Izoldia's hands, suffering sanctioned by my mother."

Saritha roared, shaking a neighboring date palm. Dates fell from the tree, scattering around the dragon's feet.

Ithsar flung her arms out toward the desert. "There's a whole world out there beyond this oasis. As your new chief prophetess, I've seen visions of our future. Visions that show us using our power to love, protect, and defend those who cannot defend themselves."

"Love is weak," Izoldia snarled. Her *sathir* muddied, turning murky brown.

Some women nodded, murmuring their assent.

"What is weaker?" Ithsar called. "To hate the people who despise you, or to love them despite what they've done?"

"Just like you loved your mother?" a slim assassin jeered. "Look where that got you."

Ithsar spun. "Just like I loved my mother. Despite her hatred, which destroyed her. Without love, there is no future. We will eventually destroy each other. I have seen this in a vision."

"How can you have visions?" someone called. "Your mother has the prism-seer under lock and key. No one can see a vision without a prism."

A larger assassin, dark hair streaked with silver, interjected, "It's uncommon, but not impossible. Some naturally have the gift of visions and don't need a prism."

Ithsar nodded. "I've had visions since I was a littling on my father's knee." Some of the women scowled—no doubt, at her referring to a male. "I've seen terrible, dark dragons plaguing Dragons' Realm, the land of the prisoner I released—Ezaara, she of the golden hair."

Startled gasps rippled through the gathered assassins.

Ithsar paused, straightening her spine. "Yes, I released Ezaara and Roberto. I did not touch Izoldia. Although she threatened me, the strangers protected me. But my *sathir* shook the ground and a palm tree swayed, dropping a bunch of dates that struck Izoldia upon the head, knocking her out."

"I saw those dates and wondered how they'd fallen," a woman said, awestruck.

"That explains the purple bruise in the sky," murmured another.

"And the fierce wind that whipped our hair as we ran around the lake." The women stared at her.

"How is it that we missed your power?" one asked.

Another fell to her knees. "I'm sorry we mistreated you."

Bala glowered, her hand drifting toward her saber. "You think you can fly back here, spin these lies, and everyone will believe you? You're the useless spawn of a dead chief prophetess."

"And you framed me by putting poison in my sleeping alcove, convincing Ashewar I was a traitor."

Bala's eyes blazed. "You have no proof."

"Oh, but I do. Saritha will show you."

Ithsar motioned Bala forward, and Bala swaggered over to stand near Saritha. Despite her bravado, her eyes nervously flitted to the dragon and her hands shook.

The dragon bowed her head, and Ithsar slid down her side. "I need three witnesses," Ithsar called.

The women hung back, eyes darting to Saritha.

"Come, be fearless. We are the Robandi."

Three women stepped forward.

"Place your hands upon Saritha's brow, and she will show you my memory of that morning," Ithsar instructed.

The women tentatively placed their hands on Saritha's brow to mind-meld with her. Ithsar also put her hand on Saritha's head, remembering yesterday morning. Saritha showed them Bala slipping into Ithsar's sleeping alcove to plant the poison.

One gasped, turning to Bala with venom in her eyes. "All these years we believed your lies about Ithsar," she hissed.

Bala lunged. In a flash, they had their sabers at each other's throats.

Ithsar motioned to the others to break them up. Misha and Nila dragged Bala over to the palm next to Izoldia's and tied her up. Ithsar's bones felt hollow. How could she command this band of bloodthirsty women?

"Show them," Saritha ordered.

"Form a line before Saritha. It's time you were introduced to her properly. You all need to witness why I have been called as your new chief prophetess."

Despite three women having just laid their hands on Saritha's brow, for a few heartbeats, no one moved.

"This challenge may be difficult, but for those who succeed, there are great rewards," Ithsar said. Good, that had made their eyes glint in anticipation, even Izoldia's. "If I, the least amongst you, can survive being thrown into the sea, overcoming my fear, and imprinting with a sea dragon, then surely you can greet that same dragon." She waved her healed fingers.

The woman with silver-streaked hair thrust her shoulders back and paced to Saritha, meeting her gaze. Alarm flashed across the faces of the others, but not wanting to be outdone, every woman joined the queue—except the three tied to the palm trunks.

"Clever," Saritha said to Ithsar. *"These fierce women like a challenge."*

§

Saritha regarded her new rider, Ithsar—so much smaller than these other orange-robed women, but more generous and courageous.

As Ithsar challenged these women to find out why she was Chief Prophetess, Saritha was determined to show them exactly why. To show them everything—much more than Ithsar intended. And to measure the mettle of every assassin in this dusty dry oasis.

The women came, laying their hands upon her scaly brow, one by one. She sensed not only the weapon-worn calluses on their palms, but also the timbre of their minds and the nature of their hearts. She of the silver-streaked hair and finely-wrinkled skin bore no malice. But not every woman was the same. Some carried dark secrets in their hearts. And even without them touching her, Saritha could see that those bound to the trees burned with violent red *sathir* and a hatred of Ithsar that made her talons itch.

When she saw dark dragons blasting Saritha's majestic cousins of Dragons' Realm with flame, the assassin with silver-streaked hair whispered, "How dare they!" And as strange yellow beams shot from the shadow dragons' eyes and sliced through the flesh of riders and dragons, her blood roiled in anger and her other hand drifted to her knife. The woman muttered when green flame shot from the hands of mages on dark dragons—mages that all looked the same.

And when Saritha shared the vision of the carcasses of dragons and riders strewn across the land, and the beautiful rivers and green pastures becoming a buzzing fly-infested swamp, and the towering snow-laden mountains becoming dry dusty gray slopes, the woman turned to face her people. "We must fight to protect Dragons' Realm before it's turned into a wasteland."

As she turned to walk away, Saritha touched her shoulder with her snout and mind-melded again. *"Wait, sister, there is more."*

The woman laid her hand upon Saritha's brow once more.

Towering sandstone rose above Saritha, waves crashing against its base. Spray misted her snout as she thrust her head above the surface to watch the tiny orange-clothed figures dancing along the top of the cliff. She and her sisters had heard the sharks in a rowdy feeding frenzy, demolishing the lone body of a woman who had fallen from the cliff.

Saritha didn't usually like to interfere with the affairs of sharks and men, but something *had whispered that she should go forth and see what this fuss was about. Queen Aquaria had also heard that same something whispering. So Saritha had decided to heed the call.*

She yawned, the green scales on her jaw glimmering with salty water in the sunlight. At the top of the cliff, two figures fought, clothed in orange. They fell—more fodder for the sharks.

She sank below the ocean, prowling the depths with her sisters, diving among the coral formations, keeping an eye on the surface. A woman with rotten sathir *as black as night plunged into the water, thrashing, hundreds of tiny braids swirling around her face as she fought her way back up to gasp air. Saritha sensed the hatred burning in this woman's heart, sensed the blood of many lives upon her hands, and turned away, diving deeper.*

Then something surged inside her. She spun, her tail lashing a baby squid.

A slip of a girl was sinking into the water, holding a lizard, pinching its nose. How dare that girl torture this lizard—a distant land cousin to Saritha. Her scales bristled. She swam closer. Above, sharks thrashed and the scent of blood wafted on the current as they devoured the evil-hearted woman. Saritha meandered along the seabed, swimming among the coral towers and waving seaweed. Her siblings dived and frolicked, scattering schools of fish.

What was that?

That tiny slip of a girl was swimming toward the cliff.

A shark butted her, dived, and butted her again, playing with its food. Saritha was about to swim away when she noticed what the girl was doing. Under the water, her legs and one arm thrashed, trying to keep her afloat. Had the littling only one arm?

Curious, Saritha swam closer. The shark was speeding at the girl, who held her other arm high out of the water, holding the lizard aloft, trying to keep it from drowning. She hadn't been torturing the lizard at all, but protecting it. And then Saritha felt the girl's sathir as a rush of pure love enveloped the lizard, and the girl cried aloud, "I'm sorry, Thika."

A shimmering radius enveloped the girl and the sweetest music coursed through the sea dragon's breast.

The shark reared out of the water and opened its jaws, leaping for the girl and lizard.

Saritha surged to the surface and slapped the water with her tail, sending a spray over the shark. Opening her maw, she crunched the shark in half and tossed its broken body over her head to its companions, who devoured it.

And then she plucked up this precious loving girl and her lizard in her jaws, careful not to hurt them, and sank beneath the ocean as her blood sang with joy. She had found a rider and her name was Ithsar.

The assassin with the silver-streaked hair met Saritha's gaze, her dark eyes shiny with tears, and nodded. Her voice was barely a whisper of breath as she said, "I pledge to follow Ithsar, the noble new chief prophetess, and will do whatever she requires."

§

Each assassin had obviously mind-melded with the beast. Izoldia knew her turn was coming. As the knowledge settled in her bones, she was determined to use it to her advantage. This beast did not know that she was stronger than Ithsar, more worthy of owning a sea dragon than Ithsar had ever been. And she'd only have one chance to convince it. So, despite her bonds, Izoldia sat tall and proud against the palm's trunk, and waited for the foul beast to approach. It paced toward her, its strong limbs rippling with muscle under its gleaming scales.

Oh, to harness such a beast and use its power—she could conquer many more enemies than with her saber and a camel. Many more than with the entire band of assassins behind her. Why, this beast could fell men, villages, and armies with a swipe of its talons or the flickering flame from its jaws.

Izoldia held her smile. Now was not the time to reveal her plans. First, she would earn this beast's trust and reveal Ithsar for what she truly was—a deformed weakling.

The monster curled its lip back, exposing gleaming white fangs, some nearly as long as her forearm. That runt stalked alongside the dragon, so close to those fangs. If only Izoldia could convince the beast to turn its head and snap Ithsar's head off, then she could ride upon its back in her rightful place.

That runty girl reached up, placing her hand inside the beast's maw to pluck out a piece of seaweed.

By the holy *dracha* gods. Izoldia gulped, fear skittering through her bones. Her hands shook.

The sea dragon snapped its jaw shut, its yellow eyes forming mean slits as it lowered its head toward Izoldia, nostrils flaring.

Ithsar, unbearably close to that glorious, powerful beast, said, "It's your turn, Izoldia. Lay your hand upon Saritha's brow."

Saritha? Izoldia nearly snorted, but refrained. Terror was a better name for this creature. Or Fang. When she killed Ithsar and imprinted with this monster, she would rename it. But for now, she would bide her time and plan. Until that opportunity arose.

A skinny assassin cut her bonds so she could touch the beast. Izoldia forced a charming smile, stretched her hand forth and placed it on the monster's snout.

And as the monster showed her a vision of the future—of a queen and her dragons waiting in the Naobian deeps for new riders, and then waging warfare in the sky—Izoldia formulated a plan. A plan that would see her triumph over that scrawny runt.

A New Challenge

Once all the women had been shown visions of their future, including Izoldia, Thut, and Bala, Ithsar stood before them as they waited in formation in the shade, protected from the hot desert sun. "If we are to imprint with sea dragons and help our sisters in the North, we must learn new skills. Who is prepared for this glory?"

Everyone thumped their fists on their hearts, although Ithsar caught Thut giving Bala and Izoldia a sly glance.

"Very clever, my friend," Saritha mind-melded. *"You have convinced everyone to follow us."*

"There are still those who will betray me," Ithsar replied.

Saritha rumbled, *"And I have my eye on them."*

"It has been a trying morning. Later, we'll learn new skills for battle on dragonback. But now, we shall eat. Please fetch food from the mess cavern and bring it up here into the shade of the palms."

Murmurs broke out. "But we always eat inside in the heat of the day."

"We usually do, but today is different. We're keeping many of our traditions, but will also usher in a few new ones. And today, we are celebrating." She motioned to six women, who scurried below ground, and then she asked four others to pick dates and oranges.

The assassins settled in the shade of the date palms while some fetched fresh water from the lake. Soon, women carried large cauldrons of warm goat stew and couscous and rounds of flatbread out under the palms.

Ithsar gaped. So much food. What was going on?

Misha sidled over. "There was a feast prepared for, ah… for your demise."

Ithsar's gut hollowed. Speechless, she stared at Misha.

Misha smiled. "I would've choked on every mouthful," she whispered, and sauntered off to help serve the food.

§

After the feast, Izoldia, Bala, and Thut were taken to the dungeons. Thut protested every step of the way, saying all she'd ever done was obey the commands given by Izoldia, and insisting that the sign of a good assassin was obeying those in command. Bala muttered under her breath.

From late that afternoon until the sun slipped in a blazing red ball toward the distant dunes, Saritha and Ithsar trained the women in dragonback archery. One at a time, Saritha took the assassins into the sky. All experienced at archery on camelback, they had to adjust their angles and perspective as they shot at the targets they'd set around the perimeter of the oasis. Most of them missed the first time, and many the second, but slowly, they learned to compensate for the breeze of the dragon's wingbeats and adjust the trajectory of their arrows.

"Leave the other three in the dungeons. I refuse to carry Bala, Izoldia, or Thut, until they have a change of heart," Saritha growled. *"Their malice for you is like a dark canker rotting them from the inside out."*

"I know." Ithsar sighed. *"You're doing a fine job, but it's frustratingly slow with only one dragon."*

"If we put up more targets, I could carry two women and they could fire arrows at targets on either side of me, so we could train them doubly fast."

"But not as fast as if they had their own sea dragons. We must get them battle-ready or they'll be slaughtered."

SEA DRAGON

"It's too early to ask them to imprint. They need more time to trust us. We can't build a new reign in a day."

"You're a wise dragon." Ithsar scratched Saritha's eye ridges, and the sea dragon leaned into her touch.

"You know, I wouldn't mind that swim we spoke of," Saritha said, eying the lake as the assassins trooped down into the entrance tunnel. *"My scales are dry and itchy. I'm not used to being out of the water so long."*

They waited until the last of the assassins had departed, and flew to the far end of the lake where they wouldn't be disturbed. As the setting sun turned the lake fiery orange, Saritha dipped beneath the surface, her bubble of *sathir* encompassing Ithsar.

Ithsar breathed deeply, letting her aching muscles relax as Saritha swam through liquid gold.

§

Ithsar sat on the grotesque throne carved from the bones of her mother's enemies, the tortured faces of dying men glaring up at her from the armrests. She gingerly placed her hands in her lap, unwilling to have her body touch more of the seat than was necessary. She wouldn't have used it, but Izoldia, Bala, and Thut had requested the right to speak and, bound by tradition, Ithsar was required to hear them. This was the only seat that would bring her remotely near Izoldia's eye level.

All the assassins were present, arrayed at the far end of the chamber near the back wall.

The doors opened and her guards Nila and Misha, flanked by four others, marched the prisoners into the throne chamber. Bala and Thut's eyes glittered.

Izoldia did nothing to mute her footsteps upon the cool tiles, her boots ringing throughout the cavern like jeers echoing off the walls. She also made no effort to disguise her labored breathing.

The guards led Izoldia and her cronies toward the throne. When they were half a camel length away, Ithsar flicked her finger, motioning them to stop. Standing in front of the throne, Izoldia dwarfed Ithsar—the way she'd dwarfed and demeaned Ithsar's entire life. Her broad shoulders were wider than the throne, her bulky body towering over Ithsar. Her eyes lowered, she stared at her feet.

Bala and Thut stood motionless behind her.

Ithsar motioned to the guards to fall back—but not too far, in case Izoldia decided to attack. Her heart thrumming in a frenzied tattoo against her ribs, Ithsar said coolly, "You may speak."

Izoldia kept her gaze downcast. "I beg your forgiveness, my Chief Prophetess."

Should Ithsar trust her? The years of taunting, insults, and pain coiled into a hard ball inside Ithsar's stomach. As Chief Prophetess, she had been preaching benevolence to her people. The gathered guards' gazes settled upon her. Unless she led by example and showed that benevolence now, none of them would respect her and do what she required in order for them to imprint with the sea dragons and help Ezaara—she of golden hair and vivid green eyes—from the North.

Ithsar drew a long, slow breath of cool subterranean air in through her nostrils. "You require my forgiveness. What will you give in return?"

Guards shuffled, eyes shifting. Bala and Thut glanced at each other, something passing between them. What was Izoldia planning?

Izoldia fell to her knees and bowed before Ithsar, her tied hands outstretched and her forehead kissing the tiles. "I pledge my undying loyalty."

Better than Ithsar had hoped for, but it had to be a trick. Izoldia was up to something. Although she wanted nothing more than to throw her dagger into this scheming sycophant's back, Ithsar forced her fingers to be still. She'd pledged to show everyone love and kindness, including this woman. Perhaps Izoldia had had a change of heart.

Fraught with risk, there was only one way to test her. Very well. "Please stand."

Izoldia rose, her face expressionless. Without her sneer, curled lip, or a glint of malice in her eyes, she looked completely different. Her face was quite pleasant. It was a shame hatred and twisted emotions had driven her to bullying.

"So you will pledge your undying obedience to me, your new revered chief prophetess?"

Without hesitation, Izoldia thumped a hand on her breast and nodded. "Yes, Chief Prophetess. I promise to obey you."

Ithsar's eyes roamed the chamber. At the back of the room, Bala was smirking. Not a good sign. "Very well," Ithsar replied. "Unbind her hands. You may live among us, but at the first sign of discontent, you will be cast out into the desert."

Izoldia closed her eyes and nodded. "I understand. As you wish, my revered Chief Prophetess."

"Bala and Thut?" Ithsar asked.

"We also pledge to obey you," Bala said.

"Yes, we do," Thut added.

It was all too easy. Misha and Nila's expressions were grim as they cut the ropes around the prisoners' hands.

Izoldia remained contrite as guards on either side led her out of the cavern. At the door, they all turned to salute Ithsar, the thud of their hands against their chests echoing in the chamber. Izoldia's eyes flashed. Bala and Thut smirked, falling in behind her.

Something cold slithered through Ithsar's belly. She swallowed. She was not Ashewar; would never be Ashewar. Perhaps her compassion would be her downfall. But she did not want to rule like her mother. She had meant what she'd said, and wanted a new reign—a reign of fairness and justice.

Everyone filed out, leaving Ithsar sitting upon her throne in an empty chamber, her belly hollow, wondering if Izoldia would murder her in her sleep.

Raven Calls

Ithsar sighed and held her hand outside the bubble of *sathir,* trailing her fingers through the deep blue lake, making a silvery trail of water as Saritha swam. The sun was rising, dawn giving the water a pale pink tinge. It was beautiful, but still wasn't as glorious as the Naobian Sea. Here, there were no coral, just endless sand and weeds and a few species of fish: tiny silver ones; some with yellow stripes and brown tails that blended against the sand; and other larger predators with jagged teeth that snapped up the small fish whenever they got too close. Still, it meant Saritha could swim—even if it was only before dawn or after dusk when their training didn't demand the sea dragon fly in shifts with the assassins.

Training had been progressing well over the last moon and a half, so well that the only time Ithsar had on her own with Saritha was during these early morning or late night swims. She cherished this time when they could relax, laugh, and be themselves. Most of the assassins had long since mastered dragonback archery and were now learning flight maneuvers and the best techniques for throwing knives from dragonback. Their usual training continued—the *Sathiri* battle dance, saber fights, and hand-to-hand combat, keeping Ithsar busy from dawn until dusk.

Despite one attempted poisoning that had never been proven, Izoldia, Bala, and Thut had been model students, acting with humility and learning the ropes as fast as anyone else. Occasionally, Ithsar caught a malicious glint in Izoldia's eyes or thought she'd glimpsed a curl of her lip, but it had always been so fleeting, she'd never been sure if she'd imagined it.

"Have you had enough? I wouldn't mind hunting fish," Saritha asked.

"Set me ashore and I'll rest while you fish." Ithsar yawned. She'd been tossing and turning half the night, wondering whether the assassins would be called upon to fight the dark dragons she'd seen in her visions. And how in the name of the flaming sun she'd convince the women to throw themselves into the Naobian Sea to meet their dragons. Yes, she'd omitted that tiny detail when she'd spoken to them about imprinting. She hadn't dared let Saritha know.

The sea dragon held out her foreleg, creating a bridge between her shoulder and the shore of the oasis. Ithsar slid down her limb, but Saritha yanked it away at the last moment, and she tumbled into knee-deep water.

Laughing, Ithsar scrambled to her feet and splashed Saritha. *"You really are a sea monster."*

"Ah, yes, I was a wild beast until you tamed me."

Ithsar slugged her dragon's dripping, scaly arm, and Saritha pretended to slash with her talons, splashing Ithsar back.

The pink tinge of dawn peeked over the tangerine sands. Drips running down her face, and saturated below the knee, Ithsar said, *"I'm going to dry off while you hunt."*

"Did you know there are mages in the North that can dry you with the touch of their hands?" Saritha winked at her and dived back under the surface of the lake.

Queen Aquaria had mentioned the dragon mage. Did he possess such wondrous powers?

For a moment, the silver sheen on Saritha's scales glistened pink in the dawn's rays, making Ithsar's chest swell, and then the dragon submerged, her tail sending one last splash across the water. Fighting was all well and good, but these were the moments she lived for.

A trail of bubbles rose to the surface, the only sign that a terrible sea monster now inhabited the lake. Ithsar gave a chuckle and laid down on the sand. It was still cool, but wouldn't be for long. Within moments, she dozed off, waiting for the sun to rise and dry her clothes.

§

Ithsar woke to a dark speck on the horizon. Her robes were nearly dry, but she lay there, watching the speck grow as it drew closer to the oasis. It was a bird, a raven, drooping with exhaustion. It fluttered its wings and dived, collapsing in the sand at Ithsar's feet with a wing outstretched and its sides heaving.

Ithsar scooped the raven up and took it to the lake. The bird trembled in her hands, its soft feathers tickling her palms. She knelt and held it near the water. The raven bent its head, eagerly scooping up water with its beak. She stroked the soft feathers between its wings at the base of its neck. "Easy now," she crooned. "Your belly will burst if you're not careful."

The raven squirmed, and something scraped against her arm. She examined the bird and found a small tube attached to its right leg—a messenger bird, then. Here in the desert? Not unheard of, but extremely unusual. This bird must've come from Dragons' Realm beyond the Naobian Sea. She cradled the tired raven in her hands, strolled back to sit under the shade of a date palm, and popped the bird in her lap. Using her dagger, she gently cut the twine that bound the tube. She uncorked the end and tapped the tube on her palm. A small scroll of parchment fell out.

Ithsar unrolled it.

My dearest friend Ithsar,
    I trust that this message finds you well. I write in the hope that you are able to come to our aid.

A scourge has risen upon the lands of Dragons' Realm. Commander Zens has created foul shadow dragons—dark beasts who are destroying towns and villages, enslaving our people, and killing our dragons, riders, and mages. As well as dragon flame, beams of golden light from their eyes slice the flesh of dragon and rider. Using his dark methods, Zens has also grown strange mages who ride these beasts, searing our dragons, riders, and mages with wizard flame.

I am calling upon all my friends in the far reaches of the realm and beyond to come to our aid. Without help, I fear the destruction of the entire realm. Our people are dying by the thousands. These beasts are clogging the skies. If there is any way you can entreat your mother and the Robandi assassins to come to our aid, I would deeply appreciate it. And if this brief letter falls into the hands of someone other than Ithsar, I plead that you will come to the aid of Dragons' Realm and help save our people from extinction.

Ezaara, Queen's Rider
Of Zaarusha, the honored Dragon Queen of Dragons' Realm.

Ithsar's hands shook as she rolled the scrap of paper and tucked it into the folds of her robe, sliding it against her skin. *"Oh, Saritha, Ezaara has requested our help."*

This was it—the visions she'd seen were coming true. Ezaara needed them. There was no time to waste. She set the bird onto the grass under a palm.

Oh gods, how was she—the deformed, useless daughter of a cutthroat assassin—going to do this?

Saritha rose from the lake, dripping, and landed nearby, shaking droplets over the sand. *"This is the moment we've been training for. We must go to their aid. My cousins in the North need us. Go, and gather your sisters."*

Ithsar swallowed. *"But, I'm just a lowly—"*

SEA DRAGON

Saritha cut her off. *"Ithsar, shake off the shackles of your birth and rise to the occasion. Dragons' Realm needs you."*

Swallowing, Ithsar nodded and rushed toward the tunnel to the subterranean caverns.

§

As Ithsar ran through the tunnels, Saritha melded with her. *"Prepare the women for imprinting. If you tell them what's required of them, they'll rise to the occasion. It's an honor to ride a sea dragon, and now that they've grown used to being with me, they're bound to imprint when they leap from the cliff."*

Saritha didn't understand. These fearless women did not like the sea or the monsters that lurked in its depths. Asking them to submit themselves willingly would be the ultimate test of Ithsar's grip on them. Asking them too soon would ruin everything. She'd wait until they had no choice. Ithsar reached the cavern and waited at the front, pounding feet rushing along the tunnels and echoing through the training chamber.

As her assassins assembled in front of her, she was too aware that she only reached the shoulders of the tallest. The women stood, hands out, poised on the balls of their feet—battle-ready. Ithsar waved a hand toward the floor. As one, the women sat.

She let her eyes travel over them, meeting everyone's gazes. Izoldia, Bala, and Thut were near the back of the cavern. Their eyes slid away—not a promising sign.

Ithsar dived right in. "A messenger bird arrived today. The vision that Saritha showed you is coming to pass. Even as we train here in the desert, isolated by the broad Naobian Sea, hundreds of people are dying in Dragons' Realm, slaughtered by evil dragons, their carcasses left to rot across the land. Ezaara—she of the golden hair, and the Queen's Rider of Dragons' Realm—has asked for our aid. I have pledged to help her. And you have pledged to obey me. So prepare your camels, pack clothes, weapons, food, and waterskins for an extended trip. We'll ride out in an hour, so you may imprint with the waiting sea dragons."

Their fists pounding their chests, the silent assassins bowed their heads. No questions asked.

Ithsar swallowed. Would they be so compliant when they got to the drop-off and realized they were required to throw themselves into the sea to prove their trust? Sharks prowled those waters. Suspicion of sea monsters was as much part of their Robandi culture as camel butter on couscous.

Perhaps she'd be flying to Dragons' Realm on her own, an army of one to fight against Commander Zens' evil shadow dragons.

A Test of Trust

Camels snorted, saddlebags creaking as the assassins tightened them around the girth of their beasts. Hooves shifted in sand, like hissing rust vipers. Ithsar strode through the camels, nodding at her women as she made her way to the front, Thika nestled on her forearm.

"I assume you've told these women what is required of them? They look resolute and willing to fight," Saritha rumbled.

Ithsar avoided answering, helping Thika onto Saritha's back. *"I assume you're ready for the long trek across the desert?"*

Saritha snorted. *"It's a mere wingbeat or two. We could be there in no time."* As Ithsar climbed into the saddle, Saritha flicked her tail toward the camels. *"Those creatures will take half a day."*

"I'm afraid we will too. I dare not take my eyes off those three at the back." Ithsar glanced at Izoldia, Thut, and Bala.

"A little jet of flame will sort them out, no problem."

"I know, but you might spook their camels," Ithsar replied.

Saritha's talons kneaded the sand, and she turned, angling her head to gaze at Ithsar. *"Well, we couldn't have that, could we?"* A mischievous twinkle gleamed in her golden eyes.

"I'm trying to lead my people by example. I can't have you upsetting them."

"Upsetting them? Who said anything about upsetting them? I was merely contemplating setting their camels' tails on fire." Her fangs gleamed in a dragonly smile, and she tossed her head, facing the camels again. *"Are we ready?"* Saritha's body quivered with impatience.

Ithsar scratched her neck. *"I don't blame you. You've been cooped up here for so long."*

"With nothing but stringy goats, the odd fish, and desert vultures to eat." Saritha eyed one of the camels.

"No, you don't. They're our transport! You can't eat them."

"Well, I could… but they do have a rather unpleasant scent." The dragon wrinkled her snout.

"Lucky for them." Ithsar stifled a smile as she turned to her assassins. She drew her saber from its sheath and raised it in the air, calling, "We'll ride out across the desert toward the Naobian Sea." Her eyes flicked to Izoldia, Bala, and Thut. "Saritha and I will ensure that nobody gets lost."

Bala leaned across her camel to say something to Izoldia, who grinned. Thut sniggered.

"Those three are trouble, all right. It's not too late to leave them behind," Saritha rumbled.

For a heartbeat, Ithsar considered it. It would be safer for all of them if Izoldia, Bala, and Thut didn't come. *"What harm can those three do against a mighty dragon like you?"*

Saritha preened her scales. Gasps echoed through the ranks of the assassins as her majestic green wings unfurled, glinting in the morning sun. She sprang into the air, spraying sand over the nearest camel's haunches, and then spiraled upward until the camels were a mere speck below them in the sand.

Exhilaration sang through Ithsar's blood as the wind swept her headscarf back, the ends trailing in the sky behind her. The full force of the hot summer sun beat down upon her, but instead of sapping her strength, she felt energized, alive, as if the world was full of wonder and possibility. Saritha's pleasure shot through her, the sea dragon's delight setting her veins on fire.

Saritha swooped, and Ithsar's belly flew straight into her throat. As far as she could see, tangerine sand was spread before her, enormous dunes rolling into hillocks. The Naobian Sea winked deep sapphire-blue in the distance.

Ithsar drew in a deep breath, the tension of these long weeks training the women unfurling and rushing out of her in a whoosh.

They dived and shot out across the desert, camels trailing them, and then Saritha circled and swooped in behind the camels, driving them forward. *"Go on, just a little flame? Please?"*

"What a tease you are." Joy blossomed inside Ithsar. Too big to contain, it felt as if her skin would burst. She whooped and laughed.

Some of the assassins gazed up, surprised. Some smiled. Others waved.

She'd soon see whether they'd still be smiling when they found out they had to throw themselves off the cliff to the monsters of the deep.

§

The lapis sea was sparkling in the blazing sun when they arrived at the Naobian coast. Saritha landed upon the dune where Ithsar had fought Ashewar, only a moon and a half ago. The rugged sandstone cliff cut away beneath them where the cliff had crumbled when she'd fought her mother. The giant waves that had battered Ithsar were only tiny crests of white from way up here. The sea rushed in, roaring as it pounded the cliff, then hissed as it was sucked back out again.

Dark brown flecks—Drida's blood—were half covered in wind-blown sand. This was a place of death.

And of the birth of her new life.

Ithsar shook a trickle of unease from between her shoulder blades. Hopefully, no more blood would be shed today.

Saritha rumbled, *"I've signaled Queen Aquaria. She and the sea dragons will be arriving shortly. I'm glad these women know what to expect."*

Ithsar slid from the saddle, not meeting Saritha's gaze.

The sea dragon nudged her shoulder. *"You have told them, haven't you? They need to be ready to jump, so they can imprint."*

The camels sat at the base of the dune. The women were traipsing up, their orange robes making the sand ripple with movement. They reached the top of the hill and stood in formation, pounding their fists upon their chests.

Misha approached. "The women are hungry, and more than a little nervous. Is it all right if we eat first? It may help settle their nerves."

Ithsar nodded. "Yes, you'll need your strength."

Nila spoke up. "Are the sea dragons meeting us up here?"

Ithsar's belly coiled tight and a trickle of unease rippled through her. "You'll see," she replied softly.

But Saritha heard. She nudged Ithsar again, this time a bit harder. *"So you haven't told them? Ithsar, I warned you—"*

"I know what I'm doing." Ithsar broke mind-meld and joined the women. She hadn't been prepared when she'd imprinted with Saritha.

She bit into her fresh flatbread, but it tasted like sand. She tried a poppyseed cake, but its usual sweetness eluded her. Even her dried fruit was tasteless pap. So, she melded with her dragon again. *"Saritha, these are my people. I know them well. Please trust me."*

A low rumble issued from Saritha's maw, but she nodded, yellow eyes glinting. *"Very well. But I hope it won't cost us the safety of Dragons' Realm. Since the messenger bird arrived, I've felt something dark slithering under my scales. But at the same time, I sense sunshine filtering down through murky waters."* Her golden eyes met Ithsar's. *"Hopefully, we shall be all right."*

Saritha unfurled her wings and leaped to perch upon the edge of the cliff. She opened her maw and roared.

Below, the water churned with shark fins. Green and blue scaly heads rose out of the sea. In the depths, more long shadowy shapes sped toward the base of the cliff.

Ithsar raised her arms and faced her fellow assassins. "Have you pledged to follow me?"

"Yes," the women cried.

"Do you trust me?"

"Yes."

Although Izoldia's eyes narrowed, and Bala nudged Thut.

Bala asked in a booming voice, "Should we stand back to leave space for the dragons to land?"

"Soon we'll be riding dragons into battle." Ithsar flung her arms out. "The sea dragons are waiting."

The women cast about, looking behind them and into the sky.

She gestured to the cliff. "In order to imprint with a sea dragon, you must show great trust. They require us to leap from the drop-off and meet them in the sea. There are more than enough dragons for all of you, but this is the test you must pass to become a rider." Ithsar waited. No one moved. "You may choose to go back to the oasis, and we will not think less of you."

Wind hissed across the sand. Waves pounded on the cliffs below.

"Misha, you've shown courage. Would you like the honor of going first?"

Misha's eyes shot wide. Her face paled and she opened her mouth, then snapped it shut.

"Your most loyal follower, gaping like a stranded fish," Saritha melded. *"I thought you knew your women."*

Ithsar turned to Nila, who gave a barely perceptible shake of her head.

Panic dug its claws deep into Ithsar's belly. If nobody imprinted, Dragons' Realm would be lost. Her eyes flitted across the women, but no one met her gaze.

A voice rang out. "I'll go first." Izoldia swaggered toward Ithsar, barely restraining herself from an arrogant sneer. "I, Ashewar's greatest warrior, do not hesitate to leap into the deep. I shall conquer a wild beast."

Shaking her head, Ithsar replied, "These dragons don't require conquering, Izoldia. They require an equal, a friend."

As quick as an asp, Izoldia's arm flashed out. She whipped Roshni's ceremonial saber from Ithsar's sheath and kicked out at Ithsar.

Ithsar palmed her dagger and spun, countering with her own kick, but Izoldia leapt off the cliff, her bellow slicing through the air. "I *will* conquer a sea dragon."

Saber flashing, she plummeted toward the sea.

Izoldia's Plot

The wind ripped Izoldia's head scarf from her head and flung it into a wild breeze. Triumph and rage thrummed through Izoldia's veins. This was it. This was her final chance at leadership. If she could obtain a dragon—the largest dragon, the queen she had glimpsed in Saritha's mind—then she had a chance of leading these people. Her last chance of being a mighty ruler.

She would subdue the beast and bend its will to hers, and then destroy the deformed runt on top of the cliff, laughing as the sea monster blasted Ithsar with flame and melted her bones.

Izoldia hurtled through the air and hit the sea, feet first, the shock jarring through her leg bones into her hips. She barely had time to snatch a gust of breath before she plummeted down deep.

When her descent slowed, she kicked up, aiming for the surface. Still holding Roshni's saber tight, she burst from the ocean.

A giant green-scaled beast, the hugest of them all, plowed through the water toward her.

All she had to do was mind-meld, and this beast would be hers. Izoldia grinned, tucking Roshni's saber in the back of her waistband, and swam closer. The beast's majestic head rose from the ocean, its jaws dripping seawater and its golden eyes glinting. Fin-like projections from the side of its face glittered like emeralds in the sun. Its maw, longer than Izoldia's torso, opened, its snarl making Izoldia's bones skitter.

Nearby, a shark cut through the water. The beast lashed out with its tail. The shark arced through the air and landed in the water a hundred camel lengths away. The power of this beast was thrilling. With such a mighty creature fighting for her, the world would be hers.

Izoldia swam nearer.

The monster slitted its eyes and lowered its head, gazing at her. A deep growling voice burst into her mind, *"You would dare imprint with me?"*

It stole Izoldia's breath. A wave lapped, crashing over her head. She spluttered and kicked upward, projecting her thoughts outward. *"Oh yes, wondrous creature of the depths, I have come to imprint with you and be your new rider."*

A dark, roiling cloud drifted through Izoldia's mind. *"You, who killed so many and taunted my daughter's rider?"*

Fierce rage surged through Izoldia's breast. Not that deformed little runt again. Ithsar had always stood between Izoldia and everything she'd ever desired. She quelled her rage, dampening it and shoving it down deep where the sea monster couldn't detect it. *"I have seen the evil of my former ways, dear gracious, wondrous sea monster. I am here to offer myself to willingly serve you and Ithsar."*

She rotated her feet and thrashed her arms, treading water, to stay above the crashing waves.

"You held her saber as you plunged into the ocean—the saber of the one who sacrificed her life to save her. Your heart is full of canker. The rotten fire of hatred burns within you."

"No, no, honored Sea Queen, you sense only the trace of my old life. I have changed."

The monster tilted its head, regarding her. Izoldia's pulse pounded against her temples. At last it spoke. *"I do believe in giving the darkest, foulest creature a second chance. Come here and I will test you."*

Izoldia swam closer. Dangerously close.

The beast lowered its head, jaws underwater, only the eyes and top of her head above the surface. *"Swim alongside me."*

SEA DRAGON

Izoldia splashed, gasping, until she was alongside the queen's giant head.

"Now place your hands upon my brow so I can see your true essence."

This stupid monster was obsessed with its dung-filled rituals—the beast had no idea what she was up to. *"I am too weary, not used to swimming. Please let me climb upon your back, for I fear I will drown."* She spluttered, letting herself be dragged under for a moment, then kicked up again, gasping in great chestfuls of air. *"Help me."*

The monster's eyes narrowed. *"Very well. Climb upon my neck."* It lowered its head, its eyes gazing at her from underwater. And then that giant head swooped under Izoldia's body.

Izoldia grasped a spinal ridge on the top of its neck, but as she laid her hands upon the beast's hide and it raised its head from the sea, a violent wave of black fury ripped through her mind.

"You have the darkest heart. You will never be my rider. The blood of too many men stains your hands, and your mind is full of foul intent."

If Izoldia could never have this beast, no one would. She wouldn't face the humiliation of another assassin imprinting with the queen of the sea dragons. It was bad enough that Ithsar had taken her rightful place as heir after she'd worked so hard to curry favor with Ashewar. Izoldia whipped Roshni's saber from the back of her waistband, and raised it high above the beast's head. Then she drove the curved blade into the monster's head above its eye. The queen of the sea dragons let out an agonizing shriek. Izoldia jumped upon the saber, driving it through the beast's skull with her full body weight.

Blood sprayed from the dragon, bathing Izoldia, but she didn't care. Hanging on as the queen's neck drooped, she drove that saber with all her strength until the monster's body went limp and slumped under the water, taking her with it.

§

Izoldia disappeared over the ledge in a flash of orange robes and a silver glint of Roshni's saber. Ithsar rushed to the edge and stared down at the churning waves. Queen Aquaria was racing to meet Izoldia, her jade body undulating through the sea.

A shudder skittered through Ithsar's bones. Nothing good could come of this—Izoldia was always scheming. A cry broke from Ithsar's lips, "Saritha."

In a flash of green and silver, Saritha was beside her. Ithsar scrambled onto her back. Saritha's mighty haunches tensed, and they dived down the sandstone cliff, the wind rushing through Ithsar's hair, the churning surf beckoning.

The queen of the sea dragons surfaced, raising her head. Izoldia burst from the ocean and clambered upon the dragon. *"No, what is Queen Aquaria thinking?"*

"She wants to test Izoldia," barked Saritha. *"I've warned her not—"*

In a flash of silver, Izoldia drove Roshni's saber deep into Queen Aquaria's head, and then leaped upon it, driving the blade through her skull.

The dragon and Izoldia submerged, disappearing from view. A bloody trail of red frothed in the sea.

An agonized roar burst from Saritha's throat, and she and Ithsar plunged into the ocean, a bubble of silver enveloping Ithsar.

It was chaos underwater. Sharks swarmed around Queen Aquaria. Saritha tore into them with her claws, rending their bodies and flinging them aside. More sharks dived in, biting at the queen's carcass, whipping the sea into a bloody frenzy with their thrashing tails.

Izoldia's limp body floated past. Saritha smacked it with her tail, sending Izoldia into the mass of frenzied sharks. In horror, Ithsar watched as they devoured the burly guard, crunching through her bones and ripping her apart. Feasting upon her remains.

More dragons dived through the water, swimming toward their queen, slashing at sharks with their talons, and driving them away with their tails. Blood swirled around Ithsar, clouding the water, and the sea reverberated with anguished cries of hundreds of dragons.

§

The sea dragons formed a ring around Queen Aquaria, protecting her from the ocean's finned vultures. Anguish ripped through Ithsar's mind as Saritha opened her maw. A mourning keen reverberated through the water, shattering through Ithsar's body. The dragons joined in. Keening came from all around her, bouncing off her—an eerie lament, muted by the water, rippling through her body and echoing in her mind.

They hung, suspended in the water around the queen's limp carcass. Ithsar lost all sense of time—there was only the eerie cry reverberating through her again and again.

The dragons dived, weaving under the queen and lifting her body. Driving upwards with their mighty forearms and lashing with their tails, the loyal dragons pushed their queen's body up toward the daylight.

Ithsar clung on, the keening still filling her ears as the dragons broke the surface. The dragons grasped hold of Queen Aquaria and flew, wings dripping, up into the clear sapphire sky, carrying their queen—a huge ring of creatures honoring their valiant leader. Their mournful cries tugged at her heartstrings, threatening to split her chest in two. This was her fault. If she'd kept Izoldia in the dungeons and not given her a chance, none of this would have happened.

Ithsar shielded her thoughts from Saritha. Her poor friend was grieving her mother and her queen. She didn't need Ithsar's guilt added to her burden.

Ithsar tasted the tang of Saritha's sadness. Izoldia was no more, but, by murdering the sea dragon queen, Izoldia had destroyed their future.

The dragons rushed upward, startling the assassins gathered on the clifftop as their wings beat higher into the sky. When the cliff and the assassins were no more than specks below, the dragons dropped Queen Aquaria. She plunged through the air. Saritha and the other sea dragons dived, belching flame at the queen's body.

Her carcass caught, blazing as it plummeted toward the sea. Burning, burning, until it grew into a towering inferno, a plume of gray smoke staining the sky. The dragons dived, flaming her until the queen of the sea dragons was nothing but ash, swept away on the surface of the sea.

Sea Dragons

The moment Izoldia jumped and Saritha and Ithsar dived after her, Misha whipped out her saber and stood back-to-back with Nila facing off Bala and Thut.

"Any trouble, and you'll feel our blades," Misha called in a strong voice—a strength she didn't feel. She willed her arm not to shake.

Nila leaped forward. "We'll wait for Ithsar. Anyone who chooses not to follow Ithsar may leave now." Behind Bala and Thut, women's hands drifted to their hilts.

Bala lunged toward Nila and Misha's legs, trying to knock them off the edge of the cliff.

Misha leaped high, spinning over Bala's body, and landed. Nila dived over Bala as she barreled toward her, then rolled to her feet.

Bala stopped, fists grasping crumbling sandstone, her head hanging over the edge of the cliff, eyes on the sea. A filthy curse rang from her lips. "Shrott and camel's dung! Izoldia's dead."

Thut cried out and flung herself forward, gazing down at the churning, bloody sea. Fins cut through the water. The sea roiled with sharks and the long undulating bodies of sea dragons. The beasts dived, pink froth staining the ocean's surface.

Misha kept her grip on her saber firm. She poked the tip into Bala's back. "Would you like to return to the oasis, or imprint with a sea dragon and follow Ithsar, or join Izoldia?"

Bala scrambled to her feet, glancing over the cliff, her face pale and hands trembling. "I'm not jumping into the mouth of some horrible monster."

Nila, pointing her saber at Thut, snapped at Bala, "Those beasts are not horrible. Izoldia was. She killed a sea dragon and caused the shark's feeding frenzy. She deserved to die."

"I'm not jumping." Bala grimaced, baring her teeth, eyes wild like a trapped beast.

Misha repressed a shudder. If it came to a fight, Bala was larger, more vicious, and desperate. "Then go back to the oasis."

Bala jerked her head toward the camels. "Come on, Thut."

But Thut stared at her feet, mumbling, "I don't care if I have to jump. I liked flying on Saritha. I'm staying."

Bala snarled at her former ally as the assassins parted, hands on hilts, letting Bala through their ranks. She stomped down the dune, sand spurting around her feet, then clambered upon a camel and made her way off into the desert in a cloud of dust.

Misha released a sigh. She and Nila sheathed their sabers.

Roars and moans filled the sky as dragons burst from the sea, carrying the body of an enormous dragon up, past Misha and the others, up, until they were as small as finches. Jets of flame plumed. The dragon's body dropped, blazing and smoking, through the sky. The dragons dived, too, burning the body until there was nothing but ash, and then dived into the sea.

"Ready to jump?" Nila asked, quirking an eyebrow.

Misha's heart pounded. She swallowed, gazing down. Waves pelted against the cliff and sharks prowled the ocean. "Ah, sure."

§

Saritha howled, arching her neck, her grief roaring through Ithsar. Tears streamed from Ithsar's eyes, dashing across her cheeks, swept away by the rushing air as they plummeted toward the sea. Oh gods, oh gods, by the flaming burning *dracha* gods, Queen Aquaria was dead. And it was her fault for not imprisoning Izoldia. The pounding waves neared, thundering against the sandstone cliff.

They plunged into the ocean. Suddenly, the thoughts of the sea dragons clamored inside Ithsar's head. *"We mourn Queen Aquaria's death."*

"Princess Saritha, you are now our queen."

"We claim you as Queen."

"Hail Saritha, the new queen."

They dived down through the archway, past the undulating fronds that brushed against Ithsar's thighs and arms, and through the inky-dark tunnel in the rock, lit only by the fish with vicious jaws and lights hanging from their heads. On they swam, through the darkness, the pinpoints of light illuminating the fishes' jagged fangs. They shot out into the sunlit spot where Ithsar had first met Queen Aquaria, weeks before.

Saritha howled, the sound reverberating through the water in waves that washed over Ithsar's body. Beneath her, the new queen's body thrummed as she howled again and again.

Saritha alighted upon the coral throne that had belonged to her mother, her talons scraping. *"It is true. I am now your new queen, a responsibility I was not anticipating this soon. I will endeavor to serve you with an open heart and a steadfast spirit to the end of my days."*

A rush of sweetness washed over Ithsar as the sea dragons bowed their heads to the sandy ocean floor.

"You need never bow to me," Saritha said. *"You are my equals and my friends. Long, we've swum these seas together, vanquishing foes, facing pirates, and restoring justice in the briny deep. My mother enjoyed the traditions of old; however, I shall usher in a new reign with this rider upon my back. Together we'll make decisions to protect the fate of Dragons' Realm. You saw Queen Aquaria's vision. Let us all find new riders, so we can help our dragon cousins in the far north."*

"These strangers have brought calamity upon us," a fierce voice growled. An older dragon at the back of the crowd charged through the water and backwinged to hover in front of Saritha. *"These strangers killed Queen Aquaria, one of my dearest friends."* She flicked her tail at Ithsar. *"Dismount, and leave us in peace. We want no part of your visions, nothing to do with you terrible orange-robed women."* She bared her fangs in a snarl.

Saritha hissed. *"You have lost your friend, but I have lost my mother. I choose not to judge everyone by the actions of one. There is greater evil afoot in Dragons' Realm, and we must aid our cousins and their riders. Will you fight with us against Commander Zens and his shadow dragons?"*

The elderly mare bowed her scaly evergreen head. *"As you wish, Queen Saritha; however, I do not like it."*

"Then you do not have to come with us."

"You're not commanding me? What sort of queen are you?" The dragon's eyes slitted.

"A queen who will let everybody have their say. I trust you. You are my family. Those who wish to stay behind may do so, but let me warn you, Queen Aquaria saw these visions. My rider Ithsar has seen them too, and shared them with me. If we do not vanquish Commander Zens, whose armies and shadow dragons are terrorizing the lands, there will be nothing left but a wasteland."

"Wasteland," a young voice called. *"That's what the northerners call the Robandi Desert."*

Saritha's gaze turned to a young turquoise dragon near the front of the crowd, his talons raking the sand.

"It'll be much worse." Ithsar opened her mind and shared her vision with all of the assembled sea dragons.

The entire landscape was barren of vegetation, the mountains bare, the forests charred blackened stumps. The swamplands issued foul stenches. What were once beautiful crystalline lakes had turned to sludge. Strangletons choked the rivers. And there were no people.

No dragons. And the bodies of hundreds of sea dragons, dead fish, and carcasses of sharks littered the ocean.

Mighty roars rippled through the water from dragons, young and old. *"Save the realm."*

"We must stop this!"

"Fight to defeat these shadow dragons and tharuks."

"Then I suggest we rise and meet your new riders," Saritha said. *"These orange-robed women know how to fight. With them upon our backs, we can be a fierce force in preventing this destruction. Ezaara, rider of Queen Zaarusha, needs us. Will you come to her aid?"*

The dragons roared, ripples radiating through the current and surging through Ithsar's body. Saritha leaped from the rock throne and swept her wings and legs, powering them up toward the sunlight.

§

Roars funneled up from the ocean. Misha and Nila peered over the cliff as a teeming, seething horde of dragons broke from the sea, rushing up at them. The sea monsters were all shades of blue and green—lapis, sapphire, emerald, jade, turquoise, and moss. Their bellows filled the sky, their wings spraying droplets, glimmering in the sun.

A massive turquoise dragon rose above the cliff, its golden eyes fastened on hers. Misha gasped, clutching her chest. She'd never seen anything as beautiful. The sea dragon landed, thrashing the sand with its tail, eyes still fixed to hers. The rushing of a thousand seas filled her ears and she gasped again, her breath stolen as exhilaration swept through her. Warmth surged through her veins, flooding her limbs with energy. Before she realized what she was doing, she was on her knees in front of the glorious sea dragon.

It lowered its head, not breaking their gaze. A gravelly voice crooned in her mind, *"You were born to be my rider, Misha. I shall now be known as Ramisha in your honor."*

Misha's fingers twitched. She was dying to touch those wondrous scales—deep turquoise, shimmering with silver in the sun. *"May I?"*

"You may indeed." A rumble filled Misha's mind, like a cat's purr, but louder. Warmer.

She ran her fingers along the scales on the sea dragon's snout. So warm, soft, and supple. She'd thought they'd be hard, like armor. Happiness blossomed inside her.

Ramisha nudged her shoulder. *"Climb on my back. I know you're dying to fly."*

"I've always wanted to fly, to be a bird, be free."

"Believe me, this is better than being a bird. There's a whole underwater world awaiting you. Hop on." Ramisha crooked a foreleg and held it out for Misha.

She climbed onto the dragon's leg, clambered up his shoulder, and sat between two spinal ridges. Misha ran her hand over Ramisha's sleek scales, then grasped the spinal ridge in front of her. Energy rushed through Misha as her dragon unfurled his wings, spraying cool droplets onto her warm skin.

Ramisha tensed his haunches and sprang. They shot up, out over the sea, and swept down over the lapis waters, Ramisha's shadow chasing a school of silver fish. Through the clear waters far below them, dark shapes of enormous sea creatures roamed the depths, and pretty-colored coral sped by.

A happy sigh broke from her. Misha rested her cheek against the dragon's spinal ridge, hugging it tight. *"You know, I lost my family when I was young. But now I have you, I have a home again."*

Ramisha rumbled and chuckled in her mind. *"I know, so do I. We belong together."* He turned and huffed warm breath over her, then flitted over the ocean's surface, flying back, the air above wheeling with dragons and the excited cries of their new riders above the pearly waves breaking at the foot of the sandstone cliffs.

SEA DRAGON

§

Thut stared at the turquoise dragon that landed in front of her, sending up puffs of sand with its mighty taloned feet. She licked her lips. Although she wanted to approach, her legs were wooden, stuck like tent pegs in the sand.

The creature stalked toward her, its scales shimmering silver and blue, like a raging ocean. The dragon flared its nostrils, scenting her.

Thut's heart hammered against her ribs. Camel's dung! Could the *dracha* hear her fear? Smell it? She licked her lips again, then stretched out a shaking hand.

The dragon's wild gold eyes narrowed. It slid its snout under her outstretched fingers. *"Do not fear, Thut. You shall be my rider."*

Wild energy coursed through Thut's veins, like a lightning storm, making her skin crackle and her hair prickle. She wanted to burst out of her skin, but she held steady, regarding the fine sea dragon. *"You're my sea dragon?"* Only the lure of riding one of these fine creatures had swayed her to follow Ithsar here today. In fact, Bala had nearly convinced her to flee the oasis instead.

"So you don't like your leader?" the dragon snarled, a rumble building in its throat.

She'd displeased the beast already, but it had read her thoughts, so there was no point in lying. *"Not really. She's new and she's… um…"*

Before Thut could explain exactly why she hated Ithsar, the dragon replied, *"That's good, because I don't like my new leader either."* The beast tossed her head. *"I shall be known as Lethutle in your honor. Together, we shall have dangerous adventures, and be rid of this new lily-livered queen and her scrawny rider."*

Thut found herself drawn to the dark menace in the dragon's words. "When?" she spluttered breathlessly, forgetting to mind-meld.

"As soon as you climb upon my back."

Thut clambered onto Lethutle's back. The dragon tensed her haunches and sprang into the sky among the cavorting sea dragons and riders. The assassins laughed and called out to each other as their dragons dived playfully.

But no one called to Thut.

Savage pride surged in her breast. She hadn't found a playful frolicking beast. Hers was strong and courageous. Willing to break rules. She'd imprinted with the best sea dragon of all.

§

Ithsar and Saritha swept over the assembled assassins. Sea dragons landed and women imprinted, clambering upon their backs and flying out over the ocean or up over the desert. Dragons wheeled in the sky, their scales glinting jade, emerald, turquoise, and lapis, as women imprinted with cries of joy that echoed out across the desert. Something tight unfurled inside Ithsar, and joy blossomed in her heart, expanding until she felt as if she'd explode.

"I don't understand," Ithsar said. *"Queen Aquaria said the women would have to jump to prove themselves."*

"Ah, but I am queen now, and I know that they have trained hard, proving themselves already." Her dragon turned a reproachful eye on her. *"Besides, someone forgot to mention that fact until we got here, and that seemed a little unfair."*

"Thank you." Ithsar swallowed, staring out over the desert. Far in the distance, a camel was heading back across the tangerine sand.

Saritha mind-melded, *"That's Bala."*

"I'd be surprised if she's at the oasis when we return."

"It doesn't matter," Saritha said. *"We have more important things to deal with. We must save Dragons' Realm."* Saritha landed

near the camels, who danced back on the sand, gazing at her, their thick double rows of lashes blinking against the gust of sand from her feet.

Ithsar clambered down and unclasped the camels' saddlebags, dropping them to the sand. When their backs were bare, she slapped the camels' haunches and sent them traipsing off after Bala toward the oasis.

Saritha spied the departing camels. *"Not even a little flame?"*

"Not even a little flame. You'll terrify them."

"I'm surprised those beasts can feel terror. Or find their way home. Don't those silly creatures get lost in those vast sands?"

"They've made this trip many times—they know the way. Besides, do you get lost in the sea?"

"Good point, although I do have superior intelligence." Saritha chuckled. *"It won't matter if I give them a hurry up, then."* Before Ithsar could protest, she opened her maw and roared.

Ithsar couldn't help but laugh as the camels took off at a rapid pace, their hooves kicking up a sandstorm as they raced across the desert after Bala. She attached extension straps to the saddlebags. Crafted by the assassins over the past moon, they would allow the bags to fit around the sea dragons' large bellies. "*In time, we'll make proper saddlebags to fit you all, but for now these will have to do."*

Saritha snorted. *"I suppose we can deign to wear the garb of camels, although the bags are rather small."*

Ithsar playfully slapped her dragon's scaly thigh. "*There's nothing wrong with small things."* She drew herself up to her full height, which made Saritha chuckle. "*Now, please call your friends over so we can fit them."* As she clambered under Saritha's belly to cinch the strap, she asked, *"Are you sure you can keep our supplies dry?"*

"I told you, we'll be fine: our sathir *bubbles can expand to encompass the supplies, you'll see."*

Sea dragons landed, their new riders' faces flushed with exhilaration and joy. The assassins busied themselves, fastening their improvised saddlebags upon the dragons' backs.

Eyes bright with anticipation, Misha asked, "Are we flying to Naobia? Wow, I've never been there, but I've heard the markets are stunning."

"We'll fly some of the way," Ithsar answered, tugging her robes shut.

"If we're not flying the whole way, how will we get there?"

"We'll be swimming." Murmurs rippled through the crowd of assassins. Ithsar climbed onto her dragon. "Follow me and Saritha."

Saritha leaped into the sky and dived down the sandstone cliff into the Naobian Sea. For a moment, Ithsar held her breath as they plunged into the water. The *sathir* bubble encompassed her, the saddlebags and Thika. This time, she didn't even get her boots wet.

"How did you do that?"

"It takes a little more sathir, *so we'll have to break the surface more often to replenish your air, but we're much faster underwater. I missed the sea life,"* Queen Saritha said.

"So did I," Ithsar answered.

Her sister assassins' faces glowed with wonder as they communed with their sea dragons and took in the beauty of the coral and the stunning multi-colored fish darting out of their way as the wing of dragons swam toward Naobia.

To Naobia

Thut and Lethutle plunged down the cliff and dived into the ocean, a flurry of wings and thrashing tails around them.

"And now?" Thut asked as a shimmering bubble enveloped her so she could breathe.

"We wait." Thut's courageous sea dragon hung back behind the other sea dragons as the women gazed at the wonders in their new underwater world.

Waiting had never been Thut's strong point, but there were plenty of coral formations and fish to look at—if you liked that sort of thing. Thut didn't particularly care.

"Why don't you like Saritha?" she asked.

"I have my reasons," Lethutle replied.

"Where are we going?" Thut asked.

"Somewhere where we can grow strong and powerful, over time, and come back to smite Saritha."

A gleeful shiver raced down Thut's spine. *"I like the sound of that."*

As the other dragons swam toward Naobia, Lethutle slowed, letting the gap between them and the others grow longer, until they looked like a school of tiny fish in the distance.

Lethutle flicked her tail and swam back to the jagged Robandi coast line. They skimmed along sandstone cliffs riddled with dark crevices. Glowing eyes peeked out at them. Occasionally, fanged jaws snapped or a tentacle slithered back into a hole.

"Where did you say we're going, again?" Thut asked, glad she was on this brave dragon, not swimming here alone. Not that she could swim.

Her dragon's grim chuckle resonated in her mind. *"I'm taking you to meet the Scarlett Hand."*

Thut's eyebrows shot up. *"You know the bloodiest pirate captain on the Naobian Sea?"*

"I certainly do. And when we next meet Saritha and her scrawny rider, we'll have our own pirate crew. We'll see how they fare then."

Again, that wild lightning surged through Thut's veins, bucking to be set free.

Lethutle responded, speeding through the water, slashing out with her talons and spearing fish then tossing them aside as they sped along the coastline.

§

The sea dragons and their riders swept through the ocean, riding the currents. Nila gave a shriek as her sea dragon plunged through the water and leapfrogged over a series of coral clusters. Her wild laughter rippled through the sea, bouncing around Ithsar. With a whoop, Nila wrapped her arms around her dragon's spinal ridge and let her body and legs float out behind her. She kicked her legs, leaving a trail of wake, her giggles drifting on the current.

"Nilanna enjoys fun, too," Saritha melded. *"They suit each other."*

Some of the other women laughed, encouraging their dragons to join in. Soon, they were cavorting through the water, diving through coral arches and scaring schools of brightly colored fish that rapidly flitted away to hide in the pink, orange, and purple coral.

A pod of curious dolphins swam over. Bounding around the sea dragons, they chittered and squealed.

"They're always so playful, so excitable, like a wing of newborn sea dragonets," said Saritha.

Ithsar couldn't believe her well-trained, highly-disciplined assassins were exhibiting so much joy and wild abandon—then again, Nila had always had a wild streak. It had just been harnessed under Ashewar's rule.

They passed a huge coral fan with square-shaped bloated yellow fish darting among its lacy fronds. *"Are those fish sick?"* asked Ithsar.

Saritha's chuckle skittered through her mind. *"Those yellow ones with the black spots? That's their natural shape. They're called box fish."*

"They do look like boxes, but with fins, bulging eyes, and fishy lips." Ithsar laughed. *"What about those orange ones with white and black bands?"*

"They're clown fish," Saritha answered. *"They're practical jokers, always pranking the lobsters and hiding among the coral to jump out and scare other fish."*

Indeed, the fish appeared as if they were playing hide and seek, darting in and out of the weeds and red coral, then stilling before they darted off again.

The farther out they got from the shore, the cooler the current and the bluer the ocean.

Misha's dragon swam through some undulating weed, and Ithsar and Saritha followed.

"See that over there? That's a puffer fish. Always so proud and haughty, but not too bad once you get to know them."

The fish was like a brownish spiky ball. *"Do their spines hurt?"*

"Very much so, and puffer fish are poisonous, so even we keep our distance." Saritha's distaste washed over Ithsar.

There were so many new things, so many unusual creatures here. Mind you, Ithsar was riding a sea dragon—and that wasn't exactly your standard camel. They swam past a rocky formation rising from the seabed. A long shape with a glowing luminous stripe along its body slithered out from a crack in the rock. The women gesticulated to each other as their sea dragons swam past.

"I didn't know you had snakes underwater," Ithsar said.

"That's not a snake, it's an electric eel."

"What does electric mean?"

"It jolts you when you touch it." Saritha chuckled. *"I tried to eat one once, but I tell you, after I bit into it, my fangs ached for days."*

A thrill surged through Ithsar's veins. This was all so different, so new, so incredible. *"This is so exciting, Saritha."* Ithsar gazed around at sea turtles drifting among waving kelp. *"It's an amazing world here. I love it."*

To either side, above and below, sea dragons undulated through the water, their jade, blue, and turquoise scales glimmering silver as they passed through shafts of sunlight. Nila whooped again, obviously excited at the beautiful sight.

"Watch this," said Saritha. Her command rippled through Ithsar's mind and the minds of all the sea dragons. *"Be still."*

All of the dragons paused in the water. Some of them dived down to rest against the ocean floor among the rocks and coral. Others were motionless, suspended among weed. Some of the blue and turquoise dragons hung in the current. When they closed their eyes, they almost blended in with the water. Almost, but not quite.

"That's our camouflage trick."

Moments later, the dragons sped off again.

Ithsar's stomach rumbled, almost painfully. *"It's been a long time since breakfast. How do we eat?"*

Saritha gave a command and the dragons rose from the sea in a massive expanse of dripping, glinting wings, like a moving, living carpet over the ocean. Ithsar's bubble of *sathir* popped, and fresh briny air rushed back into her lungs. She turned back to look toward her homeland, but all she could see was a tiny orange strip visible on the distant horizon as if they were suspended above an enormous flowing cloth that stretched on forever.

She swallowed hard. *"How far to Naobia?"*

"A while yet. Reach into the saddlebags and get your food. You must replenish your strength for the long journey ahead." Saritha kept flying.

The women around them were obviously getting the same message from their dragons. They were pulling out fruit, dried meat, and flatbread, miraculously not damp at all. *"This beats traveling by camelback."*

Saritha snorted.

When the women were finished, and the sea dragons dived underwater again, there was an enormous creature with long waving tentacles and a flowing mantle floating through the water, looking like a piece of debris. The creature was as long as a small sea dragon. One of its tendrils snaked out and snatched an enormous silver fish the length of Ithsar's leg. It used those tentacles to stuff the fish inside its mouth, devouring it in two bites.

"That's a giant squid. Sometimes they throw temper tantrums and spill their ink. Hopefully, today this one will behave, because that stuff tastes quite foul." As if the creature had heard them, as the dragons approached, the squid shot off leaving an inky-black, stinky trail in the water.

They sped on toward Naobia, rising above the ocean frequently to refresh their air supply and eat. When it was dark, the dragons flew above the water and the women tied themselves to their dragons' spinal ridges so they didn't fall off. They slept curled over the dragons' backs, and the sea dragons flew on, under a dark velvet sky studded with twinkling diamonds, over the beautiful expanse of rippling moonlit ocean below them.

§

The dragons gathered in the deep sea off the Naobian coast along white cliffs that rose from the ocean floor and towered above the surface. The rocky wall was pockmarked with crevasses and lined with undulating fronds of kelp and sea grass, turning the underwater cliff into a moving, living mass of plant life. Fish darted in and out of the sea grass, and colorful shells encrusted the rock.

After a lifetime in the endless arid sands of the Robandi desert, Ithsar had never imagined so much life and color.

Tired after their long journey, the sea dragons settled on pale patches of sand at the base of the cliff, some flattening sea grass with their haunches.

Ithsar scanned the women, looking for Thut. *"Have you seen her?"* she asked Saritha.

"Not since she imprinted with an old enemy of mine," Saritha replied. *"It's probably best we've lost them."*

Ithsar shrugged, privately relieved.

Saritha's voice rumbled through their minds, *"Ithsar and I will scout the Naobian coast and approach the green guards. The rest of you will wait here."*

Ramisha snarled. *"I won't have my queen go without a guard. It's been years since we've had contact with the green guards. We should be cautious. We don't know what to expect."*

More dragons rumbled in assent, but Saritha's voice was firm. *"You're right, we haven't seen them for years, but if too many of us go, we could provoke an attack."*

Ramisha twitched his tail. *"I refuse to let my new queen go alone. I don't want a third queen within two days."*

Saritha angled her head, observing Misha and her dragon. *"Very well, you may come with me, but the rest of you must wait here. We can't risk inciting fear in the guards. We desperately need them as friends to fight this terrible enemy in the North."* She tensed her haunches and sprang. She and Ithsar ascended through the water, Ramisha and Misha following.

They broke through the surface and flew high up the pale cliffs.

As they crested the hills, Ithsar gasped. *"Everything is so green,"* she said. *"I never imagined anything like this."*

They landed on a grassy meadow on a hilltop speckled with wildflowers and dotted with rocks. Ramisha landed beside Saritha. Ithsar and Misha gazed down across the land.

Northward, a lake glinted, nestled among verdant rolling hills. A sprawling forest lay at the foot of a mountain, but immediately in front of them was a patchwork of green, yellow, and brown fields, and a large rambling town encircled by a city wall. Roads snaked from the town through the fields to smaller villages. And everywhere, everything was green—moss, jade, emerald, lime, olive, sage, mint, and evergreen—all the shades Ithsar could ever imagine.

Orchards of fruit-laden trees sprawled on the edge of the township. People tilled the fields. Strange creatures plodded along roads, pulling wheeled contraptions laden with goods.

"What are those?" Misha asked.

"My father told me about horses and their wagons when I was young," Ithsar answered. "I think that's what they must be."

Saritha rumbled in assent.

"Those creatures look so odd. How in the sun's name do they stay balanced on their legs without a hump?" Misha asked. Saritha turned an eye to her. Misha hastily added, "Not that I mean any disrespect. I mean, I know dragons don't have humps, but…"

Ramisha and Saritha snorted, and Misha blushed.

Ithsar turned to Misha. "Queen Saritha wants you and Ramisha to stay here. She's still concerned that more than one of us approaching may alarm the Naobian green guards. We mustn't make them think we're attacking."

Ramisha clawed at the ground, his talons ripping out chunks of grass and earth, but he and Misha stayed behind on top of the hill. As Saritha flew out over the fields, Ithsar marveled. The sea glinted azure, lapis, and turquoise beneath them. The warm breeze stirred tiny white peaks far out in the deep. The distant hiss of the breakers on the shore was muted by the swish of Saritha's wings.

Ithsar gasped, clasping her hands. *"This is so beautiful. So many different shades of green, so many plants. So much that grows. I'd thought the sea was a wonder with all those creatures and plant life, but this… this is just breathtaking."* The forest was such a deep, dark green, and every field and meadow was a different brilliant green. Some were speckled with flowers. Leafy crops grew in neat rows. Yellow corn stood straight and proud, leaves fluttering in the breeze. *"What are those red things bobbing in the wind?"*

"Those are poppies," Saritha said.

Ahead, waves lapped at a broad expanse of pale sand that formed a bay. At the far end, huge wooden jetties jutted out into the sea. Ships were moored to thick poles along the jetties. People unloaded large barrels, wooden boxes, and trunks onto wagons. As they swooped lower, the bustle of activity and voices carried from the city. The clop of horse hooves on the cobbled roads drifted to them.

Just outside the town, a green dragon leaped from a low hillside, propelling itself into the sky.

"Green guard!" Saritha backwinged, slowing.

The green dragon and rider speared toward them, roaring and shooting a jet of flame.

Attacked

Flame lanced through the air, narrowly missing Saritha's tail. She twisted out of reach. *"Sorry, Ithsar, if only I wasn't so tired."* A wave of blistering heat roiled above Ithsar's back. She ducked flat against Saritha's scales as the mighty queen of the sea dragons dived. *"We have no choice but to flee. I don't want to fight,"* Saritha said.

The green guard whirled, his rider low in the saddle, and chased Saritha, blasting more flame.

Thika poked his head out of a saddlebag. "No, Thika, back inside." Ithsar fumbled, shutting the flap.

Saritha ducked and changed course.

Ice skittered through Ithsar's veins. Gods, if that dragon hit them, they'd be nothing but a ball of flame like Queen Aquaria. *"No, Saritha, I can't let that dragon hurt you."* She drew her saber from its sheath and nearly dropped it as Saritha dodged another plume of flame. The pretty green fields spun and blurred as Saritha maneuvered out of the young dragon's reach.

"If we're to secure them as friends, we must be cautious." Saritha shot through the air like an arrow, landing outside the city walls in a meadow fringed on the city side by an orchard.

Snarling, the green dragon landed.

Although Saritha was larger, she prostrated her body upon the ground with her head low.

Ithsar's temper flared, and she waved her saber. *"How dare this beast snarl at you like that. You're the new queen."*

"Not too hasty. We need them as our allies," Saritha said.

"With allies like this, who needs enemies?" Ithsar slid off Saritha, and stomped toward the green dragon.

"No," Saritha called. *"I don't want you to get hurt."* She lashed out with her tail and flicked the saber from Ithsar's hand.

The blade skittered across the grass and thunked against the roots of an enormous tree. The impact knocked ripe golden fruit from the branches to the ground. An overpowering sweet scent filled Ithsar's nostrils.

The green dragon snarled, haunches tensed and mean eyes slitted.

Ithsar stalked forward, a sea breeze whipping her robes about her waist.

A slim, lanky man slid from the dragon's back, his olive skin, lighter than hers, marking him as a Naobian. Taller than her, he gestured with his sword, motioning her to raise her hands.

She complied. She'd best him anyway, with the daggers hidden in her sleeves and boots.

He stopped near her, poised on the balls of his feet, gazing at her, but saying nothing. Tension lined his body.

Ithsar inclined her head. What was he waiting for? Well, if he wasn't going to talk, she would. "Why are you accosting Saritha, queen of the sea dragons?" she asked.

The man waved his sword, motioning her to stand against a tree trunk.

Ithsar backed up until the rough bark was at her back.

Then, his sword at her throat, he patted her down, checking for weapons. A sweet scent overpowered Ithsar as a breeze ruffled her sleeves. "Why do you not talk?" she asked. Had the green guards, too, taken a vow of silence?

His dark eyes glinted as he confiscated the daggers strapped to her arms, two blades from her boots, the knives at her waist and her favorite dagger hidden inside her robes. Still, he hadn't spoken.

Ithsar cocked her head. Now that he was closer, he appeared younger than his height suggested. His facial skin was young and unblemished, without stubble. He stepped back, sword still out.

"You can sheathe that thing. We come in peace," she said.

"In peace? If you mean us no harm, why are you carrying an arsenal of blades?"

His voice was young and boyish—no wonder he hadn't wanted to speak. Despite his lanky body, his voice betrayed his age. Ithsar grinned. "You're not much older than me," she said. "Maybe not even as old as me."

He cocked an eyebrow, his sword not wavering. "And how old would that be?"

Ithsar drew herself up to her full height, aware she only came up to his chest. "Old enough to be the new chief prophetess of the Robandi assassins."

"Chief Prophetess?" His jaw dropped. "I always imagined Ashewar taller, more… um…" His eyes flicked over her as if she were a discarded orange rind.

"Yes, she *was* taller." Ithsar's tone was flat.

"Ah." He swallowed, obviously doing mental contortions to figure out that she'd disposed of Ashewar.

Well, let him think that—her or the shark—it was all the same.

"Ah, so now *you're* the chief prophetess? Why are you riding a shadow dragon?" He gestured at Saritha, who was sitting on the grass with her forelegs tucked underneath her and her snout low, while the green dragon prowled around her, a low rumble escaping its throat.

"Don't worry, Ithsar, if things turn bad I can get us out of here." Saritha wrinkled her nose. *"I can still scent the egg shards on this young, freshly-hatched dragonling. He doesn't have much experience and neither does his rider."*

Ithsar believed her. The green was only half Saritha's size.

"Since when do Robandi have shadow dragons?" the boy asked.

"She's hardly a shadow dragon. From what I've heard, they're black."

"Then why are you attacking Naobia?" He flicked his sword toward the ocean. "And where are the rest of your tribe?"

This rider asked more questions than a littling. "Are you hard of hearing?" Ithsar snapped. It had been a long trip—a whole day and night of swimming. Her patience was wearing thin. "I told you, we're here in peace."

"Why should I believe you? You're pretty short and young for a chief prophetess. And I think—"

Ithsar spun, flinging out her foot, and kicked him in the chest.

Unprepared, he crashed to the ground, dropping his sword and her collection of blades.

She snatched up her favorite dagger and leaped onto his chest, pinning him with her legs, her blade at his neck. "Good. Now, we can talk. But I'll ask the questions. How long have you been in the green guards?"

"Two moons." His eyes blazed with indignation.

Only half a moon longer than she'd been Chief Prophetess. "You've attacked Saritha, queen of the sea dragons, and her rider Ithsar, the new chief prophetess of the Robandi assassins. What do you think the leader of the green guards would say about you starting a war with two mighty races?"

His eyes widened, but he said nothing, lying there unmoving. Aware it could be a ruse, Ithsar kept her body taut, ready for action. "Speak."

"Sea dragon? But they only leave the ocean in times of dire need."

Ithsar had never heard that. *"Saritha, is that true?"* Saritha's nod of assent was enough. Ithsar continued, "We are in dire need.

SEA DRAGON

Ezaara, the Queen's Rider of Dragons' Realm, sent me a messenger bird. She needs our help and the help of the Naobian green guards." She snorted, pressing the dagger a little more firmly against his neck so he would feel it scratch.

His eyes flew open. "Ezaara asked you? So you've heard of the shadow dragons plaguing the realm?"

Ithsar flashed her teeth in a fierce grin "Yes, and I came here to talk with the Naobian green guards, so we can fight the shadow dragons and prevent Dragons' Realm from becoming a wasteland. Somehow, I'd imagined having this conversation under different circumstances. I suggest you take me to your leader."

"I p-promise not to attack if you l-let me up," he stammered.

Roars split the sky. A wing of green dragons dived toward them, spurting fire.

The boy smirked. "I'd like to see you get out of this."

Standing, he'd be too tall for her blade to even reach his throat. Ithsar slipped off him, her knife still at his neck, and crouched next to his prone body. "Get up." Keeping her blade in position, she grabbed his arm as he clambered to his feet. Then she yanked it behind his back, and pressed her dagger between his shoulder blades.

Saritha rumbled, *"Now we're in trouble."*

Roars rang out from the hilltop. Misha and Ramisha were streaking toward them, talons out and flames blazing. Trailing in their wake were all the sea dragons.

Anger surged through Ithsar. "This is exactly what me and my wise queen were trying to avoid," she barked. "Your foolhardy actions could cause the destruction of both our people and prevent us from helping Dragons' Realm."

The boy licked his lips, eyes darting between the two wings of dragons. "I can ask my dragon to call the green guards off. But if they see you with your blade at my throat, they won't believe me." He shrugged. "It's up to you. It wouldn't be my first battle."

"If one of my people or dragons are harmed, it will be your last," Ithsar snapped.

If she let him free, she had no bargaining power. He could snatch up a weapon and attack her again. Or he could tell those fiery beasts to engage in battle.

The two wings of dragons were nearing each other. In a few heartbeats, their flames would meet.

Saritha sat up, now holding her head high. Talons still tucked beneath her, she nodded at Ithsar. The vision of those evil shadow dragons attacking the northern lands shot through Ithsar's head, and she knew what she had to do. She had vowed to rule in love and kindness, not in terror. She had to act upon her convictions.

"Very well." Ithsar drew away her blade and stepped aside.

§

Snarls filled the air, and hundreds of wings rustled, creating a breeze that stirred the leaves on the trees.

As Ithsar removed the steel from the boy's back, she put steel into her voice. "One false move, and this dagger will be embedded between your ribs, my friend." He stiffened. She continued, "However, I'd like the opportunity to be your friend and work together to free Dragons' Realm."

The young man turned his head to look her in the eye and thumped his heart. "My name is Stefan and my dragon is Fangora. We will fight for Dragons' Realm." He put his fingers in his mouth and let out a shrill whistle.

As his dragon backed away from Saritha, Stefan called out, "Fangora, did you summon the other green guards?"

Ithsar had never imagined a dragon looking sheepish, but this one managed.

"Now look what you've done! Call them off." Stefan turned to her, face stricken. "I'm sorry. He's young and impatient and didn't know better."

Rather like his rider.

"Fangora says he tried to stop them, but none of them are listening," Stefan cried.

Ithsar snatched up her blades, tucking them into their sheaths as Saritha sprang over. She leaped upon Saritha's back, and her dragon launched herself into the air as Stefan and Fangora took flight.

Flame crackled overhead. Saritha and Fangora surged up into the air between the two wings of dragons. Fangora and Stefan sped off toward flaming green guards, and Saritha and Ithsar wheeled to face the fire of the sea dragons.

Ithsar cringed at the heat. *"Saritha, tell them to stop."*

"I'm trying, but they're all fired up."

Ithsar waved her arms in the Robandi gesture for ceasefire.

Nila waved back, acknowledging her. Instantly, the flame from the sea dragons' maws guttered and died.

"I've mind-melded and told them to land," Saritha said.

Stefan somehow got through to the green guards, who stopped roaring and blasting flame.

"Thank the dracha *gods, they listened."* Ithsar's breath whooshed out of her. *"I can't believe you were joking at a time like that. 'Fired up' indeed."*

Saritha chuckled. *"Well, they were spurting flame and being rather hotheaded."*

The sea dragons spiraled down to land on the eastern side of the meadow, closest to the cliffs where they'd been hiding. The green guards landed on the other side, nearest the orchard and the city, gouging the ground with their talons. A green dragon's tail lashed a tree, sending fruit flying. That same pungent, sweet aroma filled the air, making Ithsar's belly rumble.

Saritha and Fangora landed side by side between the two wings of dragons. Stefan slid from his saddle and faced the green guards. A tall, seasoned rider with broad shoulders and a face as worn as the Robandi sandstone cliffs dismounted and stalked toward them.

"My fellow green guards and esteemed leader, Goren, please allow me to present Ithsar, the chief prophetess of the Robandi assassins," Stefan said. "She rides Saritha, queen of the sea dragons, and has an important message for us."

"So you're the new chief prophetess." Goren curled his lip, glancing down his nose at her. "I'd expected something… Well, more."

Such rudeness. Aware of her unimpressive height, Ithsar stayed upon Saritha's back. A well-aimed kick in the chest would knock that arrogant man onto his backside in the grass, but Ithsar refrained, looking him up and down. "Oh, so you're the leader of the green guards," she said graciously, refusing to be drawn into a contest of bared teeth and flexed muscles. She had to work with this arrogant man to help Ezaara, not get into a slanging match. So, although her hackles were raised, she smiled sweetly, only baring her teeth a little.

Goren crossed his arms and angled his head, brows furrowed. He gave a weary sigh. "Pleased to meet you." He sounded anything but pleased. "And your message…?"

"Ezaara, the Queen's Rider of Dragons' Realm, is gathering an army to fight Commander Zens," said Ithsar. "I've seen a vision of a terrible war against his shadow dragons and tharuks, a war that could destroy your people, your dragons, and the very land you live on. All will be lost unless we ride to aid Ezaara."

Goren's frown deepened. "Who's paying *you* to fight?" he sneered.

"No one," Ithsar snapped. "We're fighting for the good of the realm, and because Ezaara's my friend."

His eyebrows shot up. "Your friend?"

"Yes." Ithsar met his steely gaze with one of her own. "My closest friend."

He shrugged. "I received a message from Ezaara two days ago. Our troops will be flying north tonight. Ezaara was here only a week and a half ago on her hand-fasting holiday. Rumors from the North do not bode well." He narrowed his eyes. "How much do you know?"

"Not enough. However, we will share what we do know." Saritha lowered her head and Ithsar beckoned Goren to lay his hand upon her dragon's forehead.

Goren stalked over and placed his hand upon the queen's emerald scales. As Saritha shared Ithsar's vision with him, his frown deepened.

When the queen was finished, he swept a hand at the meadow. "You must be tired. Please rest here for the day. You may roam our beautiful city of Naobia as you please." He gave a disparaging glance at their makeshift saddlebags. "We'll provide you with supplies, comfortable saddles, and decent saddlebags. This evening, we'll depart."

"Thank you, that's kind of you." Ithsar inclined her head politely.

"Nothing kind about it," Goren grunted. "If we're going to fight together, it makes good battle sense to fortify your dragons and warriors. If you'd like, our dragons can show yours good hunting grounds for goats and deer."

Saritha wrinkled her nose. *Not more goats.*

Ithsar smiled. Someone had to, and she doubted Goren knew how. "Thanks again, but while we're by the coast, our sea dragons can fish."

"Of course." Goren gave a terse nod, stalked to his dragon, and swung into a finely-crafted saddle Ithsar couldn't help but envy. He pointed at Stefan. "Since you started this mess, I'll leave you to organize the supplies and saddles for our guests."

Within moments, the green guards' wings were stirring Ithsar's robes as they departed and flew back to the city.

Green Guards

The sea dragons were sprawled in the meadow, having a well-deserved rest, their riders leaning against their sides or curled up under their wings, dozing.

Stefan and Ithsar walked through the orchard, discussing what supplies Ithsar's clan would need for their journey. When they were done, Stefan reached up and plucked an enormous piece of fruit from the tree. "Would you like a peach?" he asked. "I don't know if you have them in the Robandi desert."

"This is a peach?" She inhaled the aroma. "It smells different to the dried peaches my mother got from the merchant caravans." No need to mention Ashewar's assassins had slaughtered those very merchants in order to get supplies. She ran her fingertips over the skin. "I didn't know they were fuzzy on the outside." She bit into the peach. Juice ran down her chin. "Oh, this is good." She groaned and took another bite.

"They're delicious, aren't they?" Stefan plucked a few more and sat against a tree trunk. He patted the ground beside him, chewing his own peach. As soon as she was sitting, he handed her more peaches. "Save some for Saritha. Dragons like them too."

Raising an eyebrow, Ithsar replied, "I'm not sharing. These are far too good. Saritha will have to pick her own."

The queen of the sea dragons opened an eyelid and snorted. *"I heard that."* Ithsar threw a peach and Saritha snapped it down. *"Not bad, but I still prefer fish."*

Stefan grinned. "So, what's it like to live in all that endless orange sand?"

Ithsar took another bite and shrugged. "Normal. Dry. Hot. This…" She motioned to the greenery, the trees laden with peaches, the distant mountains. "Um, this is beautiful." She took another bite. "I had no idea peaches were so juicy."

He chuckled. "It'd be hard to tell if you've only ever had them dried. I'll bet there are many things you haven't tried yet. Why don't I show you and a few of your friends around the markets?" He gazed at the sun. "We should have time. I'll organize the supplies first, and then come back and get you. We can walk. It's not far from here."

From attacking her to hosting her—Stefan certainly was full of surprises—but Ithsar liked his easy, open manner. It was refreshing after growing up under the shadow of Ashewar and Izoldia. She smiled. "I look forward to it."

§

Stefan led Ithsar, Misha, and Nila through the winding alleys of Naobia, the briny tang of sea air wafting through the streets. Ithsar had left Thika back in the orchard with her sisters, but missed his comforting weight on her shoulder. The stone houses were so close, towering three or four stories above them. The streets were narrow and winding, and there was no soft desert sand to mask their footfalls, which echoed loudly off the stone walls like a thousand horses pounding on cobbles.

Ithsar flinched at the rumble of wagon wheels. "Where are you taking us?" Her hand drifted to her hilt, her eyes scanning the mouths of the narrow alleys and lanes that riddled the city.

"To the markets." Stefan grinned as he pressed through the people meandering along the street. "I have some coin. I still feel bad about nearly causing a fight this morning, so I'd like to treat you and your friends."

Nila grinned back, right at home on these narrow, cobbled roads. "Sounds good to me. The more treats, the better." Her dark eyes sparkled in a way Ithsar had seldom seen under Ashewar's rule.

All of them had more space to breathe, to be themselves now—except in this crowded, busy city.

Ithsar sighed. She'd take the wide open spaces of the desert any day. Or maybe one of those pretty meadows, or a house on a hilltop overlooking the fields and sea.

Misha shrugged, her eyes also flitting to the alleys. "Sounds good." Her voice was overly bright, forced.

A man bustled past with a barrow laden with strange vegetables of yellow, orange, red, green, and even deep purple hues. Another wagon rattled along the alley, carrying beautiful bolts of cloth with a lovely sheen—depicting dragons, brightly colored coral, and floral patterns. A tantalizing aroma wafted through the air.

"Oh, that smells good. What is it?" Nila asked eagerly.

"Crum's bakery," Stefan answered. "One of the best. But we're not going there today. I have something better in mind."

"Better than that?" Nila laughed, shaking her dark curls. "I can't wait." They rounded a corner, Nila still laughing, and walked into a piazza.

Ithsar stopped dead in her tracks. Before them was a beautiful fountain—a tangle of sea dragons, glittering in the sun, sparkling water spraying from their maws. Sunshine played across the crystal, making rainbows dance across the scales etched into the dragons' backs. Ithsar approached, running her hand along the smooth tail of a baby sea dragon. Water droplets sprayed her fingers. "This is beautiful. Is it made of glass?"

"That's opaline crystal, from Crystal Lake, two hour's dragon flight north of here," Stefan answered. "Opaline's only found in Naobia. Some say it comes from an extinct volcano that spewed the crystals into the lake, years ago. There's thousands of them up there."

"Sounds beautiful."

"It is." Stefan shrugged. "It's a shame I don't have enough time to take you there. Maybe another time."

Maybe. If they made it back from this war. With a lingering glance at the sea dragon fountain, Ithsar left the piazza and followed Stefan, Misha, and Nila through the hustle and bustle of crowded alleys until they came to a square surrounded by four-story stone buildings with colorful flags and cascading flowers hanging from balconies.

A wave of sights, smells, and sounds crashed into Ithsar's senses. For a moment, she reeled, steadying herself on Misha's arm. The cobbles were filled with people manning stalls, touting their wares. Chickens squawked and vendors shouted. Littlings chased each other, dodging people, laughing and crying out. Voices rose in a babble that would drown out the bray of the loudest camel. And every available space was crammed with people. So many people.

Stefan led them through crowds wearing brightly-colored clothes in all manner of styles, past an old crone selling fragrant herbs, a merchant with fine leather boots, and a jewelry stand.

Ithsar grasped Stefan's arm. "Wait, what are these?" She pointed at earrings shaped like beetles.

"Jewel beetles," he replied. "They live in caves out in the hills. When they die, people collect their shells to make necklaces. Look." He pointed at beetles strung on fine silver chains. Their amber, jade, and turquoise shells were lined with tiny silver and gold veins that winked in the sun. "Would you like one?" Stefan pulled some coin from his pocket and started counting.

Something so dainty in battle? Ithsar shook her head. "No, it's all right, thanks. I was just looking."

Ithsar's mouth watered as they followed Stefan past a boar spit-roasting over an open fire, but it soon stopped watering when she spied a man with a massive cleaver chopping the heads off fish. Mages were selling sticks that shot pretty colored stars into the air. Littlings parted with their coppers with glee, waving the sticks as green and yellow stars exploded from them.

"What are those?" Nila asked. "They look like fun."

"Fire sticks. I loved them as a littling," Stefan replied. His tone made it clear the pretty stars were only for youngsters.

A shame—Ithsar would've liked to try using one.

Minstrels were singing, a flute, shakers, and drums accompanying their pretty voices. After the silence of the oasis, with only the hissing of wind on the desert sands, Ithsar was tempted to block her ears. But she didn't want to seem rude, so she smiled as Stefan pulled her through the throng.

A woman holding a basket of buns jostled her, then a burly man bumped her. "Sorry." He looked down at her. "I didn't see you down there."

True, she was shorter than most of these people, but couldn't they watch where they were going?

Misha nudged her and grimaced.

Nila turned to them, her face radiant. "Oh, isn't it wonderful?" She squeezed their hands. "My father used to bring me here when I was a littling. I loved it. Don't worry, you'll get used to the bustle."

Stefan's eyebrows shot up. "You don't have a market out in the desert?"

Only the type where Ashewar had killed people and helped herself to their wares.

"There is one in the Robandi capital to the south," Nila answered quickly. "But our former chief prophetess only took her personal guard there."

"And none of you were in that guard?" Stefan quirked an eyebrow, staring at Ithsar. "Just how long have you been chief prophetess?" he asked her.

"About as long as you've been a dragon rider," she admitted.

He threw back his head and laughed. "I should've guessed." He flung an arm out at the marketplace. "It must be a shock to see so many people in one place."

"It is a bit," Ithsar admitted.

"Definitely." Misha gave a tight-lipped nod.

He smiled again. "Don't worry, we're nearly there. It'll be worth it, I promise."

Behind his back, Misha rolled her eyes.

"You'd think he was putting you two through torture." Nila giggled. "Come on, enjoy yourselves."

This time, Stefan took Ithsar by the elbow, making sure no one jostled her as he escorted her through the crowd. A delicious aroma danced across Ithsar's tongue, tickling her taste buds and making her mouth water. Something she'd never smelled nor tasted before.

"Come with me." Stefan led her past a table of pretty hand-painted scarves to a stand piled high with little brown and white shapes.

Ithsar flared her nostrils, inhaling. So, this was the source of that mouth-watering aroma.

Stefan raised an eyebrow. "They taste even better than they smell. Your tongue will be in paradise."

Ithsar, Misha, and Nila shot glances at each other, but none of them were brave enough to ask exactly what this stuff was.

Stefan haggled with the woman behind the stall, speaking so rapidly and with such a strong Naobian accent that Ithsar couldn't keep up. He flipped the woman a silver and flashed them yet another smile. "You may each take four pieces of any shape or flavor. This one's the best." He plucked up a brown swirl shaped like a snail's shell and broke it open. A dark gooey substance ran out, revealing a nut in the middle. "It's called chocolate. See, this type has hazelnuts inside." Stefan tossed it into his mouth and licked his fingers.

The aroma hit Ithsar with full force. She couldn't stop salivating, so she picked one up too—a tiny white block with a yellow spiral of lemon rind on top. Ithsar popped the chocolate into her mouth… and couldn't help the groan that escaped her.

"That was lemon," Stefan said. "The rest are just as good, too." He swept his hand in a flourish. "Help yourself."

Misha's eyes flew wide as she tried an orange-flavored one.

Nila squealed as she bit into a dark mint chocolate, then groaned and rolled her eyes. "I'll never be able to eat another thing in my life. I have to move to Naobia and eat these every day."

A ceramic bowl full of chocolates with green leaves caught Ithsar's eye. "What are these like?" she asked shyly.

Stefan's eyes twinkled. "Oh, you'll love those. They're a little different, but you should try one."

When Ithsar bit into the leafy chocolate, her mouth was flooded with juicy sweetness. The inside was succulent, pink, fleshy, and delicious. Her tongue truly was in paradise. "This tastes like fruit, but one I've never had before. What is it?"

"That, my dear Chief Prophetess, is a strawberry ripened under the warm Naobian sun and dipped in chocolate." Stefan bowed. "I promised my treat would be worth putting up with the bustle of the marketplace."

Ithsar laughed, nearly as loud as Nila. "You did. And this is worth it. Do you mind if I have another one?"

He stopped smiling, his eyes serious. "Can you forgive me for my blunder this morning?"

It was Ithsar's turn to grin. "For chocolate, I'd forgive anything."

§

The rustle of wingbeats filled the air as Saritha shot over Naobia, trailed by sea dragons and green guards, on the journey north to join Ezaara and wage war against the shadow dragons. The vibrant, writhing mass of green wings and the pearlescent silver-shot jade and turquoise of the sea dragons merged to create a wild, rippling mosaic that flashed in the sun. Saddles creaked and dragons snorted. The breeze from their wingbeats stirred Ithsar's hair and headscarf. She'd never imagined anything this wondrous. The land was so green, studded with pockets of color—orchards, crops, and tiny settlements of houses. The air swirled with currents and snatches of exotic smells—the briny sea, the tang of fish drying along the coast, freshly turned earth, smoke from hearths, and orchards full of fruit.

The sun dipped, setting the sky on fire. Ithsar gasped as the golden light danced along the dragons' scales, making them look like burnished shimmering gold.

She gave a happy sigh. Everywhere here, people were living in harmony with one another. In the city, she'd seen beggars, but also people giving them coin. And others laughing, being joyous and celebrating their lives with open smiles or friendly hugs.

Her heart ached to feel that same love and acceptance.

"You have me," Saritha hummed. *"And Misha and Nila. And now you have a new friend. It will take time to unlearn the mistrust Ashewar caused in your heart."*

Stefan waved from Fangora's back, then swooped to call out to Nila. The assassin tipped back her head and laughed.

Now loosed from the shackles she'd grown up with, Ithsar knew how Nila felt. Her newfound sense of freedom surged through her veins, making her want to fly harder, faster, higher. But not now, not all at once. Bit by bit, she would forge a new life for her people.

"*We certainly will,*" Saritha replied, "*but first we must fight this war.*"

Ithsar's senses reeled as a vision flashed into her mind.

A seething mass of darkness blotted out the sky.

With a start, Ithsar recognized the massive dark dragons as the shadow dragons Ezaara had mentioned in her message.

Plumes of flame shot down onto a village as people fled, screaming. The dark cloud broke up as shadow dragons descended, blasting more flame. Ithsar gasped. There were only four valiant dragons defending this whole settlement against hundreds of shadow dragons.

A beautiful silver dragon with a tall, dark-haired rider shot arrows with a fierce precision that would make any Robandi assassin proud. Her arrows pierced the eyes and skulls of shadow dragons, who plummeted from the sky, shrieking. A sickly dragon with insipid pale-green scales swooped and blasted a horde of tusked furry beasts rampaging through the streets. Tharuks—Ithsar's father had told her about the feral beasts that Commander Zens used to enslave the northerners.

Then she saw Roberto leaping from Erob, the mighty blue dragon Ithsar had met in the oasis. Roberto flew through the air, barreling into Ezaara, knocking her from her gorgeous multi-hued queen. Ezaara and Roberto fought, tumbling toward the ground.

Ithsar's heart pounded as the enormous queen of the dragons dived, her scales flashing with all the colors of the prism-seer, then swooped to grasp Ezaara and Roberto in her talons.

She deposited them on the grass. Roberto straddled Ezaara, but she still fought, bucked and kicked.

And then Ithsar's vision turned cloudy.

Her hands shook. Roberto loved Ezaara. Why would he attack her? And why would her dragon help? "*Saritha, are you able to mind-meld with the green guards and show them this vision? Maybe they'll recognize the village."*

"Yes, I can," Saritha replied.

It seemed like forever before Saritha answered. Meanwhile, the vision flitted over and over through Ithsar's mind.

"They've told me this is Lush Valley, the former home of Ezaara, she of the golden hair. Wait a moment."

Ithsar waited impatiently, her fingers clenching the pommel of her new leather saddle as they rushed through the darkening sky, the landscape slowly swallowed by dusk.

"The green guards received word five days ago that Lush Valley was under attack last week. The green guards sent reinforcements immediately. Now, the war has moved farther north."

"Where, north? Was Ezaara all right? Why were she and Roberto fighting?"

Another bone-grinding wait.

"They don't know, but we'll find out soon enough."

"How long until we get to Lush Valley?"

"The green guards say we'll delay our travel by half a day if we go north-east to Lush Valley. We must fly the most direct route, north-west to Dragons' Hold."

Ithsar ground her teeth. *"And how long will that take?"*

"Five days. I know you're impatient to see how Ezaara is, but we're flying our fastest, and we'll need rest if we're to be battle-ready when we arrive."

"Thank you, Saritha. I appreciate your valiant effort." There was no point in her being grumpy with Saritha, even though dread gnawed at Ithsar's belly as the dragons flew on through the night.

Northward

They traveled all night, riders dozing in their saddles, and the next day the enormous mass of green and blue dragons flew on, spreading across the sky, blotting out entire fields with their shadows. Thika's nose twitched as he perched on Saritha's spinal ridge, enjoying the view. Littlings ran outside, laughing and pointing as they passed overhead. The dragons roared, spurting tiny gusts of flame and making the littlings shriek with joy.

Stefan and Fangora swooped and dived.

"Those two seem to like an audience," Saritha commented. *"I'm glad you're more mature. A rider befitting a queen."*

What a shame. Ithsar hesitated, then decided to ask anyway. *"Um, it actually looks like, ah… fun. Are you sure you don't want to try, too?"*

"I thought you'd never ask." Saritha chuckled. *"Hang on."*

Ithsar tucked Thika in her robes and lunged, lying flat against Saritha's back and sliding her arms through the holding straps. Thank the desert sun she now had a good quality Naobian saddle with a harness holding her in.

Saritha plunged, wings furled tightly against her body and her tail whipping up like an arrow. Ithsar's stomach shot right up into her throat. Wind streamed into her face, dragging tears from her eyes. Her headscarf ripped free and her hair flew out behind her.

She couldn't stop grinning. Trees and fields loomed ever closer. When Ithsar could see the needles of the tallest pine, Saritha swooped up and Ithsar's stomach dropped into her boots. Thank the blazing sun she hadn't eaten a heavy breakfast.

"Look at the pretty one. Her scales glimmer silver," an excited littling cried, dancing in the meadow.

"Did you hear that?" Saritha crooned. *"I'm pretty!"*

"Of course you are." Ithsar patted her sleek scales, and they shot back high into the sky.

§

When darkness fell again, the dragons landed in fields of wild grass north of the Naobian forest. The green guards unloaded cauldrons and supplies, and collected wood for a bonfire. Fangora set the wood alight, and while their dragons went off hunting, the assassins and guards set about making soup, throwing in dried vegetables and fresh roots from the nearby forest.

Goren called Stefan over to the cauldrons. "Do your magic, Stefan."

Stefan fetched pouches of herbs and sprinkled them into the soup and tended it until it bubbled for what seemed like forever. Finally, he declared it ready, and ladled soup into mugs for everyone.

Then he came over to Ithsar. "Do you mind if I sit with you?"

She patted the edge of her bedroll and he sat on it, placing two mugs of soup on the ground between them. The firelight danced across his face, making his dark eyes glitter. "You know, because I only imprinted with my dragon a couple of weeks ago, I didn't have time to train properly."

"So you can't fight?" Maybe that's why he was the cook.

Stefan shrugged. "You've seen how good I *wasn't*, the other day."

His comment made Ithsar laugh. "True, you weren't the best at deflecting my attack." She blew on her soup. "And here I was, thinking I'd beaten a mighty warrior."

He chuckled and tilted his head to gaze at the stars. "My whole life, I never thought I'd meet a sea dragon. Or the chief prophetess of the Robandi assassins, let alone have her fight me." He grinned, his teeth flashing.

Ithsar picked up her soup and blew on it. "I never thought I'd meet a sea dragon either. Did you know the former chief prophetess, Ashewar, was my mother?"

"Really?" He said, cocking an eyebrow. "What was she like? Rumors say she was fierce."

Biting her lip, Ithsar met his gaze. She'd been trying not to think about her mother lately. She forced the lump from her throat, trying to swallow, but her voice still came out croaky. "Every bit as fierce as the rumors—and more."

Stefan's smile died. His keen eyes flicked over her face. He nodded, gazing at her and reading her pain. "My parents didn't want me to be a dragon rider," he said at last. "But sometimes we have to make our own lives, despite how they raised us."

Ithsar blinked, fighting her stinging eyes and cradling the warm cup between her hands.

Stefan blew on his soup, waiting before he spoke again, his gaze not leaving her. He motioned at the fire. "See how the flames in the center of the fire burn brightly? But the flames on the edge are the most adventurous, dancing out to test the air and taste everything around them. We're like those flames at the edge of the fire, testing new territory, dancing brightly." He turned back to her, dark eyes earnest. "Dance to your own rhythm, Ithsar, not that of your mother."

Something shifted inside Ithsar. The dark gaping well inside her filled with warmth.

Stefan reached out and took her cup, placing it back on the ground, then squeezed her hand. "I'm your friend. You need not be alone."

She glanced around the fire at the forms of her sister assassins, who were quietly talking, lying in the grass, staring at stars or sitting close to the fire, warming their hands. She shook her head. "I'm not alone."

Stefan smiled, took his hand from hers and passed Ithsar her soup. "Let's eat. We need our strength. Who knows what tomorrow will bring."

Ithsar sipped her soup. A delicious blend of strange herbs danced across her tongue. "Mmm, what's in this?"

"Mint, thyme, tarragon and basil—it's quite a potent mix." He shrugged. "My parents were herbalists. I guess we bring our heritage with us when we become dragon riders."

Ithsar swallowed her soup, warmth trickling into her belly. "It's not as cold here at night as it is in the desert."

"So they say," he replied, "but wait until you get farther north where there's snow on the ground."

"Is it really as chilly as they say?"

Stefan nodded. When they'd finished their soup, he reached into his pocket and pulled out a tiny package wrapped in crumpled waxed cloth. He placed it on the grass and opened it, revealing two of the chocolate delicacies Ithsar had enjoyed at the marketplace.

She sucked in her breath. "For me?"

"Yes, for you."

Ithsar inhaled deeply, already tasting the rich aroma on her tongue. Her mouth watered.

"Go on." He nudged the cloth toward her.

"Is this all you have?" He nodded, so Ithsar took the largest chocolate and broke it, offering him half.

Stefan set the broken chocolate back on the cloth next to the other, and wrapped them and put the package back in his pocket. Then he lay back, sprawled across his bedroll in the grass, his hands tucked behind his head. "Do the stars look different in the Robandi Desert?"

Ithsar leaned back on her elbows and gazed up at the velvet sky studded with twinkling diamonds. Oh, camel dung, the silly things reminded her of her mother's nose studs. "Maybe I can help you learn to fight," she said.

"I'm fine at archery," Stefan replied. "But maybe if we wake early, you can test my sword skills—or lack of them." After a moment, he added, "Thank you."

"You're welcome." Ithsar stared into the fire, the tongues of flame around the edges dancing and reaching for the sky.

§

The next morning, as dawn broke, Ithsar and Stefan finished training.

"You're much better now that you've corrected your balance," Ithsar said, wiping her brow and sheathing her saber.

Stefan rammed his sword into its scabbard and swung his arm in a couple of practice strokes. "I think I've got the hang of those blows, now."

"It didn't take much," Ithsar said as they wandered back to their dragons. "You were already doing a lot right."

Dragons stirred, and the assassins and riders roused themselves from sleep. After a hurried breakfast of bread and fruit, Ithsar and Stefan were repacking their saddlebags as a green dragon landed. A rider staggered from the saddle, his movements sluggish with weariness, and asked after Goren.

After a few hurried words, Goren waved Ithsar over.

The recently-arrived rider nodded. "I have news, Chief Prophetess. The fighting finished in Lush Valley some time ago, but we've spent the last few days patrolling the valley, woods and mountainsides, hunting down tharuks and stray shadow dragons."

Ithsar recounted the vision she'd seen of Ezaara and Roberto fighting in midair until the dragon queen had snatched them in her talons. "Do you have any idea what happened, or is this yet to come?"

The guard nodded gravely. "The folk of Lush Valley said that the enemy turned Ezaara, but that Roberto narrowly prevented her from shooting at her own mother."

"How is that possible? Is she all right now?"

He shrugged. "I'm sorry, I don't know any details. Just that there's still fighting in the North." He turned back to Goren to discuss other business.

Goren gave Ithsar a nod. "Please, get your riders ready. We've a long day's travel ahead. Make sure your women wear the thick cloaks we gave them or they'll freeze further north."

"Thank you." Ithsar went straight back to Saritha, who relayed the message to everyone's sea dragons.

Dracha gods, an enemy that could change a leader's loyalty? She tucked Thika inside her robes to keep him warm, and glanced about at her assassins and Stefan nearby, packing their saddlebags, donning their cloaks and readying for their journey.

She hoped she would never turn on her own friends and sisters.

§

Later that day, they flew over a village. As their shadows fell over the buildings, villagers ran inside, shrieking.

A littling pointed at the sky. "Look."

A man yelled, "They're not shadow dragons, they're green guards."

"Hundreds of them," the littling yelled as her mother herded her inside.

Saritha snorted. *"Hmpff. I never thought I'd be mistaken for a common green guard."*

Ithsar patted her scales. But she couldn't help shudder at the fear the villagers had shown.

Kisha

A large tharuk with a jagged scar down its furry face slammed its tankard on the bar. Saliva dripped down its tusks and its fetid breath washed over Kisha. "Another beer," Scar Face snarled. The tharuk lashed out with its claws, the tattooed 562 flashing on the bald inside of its wrist, and knocked the wooden tankard over, spilling the dregs.

"Just one moment, sir." She took a fresh cloth and wiped the ale off the counter. These brutes seemed to think that their free beer grew on trees; that she could pluck another barrel out of nowhere. With patrons too afraid to enter the tavern after the last brawl with tharuks, she had no income. And the beer was fast running out.

Her grandmother, Anakisha—may she forever fly in peace with departed dragons—would cringe in her grave if she knew tharuks now frequented the Lost King Inn, the oldest inn in Last Stop. Although that hadn't been the name of the inn when her grandmother had been alive. For the thousandth time, Kisha wondered exactly what had happened to Anakisha and Yanir—the ex-Queen's Rider and her consort—and their dragons, when they'd died in battle.

She turned the tap on the barrel and held 562's tankard under it, filling it with the rich golden beer topped with pale foam. This was the last barrel. There'd be mayhem when it was finished and the tharuks learned their precious supply had run out.

A tankard smacked against the other end of the wooden counter and another tharuk snarled as its beer dribbled over the wood.

Cloth in hand, Kisha rushed over to mop the ale up, habitually recalling happy childhood memories to make the soul-destroying job of serving her enemies bearable.

Her favorite was the day she'd discovered she had the gift of prophecy after seeing her dead grandmother in a dream:

Only six years old, she nestled against her mother's lap. Her mother's warm arms enfolded her as she rocked Kisha in front of the fire. "Why couldn't you sleep, my precious blossom?"

"Mama, I saw a lady in my dream. She was wispy, made of clouds, and she had my eyes and the warmest smile I've ever seen."

Ma shot her a sharp look, and then smiled. "Warmer than mine?" she teased, but she'd soon grown serious, asking questions about how the woman looked and what she'd said to Kisha in her dream.

And then Ma had told her something Kisha had never forgotten. "Your grandmother was Anakisha, the last Queen's Rider. She rode upon Queen Zaarusha, the mighty dragon who rules over Dragons' Realm. When Anakisha died, Zaarusha mourned for years and refused to take a new rider." Her mother stroked Kisha's hair from her forehead and kissed her brow. "Your grandmother gave me this, and told me one day you'd be old enough to wear it." She unfastened a fine silver chain from around her neck. At the end of the chain, a pretty jade ring winked in the firelight. "Your grandmother's ring opens a world gate and will take you and a dragon anywhere in Dragons' Realm. To use it, put the ring on, rub it, and say your name, 'Kisha'. Repeat that now."

"Put the ring on, rub it, and say 'Kisha'. That's easy, Mama, because that's my name."

"Yes, we named you after her." As her mother fastened the chain around her neck, Kisha had felt the solid weight of that ring, warm and comforting, against her skin.

Absently, she mopped more beer off the counter and shot a glance at the nearest tharuk. It seemed thirsty. She poured another ale and put the tankard on the bench in front of the beast, keeping her gaze averted. It was a mind-bender. She felt its black eyes probing her as it tried to take over her mind. She slammed a wall around her thoughts.

Her mother had made her practice shielding her thoughts from mind-benders every night before bed—long, boring practices when she'd wished she was outside scampering down the alleys with her friends.

Her tavern, the Lost King, had been named after Yanir, Anakisha's husband and Kisha's grandfather. Her parents had set the tavern up as a place for dragon riders to stay during their arduous journeys across the realm. Now that tharuks frequented the bar, the only dragon rider who'd visited of late was the master healer at Dragons' Hold, Marlies, who'd helped her break up a tharuk brawl two weeks ago. She'd first met Marlies two moons ago when Kisha had given her the—

The door slammed open, jolting Kisha from her reverie. Two more furry beasts entered, their boots thudding dully on her oncefinely-polished wooden floors, now marred with mud and gouges. She didn't dare close the inn, or these monsters would probably trash the place. Not that she cared anymore. Things were about to change—not because she had a choice, but because she'd run out of options. She squeezed out the cloth and dunked it into a pail of fresh water.

Kisha forced a polite smile, filled a few more tankards and sat them on the counter. That was the last of the beer. If she didn't get out of here, she'd be ripped to shreds. "I'll get some more food for you, kind sirs."

She stepped into the kitchen and closed the door to the bar. For a moment, she leaned against the door and took a deep breath, then she leaped into action. Kisha took neatly-sliced bacon from the meat safe and threw it, with some eggs, onto the giant skillet on the hearth. She hacked chunks of bread onto an enormous tray, not bothering to arrange everything nicely or garnish it. When the eggs were sputtering and the bacon was sizzling, she slammed the eggs into two giant serving bowls, and the bacon into another. Hopefully this would keep the beasts occupied. But not yet.

First, Kisha had to take care of herself. She'd learned that much tending the bar. She shoveled a few forkfuls of egg into her mouth, straight from the tharuks' bowl—not that it would bother those heinous monsters—and scoffed a rasher of bacon as she dashed around the kitchen. This would be her last hot meal for a while.

Kisha put a waterskin, a sack of dried apples, the last loaf of bread, and a hastily-made sandwich of hot bacon and egg into a rucksack and left it near the back door. As she turned back to the kitchen, the large carving knife caught her eye, so she shoved that into her waistband and stowed an assortment of smaller knives into her rucksack. After a last sweeping glance around the kitchen, Kisha slipped back into the dining room. Stalking between the drinking beasts, she placed the bowls of eggs and bacon, and the tray of bread, onto a long table in the center of the dining area. "Enjoy your meal." She smiled sweetly. As if that would happen.

Tharuks turned from their beer and rushed the table. As the beasts fell on the food, Scar Face snarled, "I eat first. I biggest." The huge monster raked its claws across the head of another tharuk.

The beast fell to its knees, black blood spurting from its cheek and dribbling over its fur.

Another tharuk growled, "I hungry too." Head down, it charged Scar Face and impaled the monster's belly on its tusk.

Scar Face roared and slashed with its claws, but the other tharuk kept running, driving Scar Face against a nearby table. The table flipped, crashed into a wall, and splintered. Shards of wood flew, the bloody beasts brawling amid the debris.

More tharuks jumped in, kicking, slashing, and biting. Blood sprayed across the table and tufts of fur rained over the food.

Smaller beasts slunk over to the feast, stuffing their jaws with bloodied eggs, bacon, and bread as the others fought.

Unnoticed by the rampaging beasts, Kisha nipped through the kitchen, donned her rucksack, and threw her cloak over it. She slipped out the back door, across the cobbled courtyard and into the streets, with more than a twinge of guilt and breathing a gusty sigh of relief.

She'd never thought she'd abandon her post at the bar. Had promised her dying mother she wouldn't. She'd even had a vision of Anakisha telling her she was needed here. But now, she had no choice.

Her boots echoed on the cobbles.

A tharuk stepped from the shadow of a nearby building, sizing her up. "Where you going?"

Anywhere but here. In truth, she had nowhere, no one who cared. "I'm taking supplies to my mother on the edge of town," Kisha lied. Somewhere in Last Stop there was a resistance group called Anakisha's Warriors. If only she knew where to find them.

The beast gave her a tusky grin. "Supplies? Let me see."

Kisha undid her cloak and opened her rucksack.

The tharuk bent and reached inside, ripping a chunk of bread off the crusty loaf that would've fed her for days. It stuffed its face, tusks gleaming with saliva. Kisha turned, pretending to fumble with her cloak. She slipped the knife out of her waistband, heart pounding. She'd always wanted to get back at the beasts who'd killed her parents.

As the tharuk bent to snaffle another snack from her rucksack, she plunged her knife at the beast's neck. But the knife glanced off the beast's tough fur. The tharuk spun, bashing her knife away. The blade skittered across the cobbles, out of reach. Kisha was left facing a raging tharuk with a tiny slice in its fur.

Claws sprang from the tharuk's fingertips. It swiped. Kisha ducked. The beast rammed into her, driving her up against the wall of a building. Stone bit into her back as the tharuk grinned, its claws digging into her shoulders, its tattooed number 617 visible on the bald patch inside its wrist.

"Think you could kill me, did you?" 617 smirked, dark saliva dribbling off its tusks.

Dark saliva—by the First Egg, she'd walked straight into a tracker.

"You're dead meat. Tasty meat. Commander Zens say we not eat people. But he's not watching." 617 opened its ugly maw, fangs gleaming in the flickering light of a street lantern. The beast's breath blasted her face, a foul stench wafting over her.

617's dark chuckle made Kisha's spine run cold. Gods, she'd never heard of these monsters eating people. Claws still digging into her shoulder, 617 fastened its other hand around her throat and squeezed.

Kisha thrashed and kicked, but the tharuk's grip tightened. She gurgled, gasping. Stars danced before her eyes. The beast roared in triumph as it squeezed harder. Darkness edged Kisha's vision.

And then 617 slumped against Kisha, its body knocking her to the ground, slamming her elbows and backside onto the cobbles. Rear end throbbing and elbows aching, she struggled out from under the beast.

An arrow was embedded in its back. For a moment, Kisha sat there, stunned, her breath whooshing in and out of her chest in great gulps.

A rope whipped down from a neighboring rooftop. A girl's head appeared over the gutter. "Quick, climb."

Kisha scrambled to her feet, stuffed her knife into her waistband, and threw her rucksack on her back. She grabbed the rope and clambered up the side of the building using her feet against the stones. Panting and arms burning like wildfire, she reached the overhang at the top of the building.

The girl stretched her hand down. "Give me your arm," she hissed, and helped Kisha over the lip of the rooftop onto the tiles.

Kisha slumped, trying to catch her breath.

"No time to rest," the girl snapped. "There could be a tharuk patrol passing at any moment. Follow me." She scrambled nimbly across the rooftop.

Her backside throbbing and head dizzy, Kisha stumbled and slipped on the tiles, then pulled herself upright. There was no point falling to her death, so she followed, more slowly and carefully, trying to ease the pounding of her heart.

A roar shattered the sky, and then more roars. Over the forest, jets of flame lit up the inky night.

Gods, no, shadow dragons were coming to Last Stop.

Anakisha's Warriors

"*Dragon flame,*" Saritha murmured, jolting Ithsar awake.

Oh, in the name of the blazing sun, she'd dozed off on dragonback. No wonder; it was dark already. Ithsar shifted her backside to ease her aching sit bones. They'd been in the saddle most of the day. The glamour of traveling by dragonback was rapidly wearing off.

Far off in the inky night, distant flashes flared in the darkness.

"*How far away?*" Ithsar asked, snatching Thika from her robes and shoving him into a saddlebag. He clambered out immediately and scampered along Saritha's back. "How am I supposed to keep you safe in battle if you won't stay put?" Ithsar muttered.

"*Let me help.*" Saritha trumpeted and the lizard scurried back into the saddlebags, trembling. Ithsar buckled the straps. If he really wanted, he could probably still sneak out, but hopefully, Saritha's warning would help him stay put.

"*So, how far off are we?*"

"*A couple of thousand wingbeats.*"

As if that helped. Ithsar checked her weapons, pulled her cloak around her, and peered into the darkness at the distant jets of flame.

§

Kisha dashed over rooftops, glad they weren't leaping over alleys, no matter how narrow they were. Hundreds of pockets of flame lit up the far horizon over Great Spanglewood Forest. A few roiled closer to the far side of town. A huge horde of shadow dragons was coming.

The girl spun to her. "Shadow dragons. We have to hide." She grabbed hold of a rope that was anchored to a chimney top. "Follow me."

What else did that girl think she was going to do, sit on the rooftop and wave? But Kisha didn't say a word. She peered over the edge of the gutter as the girl slipped down the rope and entered an open window halfway down the building. Kisha followed, hands aching and slippery with sweat as she shimmied down the rope and clambered through the window.

In the dim light she could make out a blonde-bearded man, some bedrolls, and a cache of food and waterskins.

The man strode to the windows and pulled the shutters. "I'm Kadran, and this is my daughter Hana." He motioned at the girl who had led her across the rooftops. A door opened and a woman entered with a lantern, placing it on an old rickety table. "And my wife, Katrine."

Hana nodded. "Pleased to meet you."

Katrine approached her, took her rucksack, and placed it against the wall. Then, to Kisha's surprise, she hugged her tightly.

"Hello, Kisha. We've been wanting to reach out to you, but with so many tharuks in the Lost King we haven't had a chance." She held her at arm's distance and looked her over. "It's true, you're Anakisha's granddaughter, aren't you? You have her eyes. Welcome to Last Stop's resistance movement. We call ourselves, Anakisha's Warriors."

Kisha nodded, a lump the size of a dragon egg forming in her throat. So people hadn't forgotten her—or her grandmother.

§

Kadran gestured to a spare bedroll. "You may want to snatch some sleep. We'll be heading out soon to hunt some tharuks, and we may be up fighting all night. Will you join us? Ah, can you fight?"

"My delivery man is Giant John of Great Spanglewood Forest. He trained me."

"You mean *the* Giant John, the best warrior in Dragons' Realm? The one who started our resistance group, Anakisha's Warriors?" Hana asked, eyes round.

"Yes, that Giant John." Kisha sat on the bedroll and unpacked some of her food. "Do you mind if I eat? I'm famished." She unwrapped the waxed cloth to reveal her sandwich and cut it deftly with her dagger, then passed the three of them equal shares. "Giant John still drills me whenever he comes to town. It's been a while, though." Kisha took a bite of her bacon and egg sandwich, glad the tracker hadn't wolfed it down. "I used to train at the back of the inn with some of the locals, but lately there have been too many tharuks around."

Commander Zens' monsters had been frequenting the town for many moons now. Sometimes it felt like they'd always lived under the tharuks' shadow. Ironically, the Lost King had become one of the beasts' favorite haunts. This week, hundreds of Zens' monsters had flooded the village, taking what they wanted, killing mercilessly, their boots stomping down the alleys, their stench permeating the homes of Last Stop.

Kisha swallowed. "The tavern was running out of ale, and there were too many tharuks for me to fight, so I fled." She turned to Hana. "Thanks for saving my skin. I was a goner back there."

Hana gave her an easy, careless grin. "Anytime."

Kadran patted her shoulder. "You did well to get out. Now get some rest."

Katrine reached out to squeeze her hand. "We're glad to welcome you into Anakisha's Warriors. There are pockets of us throughout Last Stop, fighting Commander Zens and his monsters."

For the first time since her parents had died, Kisha didn't feel alone.

SEA DRAGON

§

Kisha rolled over on the bedroll. Kadran, Katrine, and Hana were already asleep, but she couldn't get comfortable. She tossed and turned, and finally drifted into a fitful sleep.

Anakisha's spirit wisped toward her, those bright blue eyes, the mirror of her own, piercing Kisha to the core.

Kisha was kneeling under a tavern table as tharuks brawled around her. A tankard smashed and its wooden shards skittered under the table, hitting her knees. The boots of furry beasts tromped past her, grinding wood chips into the floor, the way they'd grind her if they caught her. Her hands trembled. Her breath caught in her throat. "Grandmother, I have to abandon the inn. I'm sorry."

"Abandon the inn? No, my littling, you must stay."

A tharuk thudded on top of the table, its arm hanging limply off the edge. Dark blood dribbled off the tabletop, fat black drops hitting the floor. "But the inn's been overtaken by rampaging tharuks."

"You must stay."

"How much longer? What must I do?" A thud overhead. Sharp claws gripped the edge of the table. The tharuk snuffled. Its tusks and snout appeared over the edge. The monster's beady eyes gleamed.

"Follow your heart. You'll know when the time is right."

The tharuk snatched up Kisha and ripped out her throat.

§

Someone grabbed Kisha. Within a heartbeat, she was awake and had palmed her dagger.

Kadran backed away. "I was just shaking you awake. It's all right, Kisha, you're with me, Kadran. And Katrine and Hana—Anakisha's Warriors. We're your friends, remember?"

Heart still bashing against her ribs, Kisha thrust her dagger back in its sheath and grimaced. She'd grown used to sleeping with a dagger under her pillow in case tharuks pummeled down her door. "Sorry, old habits die hard." Gods, what an awful nightmare.

Roars outside made the building shudder. Boots stomped down the streets. How in the name of the First Egg had she slept through that?

Kadran handed Kisha her cloak. "The tharuks are restless tonight and shadow dragons are on the prowl. Want an adventure?" He winked and passed her a bow and quiver.

Katrine placed a hand on Kadran's arm, shooting him a warning glance. "Don't be too eager. I don't want to be responsible for the death of Anakisha's heir."

"We'll take it easy tonight," Kadran said to Katrine. "We won't go for a large troop of tharuks, just pick off some isolated beasts. All over the village, other members of Anakisha's Warriors are doing the same. We'll keep Kisha safe."

Kisha threw on her cloak, bristling and eyes blazing. "I can take care of myself. I've done so for years while hundreds of tharuks visited my tavern." Gods, she'd hoped she'd left that all behind, but now after her dream, she wasn't so sure.

"A fact I don't dispute," Katrine said. "We've been hunting tharuks here for years, too, but I'd hate to face Anakisha in the land of long-departed dragons and tell her I was responsible for her granddaughter's death before she was fully grown."

Kisha bristled again. "I'm nearly fifteen summers."

"Same age as Hana." Kadran clapped her shoulder. "It's all right, Kisha. Katrine and I are just hoping you'll have another twenty summers."

Waiting near the window in her cloak with her bow slung over her back, Hana rolled her eyes. "Come on. She'll be fine; we all will. Let's get going." Hana climbed on to the window sill and headed up the rope.

Katrine followed.

"I'll be right behind you," Kadran said, giving Kisha an encouraging smile.

Cold nipped at Kisha as she clambered up, arms aching by the time she got onto the snowy roof.

"Here." Hana's teeth flashed in a grim smile as she handed Kisha some furs for her boots.

"Good idea." Kisha took them. She didn't want to slip on the snowy tiles and land on the cobbles far below.

They sat on the ridge of the roof and tied the furs around the soles of their boots, then sneaked along the ridge until they came to a gap. The next building was only an arm's length away, but Kisha's heart pounded as she looked at the drop.

"Follow me," Hana whispered and leaped to the next roof without a second thought.

Kisha fastened her gaze upon Hana's face, took a deep breath and jumped over the gap. She landed, tiles barking her knees.

Hana grasped her by the armpits and hauled her to her feet. "That wasn't so bad, was it? You'll get used to this. We've been doing it for ages."

Heart pounding, Kisha nodded as Kadran and Katrine landed on the tiles. They all crept further along the rooftops. Tharuks' boots stomped on the cobbles below. Katrine motioned, and the four of them dropped flat on the rooftop until the beasts had passed. Around a corner, roars and snarls broke out.

"Commander Zens and his troops are up to no good tonight," Kadran muttered.

Well, that was the truth—they'd been up to no good for years. Kisha heard the unmistakable rustle of wingbeats. All four of them snapped their heads up, eyes scanning the dark skies.

"Dragons," hissed Hana.

Many of them, by the sound of those wingbeats.

"Good or evil?" Katrine asked.

Rumors had been rife about the terrible shadow dragons recently plaguing the land. Just last week, the blue guards had killed three shadow dragons outside Last Stop. But a few days ago, things had gone quiet. Then tharuks had flooded the village.

Kisha and her friends readied their bows.

§

The crackle of shadow dragon flame made Ithsar's arm hairs stand on end as they flew toward the village of Last Stop. The wind was chilly, nipping at her through her robes and the heavy archers' cloak that Stefan had given her. Nearby, Fangora skittered and bucked, eager to go into battle.

"That young one is always so keen to fight." Saritha tossed her head. *"One day, he'll get his scales charred and learn a lesson."*

"Hopefully, not today." It was more likely they'd all be charred. They weren't even at the main battle front, and ahead, the night sky was lighting up like the fire sticks at the Naobian markets. But these were not fire sticks—they were shadow dragons blasting fire and killing innocent people.

Ithsar drew her bow out of the saddlebag and pulled an arrow from her quiver. She nocked her bow as they flew over the town toward the other side where dark beasts were snarling.

"Remember Ezaara's message and be wary," Ithsar said. "These dragons shoot beams from their eyes that'll slice your skin open."

Saritha rumbled.

Although the air was chill, heat roiled toward them as they approached. The dark beasts wheeled in the sky, flapping their ragged wings and shooting spouts of flame onto houses. Screams rang out from the villagers, and stomping echoed from below as furry beasts stalked through the township. Something in Ithsar's bones shuddered. There was something *other* about those dragons—something wrong. Their *sathir* was a roiling dark blanket that coalesced around them, lit up by plumes of flame. Their snarls skittered down her bones.

Saritha rumbled and opened her maw. A shadow dragon wheeled to attack them, its high-pitched screaming splitting through Ithsar's skull. She tensed her jaw and aimed her arrow. The beast swept closer, yellow beams shooting from its eyes, slicing dangerously close to Saritha.

Ithsar loosed her arrow. It punctured the beast's neck. Shrieking, it plummeted onto a rooftop below, splintering the wood and thatched roof and sending the occupants screaming along the streets. The dragon roared and leaped from the ruins of the house, a piece of jagged wood impaled in its hind leg. In midair, the shadow dragon twisted, yanking the wood from its leg with its jaws, and flung it down into the street. The jagged timber hit a man and knocked him to the stone.

Ithsar shot another arrow, missing as the dragon swerved past her. Once again, shrieking filled her head. The next time, she shot the beast right through the eye.

In a flash of green wings, Goren, the green guard leader, speared past Saritha and gave Ithsar an encouraging nod.

That was probably as close to approval as she was going to get, so Ithsar nodded back and smiled. That man's heart was as hard as camel toenails. She nocked her arrow and spun to aim at another feral shadow dragon. Her arrow flew true, hitting the beast in the temple. Golden beams sprang from its eyes and sliced toward her. But Saritha plunged and shot a volley of flame at the beast's belly.

Suddenly, ten beasts were upon them. Stefan whooped as he and Fangora shot forward, flaming a black dragon until it fell from the sky. Nila and Misha wheeled, scales blurring in the flame from shadow dragons' maws as they fought to vanquish their enemy. Saritha roared gusts of flame at anything with ragged dark wings, and Ithsar shot arrow after arrow into their skulls, chests, and eyes.

§

Stefan hunched down over Fangora's neck as they raced over the rooftops. Screams rose from an alley. Two tharuks were chasing a littling through the streets.

Fangora roared. *"That's not playing fair, so many of them chasing a littling. Those filthy stinking beasts reek from way up here. Let's get them."*

"I'm with you." Stefan nocked his arrow and aimed, loosing it. The arrow thwacked into a tharuk's back. It slumped to the cobbles, but the other one kept running. The littling glanced back, screaming, and slipped in a patch of snow.

Stefan flung his bow onto his back, dragged a rope from the saddlebags, and tied it onto Fangora's saddle. *"I'm going down, Fangora. Swoop so I can get between those buildings."*

Fangora descended. Stefan grabbed the rope and jumped. The jolt made his dragon list to one side and nearly yanked Stefan's shoulders from his sockets. *"Sorry."* Arms burning, he lowered himself, hand over hand, down the rope. He swung between the buildings and aimed his boots at the beast chasing the littling. He kicked the tharuk in the head, knocking it to the ground. Stefan dropped to the cobbles and scooped the littling up in his arms.

She sobbed and howled.

Gods, he had to do something to keep her quiet. He reached into his pocket for his chocolate and unwrapped it, shoving it at the girl's mouth. She bit into it, her eyes wide with wonder.

"Now be nice and quiet. We're going to hide from the monster." Stefan spun and dashed off down a side alley, the littling jostling against his side. There was a roar behind him. The tharuk he'd knocked over was already after them. "Where do you live?" Stefan asked.

She shrugged, eyes wide and bottom lip trembling. Gods, oh gods, he was playing nursemaid to a littling in the middle of battle—some great warrior he was. Roars echoing behind him and flame lighting up the sky, Stefan pelted around a corner…

…and smacked into a group of three tharuks.

A beast whirled, claws out, and threw Stefan and the girl against the stone masonry of a decrepit building. Stefan cradled the girl against the impact and hit the stone with his shoulder. He scrambled to his feet and tugged the girl to hers as the monsters advanced. Gods, his shoulder was throbbing.

A burly tharuk with a jagged scar along its snout snarled, "Bought us a littling, have you?" Saliva dribbled off its tusks, splattering onto the cobbles. The three tharuks prowled toward him, claws out.

He thrust the littling behind him, near the wall, and pulled out his knives, one in each hand. "Run," he whispered.

She scampered off around the building.

A small beast swiped at him with its claws, barely missing Stefan's face. He ducked, the swish of air whistling past his cheek, its claws snagging on the end of his hair and ripping out a clump.

"Plenty more where that came from," he muttered, scalp burning. Regaining his footing, he chucked a knife at the beast's chest. But the tharuk dodged and his stupid knife bounced off its shoulder and slid across the cobbles, slamming against the building on the other side of the alley.

Great—one knife against three monsters. If only he hadn't left his sword in his dragon's saddlebag. Who'd have thought he'd need it on dragonback?

Fangora roared, shaking snow from the roof of the building above. A smattering landed on Stefan's hair, but a heavy clump hit the tharuk, distracting it. Stefan lunged and thrust his knife at the beast.

The tharuk swung its arm and sent the weapon flying out of Stefan's hand. The knife ricocheted off the building and clunked to the cobbles.

Stefan swallowed, backing up. Now he had no weapons, only his wits and his dragon. *"Fangora, where are you?"*

"Can you get away from those beasts?"

Before Stefan had a chance to tell Fangora he was cornered, a gust of flame and blistering heat roiled down through the alley. He dived onto the ground as the fire hit a tharuk. It fell screaming to the cobbles. The stench of burned fur and fried meat clogged the narrow alley.

The burnt ends of Stefan's hair stank too. Gods, his dragon was too young, keen and fire-ready. *"Ah, you nearly burned me too,"* Stefan mind-melded. *"I might have to manage this alone."* He scrambled to his feet as the remaining two tharuks got to theirs and lunged for him. They hit Stefan like a wave, slamming him to the ground and pinning him against the cobbles. One tharuk straddled his legs and the other squeezed its furry hands around his throat, its claws piercing his skin. Warm, wet blood trickled down his neck.

"Fangora?" No answer. Oh gods. Stefan swallowed. This was it.

Last Stop

Ithsar hunched low over Saritha as her dragon flamed a bunch of monsters fighting people in the village square. *"It's no good, Saritha. If I fire my arrows, I might hurt the villagers."*

"I'll let you down." Saritha swooped down between the snow-laden buildings into the square and Ithsar slipped from her saddle.

As the queen took to the sky, Ithsar exhaled forcefully, trying to expel the stench of burning fur from her nostrils, and snatched an arrow from her quiver. Misha swooped down on Ramisha. Her dragon snatched up two tharuks in his talons, knocking their heads against each other, and tossed them to the cobbles where they bounced, then lay still. Screams of women and littlings rang from the nearby alleys. Men bellowed, rushing off with their swords ready.

Upon the rooftops, foul shadow beasts breathed fire down at the men rushing to defend their families. Purple rippling stains, so dark they were almost black, wreathed the vicious creatures—the shadow dragons' *sathir*. Ithsar shot a shadow dragon in the eye. It plummeted, shrieking, to the square below, its legs thrashing against the ground. Even in its death throes, a yellow beam bounced from its good eye, slashing at nearby villagers.

"Quick, Saritha, before it hurts anyone else."

Saritha swooped down and burned the beast. Ramisha landed and Misha dismounted.

Ithsar and Misha raced toward the fighting tharuks. Ithsar fired an arrow and hit a tharuk in the thigh. It collapsed onto the cobbles, howling, and swiped its claws across a man's leg. Crimson stained the snow as the man staggered toward another tharuk and drove his sword through its neck. The beast twitched and then lay still. The man spun to meet another beast, his sword striking its breastplate and glancing off. Then he stumbled to one knee while still trying to fight off the monsters.

Ithsar flung her bow over her shoulder and yanked her saber from its sheath, charging into the fray. Her first blow took out a small wiry tharuk that had just killed a littling.

"That horrible beast, picking on small ones." Saritha swooped and plucked up a tharuk, ripping it apart with her talons.

A tharuk whirled, arm flung high to slash a man's throat. Ithsar lunged and drove her saber under its armpit, behind its breastplate. Dark sticky blood spurted from the beast's mouth. Its eyes glazed over and it slumped to the cobbles in an ever-spreading pool of black fluid.

Still more tharuks came. Ramisha flamed a group of tharuks, driving them back from the mouth of an alley to stop them from entering the square. Nila and her dragon, Nilanna, thudded to the square, and Nila raced over. Nilanna shredded a tharuk with her talons and then leaped into the air to fend off a shadow dragon.

Nila and Misha dived in, years of training kicking in as they whirled and spun, slaughtering the beasts with skill and precision that Ithsar hadn't even realized they'd possessed. Ithsar swung her saber beside them, the thrill of the battle singing through her veins. The bodies of the tharuks piled up. Soon, there were only a few left fighting.

A littling burst into the square, screaming about monsters and pointing back down an alley. "Help him," she screamed. "A dragon rider, trapped by tharuks."

The girl's face was covered in chocolate stains. Ithsar's heart sank. *"Saritha, where are Fangora and Stefan?"*

"I don't know," Saritha answered, flinging a tharuk against a building. The beast's body hit the stone and crumpled.

Only two tharuks remained in the square. Ithsar had to find Stefan. "Where's the dragon rider?" Ithsar barked at the littling.

The littling's face crumpled into tears as she pointed back down the alley.

Blood thrumming through her veins, Ithsar ran. She pounded around a corner and stopped, her blood chilling.

Stefan was lying on the ground, an enormous tharuk crouched over him with its claws digging into his throat. Another straddled his legs, pinning him in place. Stefan gurgled and spluttered, blood running from his neck.

On silent feet, Ithsar lunged and drove her saber at the beast on his legs, but as she neared, her shadow danced across Stefan's face. Alerted, the beasts both spun. The larger one barged into Ithsar, slamming her backward onto the cobbles. She rolled through a pile of ice and snow, and bounded to her feet. Then danced in, feinting left. The beast took her ruse, and lunged. She sidestepped and slashed her saber across its neck. Tufts of fur flew through the air and dark blood sprayed as the beast dropped dead.

The other beast bellowed.

Ithsar danced in close, and then sprang through the air, kicking her foot at the beast's chest. It landed in the snow and skidded backward. She landed nimbly, and drove her saber through the monster's throat. Dark blood gushed, spraying her saber and legs. The beast gurgled and was still.

Ithsar pulled her saber from its neck and wiped the blade upon its fur.

"Wow." Stefan sat up. Despite his pale face and the blood trickling down his neck, his eyes were shining. "You were amazing."

She panted, wiped her saber again, and sheathed it. As the hilt smacked the top of the sheath, she gave a grim smile. "Thank you."

"No, thank you." He scrambled to his feet. "You saved my life."

"Are you all right?" Ithsar eyed his neck.

"Nothing but a scratch." He staunched the blood with his hand. "Let's get back to our dragons."

A thundering roar shook the rooftops and snow slid to the ground, splattering into a pool of mush at their feet. Ithsar grabbed Stefan's free hand and they ran back to the square.

The cobbles were littered with charred carcasses of tharuks and shadow dragons. A smoky haze filled the air. Dead villagers lay slumped on the cobbles. Roaring shadow dragons shot overhead. Flames blazed in the distance.

Ithsar ripped a piece of fabric off her robe and wiped his neck. He was right; it wasn't too bad. "You'll need to get that treated by a healer," she said, tearing off another strip and binding his wound. Then she clasped Stefan's arms tightly. "Stay on dragonback. It's safer."

Stefan shook his head. "I had to get down. A littling was in trouble."

Ithsar nodded. "I know. I think she liked your chocolate."

Fangora landed with a thud and nuzzled Stefan. He grinned. Saritha landed, her talons clattering on the cobbles. They climbed onto their dragons and took off toward the distant roars and the flame punching through the night sky.

§

Kisha aimed her arrow and loosed it at a tharuk racing along the alley after a villager. Roars broke out on the far side of town. Snarls and answering roars thundered above and flame lit up the night sky. A wing of shadow dragons flew overhead.

An arrow swished past her cheek as Kadran fired at a tharuk who was slamming a man against the side of a building.

"Quick," hissed Katrine, grabbing her hand.

They scrambled across rooftops, slipping in the snow, as a volley of answering arrows hailed on the roof behind them. Panting, they perched between two chimneys and nocked their bows.

Hana and Kadran shot at shadow dragons wheeling in the air. Katrine and Kisha drew their bows and fired upon tharuks thundering down the street. A blaze of fire lit up the night sky as a shadow dragon shot over the rooftops, claws out, heading for the square.

Despite her thundering heart, Kisha took aim and fired. Her arrow nicked the edge of the dragon's wing, shredding its wingtip. The beast's shrieks of pain echoed through her head as if someone was pounding it with a mallet.

"Look out," Kadran yelled, thrusting Kisha to the rooftop as a volley of flame and blistering heat roiled in the air above them.

"We have to get out of here. It's too dangerous," Kadran said. "Two roofs over, there's another rope. Let's go."

Kisha scrambled to her feet and rushed along the roof after Hana and Katrine. A screech ripped through her head that made her knees buckle. She stumbled on the steep-gabled roof and started sliding. Kadran threw himself to the ridge top and flung out his bow. Kisha grabbed it and scrabbled with her feet as, slowly, he pulled her back up.

"Thank you," Kisha panted.

More roars split the sky as dragons converged over the village. Green and turquoise scales flashed in the light of surges of flame above them. Blue guards? Naobian green guards? But this was so far from Naobia…

Dark leathery wings obscured the stars. Twin beams of light shot through the night from fiery golden eyes. The beams sliced through the bow in Kisha's hands. The weapon shattered into smoldering pieces.

"Hurry," Hana cried from the end of the rooftop.

Still clutching a remnant of her bow, Kisha ran, pounding across the ridge, Kadran close behind. The shadow dragon swept over them again, its scream cutting through Kisha's mind.

"Look out," Katrine screamed, yanking her across the rooftop, nearly pulling her shoulder from its socket. When they reached a massive drop, Katrine didn't stop running. Kisha followed blindly, flying through the air.

She landed on a roof below, jarring her legs through her knees to her hip sockets, and scrambled over so Kadran could land behind her.

Ahead of them, Hana turned and screamed, "No!"

Heat roiled over them. Kisha flung herself onto the tiles. An agonized shriek rang out behind her. The stench of charred fabric and burnt flesh filled her nostrils. Kisha glanced back and her jaw dropped in horror.

Kadran was engulfed in a flaming pyre.

§

Ithsar, Stefan, and Misha sped away from the square, their dragons' wingtips nearly touching as they glided over the roofs. The fighting in this quarter had now been subdued, but on the other side of town, flame lit up the night sky and screeches made Ithsar's nape hair prickle.

"There's something off about those beasts," Saritha grumbled. *"They're strange, unnatural."*

Screeches ripped through Ithsar's head, making her temples pound and her senses reel. She gripped onto the saddle, panting, knuckles clenched tight, and gritted her teeth, trying to withstand it. This was nothing, she told herself, nothing compared to the burns, brands, and beatings Izoldia had given her. They had to save these villagers at all costs.

"Not at all costs, Ithsar," Saritha replied. *"I've only just met you—I don't want to lose you."*

Thika scrambled out of Saritha's saddlebag and across Ithsar's lap. She snatched him up and thrust him back inside as ragged dark wings flapped above them. Saritha shot up, belching a volley of flame at a shadow dragon's belly. The beast shrieked and plummeted through the air, its wings alight. It crashed through a roof, setting the thatch ablaze. A family screamed and raced outside as the dragon's burning body engulfed their house in flame.

"Gods, now we're destroying their homes." Ithsar's throat clenched.

"It's nothing compared to what those beasts are doing," Saritha answered.

In the next alley over, two shadow dragons were flaming thatch. The screams of burning people echoed up through the volley of flames, and the stench of crisped flesh filled the air. Misha and Nila shot in, Ramisha and Nilanna flaming the dark dragons from above. Fangora joined them, setting another dragon's wings alight, as Stefan fired arrows. The shadow dragons plummeted onto the buildings in a spray of cinders and sparks. The flames leaped higher, consuming their bodies.

"I want to save the villagers," Ithsar cried desperately, "not destroy them."

"Here's our chance." Saritha shot toward a shadow dragon chasing a ragged band of people running across rooftops. They slipped and slid, leaving gouges in snow-laden tiles, the dragon's flames nearly upon them. Ithsar and Saritha dived in. As they neared, the shadow dragon extinguished its flames. Yellow beams shot from its eyes, slicing into the flesh of a man at the back of the ragtag group. He stumbled and slipped off the ridge of the roof, leaving bloody red gouges in the snow.

Saritha dived, but before they could reach him, the shadow dragon dived, and his body flared in a burst of fire and fell off the roof near a horde of tharuks. Saritha sped alongside the dark dragon, and Ithsar fired an arrow into its skull. The scream in her head intensified, and then stilled. The beast's body flipped and smacked into the building, scattering roof tiles, and dropping into the street.

Saritha landed on the rooftop.

Ithsar called out, "Come, let us ferry you to a safe place." Although where a safe place was, she didn't quite know. In the dark, it was hard to tell who was winning and who was losing. Bursts of flame illuminated green scales and then black. Yellow beams sliced through the sky. Arrows whooshed. It was chaos. Three people ran back to Ithsar—two girls about her age and a woman.

The woman clambered up behind Ithsar, sobbing, "M-my husband."

"I'm sorry for your loss," Ithsar said. What else could she say? There was nothing that could erase the horror this woman had just experienced.

One of the girls climbed up, but before the other could get upon Saritha's back, a shadow dragon arrowed for them, a green guard on its tail. Saritha tensed and sprang, then swooped over the roof to snatch up the remaining girl. She soared over the village, back to the square, as the harrowing wails of shadow dragons skittered down Ithsar's bones.

The Lost King Inn

Saritha flew across the rooftops, the snow now scattered with ash and debris, and spiraled down toward the square, the girl still hanging from her talons. Avoiding the dead bodies of shadow dragons, tharuks, and villagers, she deposited the girl on the cobbles, then settled back on her haunches. Ramisha and Nilanna were picking up corpses in their talons and piling them at one end of the square.

Ithsar dismounted and helped the woman and the other girl off Saritha.

"I'm Ithsar," she said, holding out her hand, as was the custom of these northerners.

The old woman shook it. "And I'm Katrine. Thank you for rescuing us from those terrible beasts."

The sky on the far side of the village still blazed with fire, although there now seemed to be more green dragons than dark ones. Despite the shadow dragons' screeches in her head, Ithsar smiled. "Don't thank me. Please thank Saritha." She hesitated. "I'm, um, very sorry about your husband."

"He died fighting to save lives. An honorable death." The woman's eyes were bright with unshed tears and she held her head high. She gestured at the girls. "My daughter, Hana, and this is Kisha, Anakisha's granddaughter."

Ithsar shook the girls' hands too. The girl with the vibrant blue eyes and dark hair was the granddaughter of the legendary Anakisha? Even Ithsar had heard the stories of the bravery and courage of the former Queen's Rider who'd been lost in battle nineteen years ago.

Saritha nudged Ithsar with her snout. *"I'd like to meet Anakisha's heir."*

"Kisha, please place your hand on Saritha's forehead. She'd like to introduce herself to you."

"It's you." Kisha stared at Ithsar, those bright blue eyes wide. "I saw you in a vision. I knew you'd come."

"Me?" Ithsar frowned. "You have visions?"

Nodding, the girl touched Saritha's snout.

"You have much in common," Saritha thrummed in Ithsar's mind. *"She has a keen mind, special lineage, and the gift of prophecy, like you."*

Her voice breathy, Kisha murmured, "Jade scales that sparkle silver. Out of all the dragons' scales I've seen growing up, I've never seen any like hers."

"That's because Saritha is a sea dragon," Ithsar said. "I only imprinted with her a moon or two ago. She's queen of the sea dragons and I am the new chief prophetess of the Robandi assassins." It still felt strange to say it aloud.

Kisha's face lit up like the blazing desert sun. "So you see visions too? I've always wanted to meet someone else who could."

"Yes, I do. I had a terrible vision, and then received a message via raven, so I've come north to help Ezaara, the new Queen's Rider."

Kisha nodded. "Good. If you'd like a place to stay, I can offer—"

A tavern door burst open and two brawling tharuks spilled out onto the cobbles, gouging each other's eyes.

"They must've run out of food," Kisha said. "That's my tavern, the Lost King Inn, named after Anakisha's husband, Yanir. In fact, this entire town of Last Stop was the last place Anakisha stopped before they were both lost in battle. If you help me clear out the tharuks, you'll have a place to stay." Her eyes flicked to the dragons. "The riders, at least."

With a roar, one tharuk slit the gut of the other, then surged to its feet, bellowing, and dashed back inside. Crashes and the smash of splintering wood came from the tavern.

Ithsar grinned and held her sword high, issuing the battle cry of the *Sathiri*, "Avanta!"

Misha and Nila flocked to her, and with Kisha, Hana, and Katrine, they surged in through the tavern door.

Ithsar spun, slicing her sword through a tharuk's gut. Another tharuk leaped from the table through the air. Nila lunged, impaling the beast on her sword. The tharuk crashed into her, the impact driving her to her knees, the point of her saber poking through its back.

Nila kicked the tharuk away and sprang onto a table, slashing another's throat. Misha spun her saber, slicing a beast's arm as it lunged toward her. Two enormous beasts lifted a table and threw it across the room at the assassins. For a moment, their reflections glimmered in the dark polished wood as it flew toward them. Ithsar rolled, Misha lunged and Nila ducked. The table crashed into the wall, splinters and shards flying across the tavern. A large chunk of wood impaled itself in a tharuk's eye. It fell to its knees, clutching at its face, screaming, as dark blood sprayed over them.

And then Ithsar saw Thika scurrying across the floor. Oh no! That silly lizard was going to get himself killed.

§

Stefan and Fangora landed in the village square. A window in a tavern shattered as a tharuk was hurled through it into the dirt-strewn snow. More gouges in the snow showed where dragons had been. There was a pile of bodies, and corpses scattered nearby, as if someone had been interrupted while clearing away the dead.

"Saritha, Nilanna, and Ramisha are battling shadow dragons, but they told me their riders are fighting inside that building." Fangora sprang across the square. Stefan slid to the ground and ran toward the tavern.

The door smashed open, ripped off its hinges as an enormous tharuk charged outside.

Stefan was ready. He swung his sword, slashing at the brute and scoring its face. The beast's eyes slitted. Stinking breath and sticky blood washed over Stefan as a fury of claws and fur dived at him. He ducked and swooped in from the side the way Ithsar had taught him, driving his sword through the beast's thick fur. With a crunch of bone he pierced its ribs. An agonized snarl ripped from the beast as it fell to its knees. Stefan drove his sword until the hilt smacked fur, and ducked to avoid the tharuk's flailing claws. The monster twitched and stilled, lifeless.

Pressing his foot on the tharuk's torso, Stefan yanked out his sword, and raced into the Lost King.

Snarls and roars split the air. The tavern was a whirl of orange-robed assassins' swirling cloaks, tufts of flying fur, and pools of dark blood. Dead tharuks were slumped over tables and on the floor, but more were still fighting.

He gasped. A tharuk was chasing Ithsar. She nimbly leaped over a broken chair and swiped her saber at the beast. It slashed and she jumped backward—awesome footwork, but she didn't realize she was about to be cornered.

Stefan sprang onto a tabletop, raced across it, and jumped over a tharuk's sharp, swiping claws. Narrowly missing an assassin's blade, he landed amid smashed crockery and splattered egg and ran.

With rapid swipes of its claws, the tharuk drove Ithsar against the bar. It kicked her saber out of her grip and jammed her neck against the lip of the counter, snarling over her. Ithsar gurgled, eyes wide, and kneed the tharuk's stomach. She palmed a dagger from her sleeve.

Stefan wasn't taking chances. He plunged his sword between the beast's shoulder blades. It slumped over Ithsar and they fell onto the blood-slicked floor. Only black blood, thank the First Egg. Stefan kicked the beast aside and lifted Ithsar in his arms. Gods, she was so tiny. "Are you all right?"

"I'm fine." Her eyes blazed. "I could have got out of that on my own. Now, put me down."

"But—" Stefan choked on his reply and put her on her feet. He scrubbed a hand through his hair. "Oh, sorry for interfering." Like flaming dragon's breath, he was.

Ithsar grinned. "Now we're even. One save each."

He bit back a smile. She'd been teasing him. Stefan snatched his sword out of the dead tharuk's back and spun back to the fight.

KITCHEN BRAWL

One moment, Kisha had been fighting a tharuk next to Katrine, swords flashing. The next, Katrine was chasing the tharuk over a table—and Kisha was facing another beast on her own. The brute whacked her arm, smashing her sword out of her grip. And then, red eyes glinting with malice, it charged.

Kisha dashed past a lanky lad in rider's garb and Ithsar, who were fighting a tharuk near the bar. She threw a tankard at the charging brute's head. The tharuk shrugged it off and kept coming. She ran into the kitchen, scanning the benches for a weapon. Snorting, the tharuk chased her. It thundered past a counter, tusks angled to rip through her body.

Kisha yanked a heavy frying pan from the range and swung. The clang of the tharuk's tusks against metal made her ears ring and her wrists and elbows throb. Kisha swung again, but the tharuk ducked out of the way and snarled at her, its tusks dripping dark saliva.

Another tharuk crashed through the kitchen door, smashing it to pieces. "What we got here?" It grinned—the ugliest smile Kisha had ever seen.

Kisha threw the pan. It glanced off a bench and hit one of the tharuks in the knee. She grabbed the nearest thing she could—a wooden rolling pin—not as heavy as the pan, but easier to wield. As the first tharuk ran at her, she swung the rolling pin and smacked it in the head. The rolling pin shattered in two, the top half flying into a barrel. The tharuk reeled, unsteady on its feet. Kisha leaped onto the kitchen bench and thonked the tharuk on the head with the other half. The monster crashed to the floor.

Snarls ripped through the kitchen. The second tharuk lunged. Pain sliced through her calf as its claws raked her flesh. Oh gods, that *hurt*.

She scrambled over the bench, keeping her head low so she didn't bump the wooden utensil rack hanging by chains from the ceiling. There, if she could get to the empty cauldron on a hook by the hearth, she might have a chance. But the tharuk was faster. It surged over the bench, snatched Kisha up, and sprang to the floor. Roaring, it held her aloft, shaking her body until her teeth clattered.

More tharuks burst through the doorway.

"I got one," the beast roared, shaking Kisha like a rag doll.

Ithsar and her assassins surged, like a sea of orange, across the bodies of broken tharuks on the tavern floor, and through the kitchen doorway. Dodging claws, hacking with their sabers, spinning and slashing. Dark blood sprayed the kitchen. Tharuks fell among the bloody rain.

A slim assassin with dark curly hair launched herself off a bench, caught the utensil rack and, in a spray of wooden spoons, ladles, and roasting forks, swung her feet into the belly of the tharuk holding Kisha. It staggered and fell to one knee, still clutching her.

Women surrounded the beast, their sabers and daggers at its neck, belly and groin.

"Unhand that girl or die." Although Ithsar was tiny, her voice rang with steel.

The assassin with the dark curly hair gave a wicked grin. "Die anyway, brute." She plunged her sword into its neck. It slumped, dropping Kisha on the floor.

"I'm Nila," the curly-haired assassin said. "Is this your inn?"

Kisha nodded and scrambled to her feet, breathing hard. "Yes, it is."

Nila and Ithsar helped her into the taproom. Slain tharuks lay among broken crockery, blood, mashed food, and beer. A table was shattered against a wall with its legs upended. Broken chairs and wood shards littered the tavern, and there was even a tharuk whose head had been impaled with a chair leg. The stench of the beasts was overwhelming.

Kisha's foot slipped in a pool of sticky black blood, but she caught herself before she fell. Aagh, she didn't want to be bathed in the blood of those monsters. It was bad enough smelling them from here—a stench she'd put up with since they'd killed her parents.

Gods, how was she ever going to clean up this mess?

A tall, lanky boy about her age wiped his sword on a tharuk's matted fur and stepped over it. "Hopefully, that's the last of them." He cocked his head. "Must be, there's no more roaring outside."

He was right. After hours of roars, the skies were uncannily silent.

"Hey, Ithsar," he called, "maybe our dragons have slaughtered those shadow dragons too." He grinned at Kisha and held out a hand splattered in black blood. Glancing down at his fingers, he hurriedly wiped his hand on his breeches and offered it again. "I'm Stefan. Nice to meet you."

It was absurd to be fussing over niceties when she was standing ankle deep in debris and dead tharuks, but Kisha shook his hand anyway, then burst out laughing. "And I'm Kisha. Welcome to the Lost King Inn."

"Looks lovely." He wriggled his eyebrows, grinning.

"Ah, Kisha, my sisters and the green guards require a place to stay. If we help you sort out this mess, will you provide us with a roof for the night?" Ithsar asked, as if she hadn't already offered, and winked at Kisha.

The weight of a dragon lifted from Kisha's shoulders, and air rushed back into her lungs. "Oh, thank you. Cleaning up would be rather daunting on my own."

Katrine snatched up a broken chair. "Some of this furniture is beyond repair. I suggest we make a pyre in the courtyard and burn these monsters, too." She quirked an eyebrow at Ithsar. "I'm assuming your dragons wouldn't mind setting these beasts alight."

"I'm sure they'd like nothing better," Ithsar replied.

Stefan chuckled and grabbed up an armful of smashed wood. "I've asked Fangora to bring us more help."

Outside, dragons thudded down into the square. The green guards landed, looking battle-weary and haggard. Orange-robed assassins flooded through the door. Everyone got stuck in, carrying broken furniture outside, dragging tharuks out by their boots and dumping them onto the pile in the corner of the square. They cleared bodies from the rest of the square and shoved the wood from Kisha's broken furniture onto the mound.

Kisha threw some chair shards onto the hearth in the kitchen and boiled up a cauldron of water. Then, she and those valiant women and men scrubbed and cleaned until there was not a drop of tharuk blood left.

When they were finished, she invited all of the green guards, Anakisha's Warriors, and the Robandi Silent Assassins to dine. "Tharuks have devoured all the food in my kitchen, but I don't think they found my secret supplies." Kisha peeled back a rug and lifted the trapdoor that led down to the cellar.

A couple of burly green guards helped her carry up some huge jars of pickles, eggs, a barrel of salted pork, another of flour, and some apple juice. With a few herbs and spices, she soon had a hearty stew in the cauldron and some flatbread toasting over the fire.

Although half the chairs and most of the tables were still intact, there wasn't enough space for everyone to sit, so men and women leaned against walls and sat cross-legged on the floor. They used the inn's entire supply of crockery and cutlery.

Once they'd eaten their fill, Kisha stood. "Thank you so much for ridding the Lost King Inn of tharuks and helping me clean up. My grandmother, Anakisha, the former Queen's Rider, would be proud of you all."

Ithsar stood, too. "I'd like to thank everyone for rising to the challenge of preserving this village. We thank Anakisha's Warriors and mourn their losses." She nodded at Katrine. "We've been lucky that we're not mourning the loss of one of our own tonight. According to reports from Katrine, there are many more shadow dragons in the North. Tomorrow we'll fight again. But tonight, we'll rest and be thankful for the new friendships we're forging." Ithsar's eyes flitted to Stefan and Kisha. "Long may our bonds last after these adventures. Long may we protect Dragons' Realm."

Assassins, warriors, and riders cheered and raised tankards of apple juice.

§

Later that evening, Kisha carried a stray chair leg outside and threw it onto the flaming pyre. The heat was melting the snow on the cobbles, sending rivulets into the gutters on the edge of the square.

Ithsar was moving among small groups of assassins, green guards, and their dragons, as they mended injuries and tidied up the square. Nila was tending her dragon, Nilanna, her slim form bent over its foreleg as the dragon held it up for inspection. Kisha wandered over. A deep slice scored the dragon's flesh. Nila turned to Kisha, eyes bright, and blinked.

It looked as if the brave assassin was trying not to cry.

"Are there any healers in Last Stop?" Nila asked.

"Not anymore. Please, let me see." Kisha bent to examine the wound. The dragon snuffled her shoulder. "It's a clean gash. How did she get it?"

"From one of those yellow beams from a shadow dragon's eye." Nila winced. "She's in a lot of pain."

Ithsar strode over. "Kisha, do you have any of that special healing juice that Ezaara, she of the golden hair, uses?"

Kisha shook her head. "No. Tharuks have destroyed our piaua supplies and destroyed the trees. There's no piaua juice left anywhere." She cocked her head. "However, I am handy with a needle and thread."

"Your dragon is in good hands, then, Nila." Ithsar strode over to talk to a group of assassins who were gesturing at her.

Kisha went into the inn and retrieved a needle, some squirrel gut twine, and another broken chair leg. She gave the chair leg to the dragon to bite down on, and mended her leg with quick, even stitches.

When Kisha was finished, her eyes shot to a red stain blossoming on Nila's orange robes, across her ribs. She was hurt—that's why she'd been blinking back tears and grimacing, not only for her dragon.

"Nilanna wants to thank you." Nila gave a wan smile.

Kisha put her palm against the dragon's warm, leathery scales.

A rumbling voice drifted through her head. *"Thank you, Kisha, but I'm worried. Nila's hiding an injury from me, masking her pain, thinking I can't sense it. Would you tend to her too?"* The dragon's golden eyes blinked and she snuffled Kisha's shoulder.

She nodded. *"I'll tend to her when we're inside the inn, so she doesn't lose face."*

"You have a good heart, young Kisha. A true heart, that of a future dragon rider."

"*I've already been for a dragon ride today.*" Sort of—being clutched in Saritha's talons might not count.

The dragon blinked. "*You know what I mean.*"

A sense of awe stole through Kisha. She nodded. "*I do.*" She'd always longed to be a dragon rider like her grandmother.

Kisha murmured to Nila, "I'll tend your wound when we get inside. Go upstairs to the second room on the left and wait for me."

Nila's eyes shot to her dragon. "She ratted me out, didn't she? And here I was, trying to fool everyone. What a tattletale."

Nilanna snorted and twitched her tail, flicking the tip at Nila's boot.

Kisha smiled and, together, she and Nila walked back to the inn, leaving the blazing pyre of carcasses and broken furniture crackling in the square.

§

Early the next morning, Kisha assembled a rough and ready breakfast from whatever scraps she could find in the cellar. It was strange, no longer having tharuks in the bar—a huge relief. Just yesterday she would've thought it impossible, now here she was, back in the inn, up at the crack of dawn preparing bread for her guests. She kneaded the dough and formed it into rounds to toast on the hearth.

The assassins and green guards rose and then bustled about, ferrying plates of dried fruit, pickles, jam, and freshly-baked bread to the tables.

Stefan wandered into the kitchen for the tenth time, swiping a dried plum as he picked up a plate. "Hands off, Stefan. You've sneaked enough," Kisha said. "Make sure the food gets into someone's belly other than just your own."

"I'm a growing lad." He winked. "But don't worry, I'm feeling generous, so I'll share." He sauntered back out to the dining room, laden with trays and plates.

As Kisha was washing the dishes, an orange lizard with brown bands scampered across the bench, making her start. "Oh, no, you don't. Not in my kitchen." She caught the little fellow, who was nearly as long as her forearm. She'd never seen anything like it—the lizards in Last Stop were usually green and only the length of her finger.

Ithsar came into the kitchen, stepping between the flour-strewn benches and a half-full barrel of salted pork. "Oh, you've found Thika. That little scamp has been having a great time."

The lizard ran up Kisha's arm and nestled in the crook of her shoulder, rubbing his back against her neck.

Ithsar laughed. "He seems to like you."

"Is he yours?"

"For many years, Thika was my only friend." Ithsar scratched the lizard's throat, then tilted her head. "Visions of destruction have been plaguing me all night. We're heading north to battle shadow dragons. Would you mind looking after him for me? I'm worried that he might get hurt. Last night he kept leaping around Saritha's back in the middle of the fighting. I'd hate to lose him."

"Me?"

Ithsar nodded. "I'd be relieved if you could."

"What does he eat?"

"Bugs, scraps of meat. He usually catches his own beetles or flies but, right now, it's a bit cold for that here."

Kisha fed the lizard a scrap of salted pork, which he gobbled down in a heartbeat. "He's so sweet. I'd love to look after him."

"Thank you." Ithsar hugged her. The assassin's warm, dark eyes regarded Kisha. "And thank you for your hospitality. I appreciate you taking care of Nila, too." Ithsar shook her head. "She's courageous, but headstrong, and takes risks in battle, so I suspect this injury won't be her last."

"I'm happy to help. Thanks for saving my life last night." Kisha dried her hands on a dishtowel. "Are you leaving now?"

Ithsar nodded. "I fear we must hurry north, but I do sense that I'll visit you again."

Kisha swallowed and stroked Thika's chin. Although Ithsar seemed to think she'd be back, any of these assassins or green guards could end up as shadow dragon fodder. Her mother had told her, over and over again, that her grandmother Anakisha's demise had been quick, and no one had expected it. So, instead of pretty, flowery words, Kisha flung her arms around Ithsar and hugged her again.

Dragons' Hold

The sea dragons and the green guards flew north, once again, casting their shadows over the land. But instead of gleeful children greeting them, terrified villagers ran to take cover. Ithsar and Saritha passed over charred farmhouses and ruined farms on the outskirts of settlements. People cowered under the eaves of barns or in copses of trees.

They flew on.

Soon they passed over blackened meadows and came to a village that was nothing but smoking ruins. Tharuks were milling around, hunting through the wreckage.

There were no other signs of life.

Goren swooped on his dragon, Rengar, to fly alongside Saritha and Ithsar. "Do you want to go down?" he called. "We could easily wipe out those monsters."

"Let's fry those beasts," Saritha snarled.

And draw the attention of more shadow dragons that could be lurking nearby, stopping them from heading north.

Images cascaded through Ithsar's mind.

The sky was teeming with shadow dragons. Yellow eye-beams sliced rider and dragon alike. Smoke and flame wreathed the sky, and more dark dragons poured over the horizon, blackening the heavens.

An overwhelming sense of urgency rushed through her. "No," Ithsar called. "We must press north. Time is short."

Goren thrust an arm at the beasts below, calling, "You're wasting an opportunity. We should kill those tharuks."

Although Ithsar's chest ached at the destruction and the loss of lives below, and although anger surged through her veins at those awful beasts, she had to stay true to her vision. They had to help Ezaara save the realm. "These villagers are dead already. The shadow dragons in the North are a threat to everyone's future."

A scowl twisted Goren's face, and Rengar wheeled away.

The further north they flew, the worse the destruction was. Charred orchards, crops laid to waste. Bodies strewn across fields. People camped outside in the snow, in makeshift tents made of blankets, their houses in blackened ruins.

Toward nightfall, Goren wheeled his dragon to fly by Ithsar and Saritha again. "See that haze on the horizon?"

A gray pall hung over a city in the distance. Nestled between two rivers near the edge of a forest that went on forever, the town was the largest Ithsar had ever seen. Bigger than Naobia. Roads snaked into the city with bridges spanning the rivers. Towering spires caught the late evening sun, and stone buildings several stories high sat beneath a backdrop of breathtaking mountains. Even further north, more fierce mountain peaks jutted against the horizon.

The city would have been an amazing sight if not for the gray blanket shrouding its beauty.

Goren pointed east. "That's Great Spanglewood Forest." Then he gestured directly north. "The city is Montanara. We should get there by nightfall. From there, it's only a few hours to Dragons' Hold. I suggest we stop for the night just north of the city so our dragons are well rested for when they face their next battle."

Ithsar didn't voice her fears. Visions had been flitting into her mind all day. If shadow dragons and tharuks had overrun the city, perhaps they wouldn't get out of Montanara to fight the battle in the North. The only thing that mattered now was the urgent need to press on.

They flew on, over the edge of Great Spanglewood Forest. Gaping holes had been smashed in the foliage. Trees were still standing, but some were charred to a crisp, dragon carcasses strewn at their roots.

As they approached, smoke rose from pyres in the surrounding fields, coalescing in a gray cloud over the city.

"They're burning the dead," Saritha said. *"But I can't tell if the corpses are friends or foe."*

The stench of burnt foliage and flesh hung in the air. A building on the outskirts of town had chunks of missing masonry. They swooped over the city. Walls were covered in scorch marks, and there were holes in a few roofs. Other snowy rooftops had gouges where dragons had landed, and some were splattered with black and red blood. Another pyre burnt in the town square, sending a dark smoky plume skyward.

The streets were deserted. The *sathir* that hung over the city was as gray and drab as the smoke that wisped over the rooftops.

Ithsar shuddered at the destruction and desolation.

Fangora flapped up. "The green guards said this is usually a thriving city with a vibrant marketplace," Stefan said.

"Not today," Ithsar muttered.

Saritha mind-melded. *"Something's wrong. This is the territory of the blue guards, so they should be patrolling the area, but we haven't seen a single dragon."*

Had they all been killed? Or fled? Or abandoned this city and its inhabitants to their fate?

Ithsar shielded her dark thoughts from her valiant sea dragon. *"How far to Dragons' Hold?"*

"The green guards say we'll be there in a few hours, but Ithsar…"

"What?"

"The dragons are exhausted. And it's cold here, and there's nowhere to swim. Those stringy goats from Last Stop weren't as

fine as a decent feed of fish." Saritha's bone-weariness washed over Ithsar. *"We can't go on. Goren's right. We'll have to stop for the night, and then hunt in the morning, or we won't be fit to fight."*

Ithsar didn't want her sea dragons or the green guards slaughtered because they were too tired to defend themselves, so—despite her dark foreboding that they should push on—she agreed.

§

Ithsar and her wings of sea dragons and green guards spent a restless night under the stars in a freezing cold field north of Montanara. They hadn't dared light a fire in case they were attacked, so the riders huddled on blankets and their dragons draped their wings over them and tucked their snouts underneath, huffing warm breath over them to keep them from freezing.

Ithsar rose early, as usual, to train with Stefan.

After the dragons had hunted, fished in the nearby river, and replenished their strength, they flew up over the mountains behind Montanara and onward, north, toward the fierce peaks of Dragons' Hold. A dark ravine split the wild fields to the east, in a rip that led to the base of mountains that rose like jagged fangs from the plains.

Bitter air nipped at Ithsar. She tugged her cloak tighter.

After hours traversing the plains, the dragons finally ascended the piercing peaks.

Saritha mind-melded, *"Meet Dragon's Teeth, the valiant sentinels that protect Dragons' Hold."*

At last they were here, at the home of Ezaara—she of the golden hair, the Queen's Rider—and the dragons that patrolled Dragons' Realm. Ithsar let out a sigh of relief. They sped up the pristine slopes, their wingbeats thundering off the mountainside.

"Ithsar…" Saritha melded.

Her dragon's tone was ominous. *"What is it?"*

"I can't see any dragons here. The green guards are saying that the air is usually full of them."

The dragons crested the fierce peaks and glided over a beautiful basin, a silver lake glinting in the sun, nestled among bristling carpets of pines. But that beauty was marred by the carnage below. A stony clearing was strewn with carcasses of dark dragons, colored dragons, and the bodies of tharuks and dragon riders. Wisps of smoke trailed across the basin. The stench of charred flesh rose up to greet them.

Within the peaks of Dragons' Hold, everything was silent, except for the swish of the dragons' wingbeats whispering off the soot-and-blood-stained mountainsides.

Saritha snarled. Fangora, Nilanna, Rengar, and Ramisha answered. Their roars echoed across the basin and bounced off the peaks. Ithsar tugged her heavy cloak again, but the cloak and her thick winter garments did nothing to stop the chill permeating her bones.

They were too late. Dragons' Hold had been devastated.

Ithsar's throat tightened. Were Roberto and Ezaara still alive?

The *sathir* in this basin was stained gray—bleak despair hung over Dragons' Hold, making Ithsar's bones ache. Save the plants and trees, there was nothing here, no one alive, and nothing worth saving.

Misha and Nila turned to her, their faces stark with shock at the torn and bloody carcasses of the dragons below. Corpses of reds, blues, greens, and even orange and purple dragons, lay torn on the blood-congealed stones. Tharuk limbs, bodies, and heads were strewn among them. And shadow dragons, so many shadow dragons. Whoever had killed them had put up a valiant fight.

Ithsar scanned the corpses for the multi-hued dragon she'd seen in her vision, for a Naobian face, or a glimpse of golden hair.

Nothing. Not a sign of her friends.

Even Goren and Stefan's faces were wan. The other assassins and green guards mirrored their grief.

Saritha's usually comforting rumble didn't help Ithsar feel much better.

"Dragons' Hold was never our destination," the queen of the sea dragons said. *"Although this is a shock, think, Ithsar: the vision you showed me was different, over a forest. We just have to find that forest."*

Ithsar searched her memories. Her vision hadn't been of this pine forest surrounding the lake.

Saritha gained altitude, her mighty wings beating at the frigid air as they sped higher, trailed by dragons. They raced over the lake, searching, the green and blue dragons fanned out behind them, their reflections like tiny dragonets on the lake's silvery surface.

"Such a beautiful lake, but we will not swim here, not while death taints this basin. Not while we must search for our friends." Saritha soared higher. *"Look, Ithsar. What's that?"*

Ithsar gazed over the peaks of Dragon's Teeth. To the southeast, a dark stain hung over Great Spanglewood Forest, shot with tiny pinpoint flashes of light.

Dragon flame.

"That's our destination." Her fist high in the air, Ithsar let out a bloodcurdling cry.

The sea dragons and green guards twisted and backwinged, following Saritha and Ithsar as they surged up over the eastern peaks of Dragon's Teeth. The assassins and dragon riders loosed battle cries that stirred Ithsar's blood. Their dragons bellowed as they crested the peaks, their roars rumbling through Ithsar's bones.

They still had a long, hard flight east before they reached that distant smear of black lit up by bursts of flame.

They swooped down the far side of Dragon's Teeth over Great Spanglewood Forest—an enormous carpet of green bordered by the nearby Northern Alps, and spread for hours of flight, all the way to distant peaks in the east.

"*When I was young, my father wove spellbinding tales of spangles, magical beings that lived in Great Spanglewood Forest.*" Ithsar paused. Gods, how she wished her father had lived to fly on dragonback with her and see this wondrous realm. She'd been so tiny when he'd told those tales, but she'd never forgotten them. Even after he died, she'd lain awake at night, missing him and reciting his stories to keep him alive. Funnily enough, it had worked. Although it was hard to remember his face, his stories lived on inside her. "*Do you know if it's true, Saritha? Is there really magic among the trees?*"

"*My mother Queen Aquaria told me spangles exist. We have something similar in the Naobian Sea, tiny glimmering beings of light that shape the currents in the sea.*"

Dragons beat their wings, racing over the snowy pines. Here and there, Ithsar spied carcasses of shadow dragons among the trees. The northerners must have been fighting these beasts for a while.

Dark visions swirled around Ithsar.

A black swarm of screeching shadow dragons; blinding beams of yellow light slicing open blue dragons and rending limbs from greens; a silver dragon howling with grief; a strange yellow beam streaming from a metal box into the sky; roiling flame and riders screaming; strange mages with identical faces, shooting green balls of fire from the back of dark shadow dragons. Bleak despair shuddered through her bones, making them ache.

Ithsar mind-melded with the queen of the sea dragons. "*Saritha, it's been an honor to fly with you.*" She tried to force her vision to show her a glimpse of her future with the queen, but there was nothing. Only emptiness. "*You changed my life.*"

"*Ithsar,*" the queen melded. "*We've found the battle, so be of good cheer. Don't give up hope yet.*"

Ithsar nodded, throat too tight to speak, mind too tangled with dark visions to feel anything but desolation. She patted Saritha's scaly hide and they flew on, the thunder of her heart drowning out the rustle of hundreds of dragon wings.

§

As they sped across the treetops dusted with snow, another vision drifted through Ithsar's head.

A woman was riding an enormous silver dragon. The shimmering silver sathir *around the two nearly blinded Ithsar. This woman had a good heart, a strong heart. Her* sathir *was pure and vibrant, glimmering in the waning sun.*

Silver tendrils snaked out from the woman's sathir *and enveloped a man riding a bronze, a young male rider on an orange dragon, and Ezaara riding a multi-hued dragon.*

A mage on a shadow dragon blasted mage fire at Ezaara.

There was a flash of silver. The woman screamed and leaped, her dark hair flowing in the wind as her lithe body shot into the path of the roiling mage flame. Within moments, the woman was a pillar of fire.

"Ma! Ma!" Ezaara screamed. "Zaarusha! No, not Ma."

The dragon queen roared, diving after the burning woman. The silver and bronze dragons dived too, nearly colliding in their quest to snatch the burning body.

The towering pillar of green mage fire flared in the sky, and then the woman's silver sathir *and the fire snuffed out. Her ashes swirled in the wind from the dragons' wingbeats.*

The silver dragon stretched her neck skyward and howled, the mournful keening echoing through Ithsar's chest. The bronze joined her and they speared through the mass of shadow dragons, chasing the mage that had killed Ezaara's mother.

The dragon queen's roars shook the sky, making Ithsar gasp. Ezaara screamed and snatched up her bow. Roberto and Erob at her side, Ezaara shot an arrow into the breast of a mage and another at a dark dragon's eye.

As the vision cleared, Ithsar gazed out over the forest at the dark swarm of dragons they were heading for. Had this happened yet? Or was it yet to pass? Perhaps she could prevent it.

"Faster, Saritha, we must save Ezaara's mother." No sooner than she thought the words, there was a brilliant flash of silver and then a blazing green flame lit up that dark cloud, burning as it plummeted, then extinguished completely.

A jolt hit Ithsar's chest, as if she'd been punched, and she knew Ezaara's mother was dead.

Mage Gate

Straight ahead, Ithsar saw the landscape as she'd seen it in her vision: a winter forest sprawled before her, patches of snow in dark shadows, and grass peeking through in the sunlit clearing. And there was the metal chest she'd seen with the strange yellow beam of light jutting from it. Above it all, spread like a giant awning above an oasis, was a legion of foul beasts spitting fire and shooting yellow beams from their eyes. Mages rode on their backs, lobbing green flame.

There was a flash of multi-hued scales and a cry rang out, "Ithsar!" Blonde hair swirling in the breeze from thousands of wings, Ezaara punched her bow high in the air. She was riding an enormous dragon, the hundreds of hues on its scales rippling in the light as the beast flew.

Thank the *dracha* gods. Ezaara was alive.

"*Zaarusha, the dragon queen and fearless leader of Dragons' Realm, welcomes us,*" Saritha said.

Joy thrummed inside Ithsar's breast, a surging, bucking beast. Moons before, Ezaara—she of the golden hair—had healed her, making her fingers whole, and helped Ithsar discover the power of her *sathir*. And Roberto had restored her faith that kind men like her father still existed. Now, at last, she could repay them.

Ithsar punched her fist into the air, too, shrieking the ancient *Sathiri* battle cry, "Avanta!"

Saritha's jade scales glinted with silver like a brooding sea as the mighty sea dragons and brave assassins surged into the mass

SEA DRAGON

of dark dragons. Green guards speared through clusters of dark dragons, breaking groups apart so they could pick them off.

Screeches and howls ripped through Ithsar's mind. Gritting her teeth, she focused on the *sathir* of the shadow dragons—a purple so dark it was almost black, the shadowy stain rippling around the foul creatures.

A huge dragon swooped down toward Saritha, its dark, ragged wings blocking the sunlight. Saritha snarled and shot a jet of flame at the beast. Fangora dived past, chasing another shadow dragon, his flame scorching the foul beast's tail. More shadow dragons blasted flame at dragons of orange, gold, bronze, purple, blue, green, and red.

Saritha dived, spitting fire at a dark dragon who was chasing a blue. Ithsar whipped her bow from her back and an arrow from her quiver, and fired. The arrow plunged into a shadow dragon's neck, but it writhed and bucked. With a swipe of its talons, it freed the arrow and breathed a swathe of flame at the blue dragon, who roared down into the forest and crashed into the trees.

Saritha gave chase. Ithsar fired another arrow, meeting her mark. It pierced the back of the shadow dragon's skull, and in a writhing heap of flaming wings, it let out a piercing shriek, and plummeted into the trees, setting them ablaze.

With a flip of emerald wings, Goren's dragon shot past her, and the green guard leader flashed a grin. Ithsar grinned back. She didn't need his acknowledgment, but it was nice to know he'd noticed.

Heat wafted from the forest below, but they had no time to investigate as Saritha spun to deflect the attack of another shadow dragon. Diving at them, its ragged wings outstretched, it breathed fire. They wheeled, but couldn't shake the dragon off.

The dragon spurted a jet of flame at Saritha. The courageous sea dragon bucked, narrowly avoiding her flank being singed.

A yell cut through the mayhem. Roberto swooped in on Erob—the mighty blue *dracha* Ithsar had met at the oasis. Erob blasted flame at the shadow dragon. It clawed at its flaming wings, trying to extinguish the fire, but the blaze was too great.

Gods, that screaming, always that infernal screaming in her head.

Then a flaming ball of green fire shot across Saritha's head near Ithsar's face. She leaned back, the stench of her own burnt hair jamming itself up her nostrils. Ithsar whipped her head around and loosed an arrow before she was upright. It sailed toward a young female mage with blonde hair riding a shadow dragon and lobbing fireballs at the dragon riders. Behind her another dragon swooped in, an identical mage upon its back.

"A mage fighting her own kind? And two the same? I don't understand."

"Zaarusha says they're evil. Grown from real mages, but unnatural fake mages, made by Commander Zens."

"Strong magic indeed." If he was growing mages, what hope did they have? No matter how many they killed, Zens could grow more. Ithsar loosed an arrow, but one of the mages flung a fireball at it, and the arrow disintegrated in a burst of green flame. She fired two arrows in rapid succession as Saritha blasted a huge volley of flame. The mages wheeled off after a red dragon.

Ithsar was about to chase them when Fangora shot by. "Look out," Ithsar called as a shadow dragon wheeled for Stefan, opening its maw.

Ithsar fired an arrow into the beast's cavernous mouth. It screamed. Its head jerked back, its flames shooting skyward and missing Stefan. Ithsar followed up with another arrow, piercing the beast's eye ridge, the shaft driving deep into its face. It clawed at its head and plummeted to the forest below.

Face pale with shock, Stefan turned to Ithsar, held up two fingers and pointed at her.

Two saves to her.

Their dragons beat their wings and headed into the towering mass of rolling flame, dark shadows and howling beasts. Saritha breathed fire. Ithsar and Stefan fired arrows. Heat roiled around them as they bucked and twisted, trying to keep out of the paths of the fiery beasts' flames.

§

A shadow dragon charged at Ithsar.

"Let's take this one together," Stefan yelled, swooping at its stomach.

Saritha flamed the dragon's maw, while Fangora fried its wings. Stefan shot an arrow at its belly and Ithsar fired, her arrow punching through the beast's skull.

A cry of triumph rent the sky. "Nice shot," Stefan yelled.

Goren swooped past on his dragon. He punched his fist high in the air and called, "Well done."

Ithsar nearly fell out of her saddle. Knock her down with a vulture feather—Goren had actually praised her! She grinned back and rose in her stirrups to shoot at a snarling dark dragon chasing a blue.

As the dragon dropped, Ithsar cast about. A lull in battle was rare, but soon more dragons would be upon them. A dark cloud of them was rushing in. She grabbed a waterskin and held it up in a toast to Stefan. He grabbed his too, and, together, they swigged down some water, then stowed the skins back in their saddlebags. Nocking an arrow to her bow, Ithsar scanned the battle.

Below, men were battling tharuks among the trees, leaving a swathe of dead and wounded behind them—both tharuks and humans. An enormous barrel-chested man, with two strong fighters beside him, led the warrior troops. They hacked and cut their way through the tharuks, surrounded by brave woman and men fighting those beasts, tooth and nail.

"We can't help there," Ithsar said. *"We'll accidentally flame our own."*

Saritha rumbled in agreement and shot north over the trees. A towering inferno of green flame ripped through the forest, driving a horde of tharuks toward a river choked with weeds that waved greedy tentacles above the water. Green fireballs shot from the river, killing tharuks. More tharuks plunged into the water, trying to escape the fire. Bolts of green mage fire slammed into some, while tentacles grasped others and dragged them down, gurgling, to their deaths.

Some clever mage must be hiding underwater. But what were those awful tentacles?

As they flew over the inferno, unbearable heat crackled through the air, making Ithsar's skin itch, and then they were behind the green flames. Was that a man down there? *"Saritha, get lower."*

The sea dragon queen circled above a young mage—Naobian from the looks of him—extinguishing pockets of fire behind him and funneling the wall of mage flame so it drove the tharuks into that seething river. All that fire, from one man…

"By the dracha *gods, he's a powerful mage."*

"Indeed. He and the mage in the river have these beasts under control. Our help's not needed here." Saritha shot higher.

"Wait, Saritha. Look."

Two tharuks had sneaked around the side of the wall of flames and were creeping up on the mage, about to attack. Ithsar shot an arrow into the front tharuk's head. The other roared and glanced skyward as Saritha blasted it with dragon flame.

Surprised, the mage spun, waved a grateful hand and pressed on, pushing those tharuks with his mage fire into the mages' clever trap.

Saritha flipped her wings and shot up. *"The green guards told me this place is called Mage Gate. Years ago, the mages opened a world gate here and let Commander Zens into Dragons' Realm."*

SEA DRAGON

"Stefan said Zens grows those awful tharuks and shadow dragons, as well as those identical mages you told me about," Ithsar replied.

"No one really understands how, but Erob just told me that Roberto and some young mages have destroyed the place in Death Valley where Zens makes them. They say if we can win this battle and kill Zens, the war will be over."

"Now, that would be something to celebrate."

Glimmers lit up the leaves in the forest below. The foliage was a surging sea of twinkling lights that swirled as squirrels scampered from branches, down tree trunks, to attack the tharuks. Tiny sparkles of light shot from the trees and wrapped themselves around a young dark-haired boy. He flung out his arms. Foxes crawled out of holes, biting tharuks' legs. Wolves raced through the trees and flung themselves at the monsters. The ground seemed to surge as beetles and rodents swarmed Zens' beasts. Even the trees bowed their branches, thrashing the tharuks.

"Spangles, Saritha! The boy and the spangles are rallying the forest to fight back." Ithsar felt a glimmer of hope. Perhaps they could win this war, after all.

The warriors surged forward, heartened, too.

But a huge tharuk roared, and the tharuk troops rallied, too, slashing through the woodland creatures and hacking them and the men to pieces with their claws.

Saritha dived, but it was hopeless. Ithsar couldn't get a clear shot without hurting the warriors, and Saritha couldn't risk flaming their people. So, they zipped back into the sky to kill shadow dragons.

To the south in a huge clearing, that strange beam of light still streamed from the metal chest she'd seen in her vision, piercing the sky. A dark-haired man with a goatee stood near the chest, with his head back, staring at the beam, his limbs and body frozen. He looked strangely familiar.

Next to the man was an enormous being, with bulbous yellow eyes and dark stubble over his head. Dark shadowy *sathir* wafted around this menacing man, filling Ithsar with a sense of dark foreboding.

Saritha flicked her tail. *"It's no wonder that man gives you a terrible feeling—he's Commander Zens, the one who came through the world gate years ago. He created the tharuks and shadow dragons that are destroying Dragons' Realm."* She angled her head toward the dark-haired man. *"That is the man my mother spoke of, the dragon mage, Master Giddi."*

Now, Ithsar knew where she'd known him from—Queen Aquaria had shown him to her and said, *"This is the dragon mage. Years ago, he saved my life. Aid him in any way you can and send him my greetings. His role in this war is essential, but without your support he will fail and Dragons' Realm will be lost."*

It was unnatural for someone to stand so still. *"Why isn't he moving?"* Oh, by a thousand blazing suns, she hadn't seen *that*. Sickly strands of yellow *sathir* wove from the dragon mage's back toward Commander Zens. *"He's under Zens' control."*

Saritha snarled.

The key to this battle was that metal box with the golden beam streaming from it. Although the *sathir* around the box was neutral, Ithsar was sure it could be used for good or evil—but there was no doubt which course Zens was choosing.

Hordes of tharuks, twenty, thirty, sometimes a hundred deep, surrounded the clearing, protecting their commander. Swarms of shadow dragons circled overhead, staying out of the beam's rays, ready to blast anyone who got near.

"More shadow dragons are coming from the south," Saritha said. *"The blue guards have asked us to fight them."*

A Bright Flame

Ithsar and Saritha sped southward, flanked by Stefan and Nila, with Misha. Three Naobian green guards flew behind them. They charged across the clearing, avoiding the beam of yellow light that shot into the sky. The day was drawing to a close, but the fighting was not over.

A fake mage, male this time, fired an arrow at a blue dragon, and suddenly, the blue whirled upon a red, biting its wings. The red bit back and the blue slashed out and shredded the red's wing with its sharp talons. As the red plummeted, the blue chased, flaming it.

"By the bleeding First Egg!" Stefan yelled. "What was that?"

Ithsar gaped as the fake mage kept firing arrows, and more blue, orange, green and red dragons turned and attacked each other, tiny trails of sickly-yellow *sathir* issuing from their arrow wounds.

"Zaarusha has told me that these arrows contain methimium implants, yellow crystals that can turn a dragon's loyalty to Zens in a heartbeat. Ezaara was shot when she was battling in Lush Valley and only Roberto's quick action saved her."

"Methimium must be how Zens is controlling Master Giddi, the dragon mage," Ithsar mused. When the fake mage raised his bow again, Ithsar shot him in the back.

They plunged over the foliage, blasting flame down at tharuks. Ithsar let an arrow fly.

A tharuk leader fell, trampled by its own troop's boots as they marched onward, straight over the leader's carcass, their large furry bodies breaking saplings and smashing through underbrush.

"Look out," Stefan yelled. Ithsar spun in the saddle.

A cloud of shadow dragons blotted out the waning sun. Their dragons flapped, speeding through the sky to meet them.

Two shadow dragons broke off from the cloud and charged at Saritha, one on either side. Saritha belched flame, but beams from their eyes sliced toward her. She ducked the beams and shot upward, but the shadow dragons clawed at her wings. She furled her wings and dived, and then ascended again. The two dragons stayed on her tail, flanking her and blasting roiling heat. Their dark purple *sathir* enveloped Saritha and Ithsar. She nocked and fired an arrow. Another of those blonde female mages spun on her shadow dragon's back and blasted a green fireball at Ithsar's arrow. It disintegrated in midair.

She fired another and that, too, burst into flame and fell to the forest. A shadow dragon snarled, lunging for Saritha. Ithsar slung her bow into the crook of her elbow and hung onto Saritha's spinal ridge and her saddle as Saritha reared up in the air, clawing at the dragon's wings with her talons.

Another dragon behind them roared and latched on to Saritha's tail with its fangs. The three dragons twisted and plummeted. Ithsar hung onto the saddle with one hand, snatched her dagger with the other, and flung it down toward Saritha's tail. It plunged into the shadow dragon's neck, but the beast hung on, its jaw clamped tight around Saritha's bleeding tail.

Saritha arched her neck and roared in pain and fury. She flailed as the other shadow dragon locked onto her neck with its jaws.

A purple dragon angled through the air, speeding down, her scales glinting with a tinge of gold in the evening sun. Two young riders were astride her back, both blond; one tall, the other with startling green eyes and wearing a mage cloak. The mage raised his hands and a coil of blistering green flame issued from his palms, licking along the shadow dragon clamped to Saritha's tail. The dark dragon roared, opening its jaws and releasing its grip on Saritha's tail and plunging down to the forest.

Misha and her dragon dived at the dragon clutching Saritha's neck, and the purple dragon and blond rider and mage dived off to help a blue being attacked by another dark dragon.

Zens' mage shot fireballs from the shadow dragon's back. Misha ducked, but the fireball glanced her and set her headscarf alight. Her dragon backwinged from the flailing, fighting dragons as Misha dumped the contents of a waterskin over her head. The air stank of singed hair.

Ithsar threw another dagger, the dragons' screeches ripping through her head, but missed. A waste of a good blade. By the blazing *dracha* gods, if only she could let go of Saritha to use her bow.

Saritha yowled as the shadow dragon bit deeper into her neck. Her wingbeats slowed.

"No, Saritha, no!" A sob burst from Ithsar's chest. *"Come on, girl."* She tore her saber from its sheath and leaned out over Saritha's neck, trying to slash the dragon, but her arms were too short.

A battle cry sliced through the air.

Stefan fired an arrow into the shadow dragon's neck. And then Fangora was there, golden eyes blazing. He landed on the shadow dragon's back, shredding its wings with his talons and ripping out chunks of flesh with his teeth. Dark blood sprayed Fangora, Stefan, and Saritha. Fangora grasped the mage in his jaws and flung it from the dragon into the forest. Her body was speared on a massive pine and hung, twitching, in the treetops.

Fangora lashed the shadow dragon's limbs with his tail. His strong jaws lunged into the shadow dragons' neck and he crunched through bone. In a spray of blood, the monster's grip on Saritha's throat loosened and it fell away, crashing through the treetops.

A fate they'd soon share if they didn't gain height.

More dark dragons dived. Misha, Nila, and the green guards wheeled to fight them.

Saritha was panting, her neck and tail dripping blood. Ithsar slid her bow out and fired an arrow deep into the belly of a shadow dragon above. And then another, and another. Her dragon's sathir was shimmering, her waves of pain washing over Ithsar. *"We have to get you to a healer."*

"Soon. First, we must fight these beasts," Saritha muttered.

More shadow dragons dived at Saritha, fangs bared and snarling.

A mage shot a green firebolt at Misha, whose dragon shied away. And then Nila lunged in, her dragon attacking the beast with a plume of fire. Nila shot an arrow at the shadow dragon. The arrowhead buried itself deep in its belly. It roared and spun, beating its leathery wings.

Nila grinned. "Come on, you awful coward," she yelled and fired another arrow.

It hit the beast's jaw, but disintegrated in a burst of flame as the shadow dragon shot fire at Nila and knocked her from her saddle in a ball of flame. Nilanna roared and pounced on the beast, shredding it with her talons and letting out a mournful howl that shuddered down Ithsar's spine, rocking her in the saddle.

Nila's bright, vibrant orange *sathir* winked out like an oil lamp snuffed between a great god's fingertips. Her body thudded through the trees and landed in a smoking heap.

Ithsar's chest hollowed. Just like that, Nila's daring, and her wild sense of adventure and fun, were gone. Ithsar's bones ached and her head throbbed. Her throat tightened and a sob burst from her chest.

But there was no time to mourn her friend—a writhing horde of shadow dragons swept at them.

With a cry, Ithsar shot arrows into the beasts' bellies, wings, and skulls. Saritha blasted flame, lashing wings with her tail, clawing beasts with her talons, a snarling mass of vengeance.

Beams from a shadow dragon's eyes sliced at them. They missed, topping a tree.

The green guards, Stefan, and Misha fought, but Saritha's sides were now heaving, her movements slowing.

"Saritha, we must get you to a healer."

"I'm f-fine."

Goren swooped in, waving an arm out over the forest. "Toward the east, there are healers in a clearing. Take Saritha there. That's an order."

Stefan flanked them on Fangora. They headed over the trees, but Saritha lost height rapidly, flying too low, nearly scraping her belly on the treetops. The blood from the fang marks on her throat splattered on strongwoods, turning their snowy foliage pink.

Ithsar swallowed. *"I'm sorry, Saritha. I was too tempestuous. We should've stopped fighting earlier."*

"It doesn't matter," Saritha said, turning her head toward Ithsar, her eyes half-closed and wingbeats slowing.

"It does matter. You matter." Ithsar choked on a sob.

Beside them, Stefan yelled, *"Go, Saritha, we're nearly there. Fly!"*

His cry spurred on the queen of the sea dragons. She swept over the forest and landed with a thud at the edge of the woods.

A pale-faced young boy with lake-blue eyes rushed toward them, bearing a waterskin.

Ithsar slid from the saddle and held up a hand. "No, not water. Do you have any piaua? My *dracha* is badly hurt."

His eyes round, the boy nodded. "Yes, this is piaua."

Saritha's head slumped to the ground. The boy rushed over and tipped pale-green juice from the waterskin, rubbing handfuls of piaua juice into Saritha's gaping neck wounds.

"*That burns,*" Saritha murmured as her eyes slid shut.

Ithsar raced to her head and grasped her snout in her hands. "*Saritha, it's a good burn. This will heal you, just hold on.*" A dark hole gaped in Ithsar's belly, threatening to engulf her. By the *dracha* gods, Saritha had to make it. She had to. "*Hold on, Saritha. Please.*"

Saritha's eyelids flickered. "*Yes, Ithsar. For you, I will.*"

Ithsar bit her lip, unable to tear her gaze from the wounds on Saritha's neck as the boy slowly healed each layer of tissue, the muscle and flesh knitting together before Ithsar's eyes.

Fangora thudded down beside Saritha and nudged her with his snout, huffing warm breath over her and Ithsar. Stefan dismounted and rushed over to the healer, holding out a mug from his saddlebags.

Ithsar bristled. He wanted a drink at a time like this?

"Please, give me some juice so I can heal her tail wound," Stefan panted.

By the *dracha* gods, he'd only been trying to help. "Thank you, Stefan," Ithsar murmured. Nila's bright flare of *sathir* flashed through her mind again, and she was sure her chest would break in two.

Stefan reached into his pocket and pulled out a grubby package. "Here, Ithsar."

As he dashed off to Saritha's tail, she opened it and found a piece of smashed chocolate. Eyes burning, she jammed the package in a pocket of her robes, and tears slid down her cheeks.

Rampaging Tharuks

Ithsar ran her fingers over the new pale scars on Saritha's neck. *"Does it hurt anymore? Are you feeling weak? You lost quite a bit of blood."*

"No, it doesn't hurt. No, I'm not weak, and yes, I'm ready to fight again."

"I didn't ask you that."

"I know, but I'm telling you," Saritha snapped. *"For the sake of everyone we've lost today, and for their dragonets, eggs, and littlings, we must get back into the sky and win this war."* Saritha narrowed her golden eyes. *"Are you afraid?"*

"I don't want you getting hurt again."

"Ithsar, you've seen the visions. We must help."

Sighing, Ithsar nodded.

"I don't like to alarm you, when we're so busy taking care of Saritha, but look." Stefan pointed to the sky.

A dark ring of shadow dragons had surrounded Ezaara's dragons and was growing ever tighter, herding them toward something. "Where are they taking them?" Ithsar asked.

"I think they're being herded toward the clearing to that strange beam of light."

"Then whatever we do, we must avoid that light." Ithsar turned back to Saritha. *"Tell the sea dragons we're ready to fight."*

"I already have."

The healer-boy brought them a quiver of arrows. "Our master healer died, so I'm working here, not fighting. I see you're running low on arrows. Please, take these."

"Thanks." Stefan grabbed a handful and stuffed them in his quiver.

Ithsar took the rest of the arrows from the boy's quiver and put them in her own, tightening the strap across her chest. Wait, there was something familiar about this boy. "Aren't you the one who worked with the spangles against the tharuks?"

"Yes, I am. My name's Taliesin." He bowed. "Pleased to meet you."

"There's no need to bow to me." Ithsar thumped her hand on her heart.

His serious eyes regarded her, their deep blue nearly piercing her. "Yes, there is. I saw you in a vision, and knew you would help us win this battle."

He'd seen her in a vision? Winning? It didn't feel like they were winning, not with Saritha getting injured.

"Besides," he continued, "one of the green guards told me you have visions too, just like me, Lovina, and Ezaara's father, Hans. It's always nice to meet someone else with the gift." He grinned. "And it's also nice to meet a leader who's so young."

She chuckled. "I'm sure it is. Nice to meet you, Taliesin. Thank you for your help."

Their dragons rose from the healers' clearing, leaving the wounded on bedrolls in the muddy snow beneath the trees. Sea dragons joined Saritha and Fangora, forming a spearhead, and rushed over the forest, their wingbeats dislodging snow from the treetops in soft wet clumps.

Tharuks surrounded the clearing in a thick ring, fighting with warriors. Overhead, the wingbeats of hundreds of dragons thundered through the sky—shadow dragons, Dragons' Realm dragons, and those that had been turned with methimium, attacking their own. The screeching shadow dragons made it hard to think.

That metal box's gold beam of light pierced the dusky clouds.

"Where's Ezaara?" Stefan called, pointing at Zaarusha as she ascended from a low hill near the clearing, riderless, with Erob, at her side.

"Roberto's missing too." Ithsar scanned the clearing and surrounding fighters, and caught a glimpse of Ezaara's colorful sathir, wending its way from the bottom of the hill toward the clearing.

Saritha spun to flame a shadow dragon, and Fangora chased it off. By the time Ithsar glanced below again, there was a flaming tunnel of mage fire cutting through the ring of tharuks into the clearing. The huge fighter she'd seen leading the warriors charged through the tunnel with Roberto at his side, warriors pouring through behind them.

Warriors fought and battled to keep that tunnel of flickering green flame open. Ithsar gasped. They couldn't see a swarm of tharuks approaching from the southeast, about to provide reinforcements. She scanned the clearing and could only see Roberto, the barrel-chested man and other warriors. There was a tiny glimmer of multi-hued sathir, but no Ezaara. Worry gnawed at her. *"Saritha, please ask Zaarusha where Ezaara is."*

A heartbeat later, Saritha answered, *"She's down there, wearing an invisibility cloak."*

Ithsar signaled to her assassins and they speared behind her and Stefan toward the swarm of tharuk reinforcements sneaking through the forest with as much stealth as a herd of stampeding camels. Tusks glinted in the last rays of the sun as the furry monsters barged through undergrowth.

Sea dragons wheeled above the forest, trying to blast flame down between towering trunks. Tharuks ducked behind trees and slunk through bushes. Dragon fire surged past foliage, melting snow and making leaves smolder.

"We're going to set the whole forest alight if we're not careful," Ithsar said.

"Our sea dragons could surround them and set the trees on fire to cut off their path," Saritha—not so helpfully—suggested.

This was dragon fire, not mage flame that could be controlled to only burn what was intended. *"If we set the forest on fire, the casualties could be too great."*

Ithsar yanked a rope from her saddlebag and tied it around the saddle, then waved to her Robandi assassins. *"We're going down, Saritha."* Before her dragon could object, she leaped.

Ithsar swung through the trees, to Saritha's mournful howl. *"I don't want to lose you. Be careful."*

Stefan, Misha and countless orange-robed women dropped to the forest floor and ran to attack the tharuks. The assassins spun and slashed, fur flying, dark blood spraying, hewing down tharuks—an orange whirlwind against an endless mass of dark fur, tusks and beady eyes.

Ithsar cried, "Avanta." She plunged her saber into the belly of a wiry brute and kicked its body away, yanking her saber free. Oh, these beasts stank. She wrinkled her nose and spun, hacking through the arm of another tharuk. It crumpled to its knees and she drove her saber through its back and flicked her throwing knife into the neck of another running at her.

As Ithsar retrieved her weapons, Misha slashed a tharuk across the snout, and Stefan parried another's claws. A beast lunged, swiping for Ithsar's head. She ducked, but it sliced her hair and a dark lock fell to the ground.

Stefan whirled in and plunged a dagger up under the beast's chin through its jaw and into its brain. The beast keeled toward him, but he threw it backward. Panting, he bent to grab his weapon, and then grinned and held up three fingers.

She groaned and rolled her eyes.

SEA DRAGON

"Watch out!" Stefan's cry was too late.

The stench of tharuk overpowered her as a beast grabbed Ithsar, its strong furry arms a vice around her ribs.

Stefan's knife glinted. Ithsar flung her head to one side. His blade whistled past her, making a wet thud. The *dracha* gods only knew where it had hit. A spray of dark stinking blood gushed over the back of her neck and the tharuk fell away behind her.

She shook off the slick blood as Stefan held up four fingers. Shaking her head, Ithsar yanked the blade from the monster's neck and threw it to him. "Good shot."

He caught it. "Thanks. That's four to me, only three to you." He gave her another one of his infuriating grins.

Ithsar wiped her hand on her robes and hefted her hilt.

"Incoming tharuks," Misha yelled behind them.

A sword in each hand, Stefan swung them like windmills. The beasts hesitated, following the blades with their eyes.

Ithsar sneaked around behind a bush and slashed her saber across the back of a tharuk's knees as Stefan drove his sword into the eye of the other. Plunging her saber into the tharuk's back, Ithsar finished it off, and straightened.

"Behind you!" Stefan yelled.

A flash of dark fur caught on the edge of Ithsar's vision. She ducked and rolled as a tharuk slashed its sharp claws where she'd just been.

Stefan hacked at the beast. It slashed at him. *Dracha* gods, had it hurt him? He was so coated in dark tharuk blood, it was hard to tell. No, he was swinging again, hacking at the beast's arm, then its belly. It collapsed to its knees, snout open to the sky, roaring. Stefan drove his sword through the monster's maw and out the back of its throat.

He placed his hands on his knees, catching his breath. "Five," he puffed.

§

Stefan grinned, his face and clothes splattered with gore and tharuk blood.

Ithsar knew she didn't look much better.

"Did you see that? Five," he panted. "You only saved me three times—and you're the assassin." He hunched over, his hand clamped onto his side, breathing hard.

"Then we're lucky I drilled you, aren't we?" Ithsar narrowed her eyes.

Red blood was seeping over Stefan's fingers. Within moments, his hand was stained scarlet.

"Let me look at that." Ithsar tried to remove his hand, but Stefan hissed in pain. *"Saritha, come quick. Stefan's hurt."*

Ithsar waited agonizing heartbeats, but there was no answer. *"Saritha?"*

Roars ripped through the forest. Fangora landed on a sapling, crushing it with his talons, his tail lashing the underbrush.

"Sorry, I was telling Fangora." Saritha said, circling the trees.

Stefan leaned heavily on Ithsar's shoulder, still clutching his side. The blood was spreading across his jerkin. Ithsar helped him over to Fangora, who lay as flat as he could against the ground so she could shove Stefan into the saddle. She clambered up behind him.

"Quick, to the healers," she said aloud to Fangora, then mind-melded with Saritha. *"Does he know where to go?"*

"Yes, he remembers and thanks you for letting him transport his rider."

The young green dragon tensed his haunches and leaped above the trees. Teeth gritted, Stefan slumped over the spinal ridge in front of them. Ithsar wriggled forward, arms around him, jamming her short thighs against his long ones, and holding him in place. "Don't you dare let go," she threatened. "Or I'll kill you myself."

Oh gods, had she really just said that? "Just a few moments and we'll be there," she added.

She prayed to the *dracha* gods that her new friend would make it. Her throat suddenly dry, she tried to swallow, but couldn't. So, instead, she hung on to Stefan, willing him to live.

His *sathir* was still green, but shimmering. Nila's had gone out in an instant. She tried to tell herself that this was different, that the healers would fix him, that everything would be all right, but it didn't stop the pounding of her pulse at her throat or the worry that tightened her airways.

Fangora landed gently, backwinging up a storm to slow his descent. This time, a young blonde girl rushed out to meet them, accompanied by a huge warrior with a bandage on his head. The man lifted Stefan from Fangora, as if he were as light as an empty waterskin. Ithsar jumped from the saddle and spread her cloak on the grass next to Fangora. "Please heal him near his dragon."

Fangora huffed warm breath over Stefan's face. The healer lifted Stefan's shredded tunic. Two ugly gaping wounds were ripped in his side.

By the blazing sun, if those claws had gone any deeper…

"Tharuk claws. We've seen a lot of those injuries lately." The healer bit her lip. She was younger than Ithsar—and thin, with red-rimmed eyes. This young girl's *sathir* was the deep blue of mourning. "Usually I'd stitch him, but we don't have time with so many wounded, so he's going to have a scar."

"Better a scar than—" Ithsar swallowed and squeezed Stefan's bloody hand.

"Exactly. Tharuk claws are pretty dirty. Unfortunately, I don't have any clean herb left, so this will have to do." The healer sloshed water over the wound, then patted it dry and dribbled pale-green piaua juice deep into the torn and bloody muscle.

Stefan's eyes were glazed, flitting back and forth, unseeing.

"Hold on, Stefan," Ithsar pleaded. "This will burn like dragon flame, but soon you'll be back on Fangora, ready to fight again."

His eyes cleared and he gazed at her. "Too right," he said, then hissed through gritted teeth as the healer dribbled more piaua juice into his wound.

"You know," he said, "I won. Even at two saves, I won, because I helped save Saritha, queen of the sea dragons. And, without her, you'd be heartbroken."

"Yes," she said, "I would be. You won." She'd never admit that without him, she'd be heartbroken too.

He shuddered, clenching his jaw as the juice burned through him.

Ithsar recalled the burn she'd felt when Ezaara had healed her fingers. Back then, Ezaara had been captive; Izoldia, her jailer; and Ithsar, Ashewar's bullied and tormented servant. She gave Stefan a faint smile. Oh, how her life had changed.

When the deep inner layers of Stefan's muscle had kitted together, the healer dribbled in more juice, progressively healing all the tissue until his skin was whole.

Finally, Stefan's eyes cleared. He sat up and stretched his side. "Thank you." He beamed at the healer. "I didn't catch your name."

"I'm Leah." The healer smiled. "I'm glad to help. Many moons ago, Ezaara healed me, so now I share my gratitude by healing others." She packed up her leather pouch.

Stefan raced back over to Fangora. Saritha landed with an injured warrior on her back. Behind her, more dragons were alighting, bringing injured riders.

Ithsar gently touched the healer's arm. "Have you lost someone you love?"

"Yes," she whispered, eyes pooling with tears. "The Master Healer, Marlies, Ezaara's mother. She taught me, Ezaara, and Taliesin everything we know."

"Do you mind me asking if she rode a silver dragon?"

Leah nodded. "Yes, she did." She went to help the incoming wounded.

So that had been the brilliant flash of silver they'd seen in the sky on the way to Mage Gate.

Ithsar picked up her cloak, now stained with Stefan's fresh blood, and threw it over her shoulders. It was an honor to wear the blood he'd shed in saving her. Then she helped Leah get the wounded warrior off Saritha's back.

As she and Stefan mounted their dragons and sped above the trees on dragonback, that same blinding beam of light cut through the evening sky, but now it was alive, writhing with gold, silver, and black shadowy *sathir*.

WORLD GATE

Shadow dragons lunged through the air at Saritha and Fangora. Ithsar ducked a green fireball, then shot the fake mage before he could fire another. Thank the blazing sun, Taliesin had given her more arrows. Saritha blasted flame at the mage's shadow dragon and it dropped to the clearing, squashing a horde of tharuks. Hopefully, not any warriors.

A silver thread of *sathir* raced from the dragon mage's hands up the yellow beam of light, as a gold thread rushed from a slim crack in the sky down to meet it. Dark shadowy *sathir* swarmed up behind the dragon mage's silver thread, shrouding it. Ithsar knew that if the shadows overtook the silver, all would be lost.

The dragon mage, Giddi, fell to his knees, screaming, "Mazyka!" His desperate cry reverberated through the clearing and echoed through Ithsar's gut, striking a chord deep within her.

The silver thread shot above the clawing shadows and touched the gold. The world exploded in a flash of light.

A rift appeared in the sky and a golden dragon flew through, a woman with flaming red hair upon its back. A mighty battle cry ripped from the woman's throat.

Smaller golden dragons poured through the crack, ridden by mages with blue light springing from their fingers.

"Mazyka," the dragon mage cried.

"Who is she?" Ithsar asked Saritha.

"His wife—the woman who helped the dragon mage break the world and let Commander Zens in," Saritha replied.

Zens thrust his hands up. With a surge, the shadows raced from his hands up the entwined silver and gold threads, and a dark crack opened in the sky. Metal beings glimmered behind it. A shining metal weapon poked through, blasting flame. One of the smaller golden dragons dropped from the sky, dead.

The *sathir* threads grew thicker, twining around one another to form a golden rope threaded with silver. Dark shadows swirled from Zens around Master Giddi. Head swaying from side to side, the dragon mage held out his hands and roared.

Zens laughed as a metal figure flew through the dark rift, shooting its weapon, felling green, gold, and blue dragons. The legs of more metal beings poked through the rift. Another dropped down. Its metal body gleaming, it fired at a blue dragon, destroying its wing in a burst of flame. The dragon plummeted, roaring in agony.

The metal being chased it, propelled by some unseen magic, blasting more fire.

Goren swooped in. Ithsar, Goren, and Stefan fired at the beings, but their arrows clattered off their metal carapaces.

What manner of powerful beings were these—made of metal and wielding tubes of fire? Fear skittered through Ithsar's bones. They could never withstand an army of these creatures.

Below, Master Giddi ripped off his cloak and shirt, his torso naked. Dark tendrils of mist leaked from methimium arrow wounds in his back, winding around his neck and face.

Zens laughed.

White light burst from a crystal around the dragon mage's neck and swept around the clearing, banishing the shadows. Zens was thrown onto his back. Tharuks and warriors fell to their knees, shielding their eyes.

The light from the crystal on Giddi's chest blazed through the sky, hitting the dark rift. The crack closed, shutting out the metal beings—hopefully forever.

Mazyka's golden dragon swooped upon the remaining metal beings. She blasted them with plumes of blue mage fire. They exploded, metal shards spraying across the forest.

Saritha, Fangora, and Rengar rocked in the air, winging up to dodge the debris. Golden dragons dived and swooped after shadow dragons, mages on their backs shooting blue fireballs from their fingertips at the fake mages upon the dark dragons' backs. Each time a fake mage was hit, it disintegrated into ash. Suddenly, the dark dragons started attacking one another, ripping off each other's limbs and shredding wings.

"What's going on?" Ithsar asked.

"I felt a mental ripple. I think the dragon mage has wrested his control back from Zens and has commanded the shadow dragons to attack one another."

Down in the clearing, Mazyka aimed a metal tube—like the one that had spat fire through the world gate—at Master Giddi, who collapsed.

"She's hurt him!" Ithsar cried out.

"I don't think so. Look again."

Mazyka was cutting the methimium crystals out of Giddi's back, right there in the middle of the field.

Mages on dragonback chased fighting shadow dragons. Ithsar dispatched dark dragons and fake mages with her arrows, the other assassins felling more of the foul beasts. *"It's much easier picking them off when none of them are flaming us. Almost too easy."*

There was a roar, and a blast of heat roiled through the air overhead. Ithsar spun. *"Blue dragon, incoming from above."* The dragon was aiming for Saritha. *"It must have a methimium implant."*

Saritha ducked and dodged but the blue had the advantage of altitude, so Saritha sped off, heading over the forest, flame nearly singeing her wingtips.

By the blazing desert sun, she was a fool for relaxing her guard. If anything happened to Saritha—

SEA DRAGON

Fangora appeared, and the blue dragon screeched and whirled, racing back to the clearing. Stefan held up six fingers and pointed to his chest.

"That was hardly a save," Ithsar yelled, relieved all the same. "Neither of you even fired."

"I can't help it if I'm so fierce and ugly I scare away the most terrible foes," Stefan called.

Ithsar laughed. Stefan was anything but ugly, but she wasn't about to tell him that. Fangora wheeled off to fight another shadow dragon.

Back in the clearing, golden dragons dropped a shadow dragon carcass onto the grass and lured in the methimium-turned dragons to feast.

"Disgusting." Saritha's distaste washed over Ithsar. *"Those were valiant dragons, but Zens has turned them into despicable savages."*

The sight made Ithsar's stomach churn.

Mazyka and a team of warriors shot the turned dragons with metal tubes, and they collapsed, asleep. Mages from the golden dragons clambered over them, digging out their methimium arrowheads.

"Look," Ithsar said. *"Mazyka and her mages are extracting methimium implants from the colored dragons that turned."*

"The battle's not over. Look there, Zaarusha needs help." Saritha shot over the trees toward the river where they'd seen the raging wall of mage flame earlier in the day. That inferno was extinguished now, and the river was choked with tharuk bodies, the grasping tentacles of feeding plants, and a dying shadow dragon.

On the far bank, Ezaara and Roberto were fighting Commander Zens.

But below them, on this side of the river, Zaarusha was flaming a horde of tharuks that were trying to sneak through the trees. If those beasts broke through Zaarusha's defense, Ezaara and Roberto would have no chance. *"Saritha, those tharuks."*

"I was thinking the same thing."

Her dragon dived as Ithsar nocked her bow and fired at a hulking tharuk leading the troop. Her arrow hit the beast between the eyes, and it crashed to the forest floor. Zaarusha belched a swathe of flame across the front of the troop, and Saritha hit them at the back end, while Ithsar fired arrows into the thick of the horde. Tharuks roared and snarled as arrows struck them in the head, thighs, chest, and neck. They yowled, dragon fire licking over their fur and burning them.

Above Ithsar, the sky roiled with fire. Flashes of green mage flame and streaks of blue stabbed through the flames, incinerating dark dragons. Thick clumps of ash floated down, coating her hair and thighs, but still Ithsar kept firing arrows, and the dragons kept flaming until there were only a few tharuks left.

"Zaarusha has asked us to leave the last few tharuks to her, and to check the forest between here and the clearing in case there are more." Saritha ascended above the forest.

"And Ezaara and Roberto? Should we help them kill Zens?" Ithsar glanced down at the riverbank where Zens lay at Roberto's feet, with Roberto's sword at his throat.

"No. Zaarusha says they want that pleasure themselves."

As Saritha wheeled to head back across the forest, Ithsar glanced back to make sure her friends Ezaara and Roberto were safe. Ezaara stalked up behind Roberto and slashed her sword across Zens' gut, a red stain blooming. Then she drove her sword through his throat.

Even without having seen it, Ithsar would've still known Zens was dead. The *sathir* over the forest lightened, as if a great shadow had lifted from the land—like an awning being rolled back so the blazing desert sun could shine.

After the War

Bonfires crackled high in the clearing at Mage Gate as dragons incinerated piles of tharuks, shadow beasts, and even their own kind, who'd died or been killed after being turned by methimium. Ithsar shook her head at the waste of life—although, as an assassin, she would've been trained specifically to kill, had it not been for her deformed fingers.

The piles of burning, reeking flesh turned her stomach.

Stefan nudged her with his elbow. "It almost makes you want to give up fighting, doesn't it?" He scrubbed his eyes with the back of his hand. "We lost some brave riders today."

Misha nodded. "I've never really enjoyed fighting."

Holding her chin up, Ithsar squeezed Misha's hand and swallowed. Nila's bright flickering flame and her zest for life were no more. It was a sore loss for all of them, but Misha had been Nila's closest friend.

She cast about, looking for Ezaara. In the light of the fire, pockets of assassins and dragon riders were chatting, cleaning their weapons, or making food.

Ithsar paced over to the young dragon rider seated near his purple dragon whose scales glinted gold in the firelight. She inclined her head. "You helped me in battle today when those dragons had Saritha in her clutches. Thank you for killing the one latched to her tail." She clasped his hands, then released them.

"It was nothing," An easy grin lit up his soot-smudged, bloodied face. Blue-gray eyes looked from under from his battle-dirty blonde hair. Eyes that sparkled with fun. "I'm Kierion. Nice to meet you,

Ithsar. I've never shaken hands with a chief prophetess before—or an assassin, and lived to tell the tale. Can you predict my future?"

She shook her head, then realized he was teasing her. "No, but one of my assassins may be able to predict your immediate future, or lack of it, if you test their skills with a blade."

He threw back his head and laughed. "Hey, Fenni, come over here."

A tall green-eyed mage with blond hair stalked over and shook Ithsar's hand. "Pleased to meet you. I'm Fenni."

"You're the mage who was riding with Kierion," Ithsar said. "Thanks for your help. Your fireball skills helped save my dragon's life today."

"Did you hear that, Fenni?" Kierion crowed.

Fenni blushed to the tips of his ears. "He's giving me a hard time because fireballs took me ages to master." He grinned. "Seriously, I used to be hopeless."

Ithsar grinned back.

A short Naobian girl raced over and threw her arms around Ithsar, nearly bowling her over. It was strange hugging someone her own size—usually everyone towered over her.

"Hey, Ithsar, I'm Adelina," the girl said. "Thank you for saving my brother." Adelina's voice broke.

Her brother? Ithsar pulled back to gaze at Adelina's olive-back eyes and Naobian complexion. Oh, of course. "I should have realized Roberto was your brother."

Adelina waved a hand. "He's much taller than me, so most people never guess we're related."

It wasn't the height difference as much as their demeanor. Roberto had an air of distrust about him. Adelina was bubbly, her smile bright—they were worlds apart.

Adelina clasped Ithsar's hand. "Ezaara asked me to tell you she had to leave for Dragons' Hold urgently."

Ithsar swallowed a sharp pang of disappointment. So that's where Ezaara was. She'd gone to find out what was left of her shattered people. Ithsar hoped for her sake that her home was still intact. She sighed. Of course, a Queen's Rider would be far too busy to visit with a lowly assassin.

"What do you mean, a lowly assassin?" Saritha growled. *"You're a Queen's Rider too—of the queen of the sea dragons."*

"She said she'd love to see you tomorrow morning at Dragons' Hold to personally thank you for your help." Adelina gave an infectious smile.

"She did?" Ithsar grinned, warmth blossoming her breast.

§

Ithsar and Saritha swooped over the peaks of Dragon's Teeth and into Dragons' Hold. The faint scent of char remained on the breeze, the blackened stones where snow had been melted away, a testament to the bodies that had recently been burned there.

"I see Zaarusha asleep on a ledge on that mountain face," Saritha mind-melded.

The mountainsides above the stony clearing were pockmarked with caves. Some dragons were slumbering on ledges—recovering their strength after the arduous battle—while others flew above the basin, ferrying debris into piles, no doubt for another burning. It took Ithsar a moment to spot Zaarusha. There was space for several dragons on her wide, rocky ledge. An overhang protected the back end, and it was there that Zaarusha was sequestered with her head under her wing. Beside her, Erob was asleep too.

The queen of Dragons' Realm raised her head and looked right at them, tracking Saritha with her eyes as she flew.

"Did you tell her we're coming?" Ithsar's orange robes billowed in the breeze.

"In the sea, we mind-meld when we're visiting another's territory. I thought I'd give Zaarusha the same courtesy. She is another dragon queen, after all."

"Fair enough." Finally, Ithsar would see Ezaara again. Not just a distant glimpse in battle, but a chance to talk to her friend.

Saritha flew in a lazy arc and swooped in to land on the ledge, her talons scrabbling on the rock. *"Zaarusha welcomes you and has told Ezaara you're here. If you don't mind, I'll take a swim later in that beautiful lake."*

"Of course, you can, and please thank Zaarusha." Ithsar leaped off her sea dragon.

"Ithsar!" Ezaara and Roberto appeared at the back of the overhang. Ezaara ran over and they embraced.

"Thank you, Ithsar," Ezaara said. "You changed the tide of the battle. Your sea dragons and the Naobian greens helped us."

"Before I ever met you, I had a vision of us riding into battle together," Ithsar said, her blood thrumming as she remembered. "And then again, when my mother captured you."

Ezaara clasped Ithsar tighter. "I was afraid your mother had killed you because you helped. Gods, I'm glad you're alive."

"Ashewar lives no longer." Sorrow lanced through Ithsar. She would probably always feel this sadness and disappointment, but now she had much more than just a mother who'd hated her. She was the rider of Saritha, and the leader of the Robandi assassins. She'd helped win a war. And she'd found friends who valued her. "I'm now the chief prophetess of the Robandi assassins." She waved her fingers in the air. "And I have fingers that work. Thank you. None of this would've happened without you, Ezaara."

"How in the Egg's name did you become Chief Prophetess? And how did you meet your beautiful dragon?"

"That's a long story," said Ithsar. "And Saritha is hungry and needs time to recover from battle."

"As do you." Ezaara enclosed Ithsar's cool hand in her own warm one. "I suggest Zaarusha takes Saritha hunting and maybe to the lake for a swim, while you and Roberto and I catch up over breakfast."

Roberto laughed and embraced Ithsar. "We'd love to hear your tale."

"That would suit Saritha well. Although she hankers for the sea, she's keen to try your northern lakes." Ithsar grinned. "And I'm famished."

As the dragons flew off together, Ithsar followed them through Zaarusha's den, inside. The Queen's Rider's cavern was more modest than Ithsar had expected—nothing like Ashewar's grand throne room in the Robandi lair under the oasis. There were drawers, a big bed, a beautiful hand-painted wardrobe, a small table, and some chairs. And dragons. Everything was decorated with dragons—the quilt, the rug, the cushions, even the paintings on the wardrobe and the hilts of the two decorative swords mounted on the wall. A dragon tapestry on the far wall had been slashed. Probably by tharuks when they'd overrun the hold.

Ezaara waved a hand. "Sorry, it's a bit of a mess. I'll tidy up eventually, but at the moment, the welfare of my people is more important."

Again, so different to Ashewar.

Roberto pulled three chairs out from the table, and flourished a hand. "Please, take a seat." He sprinkled dried berries from a pouch into three cups, then added water from a waterskin. "I'll ask Erob to heat this brew." He brushed Ezaara's hair with his lips. "Back soon." He wandered out to the ledge as Ithsar and Ezaara sat down.

"It must be nice to have someone care about you like that," Ithsar said.

Ezaara followed him with her gaze, a faint smile on her face. "You know, he wasn't always like this. I positively hated him when we first met. He was so cold and arrogant."

"But he's such a wonderful man now. I could tell that, even back at the oasis."

"Yes, he is. He hid it well." Ezaara gestured at a basket of fruit and some bread. "I'm afraid there's not much else to eat around here. Although we do have a few preserves if you'd like me to fetch some. Tharuks rampaged through the mess cavern and destroyed most of the fresh supplies."

Ithsar bit into a roll of fluffy bread. "I never really had a chance to thank you properly for healing my fingers."

Ezaara laughed. "We were too busy trying to escape a horde of angry assassins. What happened after I left? I was sure Ashewar would be livid."

"Ashewar was. She tried to kill me." Ithsar finished her roll and told Ezaara exactly what had happened.

When she described Stefan's hopeless attack on her, there was a quiet chuckle behind her.

Roberto came over and placed the steaming cups on the table, the fragrant tang of berries wafting toward them.

"What's this?" Ithsar asked.

"Soppleberry tea. One of my favorites." Roberto took a sip. "Luckily." He winked at Ezaara.

"It sounds as if there's a story behind that," Ithsar said.

Roberto's dark eyes, so like her own, were laced with pain. "A while ago, Zens captured and tortured me, then implanted a methimium crystal in my back. When I returned to Dragons' Hold, I was determined to kill Ezaara, but at the last moment, she distracted me with soppleberry tea." He raised his eyebrows, exhaling forcefully. "Even if I hadn't liked soppleberry before, that would be a great reason to make it my favorite."

Ezaara shuddered. "I laced it with woozy weed. He fell asleep within moments. My mother, Marlies…" She bit her lip.

Roberto squeezed her hand and finished for her. "Ezaara and her mother extracted the crystal from my back. Marlies was a great woman, one of the finest healers Dragons' Hold has ever had."

A stray tear on her cheek, Ezaara murmured softly, "It was thanks to my mother that I could fix your fingers."

"She rode a silver dragon, didn't she?" Ithsar asked.

"Yes, she rode Liesar. They'd only been reunited for a few short moons. She sacrificed her life to save me in battle."

"So we've both lost our mothers recently." Ithsar clasped Ezaara's hand and Ezaara squeezed hers back.

"And Roberto lost his father," Ezaara murmured.

"My father sold me to the enemy, who tortured and abused me, and turned me against the ones I loved." Roberto grimaced. "We all have scars. Some of us have done unspeakable things, but now let's make the world a better place."

No matter what their pasts were—despite methimium crystals, murderous mothers, traitorous fathers, and despite the evil monsters that had tried to destroy Dragons' Realm—they could rebuild this realm.

Ezaara put her hand on the table. "Let's make it a place where children may laugh and play in the sun without the fear of being hurt or enslaved."

Ithsar placed her hand on top of Ezaara's. "A place where people may pursue whatever life they want, regardless of where or how they were born."

Roberto placed his hand on top. "A life where mothers and fathers respect and honor their children, and raise them with a sense of dignity and self-worth."

Then Roberto smiled. "Let's start tomorrow. Now, we'll show you around Dragons' Hold."

But Ithsar knew they'd already started rebuilding. From the pride gleaming in Roberto and Ezaara's eyes, they knew it as well.

Reunion

Kisha saw the last of her customers out the door. "Have a lovely evening."

"You too, Kisha, it was a wonderful meal. We're glad you've reopened without those *other* patrons." The gentleman winked, then surreptitiously glanced over his shoulder just to make sure no stray tharuks were listening.

He needn't have feared. The Robandi assassins and green guards had managed to kill most of them and drive the rest away. Hopefully Last Stop would be free of those awful beasts for a while. Kisha walked back to the kitchen, Thika perched upon her shoulder with his tail loosely around her neck, to finish washing the dishes.

She dunked a pan in the tub and scrubbed it. It had been a long day, but a good one. Two days ago, after the Robandi assassins had left the Lost King Inn, Kisha had spread the word around town that she'd be opening to patrons again today. Then she'd rushed back to polish the place until it gleamed. The builder had fixed the front door and the glazier had even managed to replace her window, so even though she had fewer tables and chairs, the inn was in good shape.

She was just putting away the last serving dish when a heavy thud sounded outside the square—an ominous thud, like a shadow dragon landing. Thika's tail coiled tighter as Kisha crept to the window to peek outside.

It wasn't a shadow dragon, but Ithsar on Saritha. Ramisha, Fangora, and Nilanna landed beside her. More sea dragons and green guards wheeled in the air above the town square.

Kisha raced outside as Ithsar dismounted. Ithsar's robes were stained and battle-dirty, but Kisha didn't care. She flung her arms around the chief prophetess. "I'm so glad you're back. I wasn't sure if you'd make it."

Stefan swung out of the saddle and jumped down, his boots thunking on the cobbles. "Thanks to me, she made it." He grinned cheekily. "For a moment there, she was in trouble, but I swooped in and saved her—six times, no less."

Kisha hugged him too, but Ithsar reached past Kisha to slug him on the arm.

Stefan slugged her back.

Kisha glanced around. "Where's Nila?"

Ithsar's smile died.

And Kisha knew. "She didn't make it, did she?" Her throat tightened and her eyes stung.

Nila, gone. Nila, who had laughed as she'd stitched her wound, and told her crazy tales of life in the desert and stories of the underwater world, stoically ignoring the pain in her side—pain that was so bad, she'd been pale and shaking. Nila, who'd swung on the utensil rank in her kitchen to save her from those horrible tharuks.

Nilanna hung back, hunkering down on the edge of the square. She tucked her head under her wing and went to sleep.

Ithsar jerked her head toward the dragon. "It'll take time. For all of us. Nila was a bright star in our lives."

A bright star that had burned out. Had Kisha's grandmother, Anakisha, been like Nila? Although Kisha had never met Anakisha, her mother had told her that she'd been full of life, bold, and not afraid of danger. No one had expected her to be lost in battle.

Kisha forced herself to smile brightly. "Come inside, Ithsar, and call your riders. There's hot stew on the hearth if you'd like some."

"Sounds great." Ithsar forced her own overly-bright smile, and raked a hand through her disheveled hair. Somewhere in battle she must've lost her pretty orange headscarf. Her face was covered in grime and she looked weary.

Thika scrambled from the crook of Kisha's neck, down her forearm and leaped onto Ithsar's arm, racing up to her shoulder. He snuffled her hair and chittered. Ithsar laughed. "Yes, boy, it's good to see you too."

A tiny stab of loss pinged through Kisha. It was fine. Thika was Ithsar's lizard, after all. She'd only been looking after him.

The lizard scampered down the front of Ithsar's robe and burrowed inside, then popped back out, and raced down Ithsar's leg and up Kisha's skirt, onto her forearm again. He perched there, looking back and forth between them both.

Ithsar laughed. "Now that's the funniest thing I've seen in days—apart from Stefan being caught by tharuks down that lane." She waved a hand toward a nearby alley.

"Huh! What about you?" Stefan leaned down and picked up a short end of Ithsar's hair. "You haven't told us yet about how you managed to lose one of your beautiful dark tresses. When exactly did you make the decision to hire a tharuk as a barber?"

Ithsar snorted. "At least my hair's beautiful. When did you decide to wash yours in tharuk blood?"

Misha laughed. "We all decided to do that when we followed you north. Now, will you two stop bickering. Kisha, you mentioned a hearty stew?"

Kisha laughed. "Come inside and tell me everything."

Ithsar groaned. "Don't say that! Stefan will never stop yammering about the six times he saved me."

"There! She admitted it!" Stefan crowed to Misha. "I told you I saved her six times."

Kisha wrinkled her nose. "Well, I'm sorry, but now that I've purged my inn of the stink of tharuk, you're all going to have to take hot baths before dinner."

Ithsar's eyes shone. "Sounds blissful." Her smile was matched by Misha and Stefan's grins.

§

In the end, Kisha didn't have quite enough stew to go around, so Misha and three of the green guards chopped more ingredients and threw them into the cauldron—the same cauldron she'd wanted to hit the tharuk with. They cracked open a few more jars of pickles, and Kisha rustled up some flatbread.

When the food was ready, Kisha bustled out with steaming tureens of stew and baskets of bread, and placed them on the tables.

The Lost King was crammed full of green guards and assassins—many of whom had taken advantage of the bathing facilities upstairs and changed into fresh orange robes or riders' garb. They lounged in chairs, all over the floor, and even stood around the walls as they bit into fresh bread and helped themselves to Kisha's stew.

She sighed. It had been moons and moons since the inn had been this full of anything other than tharuks. She'd only managed to keep the place going so long due to the suppliers who'd taken pity on her and knew she'd be killed if she hadn't kept providing the tharuks with food and ale. Kisha found a quiet corner, ladled herself a bowl of stew, and sat down on the stairs leading up to the bedrooms.

The babble, laughter, and murmuring were like soothing music.

When she'd finished her dinner, Kisha leaned back against the railing on the stairs.

The door opened and Goren, leader of the green guards, stalked in. He wasn't alone.

Kisha's hand flew to her mouth. No, it couldn't be. She looked again. It was. An enormous barrel-chested man filled the doorway, his beard and bushy hair like a dark halo around his friendly face.

He grinned and his voice boomed across the inn. "Kisha, it's great to see you."

Kisha leaped up and propelled herself across the room, racing to meet Giant John. A moment later, she was lifted from the ground as he enfolded her in an enormous bear hug.

"After battling tharuks for days, you're a sight for sore eyes." Giant John placed her back on her feet and grinned. "How are you, girl?"

"It's been interesting." She grinned back. By the First Egg, it was good to see him.

His eyes twinkled in the lamplight. "I like this class of patrons better than the last lot. The sight of those ugly tusky faces guzzling good ale was enough to turn any man's stomach." He slapped a hand against the flat of his stomach, and inhaled deeply. "Something smells good. Mind if we do?"

"Of course. We can't break tradition." Kisha couldn't stop grinning. Her cheeks were already getting sore. "I'm afraid we won't be able to provide your usual seating arrangements." Usually Giant John took two seats or half a bench, but with the scarcity of furniture and the number of dragon riders there tonight, that wouldn't be possible.

He gave a belly laugh. "I don't mind roughing it, as long as I have a soft bed tonight. Got any free rooms? Or have this rowdy lot taken them all?"

"That shouldn't be a problem, as long as you kick a few dragon riders out into the snow."

Giant John flexed his biceps and grinned. "I'll get right onto it."

Goren groaned. "And I thought we were done with fighting. Come on, let's eat."

Kisha went into the kitchen to fry up a few eggs, knowing they were Giant John's favorite.

Giant John followed her in. "I saw tharuk tusk gouges in the tabletops out there. I don't suppose there'd be any bacon left after those brutes have rampaged through the place, would there?"

"No, but I have salted pork. I can fry that for you, if you'd like."

The pork was soon sizzling. Giant John leaned back against a counter and folded his arms. As Kisha reached up for her spatula, he ducked to avoid the utensil rack swinging overhead. Kisha flipped the eggs.

"You look tired. Here, let me do that." Giant John picked Kisha up and sat her on an empty benchtop—something he'd been doing since she was a littling and her parents had run the inn—and then took the spatula and turned the rest of the eggs and pork.

"I have a question," Kisha said, swinging her legs. "Have you seen Marlies? She was here again, about two weeks ago, and helped me sort out a tharuk brawl, but I haven't seen her since."

"Sounds like her." He studied the eggs, avoiding her gaze.

"When Marlies first visited here, two moons ago, I gave her my grandmother's jade ring that controls the realm gate, but last time she was here, she didn't say much about what happened to her."

He gazed at her. "Last time I saw you, I told you how I took her across the flatlands to the foot of the Terramites, hidden in the base of my wagon." Kisha nodded, and he continued, "Well, I found out later that she helped free Zaarusha's orange-scaled son, Maazini, from Zens' clutches, but first, she nearly died when Zens tortured her. Afraid to spill Dragons' Realm's secrets, she took some berries that put her into a deep coma."

"Coma?"

Giant John flipped the pork. The fine aroma wafted to Kisha as the meat sizzled and browned. "She looked like she was dead, barely breathing, barely alive, until her son, Tomaaz, found her and rescued her. Together, they escaped Death Valley using the ring. Now, Tomaaz has returned and freed the slaves."

Kisha gaped. Freed the thousands of slaves in Death Valley? For as long as she'd been alive, Zens had been capturing and enslaving their people. "Death Valley's gone?"

"Well, it's still there, but the slaves are gone. They're at Dragons' Hold. Thanks to a contraption Zens made that held the realm gates open when he used one of those jade rings." Giant John shoveled the eggs onto his plate and moved the pork around the pan with the spatula.

"One of them?"

"Apparently there was another ring too." He tilted his head, grinning at her. "No more slavery. No more tharuks. It's hard to believe, isn't it?"

"So Marlies is responsible for all that? I'd love to see her again."

Giant John turned to her, his eyes full of sorrow. "She didn't make it. She sacrificed her life to save her daughter, Ezaara, the Queen's Rider."

Kisha swallowed. Another bright star had faded. Another person she'd cared about. "How did she die?"

"She leaped from her dragon to save Ezaara from a bolt of mage fire, and died in a blaze of fire that lit up the sky." Giant John shook his head. "The truth is, she was already dying. She never quite recovered from the berries she took in Death Valley."

Kisha swallowed, trying to ease the ache in her throat. It didn't work. "At least Ezaara's alive. I'd like to meet her, some day."

Giant John slid the pork onto his plate and took the pan off the fire. He grabbed a fork and leaned back against the counter, stabbing the eggs with a vengeance. "I'd love to be there when you meet her: the ex-Queen's Rider's granddaughter and the new Queen's Rider. I think you'll like her, Kisha." He put his fork on his plate, and placed his hand on Kisha's shoulder. "Come on. Although we might not feel like it, the revelry out there will probably do us good."

§

Ithsar leaned back in her chair as Stefan entertained half the inn with stories of how brave he and Fangora had been in battle. Even though they'd only known each other a week, Ithsar was going to miss his brash, cheeky smile.

Goren plonked a bowl of stew on the table and sat beside her. "You worked wonders with Stefan's swordsmanship in those few short days. How did you do it?" Eyes on her, he shoveled a spoonful of stew into his mouth.

Ithsar shrugged. "He's a fast learner, but his balance was wrong. Once we corrected that, and I showed him a few simple sword strokes and blocks that suited his build, he was fine."

Goren looked weary, his face lined with grief and his shoulders slumped as he dunked his bread into his stew and bit into it.

"Thanks for bringing Giant John back here to see Kisha," Ithsar said. "He trained her for years, so it means the world to her."

"Anakisha's granddaughter, the bartender to tharuks. I never thought I'd live to see the day. I bet she's glad that's over." Goren took another spoonful of stew. "Ithsar, I, um… you handled yourself well in battle. You're a fine leader."

Ithsar stared, speechless.

Goren grinned. "You led your wing of sea dragons extremely well. Much better than I anticipated. I'm sorry I underestimated you."

She gaped.

Goren chuckled. "Don't look so shocked. I'm not that bad."

Ithsar grinned and they lapsed into companionable silence, watching the bustle and hubbub around them.

Giant John came out of the kitchen with a massive plate of eggs and pork, Kisha at his side. They sat on a step at the bottom of the staircase to the bedrooms. Giant John shoveled eggs and pork into his mouth, gesticulating as he told Kisha wild tales. Every now and then, she answered, and he slapped his thigh, laughter shaking his enormous frame.

As soon as his eggs were gone, Giant John helped himself to a huge bowl of stew, and then another.

Ithsar nudged Goren. "I don't know how he can eat that much…"

Goren grinned, making him look more carefree than Ithsar had ever seen. "It's quite a feat, isn't it? I guess battle makes him hungry."

Just then, Stefan got to the punch line of his latest rescue, and the inn rippled with laughter.

§

The hubbub of the dragon riders perched on chairs, tables, and around the floor of the inn was strangely comforting to Kisha after so many moons of serving tharuks. Stefan was holding the floor, still teasing Ithsar. He hadn't stopped all night. Although the chief prophetess certainly didn't seem to mind, and was giving him back as much as he gave.

"So, here I am, a herbalist who imprinted with the dragon, and I saved the head of the Robandi assassins from a terrible fate." Stefan whacked his thigh, tipped his head back and crowed like a rooster at dawn.

Ithsar groaned and rolled her eyes. "I'm never going to live this down, am I?" She slapped him on the arm, playfully.

He turned to her in mock seriousness, face solemn. "Do that again, and I may not save you next time." And then he burst out laughing again.

The riders laughed too, joining in with tales of how they'd saved each other's hides. Tomorrow, Ithsar had told Kisha, they'd light candles in the square for those who hadn't made it. She'd asked Kisha to invite Katrine, so she could light a candle for Kadran too.

Kisha had seen enough dragon riders and warriors after battle to know that the laughter and camaraderie helped to hide the pain. But with the loss of Nila and the prospect of losing Thika and her new friends again so soon, Kisha needed fresh air. Besides, Nila's dragon was out there, lonely and grieving.

She slipped out into the square with the last of the salted pork on an enormous tray, and tiptoed over to Nila's dragon, Nilanna, who was still sleeping. Kisha laid the tray on the cobbles near her head. Her scales shimmered in the flickering lantern light from the inn's window. She was so beautiful, Kisha was tempted to touch her. She sighed, not wanting to wake her, and carefully stepped away.

The dragon's eyes flicked open. Her nostrils quivered. She angled her head and winked at Kisha.

Winked? Kisha hadn't even realized dragons could wink. And had never expected one to wink at her. She neared and laid her hand upon the creature's forehead.

Nilanna's voice drifted through her mind like a warm summer breeze. *"You have such a big heart, Kisha. Your friends are inside, enjoying each other's company, yet you come outside to care for me, knowing I am lonely and have lost the one I loved."*

"I understand losing the ones you love. It has happened to me too." Kisha's parents' faces swam before her eyes. Ma's lovely brown hair and twinkling blue eyes and Pa's friendly laugh.

"This was your family?"

Kisha nodded.

"Gone?" The sea dragon's voice was like a whisper in a hallowed hall.

"Yes."

"Then you are lonely too?"

Kisha nodded, tears rolling down her cheeks.

The dragon's golden eyes glowed with inner fire. *"Then I claim you as my new rider."*

Warmth washed over Kisha, and she gasped as a tight coil inside her unfurled like a new bud in spring, and blossomed into something warm and vibrant and loving. Sweet music filled her breast, like the melody of the most beautiful songbird. Slowly, the warmth and the music built, until her veins surged with the fire of new adventure.

"Now that we have imprinted, I shall no longer be known as Nilanna, but Kishanna, after you."

This? This beautiful sweet surety that she'd follow this dragon to the ends of the realm was imprinting.

But Anakisha's visions held her in their grip. She didn't dare fly, because, she knew, when she got on that dragon's back, she'd never want to get off again. And she was bound here—by her promise to her dying mother and by her promises to the spirit of her grandmother.

She'd pledged to stay until it was time to leave—and that time was not now. She could feel it in her bones.

Kisha rested her forehead against her dragon's snout as tears rolled down her cheeks.

Follow your heart. You'll know when the time is right.

Her heart was telling her to go, but she knew it wasn't time yet.

Kishanna's sadness washed over her. *"You're a free spirit, Kisha. Yet you remain chained to the past."*

Kisha nodded, sorrow and joy warring in her breast. *"It's my duty. I promised."*

"Then I will wait, and fly without a rider until you're ready."

Kisha flung her arms around Kishanna's scaly neck, and as a thrum built inside the dragon's throat, rumbling through her bones, she knew that this was right, so right. But not now.

With a heavy heart, she traipsed into the Lost King Inn, casting more than one glance back over her shoulder.

A Bizarre Surprise

The next morning, Kisha rose early and popped out into the square before anyone was awake. Kishanna nuzzled Kisha's hand, snuffing warm air over her palms. Kisha laughed and scratched her snout.

"Would you mind scratching my eye ridges?" Kishanna rumbled. *"They get terribly itchy."*

Kisha stretched up her hand and scratched the rough scales above Kishanna's eye. *"It's a shame I can't come with you,"* she said. *"But I sense I still have a purpose here."*

Kishanna blinked. *"You remained here so long, true to the visions from your grandmother, Anakisha. But surely now the war is over, it's no longer necessary."*

The dragon's words were tempting. But a sense of wrongness yawned inside Kisha, so she shook her head. *"Maybe I can follow you some day."* She rubbed a dry scale on Kishanna's jowl. *"But for now, I'll remain here. I've been true to my grandmother for all these years, so I can't sway from that path until it's time."*

There was a flurry of wingbeats above the square. Kisha glanced up, shading her eyes from the early morning sun gleaming off a golden dragon. Two riders were upon its back, a woman with flaming red hair wearing unusual garb, and a dark-haired man wearing a mage cloak. The dragon spiraled down to the square, two long cloth-wrapped packages draped across its haunches.

She swallowed. Surely not. Surely those couldn't be…

The dragon landed. The man smiled and hailed her. "Good morning, Kisha. I have a special message for you from your grandmother."

Her heart caught in her throat. Those bushy eyebrows. That mage cloak.

The man kissed the woman on the cheek and slid from the golden dragon, approaching Kisha. He held out his hand, shaking hers. A trickle of mage power zinged into her palm.

"Are you Master Giddi, the dragon mage?"

He chuckled. "Indeed, I am."

"Then that must be…" But it couldn't be.

"Yes, it is. I'd like you to meet Mazyka, my wife."

Mazyka, who'd opened a world gate with Giddi years before, and let Commander Zens in, and then been locked out when Giddi had closed the gate—along with dozens and dozens of mages.

"We have a special delivery for you. Do have a spare bedroom?"

"The inn is full, but Giant John is leaving today, so you can use his room."

The dragon mage's bushy eyebrows flew up. "Giant John's here?" The mage cupped his hands around his mouth and bellowed, "John! John, we need your help." His voice echoed off the cobbles in the square and rang amongst the buildings, probably waking every resident in Last Stop.

Moments later, the tavern door burst open and Giant John stumbled out in his breeches and nightshirt. "Giddi! You're a sight for sore eyes." He embraced Giddi and Mazyka. "I see you've met my friend, Kisha."

Giddi nodded. "We have a matter of grave importance, something that's puzzled us all for years. I need your help."

Giant John pounded his hand on his heart with a thump that might've knocked a lesser man down.

Mazyka had dismounted and was untying the packages on the dragon's haunches. "Please, John, be careful. These are precious. We must take them inside immediately."

Cradling the smaller of the long parcels as if it would shatter into a million pieces, Giddi lifted one from Mazyka's arms and

Giant John carefully eased the other off the dragon's haunches, his eyes full of questions.

Kisha's heart pounded.

Kishanna's gentle voice drifted through her mind. *"Be brave, Kisha. You have a valiant heart. I will always be here if you need me."*

A wave of comfort washed over Kisha. She squared her shoulders and followed Giant John, Master Giddi, and Mazyka inside.

§

Kisha had often wished to see her grandmother, but had never believed it would happen.

Anakisha's body rested on the bed, hands clasped over her breast, and wrinkled face peaceful, as Giddi explained. "Mazyka and I went to Death Valley and found her in Zens' quarters. He was using a strange, peculiar magic to keep her alive."

"It's called science," Mazyka interrupted. "I've told you, Giddi, if we're to teach everyone in Dragons' Realm, we need to be clear. Magic and science are quite different."

Those bushy eyebrows tugged down into a fierce frown. "All right, then. Using science, he kept her alive."

"And this is Yanir?" Her grandfather, the King's Rider, looked much younger than Anakisha, about two thirds her age.

"Yes, he was dead, but Zens pickled him. That's why he looks younger," Giddi said.

Mazyka rolled her eyes and chuckled. "It's called preserving."

"Yes," said Kisha. "I preserve my pickles too."

Mazyka muttered something indecipherable, then laughed. "Come on, let's organize their funerals."

Anakisha's Funeral

By mid-morning, most of the citizens of Last Stop had gathered on the outskirts of the village for the funeral of Anakisha and Yanir. Giant John had hastily erected a small dais at one end of a snow-crusted meadow. Mazyka had pulled wondrous bolts of gold cloth from the saddlebags of her golden dragon. And now, Yanir and Anakisha lay on the dais, wrapped in shimmering gold, with only their faces showing under the open, sun-kissed sky.

Birds flitted in and out of the evergreens along the side of the meadow, twittering.

Giant John slung a comforting arm around Kisha's shoulders. Happiness and sorrow warred in her breast. Happiness at finally seeing Anakisha, and sorrow for losing her grandmother.

Giant John squeezed her shoulder, his touch reassuring. "From what Master Giddi says, this will be the first time they've seen the open air in over nineteen years."

Standing on the other side of her, Giddi nodded. "Yes, that's right. Zens kept them both underground in tanks, all that time. The funny thing is, we always referred to Anakisha as being 'lost' in battle. We never said she'd died. But none of us ever dreamed we'd find her." He scratched one of his bushy eyebrows. "You know, she requested that we bring her back here so you could see her, Kisha. She knew you were maintaining a vigil, and listening to her spirit all these years." Master Giddi's eyes were soft.

A lump stuck in Kisha's throat.

Mazyka, red hair flaming like fire in the sun, looked at Giddi with such tenderness, it stole Kisha's breath. "Just as you maintained a vigil for me all these years, Giddi. You never gave up hope."

Giddi kissed her flaming hair. "And you, for me."

Giant John cleared his throat. "Are you two done? Yanir and Anakisha have waited for a decent funeral for over nineteen years. We don't want to keep them waiting any longer."

"Tut, tut, so impatient, John." Giddi winked at Kisha, who laughed. Then the dragon mage pointed northward.

There were specks in the sky above the forest, north of the fields. As they steadily grew larger, the crowd murmured. Dragons—lots of dragons.

Giant John's belly laugh rumbled through Kisha's bones. "You didn't tell me we were expecting guests, Giddi. But of course Anakisha's family would want to be here."

Family? Kisha scarcely dared breathe. Years ago, Anakisha's children had gone into hiding, because they'd been under threat. When Anakisha and Yanir had died, the knowledge of their children's whereabouts had been lost. Her mother had once mentioned that it was possible Kisha might have cousins in far-flung regions.

"Are my long-lost cousins the family you mean?" Kisha asked Giant John. "Or do you mean the large family of dragon riders that loved Anakisha?"

Giant John arched an eyebrow. "Tut, tut, so impatient, Kisha." He winked at Master Giddi and laughed.

Kisha gave him a sharp jab with her elbow, but that just made him laugh harder.

As the dragons neared, the rustle of their wingbeats swished across the meadow, the foliage rippling in the breeze. There were at least forty, of all colors and sizes. Most of them landed near the sea dragons and green guards in the next meadow, but some flew closer and descended to land near Kisha, Giant John, Master Giddi, and Mazyka.

The largest dragon, a multi-hued creature with a regal bearing—Zaarusha, the Dragon Queen—landed nearby and strode toward them, accompanied by an enormous blue.

A tall woman slid from Zaarusha's back, her long blonde hair stirring in the breeze of other dragons' wingbeats as an orange dragon and others dropped down behind Zaarusha.

That pretty rider must be Ezaara.

Kisha wiped her suddenly-sweaty palms on her skirt.

A Naobian with a handsome, hard-edged face dismounted from the mighty blue dragon. He held Ezaara's hand, his smile dissolving those tough edges into tenderness.

Something inside Kisha twanged. All this time, this was what she'd missed, these loving connections.

§

Ezaara strode toward a small band of people assembled near the dais that held the bodies of Anakisha and Yanir. She'd often wondered what Anakisha, the ex-Queen's Rider, had looked like, and had even been compared to her when she'd first imprinted with Zaarusha. But this chance to see her was something she'd never expected. Such a strange situation. Tomaaz's girl, Lovina, could preserve someone's likeness in a portrait, but Zens had preserved Yanir's *whole body* and kept Anakisha alive with tubes and a... Mazyka had called it a... a ventilator. That was it. She'd never thought she'd live to hear of something so bizarre.

Anakisha's wrinkled blue eyes stared at the sky of her homeland. Beside her, Yanir was younger—even handsome, despite the sallow tinge to his skin. Ezaara strode past the dais, Roberto at her side. There would be time for this later. The living were more important right now.

Giant John had his arm over the shoulders of a young girl, perhaps fourteen or fifteen summers old. From what Ma had told her, this was Kisha. Her hand in Roberto's, Ezaara strode over. She nudged Roberto and mind-melded. *"After you."*

His ebony eyes touched Ezaara's face. *"But you're the Queen's Rider."*

"You're her family."

"No, I really think you should go first as Queen's Rider." He squeezed her hand.

"Very well." Ezaara ignored Master Giddi, Mazyka, and Giant John, and made a beeline for Kisha. "Good morning, Kisha. I'm Ezaara. I believe you met my mother Marlies."

The girl's bright blue eyes were wide. She nodded.

Just saying her mother's name made Ezaara's eyes sting. But Marlies wouldn't have wanted her to cry. "Through your help, my mother helped change the fate of Dragons' Realm." Ezaara pulled the girl into a warm embrace, enfolding her in her arms. She was so tiny, so frail, yet so strong to have held out for all this time on her own. "Ma appreciated your kindness. The ring you gave her was key to her escaping Zens, and she never would've made it across the Flatlands if it weren't for you and Giant John. You've played an important part in this war, and we'll be forever grateful. If you ever need a home, you're welcome at Dragons' Hold." Ezaara stepped back and brushed away the tears that graced her cheeks.

Kisha's eyes were bright with moisture too. She gave a trembling smile. "Thank you. I needed to hear that."

Ezaara swept a hand behind her. "There's someone I'd like you to meet."

Roberto mind-melded, *"She's so dainty."*

"Yet so strong," Ezaara melded. *"She gave Ma the ring that helped her and Tomaaz save Maazini. Without Kisha, I would've lost my family, and we might not be here today."*

"True." Roberto gave a warm smile and clasped Kisha's hands. "Kisha, I'm Roberto, your cousin from Naobia. My mother Lucia

was your mother's sister, another of Anakisha's daughters." And then he hugged her.

The joy that lit up Kisha's face was worth all the pain of this war. Worth everything Ezaara had gone through. Zens' torture. Losing Ma. Everything.

"You have a kind and generous heart, Ezaara," Zaarusha rumbled in her mind.

"How could I begrudge anyone this? Look how happy she is."

Adelina raced over and threw her arms around Kisha. "I'm Adelina, Roberto's sister. I always thought that Roberto and I were the only ones left. Welcome to our family."

Ezaara didn't miss the shadow that flitted across Roberto's face. He was thinking of his father, Amato, again. How he'd survived in an underground lake for years, only to throw himself in the path of a tharuk arrow to save Adelina's life.

Her twin, Tomaaz, slid from Maazini, his royal orange-scaled dragon, as Lovina landed with Ajeurina, a royal green, and dismounted. Behind them, Taliesin's red dragon wheeled in and blue guards landed with more people for Kisha to meet.

Tomaaz and Lovina approached Kisha, smiling. Lovina's face was no longer gaunt, and she'd gained new curves since being freed from slavery. That, and her confident smile, had transformed her into a completely different person from the cowering reed-thin slave who'd been drugged on numlock and barely aware of her surroundings in Lush Valley.

Kisha beamed as Lovina said, "I'm your cousin too. Argus was my father, but sadly, the rest of my family died as slaves in Death Valley."

"May I hug you as well?" Tomaaz asked before embracing Kisha. "As Ezaara said, you helped save my life and my mother's by giving Ma Anakisha's ring." He waved a hand behind him. "There's someone else who'd like to meet you."

Maazini strode forward, the tip of his tail leaving a thin trail in the snow. His warm dragon breath huffed over them as he passed Ezaara and snuffled Kisha's hand. Tomaaz scratched his dragon's snout affectionately. "Ma and I rescued Maazini from Death Valley, where Zens kept him captive."

Kisha was weeping openly now, the smile upon her face radiant.

§

Kisha couldn't believe she had a cousin—no, cousins—Roberto, Adelina, *and* Lovina. And the Queen's Rider had thanked her.

Roberto grinned. "Wait, there are more."

More people flooded forward, forming a line. So many, she was never going to keep up with the whirl of faces and names.

A waif-thin boy with dark hair and solemn lake-blue eyes shook her hand. "I'm your cousin, Rhun Taliesin of Waykeep in the Flatlands. You can call me Taliesin," he said. "My pa, Rhun, was Anakisha's son. He died with the rest of my family in Death Valley, but Tomaaz and Marlies helped me to escape. Now, I'm training in prophecy at Dragons' Hold." He beamed. "Thank you for keeping the ring safe or we wouldn't have made it."

All this time alone, tending the bar, mopping up tharuks' spilled beer, staying out of the way when they brawled, and cleaning up the debris, had been worth it. Her loyalty to her grandmother had helped save lives.

Next in line were a woman with her husband and children, not dragon riders by the looks of their clothes. "I'm Esmeralda, your aunt. Meet your uncle Nick and your cousins, Urs, Tom, Greta, Luisa, Markus, and Rona." Urs, the oldest, was way older than Kisha, but the youngest was still a littling. "Until recently, we hailed from Western Settlement in Lush Valley where Nick and I ran the inn."

Tears streamed down Kisha's face as they each hugged her.

A middle-aged woman presented her with a beautiful hand-painted scarf of green and blue sea dragons wheeling above an ocean. "I, too, am your aunt. My name's Ana and this is my husband, Ernst, and my children, Lofty, Mari, Samuel, and Johanna, and Little Ana. We were Ezaara's neighbors in Lush Valley. I also kept a jade ring for Anakisha for many years, until it was needed."

"You did?" Kisha felt an instant sense of kinship with this woman with the kind eyes and warm smile. She wrapped the pretty scarf around her neck. "Thank you."

Kishanna's comforting voice rushed into her mind like a warm breeze. *"Not only do you belong, you are at the very heart of a family that spans Dragons' Realm—from Dragons' Hold to Naobia and all the way across the Flatlands."*

Kisha eyes skimmed over all fifteen cousins and her two aunts and uncles, and she felt as if her skin would explode with joy.

Her family members filed past her grandparents, gently placing their hands over their hearts as they paid their last respects, then stood closest to the dais, near the front of the assembled crowd. The gathered crowd's murmurs died as Kisha faced them, next to Ezaara, Master Giddi, Mazyka, and Giant John.

Zaarusha reared onto her hind legs and roared, then stalked over to Kisha.

"She wants to mind-meld with you," Ezaara said.

As the dragon queen dipped her head, Kisha was struck with awe. Zaarusha's hide glimmered with all the colors of the rainbow. When she laid her hand on the queen's scaly forehead, Zaarusha's memories rushed through her.

Anakisha as a young girl—beautiful, strong-willed, and feisty. Anakisha, the first time Zaarusha had seen her, imprinting. Her meeting Yanir. Snatches of them leading blue dragons into battle. And then the vision that Kisha had seen herself, many times over: Yanir dying and Anakisha trying to save him, but falling off Zaarusha into a swarming mass of tharuks.

"I thank you for being true to the memory of my former rider. As Ezaara said, there will always be a home for you at Dragons' Hold."

The warmth that washed over Kisha settled deep inside her. She belonged.

§

Finally, it was time to start. Kisha waited with bated breath, wondering what she could learn about her grandparents. Ezaara stood before the assembled crowd, her blonde hair shifting in the breeze. Zaarusha roared, quieting the murmurs.

"It's appropriate that we're in Last Stop, the last place Anakisha visited before she was lost in battle. It is with joy and sorrow that we meet here today," Ezaara said, her clear voice rippling through the throng and out across the fields. "Joy that slaves have been freed and families can be reunited. Joy that Zens and his evil monsters have been vanquished. And sorrow that we are mourning many we loved and lost. Today, we celebrate the actions of brave people, who stood up against evil. Alone, none of us could've battled Zens. But together, we managed to triumph. Every one of you can be proud of your actions, no matter how small. Whether you fed a hungry warrior, rode a dragon, flung mage flame, tended to wounded, repaired destruction left by tharuks, or sheltered your family behind closed doors, I thank you."

Despite the watching crowd, Kisha made no move to wipe the tears from her cheeks.

Ezaara swept a hand toward the assembled people. "Today, we're experiencing something that will never happen again. Nineteen years ago, the King Dragon, Syan, Yanir, his rider, and Anakisha, the Queen's Rider, were lost in battle. The world gate was shut and Mazyka and many other mages were locked out of Dragons' Realm. For years, we lived in darkness, with a growing rift between riders and mages that almost spanned a generation. During these dark times, Commander Zens tightened his grasp on the land. None of us suspected his plan went so much deeper. None of us ever dreamed of shadow dragons, of thousands killed in slave camps, or crystals that could turn our loyalty and make us try to kill the ones we love." Tears glimmered on Ezaara's cheeks now, but her voice remained steady. "None of us suspected that Zens had kept Yanir preserved. Or kept Anakisha alive, only to exist as a spirit, trapped in a realm gate, while he nourished her body, imprisoned in a tank." She shuddered. "So, now we'll pay our last respects to Yanir, the King's Rider, and Anakisha, the former Queen's Rider. We'll celebrate their lives, and thank them for their service to Dragons' Realm." Ezaara gestured Master Giddi forward.

Arms gesticulating and his eyebrows shooting up and down to punctuate his stories, Master Giddi recounted anecdote after anecdote of Anakisha's bravery and stubbornness, Yanir's sense of humor and courage, and the way they'd been lost in battle. The crowd was transfixed, laughing as he regaled them with funny stories, moved to tears as he spoke of their bravery and courage, and silent as he finally finished.

So many people spoke of her grandmother and grandfather— Hans, Ezaara and Tomaaz's father; Giant John, who made the crowd laugh as he described some of Anakisha's antics; Lars, the leader of the Council of the Twelve Dragon Masters; and Aidan, the master of battle.

Kisha's tears dried, and her heart filled, and then overflowed. If only Ma could hear these stories.

Finally, Kisha's newfound aunts and uncles spoke, one after the other. And then Ezaara turned to Kisha.

Kisha stood before hundreds of dragons and people, and for the first time since losing her parents, her heart was at peace.

She gazed out at people's shining faces, some damp with tears, and others blazing with happiness. And all Kisha could say was, "Thank you for bringing my grandmother and grandfather home."

The ground shook as the dragons roared.

Zaarusha sprang to the dais, accompanied by her offspring, Erob, Maazini, and Ajeurina. The dragons grasped the ends of cords that were bound to the shimmering gold cloth wrapped around Anakisha and Yanir's bodies. Between them, they lifted Kisha's grandparents high into the air, wings flapping valiantly until they were mere shadows against the sun.

The dragons let go.

Moments later, bright twin flames lit the sky, burning like comets, as the dragons chased Anakisha and Yanir, flaming them until they were nothing but ash scattered over the fields.

Dancing

Drums pounded in Last Stop's village square as the melody of flutes and a gittern wound among the flickering torches, conversation, dancing, and laughter. Villagers had pulled tables and chairs into the square, and the dragons had created fire pits for spit-roasted pigs and goats. Fruit, fresh bread, cakes, and cheese adorned the tables, and in the corner was a steaming cauldron of fine sweet potato and lemon-grass soup.

Perched on the rooftops around the square and in the fields surrounding the village, dragons slept with their heads tucked under their wings.

Roberto sat on a bench in a corner with his arm wrapped tightly around Ezaara's waist. Gods, he'd nearly lost her so many times since he'd met her—now, he was never letting go. There'd been attempts on her life and her virtue; the time he'd had to leave her in Zens' hands to be tortured so he could save Adelina—by the First Egg, what a heart-wrenching moment that had been; poisoning; a knife attack; tharuk fights; shadow dragons; and Ashewar, who'd wanted to kill them both. And more.

She turned to him and mind-melded, *"Morbid thoughts?"*

"Just thinking how much I love you."

Her smile was tinged with sadness. It would be for a while. Ezaara had been close to her mother. That wound would take time to heal. He pressed his lips against her hair, inhaling the herbal fragrance of her hair soap. *"Just remember, although many have fallen in battle, we've won the war."*

His thoughts flitted to Tonio, the spymaster who'd died at Mage Gate. Taliesin had told him that Tonio had saved Marlies by taking an arrow for her. Even though the spymaster had borne a grudge against Roberto's father and hated Roberto, in an odd twist of fate, Tonio had bought Marlies enough time to save Ezaara's life. In battle, the actions of many were woven into a complex tapestry.

"I think we should celebrate. How about a dance?" Ezaara asked. *"They're expecting us to."*

"Someone's always going to expect us to do something."

"Well, I am the Queen's Rider."

"And don't I know it." He could still see the terrified waif who'd trembled before the roaring dragons of the dragon council, moons ago, when she'd first arrived at Dragons' Hold. She'd faced down every one of them, despite her fear. And gone on to surprise everyone, time and time again, as she mastered the necessary skills to be the best Queen's Rider she could be. She still surprised him most days.

"Come on," Ezaara said, getting up and pulling him to his feet. "Let's dance."

And as Roberto took Ezaara in his arms, and held her close, he had to admit, it was a great idea.

§

"So, Mazyka's daughter?" Waggling his eyebrows suggestively, Fenni jabbed Jael in the ribs.

Next to Fenni, Gret grinned. "Go on, Jael, tell us all about her." She swung a blonde braid over her shoulder.

Although Jael's cheeks were heating, he ignored their jibes. The sooner he got this over with, the better. Serana would be back at any moment, and he didn't want her embarrassed by his friends' nosiness. "Her name's Serana," he said matter-of-factly. "She happened to heal my gut injury. I've flown on her dragon a few times, just like I fly with Kierion or Tomaaz. That's all there is to it."

Fenni winked. "Yes, we noticed that."

Jael frowned. "What?"

"You, on her dragon." Fenni's grin nearly split his face.

Gret arched an eyebrow, going in for the kill. "We also noticed you were sitting rather close. Closer than most dragon riders and mages sit when they're flying together." She leaned back and snuggled into Fenni, as if to demonstrate how close two people could actually get.

Was it that obvious? Jael snorted, feeling his blush deepen. Thank the First Egg it was dark. Maybe he should slip off and encourage Serana to take him for a flight now. Anything to get away from Fenni and Gret's embarrassing questions.

Oh gods, Serana was making her way over now, two glasses of apple juice in her hands. He couldn't take his eyes off her—the way she moved in those strange clothes from her world, her red hair ablaze with color as it glinted in the firelight. That magical smile. Oh, he was a goner.

Serana approached the table, and Jael took the glasses from her. "Would you like to dance?" he asked.

The smile that lit her face was brighter than any bonfire. "I never thought you'd ask."

He placed his arm around her waist, and glanced over his shoulder at Fenni and Gret, calling, "If you think that was close, then watch this." He led Serana over to the dancers.

"What was that about?" she asked.

He shrugged.

"Go on."

So Jael took a gamble. "They're teasing me for sitting too close when I ride with you on your dragon. It's just idle gossip."

"Is it?" She grinned, eyes blazing. "Let's give them something else to gossip about."

The bonfire crackled, and the drumbeats pulsed through them as Jael took Serana's hand and whirled her among the throng of dancers.

§

Fenni turned to Gret, gesturing at Jael and Serana, who were whirling through the crowd with huge grins on their faces. "That looks like fun. Want to try?"

Gret took his hand, her braid glistening like honey in the torchlight as she led him over to the dancers. She ducked her head shyly. "Do you realize that we haven't danced since Roberto and Ezaara's hand-fasting ceremony?"

Fenni's eyebrows shot up. "We haven't?" He took her warm hands in his. "That's a terrible mistake. We'd better make up for that, tonight."

They swayed and moved in time to the music, getting faster as the crescendo built, and as Gret whirled and spun, her face radiant with joy, Fenni vowed he'd dance with her every day.

Kierion swept past, Adelina in his arms, and winked.

Fenni had to grin. Adelina was so short, she only came up to Kierion's chest. What was Kierion up to now?

His friend lifted Adelina right off the ground as he spun her.

Gret sighed and leaned her head against Fenni's shoulder, making his bones melt.

"You know," she said, "sometimes I wish I was short and petite, like Adelina."

"Really?" Fenni gaped. "Why?"

"I don't know, just because…"

"But you're beautiful the way you are." He slipped his arms around her and let a little mage power trickle through his hands, just enough to keep her warm. "You're tall and fit and strong, and a great swordswoman, and I'd like to dance with you all night."

"Really?" Her eyes shone.

"Mmm hmm." He nodded. "Every night."

The smile that Gret gave him lit up the night sky.

§

Tomaaz held his arm up as Lovina whirled underneath, then he pulled her close, murmuring in her ear, "So what do you think of your new cousin?"

Lovina smiled, her blue eyes alight with wonder. "I'm just happy to have family again. Happy we freed the slaves. Happy to have you."

Tomaaz grinned. "I feel exactly the same." He twirled her around again.

And again.

And again.

Until Lovina was laughing, her head thrown back and her face radiant with happiness.

§

After all these years, she was in his arms again. A tendril of mage power sizzled from Mazyka's palms through Giddi's shoulder. He laughed. Gods, it was good to have his wife back. "So," he said, "did you dance in that other world?"

"Not once," Mazyka said. "There was no one I wanted to dance with." She grinned and flung her hands above her head. Blue mage flame surged from her fingers, exploding into a shower of blossoms.

Giddi tossed out sparks that turned into green birds, flapping above the heads of the dancers.

Dancing nearby, young Master Jael and Fenni joined in. Fenni's mage lights zipped above the crowd like tiny green fireflies. Jael conjured up green dragonets that flitted between the rooftops.

Mazyka nudged Giddi. "What do you think of those two?" She tilted her head toward Jael, who was dancing with their daughter

Serana—a daughter Giddi hadn't even known about until two days ago.

Giddi grinned and pulled Mazyka closer. "I hope they hold each other tightly," he said. "And never let go."

"So do I." Mazyka's dark eyes roamed his face, lit by dancing flames of the bonfire, and Giddi knew they weren't talking about Jael and Serana at all.

§

Giant John waved a haunch of goat toward the dancers, who were silhouetted by the roaring bonfire. "So, what will you do now, Hans?"

Hans shrugged and watched the young ones dance, the way he had danced many times with Marlies when they were young. It was like having an anvil on his chest, this grief—missing her. Her laugh, the quick flick of her turquoise eyes, the sparkle in them whenever she saw him, the warmth of her touch. He'd known this was coming, sooner or later, had been trying to stave off the truth—that she was dying and had been since the piaua berries she'd taken in Death Valley. It was ironic that those berries had been grown in Lush Valley, their home for eighteen years of relative peace. Eighteen years of hiding who they really were. Eighteen years of preparing Ezaara and Tomaaz for the roles they'd just played in saving the realm.

He watched Roberto lead Ezaara from the dance floor to a table in the corner, where Ithsar, the quiet but remarkable orange-robed assassin, was sitting.

Hans knew Ezaara had been down in that clearing with Giddi. He'd sensed her, masked by an invisibility cloak, lending her mental strength and *sathir* to Giddi to open the world gate. Without Ezaara, the whole realm would've been turned into a desolate wasteland.

And so he was glad Marlies had given her life for his daughter. That Ezaara could now dance with Roberto and lead their people in peace.

But it didn't stop the pain. The hurting. The anger at losing his wife.

Or the numbness that sometimes stole over him, deadening everything inside him, so he didn't have to feel anymore.

He considered Giant John's question. What would he do now, without her? "I'm not sure, John, but I'd like it to be something that honors Marlies."

Giant John cocked his head, his goat haunch raised in the air as if he was about to club someone with it, not take a bite. "Did you know that when Taliesin and Leah brought piaua juice back from the brown guards in the North, they also brought seedlings? Hundreds of tiny piaua seedlings."

Hans raised his brows. He hadn't known that. Hadn't really taken much in at all since his wife's death. When Marlies had been injured, the two young ones had gone north in search of the life-giving juice for her. As Master Healer, she'd relied on the juice to heal their wounded riders and dragons. Someone would have to tend to those seedlings, grow and nurture them. "Now that might be worth thinking about," Hans said.

"I think it would," said Giant John, finally taking a bite.

§

Katrine was sitting at a table at the edge of the square, watching Hana and a handsome blue guard dancing.

Kisha made her way past the dancers to Katrine's table. "How are you doing?" she asked.

Katrine shrugged, dabbing at her eyes with a kerchief. "I miss Kadran."

She gestured at Hana and her dance partner. Their gazes were locked upon each other, and their movements were not in time to the music, but to an inner rhythm that no one else could hear. Hana tipped back her head and smiled, then rested her cheek on the blue guard's chest. He stroked her hair and whispered something that made her laugh.

"At least they're happy," Katrine said, dabbing her eyes again.

Kisha squeezed Katrine's hand. "What will you do now?"

"I don't know," Katrine replied. She smiled. "But I'll find something."

Kisha hesitated. Heart pounding, she asked, "How would you like to run the Lost King inn?"

You'll know when the time is right.

Katrine stared at her, gaping. A few heartbeats later, she asked, "What will you do?"

Kisha tilted her head, gazing around the square at the happy, battle-worn faces. "I'm not sure," she said, "but I think it's time for an adventure."

§

After dancing with each of her new family members, her skin nearly exploding with joy, Kisha slipped away from the revelry, down the alley to the courtyard at the back of the Lost King inn. Kishanna was curled up on some hay in a corner outside the stables.

"You're ready for your first flight, now, aren't you?" Her dragon's golden eyes were lit with an inner fire.

Kisha gazed into those beautiful, warm golden eyes. "Yes, I am," she said.

She hadn't thought it was possible for a dragon to raise an eye ridge, but somehow it looked as if Kishanna was doing exactly that. Kisha laughed and flung her arms around her dragon's neck. Kishanna tucked her head over Kisha's shoulder, snuffing warm breath over her. She crooked a hind leg, and Kisha clambered up the smooth scales and rippling muscle onto Kishanna's back. She slid into Nila's old saddle.

"You know, for a long time, I believed that everyone I loved would die. Nila was the last in a long line of people I cared about. Even Kadran, who only helped me for a few hours, was killed. Before that, my parents, my friends..."

"And now?" the dragon rumbled.

"Now, I'm surrounded by people I love or can grow to love."

"Good," Kishanna answered. A wave of love so sweet that Kisha could taste it, washed over her. *"Are you ready?"*

"I am."

Kishanna tensed her haunches and leaped above the stables and the courtyard, circling over the square. Below, Kisha's family and friends were dancing, the bonfire's flames casting a glow over their wheeling cavorting figures.

The faint rhythm of drumbeats and the high trill of a flute accompanied Kisha and Kishanna as they flew over the village, and out over the fields beyond. Moonlight glinted off Kishanna's scales, making them shimmer with jade, emerald, and silver. Kisha unbound her braid and shook her head, the wind tugging its icy fingers through her hair. But Kisha didn't care about the chilly wind. Inside she was warm and glowing, the fire of new adventure in her veins.

§

Ithsar leaned back in her chair and stretched as the music and heat from the bonfire swirled around her. The *sathir* of the people wended its way among the dancers in a bright tapestry, rich with color. The mages were playful tonight. Tiny birds made of green mage flame zipped between the dancers, chased by green dragonets, and blue blossoms shot above the crowd, with fireflies darting among them. Ithsar hadn't ever seen anything like it.

A voice broke through her thoughts. Someone was mind-melding with her and it wasn't Saritha. *"Ithsar, you did a valiant job."* It was a rich, deep voice steeped with wisdom.

She cast about, but couldn't tell who was speaking in her head. *"Who are you?"*

"Look a little further."

Her eyes roved across the dancers. Master Giddi, the dragon mage, was watching her, his keen eyes steadfastly upon her as he swayed with his daughter Serana in his arms.

Well, that was a surprise. *"They said you could mind-meld at will, but I wasn't expecting this."*

He smiled as he danced. *"You did admirably. Although I was trapped within Zens' thrall, I saw the wings of green guards and sea dragons that you brought with you. They turned the tide of the battle. Without you, we would've lost long before I opened the world gate and let Mazyka through. I thank you and honor you."*

His praise was unexpected. A shock. *"I bring you greetings from Queen Aquaria."*

His eyes crinkled as he smiled over Serana's shoulder. *"Give her my greetings too, when you next see her."*

"I'm sorry, she was murdered by an unruly, hateful assassin." Ithsar shared her memory of Izoldia's treachery.

"That saddens me. I met her years ago when she was a dragonet."

"She said you saved her life. She was still grateful."

"As people will be to you, for many years to come."

Serana spoke to the dragon mage and he broke mind-meld sending a plume of mage flame butterflies into the air to dance around Ithsar.

Next to Ithsar, Roberto's arm around her shoulders, Ezaara grinned. "Let me guess, Master Giddi?"

Ithsar shrugged. "It seems he's happy I came to help."

"As we all are. So, what are your plans?" Roberto asked. "Now that Ashewar is gone, and your women have imprinted, will the sea dragons go with you to live at the oasis? I mean, it's not as if you can live underwater."

Goren put down his ale and cleared his throat. "I've been thinking about that," he said.

Ithsar nearly fell off her chair. "You have?"

He nodded sagely. "The Scarlet Hand and his pirate crews have been raging upon the Naobian Sea for years. We could use your help in keeping the seas a safe place for ships."

Ezaara raised her eyebrows. "That's well worth thinking about." She nudged Roberto. "Tell Ithsar about the time you fought the Scarlet Hand."

Roberto ran a hand through his dark hair. "It wasn't the Scarlet Hand himself, just one of his pirate ships—nonetheless, just as fierce. They attacked us when we were sneaking into Death Valley." He shook his head at Goren. "That's no mean feat you're asking of her, but I'm sure Ithsar and the Robandi assassins are up to the task."

"I'm not sure what we'll do," Ithsar replied. "I'll have to talk to my sisters." She watched the whirling orange robes of her assassins as they danced to the wild, bucking music—a different dance than the dance of the ancient *Sathiri*, but one that suited them just as well. Misha was graceful, her robes swirling around her as she danced with a green guard, her eyes alight.

Stefan appeared, cheeks pink and chest heaving. He bowed and held a hand to Ithsar. "My most revered Chief Prophetess, would you care to dance?"

Ithsar smiled and took his hand. "I would like that, thank you."

Stefan whirled her across the cobbles amongst the throng of joyous, dancing people.

"One moment, I have something to give you." Ithsar pulled him aside and took the wrapped smashed chocolate out of her pocket. She passed it to him.

Stefan opened the wrapping and popped the chocolate in his mouth. He stuffed the cloth back in his pocket and bowed. "And I have something for you." He tugged a cloth, decorated with orange and gold butterflies, out of his jerkin. "For my new best friend."

Ithsar stared at him. "For me?" She opened the cloth to reveal a dragon-shaped chocolate. "Oh, it's too pretty. I couldn't possibly eat it."

"I think you should. It's orange-flavored." He gestured at her robes, then the bonfire. "Besides, if you don't, it'll melt."

Ithsar broke the chocolate in half and grinned. "For my new best friend."

Stefan chuckled and ate his half.

The sweet chocolate and tart orange made Ithsar's taste buds explode.

Stefan grabbed her hand and tugged her into the throng.

The drumbeats throbbed through her feet, her bones, her heart. The flute made her veins sing with magic. Stefan laughed, pulled her close and flung her out to whirl with the dancers. *Sathir* swirled around them, rich and vibrant and full of life. And Ithsar knew the future was bright, and that she and her Robandi assassins would soon be dancing to a different tune. Their own tune.

Anakisha's Dragon,
Riders of Fire Dragon Masters, Book 1

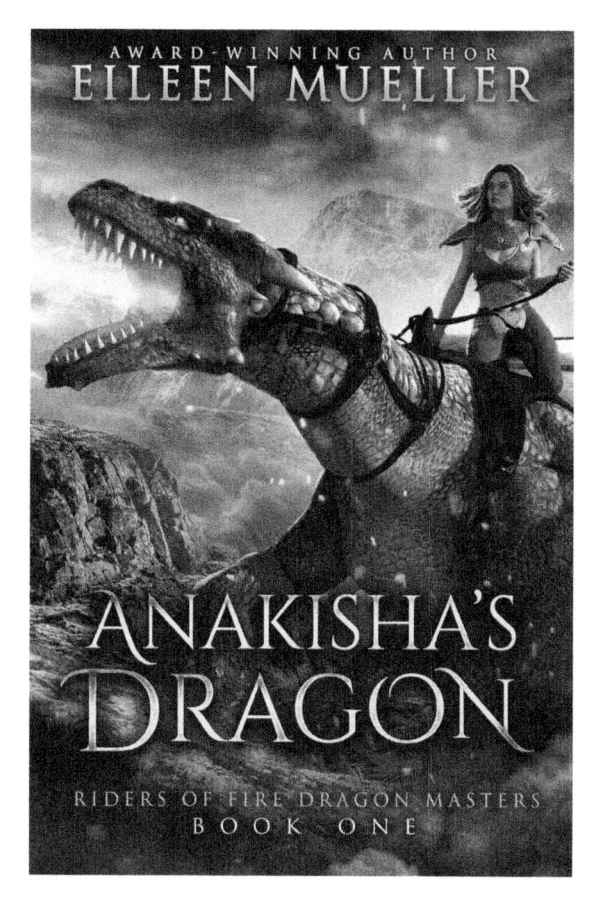

Being a dragon rider is not in Anakisha's plans. And Anakisha's stubborn. She's not giving up her dreams anytime soon.

Even the dashing Yanir—the King's Rider, who patrols the skies on the ebony King Syan—can't convince her to train at Dragons' Hold. Then again, Yanir's as irritating as he is good looking.

But then Anakisha's gifts unfold. A dragon comes calling.

And a crisis calls her into action.

Riders of Fire
Dragon Masters

Coming Soon

Anakisha's Dragon—Book 1

Dragon Mage—Book 2

Dragon Spy —Book 3

Dragon Healer—Book 4

Prequel

Ruby Dragon

To find out how Tonio, the spymaster who saved Marlies' life, met Antonika, his dragon, read Ruby Dragon, a Riders of Fire short prequel.

Riders of Fire

Complete Series Available Now

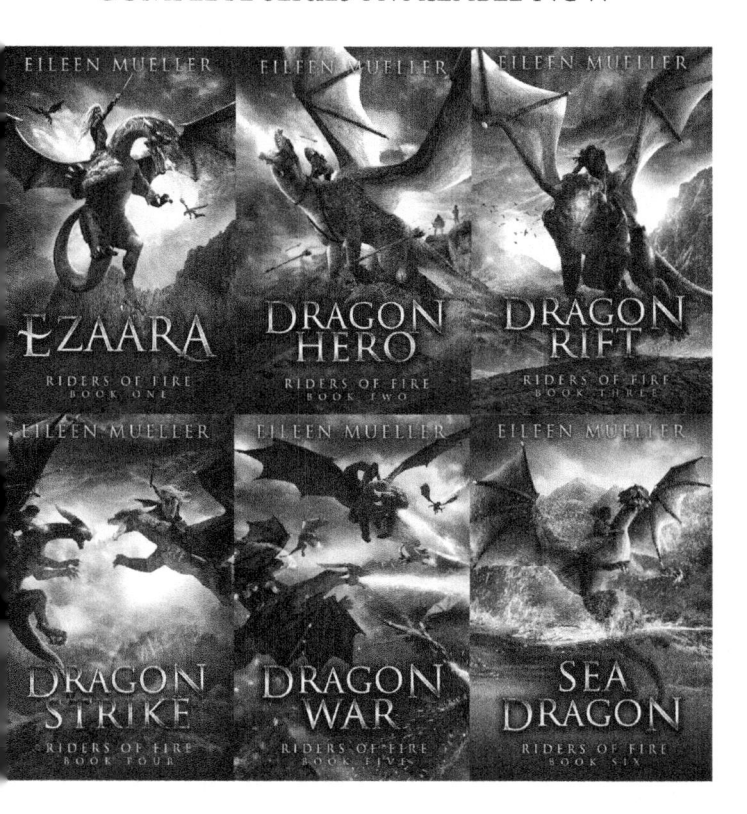

Ezaara—Book 1

Dragon Hero—Book 2

Dragon Rift—Book 3

Dragon Strike—Book 4

Dragon War—Book 5

Sea Dragon—Book 6

Herbal Lore in Dragons' Realm

Arnica—Small yellow flower with hairy leaves. Reduces pain, swelling and inflammation. The flower and root are used in Marlies' healing salve.

Bear's bane—Pungent oniony numbing salve with bear leek as the primary ingredient.

Bergamot—Citrus fruit with a refreshing scent.

Clean herb—Tangy, pale green leaves with antibacterial properties.

Clear-mind—Orange berries, used to combat numlock. Stronger when dried, but effective when fresh.

Dragon's bane—Clear poison that, when it enters the blood, makes wounds bleed excessively, and then slowly shuts down circulation and breathing.

Dragon's breath—A rare mountain flower that, when shaken, produces a soft glow.

Dragon scale—A gray powder that when swallowed gives the appearance of being numlocked, i.e. gray eyes and fingernails.

Freshweed—A weed that is chewed to mask the user's scent.

Healing salve—A healing paste that contains arnica, piaua juice, peppermint, and clean herb, and promotes healing.

Jasmine—Highly-scented white tubular flowers. Promotes relaxation.

Koromiko—Thin green leaves that, when brewed as a tea, prevent belly gripe.

Lavender—Highly-scented lilac whorled flowers. Relaxant, refreshing.

Limplock—Green sticky paste with an acrid scent used to coat tharuk weapons. Acts on the victim's nervous system, causing slow paralysis, starting with peripheries and making its way to the vital organs.

Limplock remedy—Fine yellow granules that reverse the effect of limplock. Dose: one vial for an adult; three vials for a dragon.

Numlock—Thin gray leaves, ground into a tangy powder. Saps victim's will, determination and coherent thought. Used by Zens and tharuks to keep slaves in submission. Creates a gray sheen over the eyes and fingernails.

Owl-wort—Small leaves that enable sight in the dark.

Peppermint—Dark green leaves with aromatic scent. Good for circulation, headaches and as a relaxant.

Piaua juice—Pale green juice from succulent piaua leaves. Heals wounds and knits flesh back together in moments.

Piaua Berries —When eaten, these berries cause a coma that simulates death. The only remedy is piaua juice.

Rubaka—Crushed leaves produce a pale green powder used as a remedy against dragon's bane.

Skarkrak—Bitter gray leaves. A Robandi poison. In mild doses causes sleepiness and vomiting; in strong doses, death.

Swayweed—Fine green tea. Reverses loyalties and allegiances.

Woozy weed—Leaves that causes sleepiness and forgetfulness.

Acknowledgements – Is your name here?

Ezaara and Roberto stumbled across Ithsar in the Robandi desert in *Ezaara, Riders of Fire book 1*. I must admit that I have to thank Ava Fairhall, my map designer, for planting sea dragons in my head. When we were designing the map of Dragons' Realm, Ava asked me if I wanted anything in the enormous expanse of the deep blue Naobian Sea.

"You know, a ship or a sea dragon, or an island," she said.

"Yes, I'd like a sea dragon off the coast of the Robandi Desert," I replied. "And a couple of pirate ships and a few jagged rocks near Death Valley."

Sea Dragon was born!

The pirate ships and jagged rocks featured in *Dragon Strike and Dragon War*. Ava has a lot to answer for!

Sea Dragon fleshes out some details that have been omitted from Ezaara's adventures as the new Queen's Rider, and concludes the war against Zens. But wait, *Riders of Fire* isn't over yet!

Riders of Fire Dragon Masters is a series that features the events that led up to Ezaara's birth. Some of these books were originally planned as books 7-9 of the *Riders of Fire* series, however, I realized that new readers may want to read the *Riders of Fire* adventures in chronological order. Splitting out the prequels into a separate series allows people to do this.

A big thank you to my readers. Your energy and enthusiasm for my stories keeps me writing. I love your emails, messages and having fun with you on social media. It's wonderful knowing you're waiting for my stories!

Now, for the drumroll… Did you name a character in *Sea Dragon*?

My readers suggested 1005 names for characters and dragons. And I loved them all. I wish I had more characters and dragons for them. On the other hand, I'm thankful I don't have to write 1005 characters in my adventures! So, thank you everyone for participating.

Catherine Ellis named Queen Aquaria, the queen of the sea dragons; Stacy Floyd named Misha, an orphaned teen Robandi assassin and her dragon Ramisha; Charlotte Kieft named Roshni, a valiant Robandi assassin; Cathy Wellman named Nila, a wild Robandi assassin and her dragon, Nilanna, and also a dragon, Kishanna. Pierre Rutherford named Drida, the eldest Robandi assassin; Douglas La Grow named the bully, Thut, Izodia's sidekick; Jeanine Thornton named Bala, also a bully and Izodia's sidekick; Drea Dean named Goren, the leader of the green guards & his dragon Rengar; Marvin Smith named Stefan, a hot-headed young green dragon rider & his brash dragon Fangora; Brittany Timmins named Kadran, a father and member of the Last Stop resistance called Anakisha's Warriors; Lucy Ladeira named Katrine, Kadran's wife and Hana's mother, also a member of Anakisha's Warriors; and Cecilia Rodriguez named Hana, their daughter and member of Anakisha's Warriors.

Readers and reviewers, you are an awesome team that carries me through the long hours writing and editing!! Thank you. ☺

Thank you to my editor, Charlotte Kieft, who has a fine eye for detail and a great sense of humor. Her hilarious comments made me laugh as I edited my manuscript. A shout out to the rest of my writing tribe, Alicia, Peter and Kevin, for their support, and to Christian Bentulan who designs my exquisite covers!

I'd also like to thank my four amazing kids, who put up with Mum at the keyboard for long hours, laughing, crying or groaning, as I create another adventure for you. What? You thought writing was a quiet, solitary occupation? Not in my house!

Please check out my reader's group on facebook, if you'd like to say hi! Riders of Fire: Eileen Mueller's Fan Zone

About Eileen

Eileen Mueller is a multiple-award-winning author of heart-pounding fantasy novels that will keep you turning the page. Dive into her worlds, full of magic, love, adventure and dragons! Eileen lives in New Zealand, in a cave, with four dragonets and a shape shifter. She writes action-packed tales for young adults, children and everyone who loves adventure.

Visit her website at www.EileenMuellerAuthor.com for Eileen's FREE books and new releases or to become a Rider of Fire!

Please place a review

I absolutely love reviews! Hear the dragons roar and me squeal with enthusiasm when you post one. Readers are my lifeblood, so I'd love you to pop a line or two on Amazon or Goodreads. Thank you.

Become a Rider of Fire

Every author needs a team on their side to help them fight tharuks, imprint with dragons, and keep the realm safe. Being a Rider of Fire gives you early copies of my books, the chance to name characters, dragons and villages, and other special glimpses into Dragons' Realm, the world of Riders of Fire. I would be grateful for reviews, social media shares and recommendations. If you're keen, please contact me at www.EileenMuellerAuthor.com

Printed in Great Britain
by Amazon